SIGMA

JASINDA WILDER

SIGMA

ISBN: 978-1-948445-72-6

A NOTE FROM THE AUTHOR

Sigma is set in the theoretical future, twenty-ish years after the events of Alpha and Alpha One Security. But, in the interest of storytelling simplicity, I've written this without worrying overmuch about silly things like the technicalities of linear time progression. Valentine, Kyrie, Harris, and Layla are in their 50s and 60s, and their kids are young adults. I've not attempted to guess at what the future society is like, since this isn't sci-fi, it's romantic suspense. Basically, if I've done my job right, you'll be able to just enjoy the story and not even really think about anachronistic continuity.

1

ISLAND TIME

"Do you *have* to go, Val?" I hear the whine in my voice, and even I'm irritated by it; I sidle up against my husband of twenty years and flatten my palms against his broad hard chest. "Can't you just handle it via video conference?"

He's not lost any of his sex appeal, to me, my man Valentine Roth. Six feet four inches, with a powerful physique he's kept rock hard, lean and muscular. His blond hair is shot through with touches of gray, now, and there's some silver at his temples and in his beard. But to me, that just makes him all the sexier.

And, for the curious, no, we've not lost any of our sexual chemistry. It's heightened, if anything. Sure, when Rinna and Cal were young and he was running his empire as a stay-at-home dad and I was running the philanthropic arm of St. Claire, Incorporated, we were often too busy and too tired to have sex as frequently as we used to or wanted to. Yeah, his—our—entire business empire was named after me. He'd named it that when he sold the tower in Manhattan where I'd first met him, and kept the name. I had sort of expected him to change it to something else, but he never did. But Rinna and Cal grew up, and we learned how to slow down, and now we make love as much if not more than we did when we were in our thirties.

"Unfortunately," Valentine says, his hands cradling my waist, "I do have to. I can do ninety-nine percent of my work from here. Ninety-nine-point-five percent, even. But this is one of those rare instances where my personal presence is required."

"It's a merger?"

He shakes his head. "I'm selling off Heart Space Medical Technology. It's gotten too bloated, too corporate. Streamlining it would take more time, money, and effort than I'm willing to invest at the moment, so I'm selling it off to a competitor." He grins. "Plus, the proceeds from the sale will balloon our cash supply, which I'm going to need to get Valkyrie off the ground."

I roll my eyes. "Such a melodramatic name."

He smirks. "It's a cool as hell name, is what it is. This is the future, babe. Stellar exploration is where the real fun happens, and we're getting in on the ground floor."

"Stellar exploration," I echo. "Spaceships, you mean."

"Exactly!" His eyes light up, as they always do when he talks about his latest business baby. This one, though, is seriously next level, even for my husband, who has never done anything in half measures. "Everyone else is focused on reusable rockets and technologies for a colony on Mars. Good, great—but I've got different plans."

"Like?" I can't say I get excited about all this space stuff, not like he does, but his excitement is contagious, and the passion he exudes is, frankly, arousing.

"Orbital construction." He has his Thinking Face on, where he's mentally rolling around all the billion facets and functions and obstacles. "If you're limited to building your ships here on earth, you're never going to reach full potential. Think about all the science fiction from the last fifty to a hundred years: the *really* big ships all get built in space, in orbit, right? Because you're no longer limited by the constraints of gravity. Well, someone has to learn how to do that. It's got to start somewhere. Valkyrie is where it starts."

I sigh, breathy and smiling. "You're such a nerd." I tangle my fingers in his beard and pull him down to me. "It's hot." I kiss him until we're both out of breath. "When do you leave?"

"Mercedes will be here in thirty."

Mercedes Felix—his personal transportation chief; driver, pilot, and logistical coordinator.

She's thirty, Black, beautiful, and one of the most terrifyingly intelligent and competent human beings I've ever met. She can drive anything with wheels, fly anything with wings or rotors, speaks five languages that I know of, has a black belt in three martial arts disciplines, and is capable of feats of mental arithmetic that boggle the mind...and she can do it all in a cocktail dress and six-inch heels—I've seen her do it. She's more comfortable in a pilot's jumpsuit and combat boots, of course. She's also fiercely private, as are most of the crew in our inner circle. But most of all, her loyalty to our family is without question.

"Are you packed?" I ask.

He pulls me closer to him, grabbing a double handful of my ass to do so. "I'll be gone less than seventy-two hours, if all goes according to plan, so packing took all of ten minutes." His eyes spark fire. "Why? You got something in mind for the next thirty minutes?"

I glance around us—we're in the kitchen of our Caribbean compound on our private island. Cal, fifteen, is on the other side of the island, hanging out at the beach with Killian Harris—Layla and Harris's son—and a group of friends from St. Croix. Rin, twenty, is shopping in Charlotte Amalie with Layla and Layla's daughter, Bryn, who's the same age as Rin. Those two are like twins, inseparable—Rin and Bryn.

We only have Marta, our housekeeper and personal chef, here at the house three days a week. Which means the house is empty.

There's security out there, of course. A small army of elite security contractors, all ex-Special Forces employed by Alpha One Security, Harris's company. But they're invisible to us, and trained to keep watch on the premises, not us personally.

"I might have something in mind," I whisper, pivoting away from him.

He follows me as I hop up onto the island counter, and his eyes light up. He knows what I want, and he will enjoy giving it to me, thoroughly. Several times, probably, before he takes anything for himself.

It's fairly early, just past nine, so I'm still in my bathrobe; I've got nowhere to be and the house to myself after Valentine leaves, so why bother getting dressed at all? Now, though, it provides easy access for him. He tugs at the loose knot of the belt keeping the robe closed, and it drapes open, baring my naked body. He leaves it like that, for a moment, the edges of the robe just outside my erect nipples, core exposed. His eyes rake over my body, pupils dilating, nostrils flaring, jaw grinding. His zipper tightens, bulges. Even now, after twenty years, he still gets hard as a rock at the mere sight of me. I'm not a young woman anymore, past fifty and never you mind the exact number. I've nursed two children, and things aren't as taut and perky as they used to be. There may be some dimples on my thighs. Some new wrinkles here and there. But he doesn't see any of that. He sees his wife, the love of his life, and I arouse him.

It's a heady thought, if I dwell on it. Twenty years, two children, and he loves me and is every bit as turned on by me now as he was the day I entered his high-rise, blindfolded and scared shitless.

He brushes the robe off my arms, and the delicate silk floats to the counter around my hips. He's in no rush. He fits his hips between my thighs, caressing my breasts and kissing the side of my jaw. My throat. My shoulder. His hands caress and arouse, tweaking my nipples and hefting the weight of my breasts, letting them fall free only to toy with them again. I tilt my head back and gasp as he kisses my breastbone, and my hands sink into his hair, cupping his head to me as he kisses lower and lower, down the valley between my breasts.

"Valentine," I breathe. "Don't make me wait."

He growls a laugh. "Eager, are you?"

"You were busy yesterday," I grumble, "And I was horny all day."

"You were?"

I laugh. "Yeah, I was. I tried to get your attention, but you were too focused on work."

He sighs. "I'm sorry, my love. This sale has taken up too much of my attention." His lips close over my nipple, suckling it until I gasp. "I shall rectify the lack of attention, posthaste."

"You better, buster." I knot my fingers in his hair as I anticipate his lips where I need them most—on my sex. "I had to take care of things myself. It was awful."

"You did?" He looks up at me. "Bad girl. That's for me."

"Well, I was touching your hair and bending over in front of you, and you didn't even look at me. I even very suggestively told you I was going to go take a bath. What was I supposed to do?"

"And I missed all of these hints, did I?"

"Every single one."

He spends a moment on my breasts, kissing them, caressing and licking and nuzzling until I'm about to shove his face where I need it. But then, finally, he drops to his knees. His mouth grazes my inner thigh, and I hiss, opening my thighs, guiding him to me.

"Are you going to punish me?" he says, smirking up at me from between my legs.

"Yeah," I breathe. "I'm going to make you eat me out until I come at least three times before I touch your cock."

He rumbles wordlessly, something between a

growl of arousal and a laugh. "Threaten me with a good time, why don't you?"

I huff. "I don't want to punish you, love, I just want you to fuck me six ways to Sunday."

"Request granted."

His tongue grazes up my seam, teasing, teasing. I hook my knees over his shoulders, lock my feet around each other on his back, brace my hands behind me on the countertop, and throw my head back as he begins ratcheting me up the mountain of climax. God, his mouth. Twenty years of discovering all the ways to make me scream has made him freakishly good at going down on me—he can get me to orgasm within seconds if he wants—mostly, though, he likes to draw it out. Bring me right to the edge and hold me there, about to come but not quite there. Screaming. Begging. Thrusting toward his mouth, seeking the edge.

He doesn't let me, though. He keeps me wild with just his tongue, hands holding my hips.

"Val, *please*," I gasp. "Please."

I feel his smile, feel the curve of his lips against my sex. Feel it in the energy sizzling between us.

"What do you want, Key?"

"Let me come," I whisper, sitting upright to cradle his head, pulling him closer. "Make me come, Val. Then give me your cock."

He nuzzles my pussy, licks. Kisses. Suckles my

clit into his mouth and teases me to the edge. But this time, he slides fingers into me and hooks them inside me just so, and his tongue thrashes side to side, and I fly over the peak and into orgasm, biting down on a scream and lifting my ass off the counter as I thrust against his mouth and fingers.

While I'm still caught up in the gnashing throes of climax, he pulls me down off the counter and sets me on my feet, facing the island. Pushes me forward so my ass is sticking out. I lie forward on the counter, breasts smashed against the cold marble, spread my thighs open and lift up on my toes, presenting my opening for him. I hear his belt jingle and hear his slacks drop to the kitchen floor with a thump. I feel him brush my ass with his cock, and then he notches himself against me, preparing to fill me—I whimper with anticipation.

"Fast or slow, baby?" he murmurs.

"Fast," I gasp. "Hard."

He caresses my ass with both hands as he ignores my request, slowly pushing into me, inch by inch, until his hips smash against my ass and I feel him fully within me, stretched and aching around him.

He pulls back just as slowly as he thrusted in, feathers a series of short, shallow thrusts, just the first few inches of him gliding through my slick sex; and then, with an unexpected crack of his hand against my ass cheek, he fucks into me.

Hard.

I scream.

Loudly.

"Hush, love," he growls. "The kitchen is open, and this is a small island."

Our kitchen is open concept of a different kind: all four walls are doors which accordion open to each of the four corners, so the entirety of the kitchen can be open to the Caribbean breeze and the soft shush of waves in the distance.

I grit my teeth and scream more quietly the next time he fucks into me, spanking the other side. Each thrust is hard, but the pace is slow, withdrawing achingly slowly, occasionally pausing to thrust shallowly as he pets and soothes the reddened flesh of my buttocks where he's spanked me.

I need to come again—I'm stuck just this side of climax.

I wedge my arm between my body and the counter and touch myself, fingering my clit to drive myself to the edge—if I come, he'll come. And what I want more than anything, right now, is to come in unison with my husband. That's the ultimate pleasure, for us both. We may not have two- or three-hour sex marathons anymore, or fuck four times before breakfast, but when we do, it's fiercely intimate, wildly powerful, and when we orgasm together, it feels like the universe resonates at a frequency only we can feel, where our hearts and souls sing harmonizing arias, our bodies the instrument of the song.

As I circle my clit with increasing speed, I begin thrusting back against him, screams turning to soft hoarse grunts and whimpers as I near the edge, ass flexing back against him, lifting up on my toes and sinking down to take his thrusts. He forgets the spanking and the hard, measured thrusts, and begins chasing his own climax. He snarls and gasps, whispers my name, whispers his love for me. Whispers to me that I'm beautiful. That I'm so sexy when I come.

I can't summon words, only try to keep my building howl of climax something like quiet.

Finally, my orgasm breaks through me like a detonating bomb, and I feel my sex clench him, and I cry out his name. "Valentine! Come with me, Val."

He obeys.

With a soft, growling groan, he lets loose, pounding into me hard and fast until I feel him unleash, feel him explode inside me, filling me with his cum in burst after hot wet burst, and when he comes, he thrusts deep and pushes deeper with each spasm of ecstasy.

At that moment, we hear voices.

Young male voices, laughing, shouting, overlapping.

"Shit!" Valentine hisses, quickly withdrawing from me and bending to yank his pants up, fastening them around his still hard, still sex-slick cock. I'm gasping, still shaking with the quaking aftershocks of my orgasm, dripping with his seed, still naked. He snatches my robe off the counter and I hurriedly shove my arms in. I'm still belting it when Cal rounds the corner from the direction of the beach, Killian beside him, three of their friends from St. Croix trailing behind.

I'm facing my husband, and he's embracing me, as if we've just kissed, hiding the bulging zipper.

"My god, you two," Cal grumps as he sees us, half joking, "get a damn room."

I snicker. "We have a room, Cal. We just don't always use it."

He reddens. "MOM!"

His friends groan, but Killian, I notice just laughs and shakes his head. Of course, his parents are Nick and Layla, and their sex life is every bit as...healthy, shall we say...as ours. So this is nothing new for him.

Cal yanks open the fridge and grabs the partially empty case of cola, tossing cans to each of his friends without looking at them. "But I mean, we eat in this room, you know?"

Valentine bends to kiss me. "Your friends' parents don't make out in the kitchen?"

Cal snorts. "If all you were doing is making out, then I'm freaking Santa Claus."

One of his friends, a local native to the islands,

speaks up with a laugh. "My parents get it on like teenagers, man. I accidentally walked in on them in the shower the other day. I'm still blind in one eye from it."

"It's the sign of a healthy marriage, Thomas," Valentine says.

"Sure, I know," Thomas shoots back, shaking his head. "And I respect that. Shit, I want it for myself, some day. I just don't wanna see it, you know?"

I press my thighs together, stifling a face as I feel myself dripping. I lift up on my toes, press my lips to Valentine's ear and whisper, "You made a mess of me."

He snorts softly. "Something to remember me by while I'm gone," he whispers back.

"I'll probably still be leaking your cum when you get back."

He smooths his hands over my ass. "Go get cleaned up and put some clothes on so you can see me off."

"You're gonna smell like me all day if you don't clean up yourself," I tell him.

He just nips my earlobe. "I know. That's the plan."

"Dirty old man," I say, sashaying away from him.

The teenage boys are studiously attempting to not hear our whispered conversation

A few minutes later, I've done a quick cleanup and put on a loose skirt and tank top. I find my husband and son and his friends at the dock where our seaplane will tie up. I hear it, a distant hum approaching from the direction of St. Croix.

I watch Valentine roughhouse with Cal and Killy—he hates that nickname with a passion, but it's been his nickname to those closest to him since birth, and it's not going anywhere. Cal is almost as tall as his father, already several inches taller than me at six-one. An active kid, he's lean and wiry, but shows signs that he'll be built like his father. His blond hair is long and shaggy, brushing his shoulders and always in his blue eyes; he's the spitting image of Valentine, with only hints here and there of my genes, the angle of his nose, the tilt of his eyes. I'm more apparent in his mannerisms, prone to emotional outbursts where Valentine tends to be more reserved.

Killian is the opposite, looking more like his mother, Layla, with the personality of Harris; Killy is medium height and densely built with his mother's complexion and black, densely curled hair, but he has his father's eyes and calm, quiet, reserved demeanor.

They're playing at the water's edge, Valentine barefoot with his suit slacks rolled up to his knees, jacket draped over his valise, shirt sleeves rolled up to just beneath his elbows, no tie. He's so freaking handsome, my man. Especially when that playful smile lights up his face. He dodges and ducks and weaves as Cal and Killy try to wrestle him into the water, each of them laughing. The St. Croix boys watch the game, laughing as well...until Valentine surreptitiously moves the roughhousing closer and closer to them...and then whirls on them, tossing them each with lightning-fast speed into the water.

And then it's a free-for-all, all five boys trying to tackle Valentine into the water. They nearly succeed several times, but Valentine always manages to keep his balance and elude their grasp.

The game continues until Mercedes brings the seaplane in for a smooth landing. The seaplane is, of course, a custom design by RTI—Roth Transportation Industries. It's sleek, jet-powered, utilizing a buoyant body design rather than external floats, capable of seating twelve not including the pilot and copilot. It's also designed to minimize radar profile, and features all the latest defense technology. The base model can be configured as an executive transport, like this one, with bedroom suites, office space, a full kitchen, and a theater, or as a supply transport.

"I never get tired of seeing that thing," Thomas says.

It really is an impressive aircraft, but then, everything Roth does is impressive.

Roth says goodbye to Killian and the boys, Cal following him to the dock to say goodbye. They're arguing about something, unexpectedly, and I hurry up onto the dock to soothe the ruffled feathers. Cal and Valentine can butt heads, sometimes. They have a loving, affectionate relationship, but Cal is a teenager and Roth has little patience for attitude, which can lead to conflict like I see brewing right now, and I don't want them to part on a bad note.

"...I'm not a kid anymore, Dad. I can help. I know I'm not as...everything...as Rin is, but..." Cal drags his long shaggy blond hair back with an angry, frustrated swipe of his hand. "I just don't see why I can't go. Just to watch." A long pause. He sighs harshly. "I want to be a part of things."

Valentine is gathering his valise, jacket, and socks and shoes. "You're not ready, Cal. This deal is vitally important to my plans for the future of St. Claire, and I need to be focused."

"I can just watch and listen. I won't interfere or ask any questions until after. I promise."

Valentine is conflicted, tension in every line of his body. He looks to me, and I come up and stand between them, put a hand on each shoulder.

I look up at my husband. "It could be good for him. For you both."

Valentine frowns, not expecting me to come in on Cal's side. I'm usually the conservative, hyper-protective one, not inclined to let my precious kids take unnecessary risks before I think they're ready.

"You're taking security, right?" I ask.

Valentine nods, shrugs. "Yeah, of course. Sasha and two new hires from A1S HQ."

"And the deal is all done except signing the contracts, right? The negotiations are over?"

He nods again, the tension bleeding away. "Yeah—yeah, you're right," he sighs.

I turn to face him, resting my hands on his chest. "He's expressing a desire to learn the ropes. Rin was younger than him when you started taking her on business trips."

Valentine rakes his hand through his hair, a mirror of Cal's gesture from a moment ago. "Fine. Go pack. Wear your suit, dress shoes, white button-down and a black tie. Pack a pair of jeans, a T-shirt, underwear, and sneakers. Nothing else—you have ten minutes."

"You won't regret it, Dad." Cal says, already jogging for the house—Killian and the others follow him.

Valentine watches him go, then looks down at me. "He doesn't have Corinna's killer instinct."

"He doesn't need it," I say. "And she needs someone around to balance that out. She needs Cal's optimism and sweetness."

A thoughtful nod. "You're right, I suppose. I guess I just wonder what suddenly has him so interested. He's never shown much interest in anything except surfing and gaming with his buddies."

"Something to talk to him about on the flight," I say, lifting up onto my tiptoes to kiss Valentine. "I think maybe he sees this as an opportunity to have you to himself."

A rough sigh. "Do you think he feels like Corinna is my favorite? Like over him?"

Valentine is the only one of us who ever calls our eldest by her full name, and he's the only one she'll allow to call her that. To close friends and family, she's Rin, to acquaintances and the world at large, she's Rinna. To her father, she's Corinna. Or, when he wants to tease her, Rinny. Which sends her into a paroxysm of explosive rage.

I think about his question. "Maybe? You do, sometimes, occasionally, show a little bit of favoritism. Mainly just because she's shown an interest in the family business since she was old enough to walk into your office on her own. And Cal has generally been more interested in fun. In being a boy, and then a teenager, whereas Rin has always been…an old soul, I suppose."

He chuckles. "Remember her 'office?'" He uses air quotes to emphasize the last word. "She had her little chair, toy computer, toy cell phone, and a notebook and a marker, and she'd sit in my office with me and play businesswoman. She'd have these intense conversations with herself. That, or she'd sit and parrot back every word I said."

I laugh. "Do you remember when she caught you in a mistake?"

He rolls his eyes. "I thought Rob Howell was skimming. She caught the discrepancy in the books while looking over my shoulder—an error I'd introduced myself."

"You were so mad at yourself."

"It was a dumb, rookie mistake, and my eight-year-old daughter caught it."

"No one is perfect, and she's smarter than both of us put together."

He sighs. "And…it's not that Cal's not. And I don't have a favorite."

I pat his chest. "He just needs some special time with you, that's all. Make him feel special and included. Part of the team."

"I will." He lifts me up, cupping my ass in his hands to support my weight. "Thank you."

I nuzzle his cheek. "You're an amazing father." I kiss him. "Make sure you call Rin. She'll go through the roof if you don't say goodbye."

He snorts. "We're stopping in Charlotte Amalie to pick up the new hires anyway, so I've already made plans with her to meet up for a quick goodbye."

I frown. "Are you sure it's a good idea to travel to the mainland with new hires?"

He shrugs. "These guys have been trained by Puck himself. He says they're some of the most promising recruits he's ever worked with. Plus, I'll have Sasha, and I'd take him over any other three people."

Sasha is one of the core A1S members, hired by Harris when A1S was first formed, and Sasha has been head of our personal security detail for over twenty years. Former Spetznaz, he's fiercely protective of our family—he has taken bullets for us, and we all trust him with our lives.

"I still wish you could do this from here. Have them meet you down here."

He sighs. "I do too. But it's important I make this appearance. Heart First is one of our largest and most financially successful corporations, and this deal is worth billions. It's not something I can do remotely."

"I understand." I cling to him. "I'm just…nervous, I guess. I never like it when you leave me."

He cradles me to his chest, one arm under me and the other an iron band around me. "I know. But, honey, we settled everything twenty years ago. There's nothing to be afraid of anymore."

"Just be careful, okay." I voice the thing that's been niggling at me ever since he told me about this trip, two weeks ago. "I just have a bad feeling. I don't know."

"I'll have Harris send some extra men to meet us Stateside."

"Who do we have here, since you're taking Sasha?"

"Bishop, Stone Crow, Vincent, Marquez, and Alinov."

I wiggle down to my feet but don't let go of him. "Can I get someone I know? I know those guys by face and name, but I don't...*know* them, you know?"

He whips out his phone. "Hey Harris, how's things in the Keys?"

Layla and Nick have their personal compound in the Florida Keys, on a small, remote island only a few hours from here by plane. It's a fully self-contained, off-grid compound, with its own water supply, and solar and wind power. They had fiber optic cable piped in, and the only way in or out is by plane or boat, and obviously all approaches are closely monitored—Harris being Harris, this means military-grade radar, with armed drones on Standby, and a fully fueled and armed fighter jet ready to scramble. Harris doesn't fuck around. Those same drones and jets can be here, flying at top speed, in a matter of minutes, if need be.

"Yeah, good. I'm just getting ready to go here, but Kyrie is feeling a little nervous. One of those feelings, you know? Is anyone from the inner circle available to get down here, like today?" A pause as he listens. "Awesome, that'd be great...no, on the island itself. Kyrie can get one of the guest rooms ready for them. Thanks, Harris."

"So who's coming?" I ask.

"Duke and Temple," he answers. "Their kids

are spending the summer with Temple's parents in California, so they're at odd ends."

Duke Silver and his wife, Temple Kennedy—Temple started as a reality TV star, eventually transitioned into stage and big screen, and is now one of the most celebrated actresses in the world. She just wrapped a major production, last I heard, so if their kids are spending the summer with the grandparents, I can see how she and Duke would be looking for something to do. Duke, as a founding member of Alpha One Security, is the hiring director, in charge of recruiting from the ranks of the Special Forces community around the world—A1S only hires the best of the best. To be hired by A1S after discharging from Special Forces is, within that community, a badge of honor, which means the hiring process is brutally competitive. Plus, the pay, if you can hack it, is best in class.

"Thank you," I say. "I'll feel better with Duke around."

"None of those guys are spring chickens anymore," Valentine says, "but I trust them over anyone else. Duke still spars with the recruits, and they're all scared shitless of him. He also runs that close quarters and urban combat training facility at their place in Colorado you and Layla trained at recently, so you know his combat skill are as sharp as ever."

I glance over my shoulder—Cal is dressed in

his suit, hair pulled back in a neat man-bun, carrying a black necktie in one hand and a small duffel bag in the other. I tug at Valentine's phone to check the time—less than ten minutes. A small victory, for Cal—having been born and raised in the Caribbean, he definitely has an intrinsic sense of "island time."

Valentine claps Cal on the back as he approaches. "There you go, son. Looking crisp."

Cal rolls his eyes. "Crisp? No one says that, Dad."

"I say it." Valentine gives him a playful push toward the edge of the dock, causing Cal to windmill his arms to stay out of the water. "Once upon a time, if I was quoted as having said something was crisp, that phrase would have been on trend within twenty-four hours."

Cal just laughs. "Yeah, once upon a time, a long, long time ago, in a galaxy far, far away...in your dreams."

Valentine gives him another playful shove toward the sea jet. "Get in there, doofus, before I change my mind." He follows Cal to the open door of the idling aircraft. "Say goodbye to your mother, boy."

I've followed them to the doorway, and Cal turns around and lifts me in a big, boyish bear hug.

"Be good, Cal. Listen and learn." I kiss his cheek, and, good boy that he is, he allows it with a minimum of embarrassed squawking. "I'm proud of you for stepping up like this."

"Where's Killian and the others?" Valentine asks.

"Killian is seeing the guys off—he's going to ride with us to Charlotte and hang with Auntie Lay-Lay, Rin, and Bryn."

Killian and Bryn often stay summers down here with us, and other times Cal and Rin spend the summers up in the Keys with Layla and Harris—or, as the kids refer to them, Auntie Lay-Lay and Uncle Harry. I'm not sure they're even aware that his name is actually Nicholas, come to think of it—he's been Uncle Harry since Rin started talking.

The other guys, living locally, have a small island-hopper boat they take to get from here to St. Croix. I'm not really even sure who owns it or the legality of minors operating it; but then, little do they know, they're always monitored from a discreet distance by our security team from point to point, to ensure they arrive safely.

Cal pats me on the head. "Thanks, Mom. Love you. I gotta go, now." He wriggles in my hold. "Okay, you can let go, now."

I reluctantly let go of him, pat him on the chest and back away. "Okay, fine. But be safe, okay?"

"It's two or three days in New York, Mom. I think we'll be okay."

"I know," I say. "But it's my job as your mom to worry."

"And you do a wonderful job at it," he quips.

"You're, like, a professional worrier. What could possibly happen?"

I snort. "Do *not* ask that question, buddy. The world likes to answer it, I've discovered."

He rolls his eyes. "We'll be *fine*."

Killian comes running, still in board shorts but now with a tank top and flip-flops.

Valentine waves him aboard, and once they're both seated and buckled, he pulls me close for one more hug and a deep, hot kiss. "We'll be back before you know it, babe. Love you."

"Love you, too. Bring my boy back safe, okay?"

He taps me on the nose. "Don't miss me too much."

I wink at him. "You know I will."

He sniffs his fingers surreptitiously, grins at me, and then closes the door. A moment later, the aircraft backs away from the dock, pushes away and heads for open water. Once they're a safe distance from shore, I hear the engines spool up, and the ocean is churned into white spray, and the sea jet picks up speed. Then they're airborne, and then they're a speck…

And then I'm alone on the island.

For the first time…ever, actually.

I really don't like it.

A whole island, and I'm alone on it.

Well, except for the security dudes, but I'll never even lay eyes on them—that's the very definition of their job, invisible protectors, so good at their job that I mostly forget they're even there.

But with Layla and everyone not due back till evening, I'm tempted to call one of them in to the house just for someone to talk to.

Ugh.

Duke and Temple should be here in a few hours, too. That makes me feel better.

But still…

A worm of unease wriggles in my gut.

It's been twenty years, but I recognize this feeling: something isn't right. I just don't know what.

I can only hope I'm imagining it.

2

ABDUCTED

Aunt Layla's phone buzzes; after a brief pause, she announces, "Killy is joining us."

Bryn snorts. "It's a girl's shopping trip, Mom. Why does Killy have to come?"

"I guess Cal is going with Uncle Val last minute," Aunt Layla says.

This gives me pause. "He is?"

Layla shrugs. "That's what your mom just texted me."

I stop, and the others stop with me. "Why?"

Layla hands me her phone. "Call her and ask, Rin, I don't know. I just know your mom just let me know to expect Killian. Your dad and Cal are dropping him off here."

"Cal, my surf bro gamer nerd brother, is going

with Dad to sign the sale of his four-billion-dollar medical company?" I have to remind myself to breathe. "He told me I couldn't go. But now he's bringing Cal?"

"Rin," Layla starts.

But I'm not done—I'm just getting started. "Cal wouldn't know a noncompete clause from a nondisclosure agreement."

"Rin."

"I mean, sure, Cal is smart, I'm not saying he's not, but *I'm* the business-minded one of the two of us."

"*Rin*." Layla's voice breaks through my rant.

"What." It comes out monotone and petulant—childish, and I immediately regret it.

She holds me by the shoulders. "He's got to start somewhere, right? And besides, we've got plans."

"Yeah, but not with Killy," Bryn says—they have a relationship much like Cal and I do, equal parts antagonistic and affectionate and competitive.

"We can include your brother."

"He's going to get a manicure?" Bryn arches an eyebrow.

Layla laughs. "He can look at surfboards or something." She puts an arm around both Bryn and me. "The point is, we have fun stuff planned, so don't get all bent out of shape about Cal doing this trip with your dad. You've been on plenty of business trips with him, Rin. It can be Cal's turn for once, right?"

I sigh. "Yeah, I guess so."

I give my best friend a knowing look; she's basically a best friend, cousin, and sister all rolled into one, even though we're not actually related in any way.

She's a perfect mixture of her father's and mother's physical characteristics: tall and lean like Uncle Harry—a fact which she regularly bemoans, complaining that she got scammed out of having boobs or butt—with dark, tightly curled brown hair and dark brown eyes. She's all Auntie Lay-Lay in personality, however, with a hair-trigger temper, stubborn as a mule, but fiercely loyal and open with her affection for those whom she loves.

In a sense, Bryn and I are alike, in that I'm equal Mom and Dad, but where Cal is essentially all Mom in his personality, I again am a mixture of their tendencies. I'm tall like Dad, standing just shy of six feet—that quarter of an inch bugs me to no end, because I know I'll never get any taller; I mean, c'mon, genetics, you couldn't have given me a solid six feet? But unlike most six-foot-tall girls, I'm not…thin. No Skinny Minnie here. I also happened to have received Mom's more than generous helping of curves. I stay active and our whole family eats healthy—I lift weights with Dad three or four times a week, and I surf with Cal, and I run around the island now and then, a run which equates to five or so miles, and we all train in martial arts with Sasha. I have Dad's eyes, pale blue and a tendency to come across as icy, intimidating, and cold. Mom and Dad are both blond, so my hair is platinum, almost white-blond, but thankfully I was blessed with skin which tans easily to a nice golden brown.

The sound of a jet engine in the distance means Dad is close. Aunt Layla hears it, cocks her head to listen, and then detours us away from the shops toward the docks where Mercedes will pull in. We arrive in time to see the sleek, aggressive-looking aircraft making its descent toward the water. Still a couple hundred feet above the water and a good quarter of a mile from the docks, the jet engines cut out, meaning Mercedes is making the landing on a glide.

I watch Layla watch the landing, noting her obvious admiration. The sea jet makes barely a splash as it touches down with deft, delicate smoothness, floating up to the dock with a bump, having bled momentum with perfect calculation.

Layla shakes her head and whistles. "That woman is a miracle worker."

Layla has had her own pilot's license since before I was born, and is herself a skilled, competent pilot, but even I, a layman in the world of flying, can tell there's a world of difference between Aunt Layla's competency and Mercedes's mind-boggling amount of talent and hyper-attuned skill.

The side door slides open, and Dad unfolds out of the craft, ducking under the wing as he ties it off with practiced speed. Cal climbs out next—and you could knock me over with a feather: he's wearing a suit. With a TIE. His hair is neatly combed back and tied into a low man bun.

He looks like an adult.

And he's *handsome.*

I mean, he's my brother so let's not make this weird, but it's not something I typically think about. He's my annoying as shit little brother, and usually I just want him to leave me alone for five minutes, but...damn.

Beside me, Bryn is frozen solid. I hear her gulp, audibly.

I glance over at her, and her jaw is literally hanging open. "BRYN!" I tap the underside of her chin. "That's my *brother*."

"I know," she whispers. "When did he get hot?"

"Ew. That's my freaking brother, Bryn." I turn on her. "You were raised with him, so he's as good as your brother."

"Well yeah, that's what makes this such a confusing hard-on. Because I'm not actually related to him, like at all. He's not even, like, a stepbrother. Our moms are best friends. But he's been like my brother our whole lives." A pause. "Until now."

I look at Layla, on my other side. "Auntie Lay-Lay. Do something."

Layla just makes a wry face. "Ah yes, let me just dig my fairy godmother wand out of my purse—" she digs into her purse and withdraws a wrapped tampon, waves it in an elaborate pattern in front of her daughter. "Ala-ca-dabra-ca-doo! You're no longer attracted to that fine-as-hell young man to whom you are not in way, legally or genetically, related, because Rinny is jealous."

Bryn snickers, and I feel my temper rising.

"Hysterical. That's your *nephew.*" I glare at her. "And don't call me Rinny."

"Nephew of my heart," Layla corrects. "No relation."

"So you're fine with your daughter drooling over him like a thirsty little—"

"Watch it, Rin," Layla says, her tone conveying a very serious lack of fucking around. She immediately softens. "I know it's weird for you. And I'm not saying I'd be fine with them, like, hooking up. Because that would in fact be super weird. But your brother is an extremely handsome young man. And since none of us have ever seen him cleaned up like this, it's kind of a shock to the system." She grabs me by the arms. "I'm fairly certain you did a double-take yourself when he climbed out."

"Did not," I grumble.

Layla cackles. "Okay, now you're just being childish. You're twenty, Rin—almost twenty-one. Act like it."

Bryn checks me with her shoulder, not exactly gently. "Chill, Rin. I'm saying he's hot, not that I'm planning on seducing him."

"Who are you seducing?" Cal says, arriving at that moment, hands shoved into his pockets, mirrored aviators on his face, grinning happily.

"No one," Bryn says. "Why are you here?"

"I'm going with Dad." He glances at me as he says this, clearly anticipating an outburst from me.

Between Layla's words a few minutes ago and him clearly expecting me to blow up, I force myself not to. I've already been called childish once in the last minute, I'm not about to go making it worse.

I'm an adult, if a young one. I'm a ranking executive in St. Claire Industries, earned mostly on my own merits, with the assistance of just a teeny, tiny little amount of nepotism.

I'm not going to act like a childish, jealous bitch to my brother, who is clearly over the moon to be going on this trip with our dad.

"What prompted the sudden interest in the company?" I asked. "Get bored of surfing?"

"Psssh. As if *that* were possible," he says, still eying me suspiciously. "Nah. I just…I dunno. I want to see what it's like when Dad actually does stuff. Like, out in the world. Most of the time he's working, he's on the computer or video conference. Plus, I haven't been away from the islands except for the Keys in forever. So." A shrug, and another glance, eyes narrowed at me. "Why are you not flipping your shit, Rin? I was all ready for you to hit the roof."

"We're outside, dumbass—there's no roof to hit, for one thing."

"It's an expression, stupid."

"Don't call me stupid, stupid." I close my eyes and collect myself. "I've been on plenty of trips with Dad. I figure it can be your turn."

He looks at Layla. "I'm guessing I have you to thank for this suspiciously adult-like calm from my normally rabid sister."

Layla snorts. "Maybe, but I wouldn't set about trying to ruin it if I were you."

Dad has been watching this exchange silently. He reaches out, pulls me into a hug, tucking me against his side. "Proud of you," he whispers, kissing me on the top of the head.

"Any news on whether Musk is going to invest?" I ask.

"We've been in talks," he answers. "He wants more data."

"What data? We've given him everything we have."

"He's hedging," Dad answers. "I've got him on the hook for at least two billion, so he's not going to make the decision overnight, and I can't pester him."

"We have to get him on board though," I say. "He's the O-G of reusable rocketry. We need his infrastructure to get our materials into orbit."

Dad laughs. "You've proven yourself to me, already, Rin. To everyone. Me taking Cal to this contract signing doesn't threaten your position in the company."

I deflate—Dad can always see right through me. "Why's he looking all fancy?"

"Jealous of that, too?" He ruffles my hair, which he knows infuriates me. "He can't very well appear at a four-billion-dollar deal signing wearing board shorts and flip-flops."

"Guess not."

"Duke and Temple are coming down while I'm gone," he says.

"Oh good, I like them. Duke is funny."

Mercedes swaggers up to the group, having done whatever she needed to do ashore. "All right, ya'll. Ready to head out when you are, sir."

She's five-eight, whipcord lean with muscle definition I'm jealous of, her hair in long box braids draped over one shoulder. Light brown, almost tan eyes, incredible facial structure, and a quick smile. She's wearing a pilot's jumpsuit, the top unzipped a few inches, showing just a hint of cleavage, enough to accentuate her femininity.

I hug Dad one more time, and then I pull Cal aside. "Have fun, okay?"

He frowns at me. "You're not mad?"

"I was at first. I'm over it. You deserve it. Just… listen more than you speak, okay?"

"Seems like that's hard-won advice from you, huh?" he says, with a teasing smirk.

"Shut up," I say, shoving him. "You look nice."

"I like wearing the suit, actually. It makes me feel…I dunno. Cool." He glances at Bryn. "Is it just me, or is she's looking at me weird?"

"Just you." Not touching that one with a fifty-foot pole.

"Huh. Okay, well, gotta go. Love you, sis. Have fun while I'm gone."

"Duke and Temple are coming over, so you know it's gonna be fun."

He frowns. "I'm missing Uncle Duke? Sucks, he's so much fun."

I give Cal a quick hug and then back away as Mercedes fires up the jet engines. Cal climbs in first, followed by Dad. The last I see of them is Dad giving me a big smile and a wave as the door closes.

There's a weird, heavy feeling in my stomach as

they slide away from the dock and away from the island into open water, where, far enough from the docked and moored boats, Mercedes can finally gun the throttle.

I look at Layla, and she too has a speculative look on her face. Then, she brightens, and claps her hands. "All right, kids. I've got one more shop to hit, then lunch, and then back to the island."

Killian is with us, now, still clad in his board shorts and flip-flops, shirtless. He's darker complected than Bryn is, with thicker and more tightly coiled black hair. His eyes are striking, being exact copies of Uncle Harry's vivid green. I'd never admit this to Bryn, especially not after my outburst about her drooling over Cal, but I do find Killian unbearably attractive. He's off-limits, of course—even if Bryn and I aren't actually related, she's at very least my best friend, and everyone knows your best friend's little brother is the most off-limits a guy can get.

But like Bryn said about Cal, Killy is just…hot.

He hates being called Killy. He went on a years-long campaign to get himself called Kill, but no one cooperated and he stopped speaking to us all for at least a month. Eventually, he acquiesced to the fact that to us, his family, he's Killy. But if anyone else tries to call him that, he'll go ape-shit. Like me and being called Rinny.

Killy is like his father, in that he's quiet and

laid-back, and often rather serious and intense. He makes a counterpoint to Cal, who's outgoing, loud, energetic, rarely serious, and lackadaisical about just about everything.

When Auntie Layla says "one more shop," what she actually means is five or six more. I love shopping. I mean, I *really* love shopping. But Auntie Lay-Lay? The woman is a shopping goddess. She's tireless and has an absolutely uncanny knack for finding the best deals. Which is funny, because Uncle Harry and Aunt Layla have a ton of money—not as much as Mom and Dad, but few people on the planet do, a fact of which I am acutely aware—so she really doesn't have to look for deals, since she can afford anything she wants. I asked her about this once, and she told me a new purse is great, but a purse you got for thirty percent off is even better, and despite being wealthy, she's never lost that mentality.

Once she's finally done shopping and a porter has been hired to transport the mountain of bags back to the plane, we hit up our favorite lunch, the Side Street Pub.

Killy is unusually quiet throughout lunch, even for him, prompting Bryn to elbow him in the belly. "What's eating you, bro-ski?"

He ignores the elbow jab, simply rolling a shoulder in a quintessentially teenage male gesture. "Nothin'."

Layla snorts. "Yeah, okay, buddy. We believe you."

"I don't wanna talk about it," he says, dragging a French fry through ketchup.

Layla tosses some bills on the table. "I wasn't asking."

"C'mon, Mom."

"Killian."

He huffs. "I've never gotten to do anything like that with Dad. That's all. And I'm a little pissed off that Cal just...ditched us like a rotten egg to go with Uncle Val. I mean, I get it, but we had a whole thing planned, and he just ditched us without so much as a second thought. It's just kinda shitty."

Layla wrinkles her nose. "Well, second point first—if Rin and Cal were up in the Keys with us, and Dad asked you last minute if you wanted to go to HQ in Montana with him, would you or would you not go without a second thought?"

Killian shrugs again. "Yeah, I guess I would."

"I know you would." She pats his forearm. "So just look at it that way. Cal ditched you, and I get that it stings a little. But just remember what you'd do in his place." She pokes him in the forehead, so he has to look at her. "As for your first point...have you expressed an interest in helping Dad with work?"

Killian squirms uncomfortably. "Um. No?"

"Right. Exactly. So no whining. You want to help? We'll give you a job and you can help. But Dad's work can be dangerous, so don't think we're gonna, like, put you in the field with the guys or anything."

He rolls his eyes. "I'm not a hundred feet tall with a billion muscles, capable of shooting the wings off a fly with a bazooka from a mile away. So no. I wouldn't think so."

Layla cackles. "That's just Bubba Thresh, honey. And there ain't no one on the planet like him."

I snicker. "I can't believe Thresh lets you call him that."

"Oh, he doesn't. He hates it. But what is he gonna do about it?" She nudges Killian. "Sorta like you and being called Killy." She nuzzles his cheek with her nose, adopting the simpering tone you'd use with an especially adorable puppy. "Don't you hate it, Killy-willy-dilly bear?"

He freezes, except to turn to stare at with the nastiest stink eye I've ever seen. "Mom. You're so embarrassing."

"Only to you, kiddo." She gestures around us. "Look at all these people, pointing and laughing at you, right now."

Killian just huffs and leaves the table. "I'm going to the plane."

Bryn and I hold in our laughter till he's out of earshot.

Bryn bursts into gales of laughter. "You are so mean to him sometimes, Mom."

Layla watches her son go, an affectionate look on her face. "He's like his dad—he takes himself and just about everything way too seriously. It's my job to loosen him up. It's taken me twenty years, but your father is *almost* able to take a joke. Almost."

Bryn just snorts. "Or not. He was riding me about how I didn't refill the gas in the ski boat, and I told him he was being a dick about it. He didn't seem to find that as funny as I meant it."

Layla just arches an eyebrow. "Kind of like how well it went when you called me a bitch?"

"I was teasing! You call me bitch all the time!"

"That's different. You were not teasing, you were being rude and disrespectful. Me jokingly saying, 'Bryn, c'mon, bitch, we're getting mani-pedis' is not the same as you saying to me, '*god*, Mom, you're being such a bitch.' Because I wouldn't let you go tubing with your friends until you did the chores I'd assigned."

Bryn rolls her eyes. "I'm twenty and still have chores. It's lame."

Layla's eyebrow can't arch any higher, so she opts for leaning toward her daughter. "You turned down a job. Therefore you do chores."

"We own an island. Why do I have to do chores *or* have a job?"

I answer. "*She* owns an island, Bryn. Not you. Just like my parents own that island, not me. I'm not rich, they are. It's different."

She frowns at me. "Whose side are you on, anyway?"

I shrug and examine my nails—I've chewed on and picked at them until the ends are ragged and the nail polish I put on two weeks ago is more gone than there. Thus the mani-pedis we're getting when we get back home—Mom's nail lady is coming over later.

"I've been telling you for months you need to quit being a baby and ask your parents for a job. So, sorry, bestie, but I'm actually not on your side on this one."

Layla points at me. "She gets it. Just because your father and I have been lucky enough to have a shit ton of money doesn't mean we want you thinking you earned shit, that you deserve shit, and that we're gonna give you everything in life. You haven't, you don't, and we're not. We've given you the most comfortable upbringing imaginable, we expect very little of you, and give you a lot. But you're twenty, Bryn. You have no college aspirations, but that's fine because college is mostly a racket anyway and I wouldn't let you go unless you had a business plan, a five-year schedule, and a specific goal in mind. But you need to do something with your life, Bryn, and social media is *not* a life. You don't want to work for Dad and me? Fine. Get a job somewhere. We'll let you take the boat or a car. If you don't want to do that, well, we'll coddle you a little longer, but you gotta do chores, at least."

Bryn rolls her eyes. "What kind of job?"

"With us or elsewhere?"

Another shrug and an eye roll. "I don't know, whatever."

I laugh. "Careful, there, Bryn, or you'll end up flipping burgers. Which, there's nothing wrong with that, but I don't think that's what you have in mind."

Bryn points at her mom. "If you say anything like, 'why can't you be more like her,' I swear I'm going to flip this table."

Layla snorts. "I'd never say that. I don't want you to be more like Rin, I want you to be more like you, just a more ambitious you."

Bryn sighs. "I'll figure something out. As long as it doesn't involve cleaning toilets. Killian's is dis-*gus*-ting."

Layla just laughs. "If you ask him nicely, your father would probably help you decide what you would be good at and what you would enjoy. He's got a knack for that sort of thing."

Bryn shrugs. "That's not a bad idea."

Layla checks her phone. "Okay, well, we'd better head to the island. Kyrie is there alone, and she goes stir-crazy if she's alone for too long."

It's a good day. Mom, Auntie Layla, Bryn, and I get our nails done and spend the afternoon chatting and gossiping. Killian, the only male on the island, seeks out the security guards just for someone with testicles to talk to. Around six or so, Duke and Temple show up, flown in by one of Uncle Harry's pilots; Duke is a licensed pilot himself, but for longer hauls and water landings, he leaves it to the professionals.

Duke has always seemed the most ageless, of all of Uncle Harry's inner circle. He's the youngest, granted, but he's still in his fifties—you wouldn't know it, though, looking at him. His hair is every bit as thick and red as it was in the photos I've seen of him in his prime, with only hints of silver at the temples. He used to have it shaved on the sides and long on top, but abandoned the style at some point; now, it's simply long all over, tied back in a low ponytail. If he hasn't shaved in a few days, you can see some gray in his stubble, and there are deep crow's feet around his eyes. But other than that? He could pass for thirty-five. He's not lost a single pound of muscle mass since his prime, either, I'd guess, standing six-six in his socks and weighing at least two-eighty. In other words, Duke is simply massive. And, for an old guy, fine as hell.

Temple, his wife, is similarly ageless-seeming, five-seven and still a blonde bombshell to rule all bombshells, with very few hints of her true age. Together, they're a couple with star power—Temple because after meeting and marrying Duke, she transitioned from reality star to business executive and touring speaker, and Duke simply by virtue of his looks and charm and constant presence wherever Temple went; Temple had been famous when she met Duke, and her fame never lessened, even though she had stopped filming her reality series to focus on running her businesses, and then to raise their children.

Duke is hysterical, which is why Cal and I both love it so much when he comes over. He has no filter over his words whatsoever, saying things that are outrageous, wildly inappropriate, and ridiculous.

We have a wild evening over wine and a smorgasbord of food, the conviviality lasting well into the night. The drinking age in the islands is eighteen, so even though I'm legally allowed to drink, Mom still monitors my consumption rate. By the time Mom, Layla, Duke, and Temple are ready to call it a night, I'm tipsy and giggly, and Bryn and I decide to walk our buzzes off on the beach…with the last of a bottle of wine.

The stars are high and bright and innumerable, and Bryn and I are arm in arm, keeping each other balanced and upright, mostly.

"Rin?" She leans her head on my shoulder. "You're not mad about Cal, are you? About earlier?"

I blow a raspberry. "Nah. He did look really handsome in that suit. But he's my brother. And we're like sisters, you know? So, our brothers are off-limits… right?"

She lifts her head from my shoulders. "You say that like you've had thoughts about Killy."

"He's good-looking. There's no denying that. But…he's your little brother."

"Right." A pause. "And Cal is your little brother."

"Right."

A long silence, in which we turn and walk back toward the house. "It's just…I don't really think about Cal like a brother, or a cousin, or anything. He's your little brother, yeah, but…"

"Bryn, what are you saying?"

She shrugs. "I like him. That's all." A sigh. "He's funny and cool, and fun."

"I don't know what to do with what you're implying, Bryn."

"I'm not implying anything. Chicks before dicks, and all that, right?"

"Bryn, ew."

"What?"

"Chicks before dicks? Really?"

She laughs. "It's what they say. Bros before hoes and chicks before dicks."

"Yeah, but you're saying it in reference to my brother."

"No, just in general. You come before anyone I like. Especially your brother."

I huff. "Can we just…not talk about this?"

We've woven an uneven path back along the beach toward the house, which is a spread of low blocky shapes in the shadows, moonlight reflecting off glass, shimmering on the surface of the ocean on our right. I stop, blinking against the blurriness of my vision. There's something out in the water, a darker shadow against the waves—there's a buoy way out there, a green light blinking steadily in the distance, marking the channel; a shadow moves across it, but if it's a boat, it's unlit and unmarked, which is weird.

I dismiss it—we have Duke here, for one thing, plus the regular guards. It's always seemed like overkill to have four to six armed guards on the island at all times, considering nothing has ever even remotely happened. I know the stories and legends of what happened, before any of us were born, but that was twenty years ago and everyone involved that could threaten my parents or Bryn and Killian's is dead.

Bryn stumbles a little, and I go with her, and we topple to the sand, laughing. Make our way to feet, and I leave Bryn at the door to her room.

My own suite of rooms is huge, a small kitchenette open to the expansive living room, which, like all the rooms of this house, opens on all four walls to the elements. The only rooms that don't open that way are bathrooms, but even those feature skylights of one-way tinted glass, with outdoor showers cleverly concealed behind concentric walls. I tend to leave the doors all open, for the most part, since each set of personal quarters is out of sight of the others, hidden behind copses of trees, with the only approaches angled so that you arrive at the kitchen or living room and not in view of the bedrooms. I like having the walls open so the breeze wafts over me, so the sun wakes me.

I collapse into bed, half drunk and exhausted from a day on my feet that began just past dawn.

I don't know what wakes me, but I sit up, suddenly totally awake. It's still before dawn, the darkness just beginning to be leavened by gray. I look around—stars, my dresser, nightstand with my alarm clock reading 4:24 a.m., trees standing in the stillness. Nothing.

I don't hear anything, and that's what sends my heart to pounding. Usually, a few birds are up and chirping by this time. Or maybe a few late crickets, or frogs.

Nothing. Dead silence.

And then the world goes dark, something wrapping around my face, occluding my vision. Something sharp and cold touches my throat.

"Don't move," a voice hisses. "Don't move, don't make a sound. Cooperate and you will not be harmed." The voice is nothing but a barely audible hiss in the darkness, indeterminate age and gender.

I do nothing, just hold still, frozen, tears of terror and confusion trickling down my cheeks.

"Open your mouth."

I do as I'm told, and the moment my lips part, something soft and smelling of fabric softener is shoved into my mouth—a sock. Then I feel something pressed over my lips—tape, wrapped around my head several times. Even if I tried, now, any sound I made would be muffled and inaudible unless you were within a few feet of me. The blindfold or hood is left over my eyes.

My hands are bound behind my back with thin, hard cord; whoever it is abducting me doesn't just tie my wrists together, he—I'm assuming it's a he, despite no hard evidence either way—forces me to clasp my fingers together like I'm praying, fingertips angled down, shoulders pulled back into an unnatural and uncomfortable position, and then my wrists are bound tightly, the cord wrapping around my fingers to keep my fingers tangled, and then another cord is wrapped tightly around my elbows—I'm trussed into helplessness, unable to move my arms except an inch or two away from my body, and that with increasing discomfort.

I'm hauled to my feet, and a hand wraps into my hair, using it as reins to guide me in a forced march.

I'm barefoot, and still dressed in my outfit from yesterday: a short, lime green tennis skirt and a halter top shirt that leaves my entire back bare. I'm not wearing a bra, a tendency of mine that drives Mom nuts. I'm barefoot.

My captor guides me away from the house, into the woods behind it, frog-marching me at a quick clip through the trees. Abruptly, I'm shoved to the ground, tripped off my feet and shoved face-first in the dirt.

"Down—silent." The hissed commands are directly in my ear.

I can hear the maleness, now. A hint of an accent, maybe, something indeterminate in the formation of the vowel sounds and the harshness of the consonants. The hand stays knotted in my hair, pulling painfully at the roots. I'm too afraid to resist, and I remember the feel of the knife edge at my throat; I'm surprisingly calm, despite my fear. Perhaps it's shock, or adrenaline, or just something in my nature, but I know somehow that if I were to throw a fit or struggle, I'd be dead before I got a second breath out. I can feel it in my gut, in the way he holds my hair, the brusque efficiency of the way he maneuvers me—this isn't for pleasure. He's got no immediate plans of doing anything like raping me. No, this is a kidnapping. This is about Mom and Dad.

They'll get me back. Mom, Dad, Duke, Uncle

Harry—they'll get me back. I just have to stay alive, and keep my wits about me.

So, I stay down, my cheek biting into the dirt. I smell the earth, the faint musk of rotting vegetation. Something wriggles past my nose, and I force myself to not react.

A long moment passes, and then I'm unceremoniously yanked to my feet by my waist, the hand retakes its hold in my hair, winding my long sheaf of hair around his hand until it's pulled painfully tight, and then I'm marched forward again, slowly, silently. Whomever it is behind me, abducting me, he's utterly silent. His feet make barely a crunch in the dirt.

The trip is long, since we go slow, step by step, often halting for long moments—fortunately, I'm not shoved into the dirt on my face again, but several times he does kick at the back of my knees to make me go down to my knees, waiting until—I assume—the security guard has passed us on his rounds through his section of the island.

Slowly, slowly, the shushing of the surf becomes louder. Then I can tell by the damp sand underfoot that we're at the water's edge. He lifts me bodily, his hands around my waist, efficient and businesslike, and sets me in what feels like a rubber boat.

I'm jerked forward as he shoves off, and I hear his feet in the water.

Splashing, but quietly. And then the boat rocks

as he rolls in. A moment of still silence, and then a rhythmic, nearly silent splashing, and movement—he's rowing us away from the island.

The rowing lasts for a long time, or so it seems. I have little means of measuring the passage of time except my own heartbeats and the endless chuck of the paddle. Eventually, the boat bumps to a halt. Something is said, far above me, in a language I don't recognize, and there's the mechanical whir of a winch or something like that. Something bumps against the rubber of the boat.

I'm lifted by hands under my legs and around my shoulders, transferred to a seat or a basket, and then I'm rising in the air for several long seconds. Then the upward movement stops, and I twist, sway. Hands grab me—again with businesslike impersonality. Set me on my feet.

The same hissing voice, louder now, but not by much. "Walk forward. No sounds. Resist, and this is over quickly but painfully."

I walk forward—we're on a boat, and a rather large one, I can tell, by the slow shallow rocking. I'm stopped, hinges creak, a body moves past me, and I'm lifted again, lowered and then dropped. I fall a few feet, hit the deck and topple over. It's painful, but I'm not injured. Back to my feet, and now I hear our footsteps echoing closely, meaning we're inside the boat, in the narrow hallways.

Turning this way and that, walking for several minutes. Another drop, more walking.

We're in the bowels of the boat, now. I can feel and hear the massive engines chugging.

Stop.

A door creaks open, and I'm pushed through. The sharp edge touches my chin. "I'm going to free your hands. Do not move even to breathe or blink until you hear the door close."

My only answer is to wait, motionless.

"If you continue to cooperate, you will be treated well. We will feed you. Allow you to use the toilet. You will not be harmed." This voice is low and rough, as if this is as loud as he's capable of speaking. There's definitely a hint of an accent. European, somewhere. German, possibly, or Scandinavian. "No screaming. No trying to escape. You're at sea, so there's nowhere to go, unless you can swim for days." The knife presses a little harder, pricking with a hot point of pain. "Understand?"

I nod once.

"Good."

A couple quick movements of the knife, and my hands are freed.

I don't move. I don't even breathe, my lungs aching as I wait.

The door closes, and I hear the grinding thunk of a heavy lock. Another moment I wait, and then I yank the hood off—it was a black cloth bag. Next, the gag, which requires unwinding the tape from my head, which pulls out long strands of my hair, since he wasn't exactly careful to keep my hair out of the tape. I spit out the sock, working my jaw and tongue, spitting again to rid my mouth of the taste of it.

The room is tiny, small enough I can almost touch all four walls with arms outspread. Metal walls, metal floor. No light. Nothing on the floor, no furniture.

The air is close, thick.

Now, I panic.

But I do so quietly, hyperventilating and sobbing without sound for who knows how long.

Eventually, I find my composure.

Dad will rescue me.

Uncle Harry will rescue me.

Duke, and Bubba Thresh.

Whoever has abducted me, I almost pity. He really, really doesn't know who he kidnapped.

More accurately, perhaps, who he pissed off by doing so.

I just have to stay alive and in one piece until they can find me.

Preferably, unviolated as well.

Don't think about that, I tell myself.

Just breathe, just wait. Obey. Keep calm. Remember anything I hear or see, just in case.

My mental pep talk works a little.

For a moment, I allow myself to feel scared—I want my mom.

I put it aside. Shove it down. I'm not a little girl. I'm twenty, an adult, a competent one. I can do this. Whatever happens, I can handle it.

I'm the daughter of Kyrie and Valentine Roth. I can do this.

3

AN UNKNOWN ENEMY

It's late when I wake up—late for me, at least. My Valentine has always been a very early riser, so over the years I've become one as well. I'm considering maybe getting up, although I'd rather just stay in bed and daydream about my husband a little longer; I was having the most delicious dream, remembering the lovely, dirty things we did his in tower, all those years ago.

Footsteps clomp noisily outside my bedroom door—I know that distinctive tread. It's Duke, running.

I lurch out of bed and wrap the blanket around me just as Duke bursts through, all but breaking the door down—I've got the walls closed, so the only way into my bedroom is through the door leading to the kitchen.

His eyes are wild and angry, his jaw pulsing. Every line of muscle in his body is taut—this is Duke as I haven't seen him in many, many years, action Duke, ready to kill. "Someone snatched Corinna," he bites out. "Right out of her room. Under my fucking nose, all of our noses."

My breath leaves my lungs, and I nearly collapse, only a hand on the wall keeping me upright. "*What*?"

"I'll show you."

I forget modesty, forget that I'm only wearing a bikini bottom and a tank top, running after Duke. The guards are visible, called in from the perimeter, now that it's too late—I see them all, pacing, weapons at the ready, fingers across the trigger guards.

Rin's room is open on three sides, the wall behind her bed shut, the rest open. No sign of struggle, although Rin's room always looks like a battle royale had happened. Nothing out of the ordinary.

On the center of her bed, a blank check, pinned to the mattress by a big black KA-BAR knife. Written in neat block letters, in red ink, one word:

SHE

That's it. Nothing else.

Three letters.

The check has no identifying marks, no account holder, no address, not even account number or routing number, just the plain, pale-blue paper, the Payable To line, In The Amount Of line, the box, date, the notes and signature lines.

Duke looks at me. "Who?"

I swallow hard, shake my head. "I don't know." I choke on a sob. "I don't know, Duke. Who? You tell me! We've made no enemies since Cain was taken out. The opposite, if anything. We've donated billions of dollars to charities, built hospitals, schools, dug wells, sent cargo planes of food, organized search parties and rebuilds after earthquakes and floods. Every takeover and acquisition has been friendly and professional. Who…" I shake my head, confusion and fear now mixing with pure, unadulterated rage. "Who would do this?"

"I don't know either."

"Have you called Harris or my husband?" I ask.

He shakes his head. "No. I showed you first."

"Call Harris. Get things in motion—do what A1S does." I hold his eyes. "When it was me, or Layla, that was one thing. Whoever did this? He took my fucking *daughter*."

Duke's eyes are the scary eyes of a man who has done awful things in the name of protection and war. "Understood. We'll get her back in one piece, Key."

"You had fucking better." I know it's not his fault—if they could snatch my daughter out of her room, off a private island guarded by five armed guards as well as Duke freaking Silver, without making a sound or firing a single shot? This was a professionally executed grab.

Duke's jaw grinds. "Out from under my fucking nose." He closes his eyes, breathes out slowly, carefully. "I can't fucking believe it. How fucking sloppy have I gotten?"

Temple touches his shoulder. "Don't, Duke. Clearly, whoever did this was a consummate professional. There's not so much as a footprint."

I knife downward with my hand. "Enough. There's no point assigning blame. It's done. Now we get my daughter back."

Duke whirls, phone at his ear. "Yeah, boss—we've got a situation…"

I'm outside, still heedless of my state of undress, dialing Valentine's number. It rings twice, and he answers. "About to start the meeting. What's up, babe?"

I don't waste time or words. "Someone has kidnapped Corinna. Right off the island, under our noses. No one was hurt, not a shot was fired, there's no footprints, no struggle, nothing. Duke is sending Harris the only…evidence."

The silence is long and profound. "Fuck."

"Who would do this, Val? After all these years, who?"

"I don't know." A pause. "One moment, gentlemen. I've just become aware of a family emergency."

To me, then. "Get off the island. Take everyone to the penthouse in Miami. It's fortified, guarded, and monitored. Leave your phones, leave everything. Get dressed and go."

"Okay."

"Key?" His voice is like ice. "We'll get her back."

"And god help whoever took her."

He hangs up, then, and I merely toss the phone aside, into the dirt at my feet. Moving on autopilot, I get dressed quickly in sensible clothing, jeans, a bra, T-shirt, socks, sneakers, hair in a ponytail and a ball cap. By the time I'm done, Killian, Layla, and Bryn have been apprised of the situation and are dressed, gathered in the kitchen.

"We leave our phones, take nothing but the clothes we're wearing." I scan the faces of my loved ones—including Duke and Temple. "We don't know who, how, or why, so we're operating under the assumption that whoever took Corinna is a threat to all of us." I glance at Duke. "We have transportation out of here?"

He nods. "A seaplane to get us to St. Thomas, and a jet to Miami from there." He's armed to the teeth, wearing a bulletproof vest over a plain black T-shirt, magazines for an assault rifle as well as sidearms in the webbing. He's carrying a full auto submachine gun by a strap clipped to the front of the vest. "Let's go." He points, and two of the guards lead the way, moving in the tactical crouch, weapons at shoulders.

The guards on our island change every day, and I rarely see them—it's that way on purpose, so no one gets familiar, so security doesn't get lax through routine, and so we who live on the island are as unaware as possible that they're even here, in order to maintain some semblance of normalcy. Or, at least as close to a semblance of normalcy as you can get when you're living on a private island, that is.

By the time we reach the docks, I've gotten my panic and fury on lockdown—I've experienced enough to know those emotions will only hamper my judgment, so I simply cannot indulge in them. They're there, simmering on the back burner, but I focus on the moment at hand, on getting everyone else to safety and figuring out a game plan.

Two guards precede us to the seaplane, Duke on one side of the small group comprised of Bryn, Killian, Layla, and me, with another guard on the other side of us and two more behind, each man with a full-size assault rifle, body armor, their heads swiveling constantly, faces impassive. This is a standard-issue twin-prop seaplane rather than an RTI special. Once Duke is in, one of the guards takes the pilot's seat, his rifle hanging at his side, another sitting on the back of the boat, clipped by a harness to a ring in the boat so he can face aft.

Layla seated beside me, gestures at the sidearm holstered low on Duke's thigh. "I need a piece," she says. "If this shit goes sideway, no way in fuck-bananas am I going into it unarmed."

Bryn and Killian stare at her.

"Did she just say…fuck-bananas?" Killian whispers to Bryn—they're next to Layla, Bryn closest, then Killian.

"Yes, I did," Layla answers, having heard him.

"More to the point," Bryn says, not bothering to whisper, "since when do you know how to shoot, Mom? I haven't seen you even hold a gun in my entire life."

Duke laughs outright, a belly laugh. "Why shit, son, yo mama is a legit, true-blue badass, a certified ball-busting killer."

Bryn and Killian laugh with him, but their laughter quickly fades when they cotton on 6to the fact that Duke isn't joking.

"Wait, really?" Killian says.

Bryn just looks skeptical.

Duke laughs again. "Kid, you don't know shit about the woman your mother really is. The loving mother, the doting wife? Yeah, that's not the whole story."

Layla huffs. "It's been the story for the last twenty years, and I was pretty damn content for it to keep being the story. So, I'm feeling kinda salty at whichever dick-licker is ruining my peaceful mama vibes."

Bryn claps her hand over her mouth, stifling a laugh. "Mom!"

Layla waves her off. "Oh hush, Bryn. You've heard me curse your whole lives."

"Yeah, but this...a different side of you."

Duke unbuckles and pulls a small black hard-plastic case from under his seat and retrieves a pistol, two magazines, and a holster with a shoulder harness. Layla unbuckles, sits forward on the seat, shrugging into the harness with practiced ease, clipping it and adjusting it, and then slotting the gun into the holster. She practices drawing the pistol, adjusting the position of the holster and harness at each draw, until it's smooth and quick. Then, she disassembles the gun to its components, balancing each component on her thighs, sighting through the barrel to check the cleanliness of the weapon, and then reassembles it so smoothly it's clear she could do it blindfolded.

"Mom can strip a pistol?" Killian mutters. "What next?"

"Let's hope you don't have to find out what your mom can actually do," Layla says, half to herself. "I was very much hoping I was done killing people."

Bryn's eyes widen. "You've...*killed* people?"

Duke arches an eyebrow. "When I told you she was a badass killer, did you think I was joking?"

"Yeah, kinda." Bryn shrugs, eying her mom as if seeing her for the first time. "I mean, she's...*Mom*."

Layla re-buckles, meeting Bryn's eyes and then Killian's. "Listen, kids. I'm really, really hoping this will all be solved without bloodshed, without you two being involved, or having to see anything gross. But if this is anything like the shit that went down before we had you two, it could very well get pretty gnarly." She's utterly serious, now, a rarity for Layla. "I just want you to hear it from me, now: I'm your mom. Nothing you may see me do changes who I am. I breastfed each of you, changed your diapers, taught you to walk, kissed your boo-boos, everything. I'm still and always your mama. But...I'm not *just* your mama."

"Give 'em the marching orders on how to act if shit goes sideways," Duke suggests.

Layla nods, and then points to Duke and herself. "If we tell you to drop, you hit your bellies and you put your face in the dirt and you don't move a goddamn muscle until we say so. If we tell you to run, you run like the devil himself is on your six."

"Six?" Bryn asks.

"Behind you," Killian murmurs.

Bryn's nose wrinkles. "Oh, okay."

Layla continues. "You can't freeze. You can't decide you can't handle it. You push through and you keep your shit together, and you fall apart when it's over." She taps their chests in turn. "You're Harrises. You do what's gotta get done and you deal with it."

Bryn and Killian seem to finally be coming to grips with the reality of this side of their mother, and recognizing that this situation is deadly serious—of course it is, but there's a difference between knowing Rin is missing and understanding that getting her back may not be a simple scenario.

I glance at Duke. "Who's meeting us in Miami?"

"Thresh and Harris." He adjusts his rifle. "Lear is wherever Lear is, doing what Lear does best, which is technological wizardry, trying to figure out if there's any chatter about who's behind this grab. Anselm? Well, I honestly don't know. Once Story left home for university in Geneva, Anselm and Selah went pretty well off-grid. I think Harris has a means of contacting him, and I'm guessing he will be if he hasn't already, seeing as one of our own has been snatched."

I nod. "And Puck?"

"He's heading to the island to see if he can find any evidence or leads."

"What about the cameras?" I ask. "I know we have video surveillance."

"I looked it over myself, if briefly. Either a real pro altered it, or the operative managed to avoid being seen. The cameras, for privacy reasons, don't cover actual bedrooms themselves, only the approaches." He rubs his forehead with a knuckle. "Again, whoever did this knew exactly what the fuck they were doing. It was, in all honesty, probably the most surgical grab I've ever seen in my life."

"And the note?"

"It's en route to a forensic specialist," he says, "but my guess is they won't find shit. The check is generic, possibly even just printed at a Kinkos or something, same with the ink, and handwriting doesn't mean shit. The knife is a paramilitary piece you can get for twenty, thirty bucks at any surplus store, and again there won't be prints. No-go, there."

"So we have zero leads." I lick my lips, force myself to breathe slowly and deeply. Keep the emotions on lockdown.

"So far," Duke says with a wince. "But you know the guys." He fiddles with the butt of his rifle, tracing the outline with a fingertip. "And I guess I would say it's good news that there's no sign of a struggle—it means she's likely unhurt. The weird note complicates it, but I'm guessing this is about money."

I shake my head. "No, I don't think so, Duke." I frown. "Something is off. The check, the one word. It…it smacks of something personal. Someone copycatting off of how Valentine and I met, somehow. Why, I don't know. But that's my personal intuition."

Duke nods. "Well, I know better than to doubt a woman's intuition, especially a mother's."

The rest of the flight to Miami is silent. I'm lost

in thought, praying to God or the universe or whomever for my Rin to be safe.

I barely notice when we touch down on the roof of the building we own in Miami. Duke herds me out of the jet and into the elevator just off the landing pad which leads directly into the living quarters. I'm in a daze, now, adrenaline and jet-fuel emotions giving way to shock. I allow it to roll over me, for now. I'll need my wits about me, and soon, but for a moment or two, I have to simply allow myself to wallow in shock. Duke and Temple and Layla get everyone situated, and I hear Duke on the phone with Harris, but nothing really enters my brain.

At some point, I find myself in bed, lights out, staring at the ceiling, one sentence echoing in my head over and over again: *please be safe, Rin—please be safe, Rin—please be safe, Rin.*

"Key?" It's Layla, shaking me awake. "Sorry, babe, but the building manager needs to speak with you."

I frown at her. "Okay?"

She pats me on the thigh. "Come on, babe. He needs to see you. Now."

I roll out of bed—I'm still fully dressed, shoes included. "What time is it?"

"Just past nine."

"A-M or P-M?"

"The next day. You slept all night." She rubs my back. "You needed it."

"My husband?"

She shrugs. "Not here."

I follow her out of the bedroom and into the main living area—Harris and Thresh are at the large, rectangular, eight-person table between the kitchen and the den, clutching mugs of steaming coffee, poring over a mess of printouts and folders of documents.

Harris sees me and comes over to me. "Key, hi."

"Layla says the building manager is asking for me?" I ask.

This is highly unusual. When we're here, the standing orders are that we are left alone except in cases of extreme emergency, and all staff is to hold to a basic statement along the lines of *I cannot give out any information, thank you.*

The building manager never sees us. We clean the penthouse ourselves while we're here, and once we're gone, it's cleaned by a dedicated crew of cleaners specifically selected for that purpose.

Harris nods, expression grim and serious. "Yes. Follow me."

He leads me to the foyer area—a rather spacious room between the private elevator and the living quarters. The elevator goes to our private parking garage, a private ground-level exit, and the roof. Not even the manager has access to it—to contact us, he has to call a specific phone number with a prearranged code.

All these layers of security, and my daughter was kidnapped? It doesn't seem possible.

I accompany Harris onto the elevator, once it's in motion down to the ground level exit, I glance at him. "Where are my husband and son?"

"New York, still," he answers. "We thought it safest to keep everyone separate for now. They're at a safe house, guarded by two full fireteams. When I told him you were asleep, he told me to let you sleep and to have you call him when you woke up. There're no developments as yet—forensics of the island reveal nothing except a couple partial footprints which tell us nothing. Same with the note and knife, and security footage. We have a glimpse of a figure in the shadows approaching Rin's quarters, but not enough to tell us anything."

"Okay, well, I'll see what the manager wants and then call Val."

The elevator halts and the doors open—Harris has a pistol in hand, held down by his thigh, and he scans as the doors open—there are four A1S guards in the small foyer just outside the elevator. Each guard is in full body armor, carrying an assault rifle.

They surround the building manager and an additional person; the manager looks…rattled.

He's middle-aged, with a receding hairline, wearing a very fine charcoal suit with a crimson tie and matching pocket square. "M-Miss Roth, good morning. My apologies for bothering you this way, but…"

Harris gestures at the additional individual, a young woman in a tailored power suit, wearing sensible pumps. She's white, pretty enough, brunette… she could be anyone, and you'd never pick her out in a crowd. "Who's she?" He holds her gaze. "Who're you?"

She has a DHL document mailer in her hands. "My name is Emily, I'm with Next Day Courier Services. I have instructions to deliver this package to Mrs. Kyrie St. Claire Roth, at this address, at this time. I am not allowed to release the package to anyone except the recipient." She holds my gaze. "May I see your identification, please?"

I shrug, frowning. "My ID? It's upstairs in my purse."

Harris motions to one of the guards. "Kitchen counter. White clutch. Get it."

The guard nods once, enters the elevator, and Harris leans in, uses a key to send the car up. A couple moments later, the elevator returns, and the guard emerges with my purse in his gloved hand—his or her, I should say, since the guard is of medium height and build and is wearing a full helmet with visor and balaclava, obscuring identifying features.

I take the clutch and produce my ID, show it to

the courier, who examines it, nods. "Very good. Sign here, please." She hands me a clipboard with a triplicate receipt, which I sign and receive a copy, and then I'm finally handed the mailer. "Thank you, and have a nice day, ma'am." She turns to leave.

"Wait," I say. "Who sent it?"

She shrugs. "I have no idea, ma'am, and even if I did, I couldn't tell you. All I know is I received the package from my boss with my instructions. Deliver to the recipient only, with proof of identification."

"I see. Thank you, Emily." I take the package onto the elevator, and wait.

Harris glances at the manager. "I'm giving you my personal number. Any other deliveries or anything of the sort, you call me directly." Harris produces a business card and hands it to the manager. "Needless to say, that number is for your eyes only, and only in the event of another delivery or if anyone asks about Mrs. Roth."

"Understood, sir," the manager says.

Harris merely nods, and joins me on the elevator. "Wait to open it," he tells me.

We reach the penthouse and Harris takes the mailer from me and examines it, probing it with his fingers, examining the seal, and attempting to determine the contents by feel.

"Everyone back," he orders. "Not taking any chances. Out of the room, everyone."

"Nick, now hold on," Layla says. "Why are you opening it, if you're worried it's a bomb or something?"

"I don't think it is, but I'm not taking any chances. Now out." He doesn't look at his wife, and she seems to recognize that this is an instance where it's best to not argue. All of us retreat into my bedroom, as Harris draws a folding knife from his pocket and opens it. A moment later, he calls out. "All clear."

When I get to his side, he has the envelope open and has dumped the contents onto the table. Another generic check without any identifying features, with another word in the same ink and same block letters:

BELONGS

Harris swears, a long, florid, creative string of curses. "Starting to sound familiar," he says.

I'm already dialing my husband. He answers on the first ring, his face and shoulders appearing on the screen.

I angle the device to show him the note. "This just arrived."

He lets out a long, ragged sigh. "Someone seems to think this is a fucking game, clearly."

"Who *is* this, Valentine?" I demand. "Gina's dead, Vitaly's dead, Cain is dead. Who else could be doing this to us? Using our own story against us?"

At this point in our lives, the details of how we met have been the subject of news articles, documentaries, streaming specials, and even a feature film with A-list actors.

"I have no idea," Valentine growls. "We're looking into it. But so far, whoever is behind this has covered their tracks pretty damn well."

"I'm guessing I'll get another delivery tomorrow," I say.

"Agreed."

"If they follow the story, after the last check is delivered, someone will come for me."

Valentine snarls wordlessly. "And you will *not* be getting in."

"The *fuck* I won't," I snap. "If this asshole has my daughter and wants me in return, I'm going and you'll just have to figure out how to get us both back."

"Kyrie—" he starts.

"This isn't a discussion, my love," I say, gentling my voice. "There is nothing I will not do for my children. *Nothing*."

He's silent. "Same. But…"

"There's nothing to say." I pause. "He has Rinna."

"Harris," Valentine says.

"I'm here," Harris answers, taking my phone from me. "We're working on it, you know we are."

"Work harder, goddammit," Valentine growls.

Harris breathes out softly, knuckling the bridge of his nose. "Valentine, you know I'm doing everything I can. That girl is a second daughter to me."

"I know, I know," Valentine sighs. "If something happens to Rin…"

"Nothing will happen to her. That serves no purpose. This is about you guys, not Rin. She's just a point of leverage."

"You don't know that," I say.

"No, I don't, not for sure," he answers, "but it's just logical. What value is there in Rin by herself except as your daughter—as an avenue to you guys?"

"This isn't some grab to get ransom," Duke says, joining us. "It was too precise. Some yahoos out for a few million in a cash ransom, it'd be sloppy and messy and you'd be getting fingers or some shit. This is personal."

"Getting fingers, Duke?" Layla snaps. "Really, asshole?"

"Sorry, I'm just—" Duke starts.

"Duke is right," I cut in. "As far as we know, she's unharmed. This is absolutely personal. We just have no clue who could be behind it, because as far as we know, all of our enemies are dead."

Harris blows out a breath. "Right. So, for now, we wait. I hate it, but we need more to go on. I'll have this most recent note examined by forensics as well, but so far, there's been nothing."

I look around at Duke, Layla, and Harris. "I need to talk to Val alone."

They nod and I take my phone into the bedroom. Close the door. "You really have no idea, Val?"

"You know all my secrets, Key."

"What do we do?" I whisper.

"Like you said, there's nothing I won't do for my daughter. If it's money they want, I'll drown them in it. But I do think this is personal, for all that I can't fathom who could hate us enough to kidnap our daughter like this. I don't think whoever this is interested in our money."

"What could they want?"

"To hurt us," he whispers. "Just hopefully…not through her."

"If they send someone, I'm going," I say.

"I know." He looks like he hasn't slept; I feel bad that I did, as if through sleeping I've lessened the emotional impact of this. "I hate it, but I know."

"I wish you were here," I whisper.

"Me too." He scrapes his hand through his hair. "I need to be with you. But if there's more to the plot than merely snatching Rin, it's safer if we're not all in one place. This safe house is a location known only to Harris, and it's not traceable back to us in any way. Even this phone I'm using is untraceable."

"Which begs the question of how they knew about this place? I thought we owned this building through a series of fronts?"

"Not fronts, exactly, but a complicated web of

subsidiaries. Still theoretical traceable, we just thought it extraordinarily unlikely." A pause. "But if you'd asked me a few hours ago, I'd have said our island was nigh impregnable."

"I'm scared, Val," I whisper.

"Me too," he answers. "But…I suppose I take a little comfort in one thing."

I sniffle. "What's that?"

"He has Rinna."

"God help him," I say, laughing.

"Do you think he has any clue what she's like?"

"I remember when Duke was missing, Harris said something about how they'd be rescuing them from Duke." I sniffle a laugh. "If anyone could come out of a kidnapping on top, it's that girl."

"Exactly," he says.

A different courier brings another note, the next day, as expected, with two more words:

TO ME

After that, nothing, for two more days.

4

THE LIMOUSINE

It's 5 p.m., two days after the last note arrived.

Duke has his phone to his ear. His face his pale, jaw grinding. He extends it to me without a word.

I take it. "Hello, this is Kyrie Roth."

"Mrs. Roth? This is Ernest, the building manager."

"Another courier?"

"No, ma'am." His voice is shaky. "A person. A man. With…with a gun…to my head. Demanding I allow him up to the penthouse. He says he's here to…to collect you."

I swallow hard. "Send him up."

"Kyrie!" Duke snaps. "Are you out of your fucking mind?"

I chop my hand sharply downward for silence. "Do as he says, Ernest."

"Yes ma'am." A pause. "I…I don't have the key for the elevator, ma'am."

"I'll send it down," I say.

A silence, then his scared, shaky voice. "Very good, ma'am. He says his patience is short, so the elevator had better be fast."

"It will be. Thank you, Ernest. And I'm sorry you've become involved in this."

"Not at all, Mrs. Roth."

It's all absurdly polite.

I end the call and turn to face the room. "Everyone out. To the jet, now. No questions."

"Key," Layla begins.

"If it was Bryn?"

Layla's teeth click down on the rest of her protest. "I'd go. And I'd be figuring out how I can kill some motherfuckers."

Duke is already ushering Bryn and Killian to the elevator up to the pad, while Harris and Layla hang back.

Harris withdraws a slim black case from his jacket pocket. "Lift your shirt up, Kyrie."

I don't hesitate or ask questions—I lift the hem of my T-shirt, exposing my belly and bra. The case contains a syringe, a red safety cap over the end of the needle. Harris stands perpendicular to me, facing my left side.

"Apologies, Kyrie," he murmurs, pinching a fold

of skin and subcutaneous fat where my armpit meets the edge of my breast, near the transition between strap and cup of my bra. He uses his teeth to remove the safety cap and presses the tip of the syringe to the fold of skin between his thumbs and forefinger. "Deep breath, don't tense."

I suck in a deep breath, and let it out. I feel a pinch as he inserts the needle under the skin at an angle. Depresses the plunger. Withdraws the needle and replaces the syringe into the case.

"Tracking device," Harris explains. "There's a chance you might be scanned, but it's a prototype designed to not show up. At the least, we'll be able to follow your movements until they notice it, and hopefully they won't."

I nod, letting my shirt drop into place. I toss my phone to Layla—she already has my purse. I let out a breath. "Go," I say. "I'll be fine."

Layla holds my eyes as she steps onto the elevator with her husband—and then they're gone. I send the other elevator down—there are two elevators in the suite, one up to the roof, and one down to the garage and exit.

I hear the jet overhead, loud and shaking the room slightly, and then it's gone.

I go back into the main area, closing the door between that and the foyer, needing a moment to collect myself.

The last time I did this, it turned out to be the best thing that had ever happened to me.

Something tells me this won't be anything like that.

I breathe slowly and deeply as I wait.

A few moments later, there's a knock at the door.

I open it, heart pounding…

The man on the other side is very tall, at least six-six. A complexion that could be Hispanic, Italian, Middle Eastern…anything. Slender, with a hard jawline stubbled with a new beard. Dark hair and beard, not quite black, but darker than brown. His brown eyes are so cold and lifeless as to be almost alien.

"It is time to pay your debt," he says.

His voice is a venomous purr. Accentless, not European, not American, not anything. Flat, impossible to place.

I say nothing. I have a million questions, but I know how this goes—this guy is a lackey. He knows nothing. Won't answer any questions if he did, and might hurt me to make a point about not asking those questions. So I just stay silent and wait for the instructions.

He scans me visually, then steps toward me. "Arms out."

I hold my arms out and wait as he frisks me—thoroughly but with professional and impersonal efficiency.

He gestures for me to enter the elevator, which I do; he turns the key to send us to the exit. The doors open—the guards are still there, clearly watching me for instructions. The man ushers me to the door. He even holds it open for me, but holds my arm to keep me in place.

"Get on the elevator," he instructs, eying the four guards. "Ride up."

They look at me, and I nod. "Do as he says."

The guards take the elevator up, and once they're gone, he gives me a gentle push out the door.

There's a long black limousine waiting. Utterly ordinary, a Lincoln limousine such as you'd hire from a service available anywhere. He opens the door for me, like a proper driver.

I do hesitate now, just for a moment.

Would you get in?

If it was your daughter?

I got in.

5

A GILDED CAGE

I HAVE NO CONCEPT OF TIME.

There's no light in my little prison, and when a man arrives—after an eternity, or a few minutes—to bring me food, there's no light beyond the door, either.

The door clunks, and a light turns on overhead, a dim yellow/amber can light recessed in the ceiling, dull but still bright enough to blind me, momentarily. The door opens, and a man steps through—he's short, dark-skinned but not black; he's wearing a bandanna around his face, covering his mouth and nose, so all I can see of him is his eyes. He has a red plastic cafeteria-type tray in his hands. On it, a bottle of water, a Styrofoam clamshell container, a package of plasticware, and a cup of chocolate pudding.

I wait, but all he does is set the tray on the floor.

I wait, but he doesn't leave. "Eat food all up," he says, in a thick accent I place as possibly Indian, "all finish, you hit on door." He slams his fist against the door twice, hard. "So. Yes?"

I nod. "Okay."

He frowns at me. "Eat all up the food."

Strange injunction. I shrug, make a confused face. "All right. I will."

He nods once, and steps backward out of the room. The door closes and the lock thunks. The light stays on, mercifully.

The clamshell contains a salad surprisingly with a piece of grilled chicken and a small plastic ramekin of oil-and-vinegar dressing. It is, against all expectations, delicious. I wonder at the command to eat it all, repeated twice, as if my preferred tactic would be a hunger strike. Like that'd do anything but hurt me and make me foggy-headed when I need above all to have my wits at full capacity.

The pudding is too sugary for my taste, but simply to avoid any unnecessary drama with the guard or whoever he is, I eat it all. I'm hoping to conserve the water, however, since the passage of time between arriving on the ship and now was marked mainly by my increasing thirst.

I pound on the door twice, and it is opened immediately. I back away. The same man enters, picks up the tray, but pauses when he sees me holding the half-finished water bottle.

“Finish,” he says, pointing at it.

I frown. “Can’t I save it?”

He shakes his head once, curtly. “Drink.”

I sigh in frustration, but finish the water—albeit slowly, in small sips. I feel him waiting, and getting impatient, but chugging it won’t do me any good. When I’m done, I cap the empty bottle and hand it to him.

He holds the tray with the trash on it one-handed. Eyes me. “Toilet?”

So considerate.

I only shake my head. “Not yet.”

“Hit on door, two time. Then back.”

I nod my understanding, and he withdraws. Closes the door, and I hear it thunk as it locks.

The light turns off.

And so passes the time. Am I fed three times a day? I don’t know. No two meals are the same. There’s thick oatmeal with blueberries once, which could mark the beginning of a second day. Maybe. A gyro, with potato chips. Stew, rich and hearty. It’s all very good food. The same guard, every time.

Finally, I do have to use the bathroom, so I pound on the door twice, and then step back to the far side of the small room. The man opens the door, and this time he has a shotgun in his hands, pistol grip, sawed-off double barrels. Pointed at me. He gestures with it for me to step out—I do so, blinking at the light.

The walls are narrow, the ceiling low and writhing with plumbing and electrical. It's clean, but aged. He touches the center of my back with the shotgun, which I take to be instructions to walk. There's a left turn, and then a right, the hallways branching at each turn so that unless I count turns I'd be lost quickly. No other doors that we pass. Finally, there's a bulkhead, and on the other side, an open door to a bathroom. Or, rather, in broader world terms, a toilet or water closet, just a tiny room with a metal toilet and a small foot-pump sink. For sure no escape from here, even if I was so inclined.

I use the bathroom, wash my hands, and when I emerge, he brings me back to my room—except, he takes me a different route than we used to get here, passing a few closed doors and going through more than one bulkhead. Keeping me disoriented, I suppose.

It works.

Back to the cell.

The engine rumbles always, sometimes increasing in tempo and thus pitch, but for the most part, it's a constant grumbling rumble.

I lose count of meals—if I had to guess, and if I'm

assuming three meals a day, then it's probably going on four days? Maybe.

It's honestly so boring it's impossible to sustain fear. The only break in the monotony is when my guard brings me food and the occasional trip to the bathroom—the hallways in the belly of this ship must be a hell of a maze, because we never take exactly the same route twice, and I know I have no chance of finding my way out on my own, even if I were to be able to leave the room and overpower the guard.

My best bet, still, is just play along and pay attention.

At some point, I notice a difference in the sound of the engine—an abrupt increase, in pitch meaning acceleration, and then a decrease, and then another increase.

Docking?

My guess is confirmed when the sound of the engine reduces to an almost inaudible idle. A long stretch of more nothing. Then, finally, the door unlocks and the light turns on. My constant guard is there, again with the sawed-off shotgun.

He has a black bundle of cloth in his hands. He tucks the shotgun under his arm, clearly assured by my track record of behavior that I'm not going to rush him, and digs in his back pocket, producing a sock and a roll of duct tape.

He hesitates. Eyes me. “You quiet?”

I nod eagerly. “You don’t need to gag me. I’ll keep quiet.”

His eyes harden. “Silent.”

I hold my hands together in a praying gesture. “Promise.”

“Make noise, very bad,” he warns. “Trouble for me, trouble for you.”

“I promise.” The thought of being gagged again is worse than anything else. The taste of the sock, the ache in my jaw, the tape around my face pulling my hair and skin…ughh, no. I’ll keep my damn mouth shut on my own, thank you very much. Mama didn’t raise a fool—I know that whatever this is about, my best bet is to keep cooperating until I see a clear opportunity. I’d really like to not be beaten up or raped, thank you, and so far, it seems like as long as I’m good, I’ll be left alone.

And fed some pretty damn good food, honestly.

“The food was very good,” I say. “Thank you.”

He grins. “Good? Good.” He taps his chest. “I make.”

“It was excellent. I’m grateful.”

He shoves the sock and tape back in his back pocket. Fiddles with the hood. Taps his chest again.

"No bad man, me. This?" He gestures at me. "No good. But…" a shrug. "Need money. So."

"You've been kind, and I'm grateful. What's your name?"

"Arnau Cadenes."

"I'll remember you, Arnau Cadenes."

He frowns, as if perhaps this came across as more of a threat than I meant it. But then he shakes his head and lifts the hood. "Put on."

I take it and put it on.

His hands are work-roughened and hard as he takes my hands in his, brings them behind my back. I hear duct tape, and my hands and wrists are taped tightly together. He then tests the tightness of my bonds. Satisfied, he puts a hand to my back and nudges me forward.

"Step."

I take an exaggerated step, and then he turns me to the left. Walk forward. His guiding is gentle but firm. Finally, we come to a stop. His hands grab me by the waist, and I'm lifted—he grunts slightly, because I'm not a delicate little thing.

I'm tempted to tell him it'd be easier to just let me climb on my own, but I hold my tongue. Another pair of hands grasps me, heaves me upward, and I'm set on my feet.

This time, these new hands cop a feel, groping my breasts with a rough, lingering squeeze.

A harsh voice snaps something, and there's the distinctive sound of a fist hitting flesh. A grunt. Voices confer, briefly.

BLAM!

The report of the pistol is loud, but I can tell we're outside. I hear something wet, and then a thud.

Another rapid exchange.

My guard's voice, low, near my ear. "He touch, he die."

My heart is hammering—I've been groped worse at the bar and dealt with it myself. But in this case, the hammering of my heart is because I just heard someone get shot and killed.

My stomach roils.

I bite it back, because If I vomit, I'll likely be gagged again, and I don't know if I can handle that again.

I'm marched forward, and now I can hear a chaos of sounds: ships' horns blaring far off, an overlapping of chattering voices and laughter and shouts, squeaking of metal on metal, clanging, engines idling and roaring up to speed and rattling, metal banging off metal in deafening booms...a port, I would guess.

The air is hot, humid.

They're going to bundle a bound and hooded kidnap victim off the ship in broad daylight at a busy port? Bold.

But then I hear the answer: a helicopter

approaching. It's landing close, too, I realize, as the downdraft nearly batters me off my feet—only Arnau's hold on me keeps me upright. And then he's hustling me forward, hand on my head to keep me ducked and bent, my belly meets an edge, and new hands lift me.

A hand grips my ankle and squeezes, briefly. I only nod my head.

Arnau Cadenes. He was kind.

The noise inside the helicopter is deafening. I'm seated in a chair, and hands buckle a lap belt across my hips, yet again with impersonality. It's awkward and uncomfortable, being buckled in with my hands behind my back.

A door closes, and the noise lessens, but I'd still have to shout to be heard—not that I'm planning on talking.

My stomach lurches as we lift up, up, up, and then tilt to the side and forward. It's disorienting, feeling movement but not being able to see.

I know there's someone else in the cabin with me—I feel a thigh touching mine occasionally as the aircraft jostles.

Sense of motion recedes once we're moving. I'd estimate a trip of over an hour, at least, and then we're circling and descending. Touching down. I'm unbuckled, handed down to my feet, a hand once again pressing my head down as the downdraft beats on me.

Through a doorway, which closes with a loud

slam, abruptly cutting the noise of the helicopter to a muffled roar.

Walked forward a few steps, then a hand on my arm stops me. "Stairs down." The voice is an accented growl.

I cast around with my foot, find the edge, and step down. His hand remains on my arm, but I manage to make it down the staircase mostly on my own without incident.

Man, by the time this is over, I'm going to be an expert at walking around blindfolded.

It's a long trip down, and we emerge in what sounds like an underground parking garage.

I hear an engine idling, and a car door opens, closes. Another opens, and I'm guided into a car, a hand pushing on the outside of my hip to rotate me so I'm sitting sideways in the car—a limousine.

Silence, then, and a long, long drive, swaying this way and that around occasional curves.

Stop.

Guided out. Same person, different? No way to know and it doesn't matter. This time, I'm guided by two people, a hand at each arm. This feels more final. Two guards is...official.

An elevator ride up.

The doors open.

I'm pushed forward, stumbling a step. Behind me, the elevator doors close. The sound of something heavy scraping across stone, metal hinges squeaking gently. Another push forward, half a dozen steps, and I stop. The same scraping as of enormous doors sliding across stone or tile, and a resounding slam of the doors closing, the noise echoing as if I'm in a fairly large room.

I can sense, somehow, that I'm alone, now.

My heart pounds.

I'm sweating.

I can smell myself—I don't smell very nice.

I swore I wouldn't say anything, so I wait.

And wait.

I sense nothing, no one.

Finally, I break. "Hello?"

Nothing.

I cast out with my toe in a sweeping arc. Forward, sweep. I reach something—a wall. I put my back to it and sit down.

How long, then? Hours?

Despite being bound, I manage to doze off.

Like the night I was taken, I'm not sure what wakes me up.

A sense.

A…something.

A smell.

Soap, and expensive cologne.

I inhale—it's a good smell. Male. Clean. The fragrance is quite frankly intoxicating—spicy, a hint of something musky, a hint of sweet.

I don't move. Barely breathe.

"You're awake, Corinna Roth." His voice is deep, smooth, strong. Accented. Greek?

I don't answer.

"Are you gagged? They were supposed to gag you."

I don't answer. I don't want to get Arnau in trouble.

Fingers touch my breastbone where the hood ends, slip under. Touch my lips. His fingers are smooth. Warm.

"No, they didn't." A sigh. "Well, no matter. If you'd caused trouble they would have told me."

I don't answer. What is there to say? The thousand questions I have I assume will be not answered.

"You may speak."

I don't.

"You must have questions."

"W-would..." I clear my throat, start again. "Would you answer them?"

A laugh. "Not likely, no."

I shrug. "Well then."

"Nothing else to say?"

"Are you going to kill me?"

A pause. "No. If you cause too much trouble, perhaps. I'd rather not. You're far more valuable to me alive."

"Surely there are easier ways of acquiring money."

A laugh, then. "Money? No."

"They're not going to negotiate with you."

"They will." A sense of absolute certainty.

A long pause. If I had to quantify the silence, I would say he's thinking about something. Considering.

"Will you behave?"

"For now."

A laugh—his laugh is sharp, predatory. Amused. "Allow me to demonstrate for you that you should amend your answer."

Something sharp touches my thigh where my tennis skirt ends. A prick—a very, *very* sharp knife. It stings, burns. Drags down, a short line, splitting the top layer of skin.

I hiss at the pain.

He tuts. "Such beautiful skin, such a shame to sully it." Something touches my skin where he cut me, a napkin or handkerchief. "All better."

The tip of the knife taps the end of my nose—the flat of it, I assume. "Do you understand?"

"Yes."

"Good. Can you stand up?"

I wiggle forward, but I've been sitting for enough that my legs are numb. "No."

Two large, strong hands grip my arms and he helps me upright. My legs go from numb to afire with pins and needles, and I shake them out, flex them to get the blood pumping.

"Steady?"

I nod. "Yes."

I feel him move, a breath of his cologne wafting past my nose. Behind me.

"Ach," he says, a nonword sound of irritation. "Duct tape? Barbarians." I feel the duct tape loosening as he cuts through it. "Spread your wrists apart."

I do so, and he cuts through it the rest of the way, and then he removes it completely. I hear what sounds like him wadding the tape up into a ball, and I hear it hit the ground and skitter away.

"Did they treat you well?"

"My kidnappers, you mean?"

"Your…custodians. I am your kidnapper, if you wish to be accurate."

"Yes. I was well treated. Except for the part where I was snatched out of my bed in the middle of the night, hauled away from my home and my family, put in a tiny metal cell in the dark for who knows how many days. Except for that, yeah, I was well fucking treated." My temper is flaring.

I struggle to suppress it. Cool it off.

"What I mean to ask is if any of the men did anything inappropriate or untoward." Calm, as if my outburst went unnoticed.

"Once. As I was leaving the ship. Someone grabbed my boobs." I let out a breath. "He was shot."

"Ah, good." A pause. "That he was shot, not that you were handled thus."

"Yeah, wouldn't want that."

I feel him close. "No, you wouldn't, would you? So far, you've been unexpectedly…removed…and had a rather boring boat ride, Corinna. Would you like it to have been more…eventful?" His voice is low and razor-sharp.

I swallow. His presence is…intimidating. "No."

"I thought not." He's behind me. "I'm going to remove your hood."

"Okay."

He rips it off quickly. The light is abrupt and blinding—when I've blinked and become accustomed to it, I take in my surroundings. A huge foyer. The ceiling rises a good fifty feet overhead, with an ornate chandelier in a vaulted, wood-ribbed ceiling. The walls are stone, huge blocks of gray stone fitted together with artistic precision. Underfoot, blue and white tile—Spanish. Before me, fifteen-foot-tall French doors with pointed gothic arches, elaborately-carved scrolling in the stonework of the frame, the doors massively heavy, strapped with black powder-coated iron—in place of door handles, there are rings of metal as thick as my wrist, wide enough in circumference that I could wear it like a crown.

My heart is hammering, now, pounding in my chest so hard it hurts.

I turn, slowly, and face my captor.

My breath leaves my lungs with an involuntary *whoosh.*

He's the most beautiful creature I've ever laid eyes on in my life. I couldn't have imagined a male as exquisite as this one.

It's unfair. Cruel, even.

He's my height, maybe a touch taller. His shoulders are broad, his arms thick with muscle—that's the first thing I notice. Silly of me, I know, but a good set of shoulders and nice arms? Mmm. My mind is haywire, clearly.

But his face? Good god. Crafted by heavenly artisans, chiseled by the hands of angels from a block of the finest marble.

Each angle is perfect. His cheekbones, his jaw, his temples. His lips. His eyes. Lord, his eyes. Black as night, wide and deep. Radiating cunning and calculated intelligence. Not kind, oh no. But not evil, either. Something…else. Those wild dark eyes rake over me, sear and search, pierce.

His skin is golden, sun-kissed. His hair is glossy jet, swept back behind his ears to drape and curl around his shoulders. His jaw is stubbled, a shadow on the dusky sun-browned skin.

My god.

I can't breathe.

He exudes confidence and power and arrogance. God, the arrogance just breathes off him in a palpable aura. But…it's the arrogance of a man who knows exactly who he is. Not the hubris of an un-self-aware asshole who can't back up that arrogance, oh no. He's utterly aware of his powers, of his place in this world.

He needs nothing and no one. Answers to no one.

It's almost a crushing pressure, his presence. Physical, palpable.

There's violence in him. I've grown up around violent men, men who can and have used their hands to kill in a thousand different ways. Good men, kind and gentle and loving and affectionate with me and those whom they care for, but…violent men nonetheless.

This is one such man. Perhaps without the same leavening of kindness, however.

He withstands my scrutiny with easy patience.

He's wearing black slacks over expensive leather boots, a maroon polo shirt French tucked behind a black leather belt with a simple silver buckle. One hand in his hip pocket, the other casually toying with a short, thin, black fixed-blade knife, wicked-looking with a S-shaped blade. He's spinning it between his fingers with astonishing dexterity, without looking away from me. He vanishes the blade behind his back—a sheath at the small of his back, likely, but it's a neat trick nonetheless.

He steps closer to me, an inch between us, no more. His presence bears on me like a weight, and I find myself impatiently waiting for him to speak. I swallow hard.

"You're mine, now, Corinna Roth."

"My name is Rin." I'm proud of how steady and firm my voice is. "And I belong to no man."

He smiles, a vulpine curl of his lips. "I admire your spirit, Rin." The smile shifts, somehow. Becomes…threatening. Full of the weight of promise. "You'll see."

He breezes past me, and I can suddenly breathe again, now that he's farther away. He heads for a door across the room, a heavy thing of dark oak and black metal straps and heavy black hardware. Pauses at it. "Unless you'd like to spend your stay with me here in the vestibule, follow me."

I follow.

He doesn't look back at me to make sure I'm following, or that I'm not going to attack him. I have no doubt he'd have that knife at my throat before I got within three feet of him, so I merely follow along. The door leads to a high-ceilinged hallway, the same heavy beams of dark, aged wood crisscrossing the ceiling here. The walls are neutral, pale. More wood dark with age underfoot. This place is not only expensive, it's *old*; and not merely made to *look* old, but is actually ancient. You can just…sense it. Feel it in the spirit of the walls and the floors and the wood.

There's an opening on the left—a library, the ceiling soaring up to two or even three stories, with ladders and a fireplace and reading nooks. I stop, involuntarily, drawn to it.

"Wow," I breathe. "That's…amazing."

He stops with me. Hands in his pockets, turns to the library, and his gaze is admiring. "It's really something, isn't it? Took me forever to accumulate all those books, and it cost a fortune to boot. Most of them are classics, rare editions, first editions, the like." His eyes find mine. "Do you read, Corinna?"

"Rin," I correct automatically. "And yes. Most definitely. We've never had a TV at home."

He arches an eyebrow. "Really?"

"Well, we have a theater and a service that lets us privately screen movies when they come out. I have a tablet, and I could stream on it if I want. But…no, mostly, we read or do other stuff. Our library at home is incredible, but this puts even that to shame."

"Good to know," he says. Then he turns away and strides forward, his pace smooth and unhurried. "Come."

I follow him reluctantly, jittery with anticipation,

not knowing what he wants from me or what's going to happen to me. The halls wind and meander, branch off here and there with doors sporadically spaced here and there—each doorway features a Gothic arch, and the ceilings are all vaulted and ribbed with the same aged beams.

Despite the heat I'd felt when we arrived wherever we are, the air in this castle—or so I'm assuming it is—is cool and comfortable.

The walk is long, and I get the sense that this place is absolutely massive. Finally, we reach a doorway at the end of a long, straight hall—this door is as massive as the double front doors I'd seen in what my captor called the vestibule, fifteen feet tall with ornate scrollwork framing, which I take to mean it's an exit to the outside. He pushes on the enormous door, which is heavy enough that he has to use his body weight to move it; as the door swings outward, I see that the beams used are all of six inches thick of dense, aged hardwood. He ushers me through the doorway with a polite sweep of his hand, using both hands and his weight again to push the door closed. We're in a covered walkway, two-foot-thick stone columns rising twenty feet overhead into more pointed arches supported by elaborate flying buttresses. It's hot and humid outside, the sun bright after the darkness of the interior. To either side of the walkway, flagstones give way to hedge-lined pathways in serpentine mazes, leading to vineyards as far as the eye can see in row after row, arching over gently rolling hillsides.

Spain or Italy, if I were to guess.

"Where are we?" I ask.

Breezing past me, my captor merely smiles.

The covered walkway extends almost a hundred feet, leading to an actual, honest-to-goodness cylindrical tower spiking a hundred and fifty feet up, with pointed arch slit windows dotting the stone face on the way up. Another heavy door, but this one features a keyhole as well as the ring. My captor reaches into a hip pocket and produces a heavy black iron key, the kind which, in a movie, you'd expect to see on a thick ring with others like it. This key, however, is by itself; he inserts it, using both hands to twist it to the left, the lock disengaging with an audible *thunk*.

He pulls the door open, gestures me through into a dark landing at the bottom of a narrow staircase winding around upward. Once I'm in, he hauls the door closed and precedes me up the stairs. Lances of sunlight pour through the slit windows as we ascend the tower. By the time we reach the top, my thighs are burning. Another arched doorway, another heavy door with a keyhole, using the same key.

When he opens the door and ushers me through, I take a step inside and stop, stunned. I was expecting another dark room with narrow windows and thick walls. Instead, the room is…incredible.

Modern.

The same dark, aged wood floors as throughout the castle are softened here with thick-piled rugs in a pale cream. Floor-to-ceiling windows ten feet tall run the entire perimeter of the tower, bathing the room in a flood of natural sunlight; the windows are tinted, I can tell, to block UV and lessen the glare. Overhead, a vaulted, ribbed ceiling.

The room is essentially a loft, a single large open space. A free-standing wood-paneled wall curves in a graceful parabola away from the wall of windows, stopping short of the glass on either end to create mirrored openings; a bathroom is on the other side, I would imagine. Backed up against the wooden wall, a massive bed. Custom made, I think, since it's larger even than a California king. Four poster, the posts carved to look like gothic columns, gauzy white curtains gathered and tied off at all four corners. The bed is made up with a white comforter and a mountain of pillows, a heavy, old-looking seaman's chest at the foot of the bed. A pair of white leather couches face each other a few feet away from the bed in the center of the room, a low coffee table between them decorated with heavy, varnished, ancient-looking silver candlesticks topped with thick white beeswax candles, dried and hardened droplets and rivulets of wax indicating that they are for use and not merely decoration. Stacks of books in haphazard piles, of varying sizes in both hardcover and paperback litter the table between the candlesticks.

This room is…lived in. Comfortable.

"This is your room," I say out loud, as the realization hits me.

"The whole castle is mine," he says.

"Well yes, but I mean, these are your personal quarters."

"And now yours, as well."

I turn to face him, hardening my expression. "Do what you will, whoever you are, but I'm *not* sleeping with you. Lock me in a dungeon, fine. But if you think I'm going to peaceably share a bedroom with you as if we're…*lovers*…then you'd better think again, and swiftly."

Both hands in his pockets, he strides over to me, swaggering with languorous insouciance. Stops when he's an inch from me, too close, too much, his eyes and his scent and his presence simply overpowering.

"You'd rather sleep in a dungeon than share space with me?" His voice is arch, and wry.

"Yes," I snap. "I would."

He slides a phone from a back pocket, unlocks it and opens an app. A moment of loading, and then the screen resolves into a grayscale night vision view of a room. Stone walls and floors, and ceiling. Blocks of stone for a bench. There's audio—a rhythmic dripping noise echoes.

On the bench is slumped a figure, facing the camera. Male. Naked. Even in the grayscale night vision of the surveillance camera, it's obvious the person has been beaten to within an inch of his life.

"Who—who's that?" I ask, the question tripping out of me unbidden.

"An employee who was caught skimming." He allows me a long look, then returns the device to his pocket. "There are dungeons here, of course. Far underground. Dark, lightless, cold, and wet. There are rats, as well as venomous centipedes and spiders. I think there may be an empty dungeon for you, but if someone needs punishing, you may very well find yourself sharing with…well, a hurt, scared, and angry male with nothing to lose." His smile communicates the simplicity of the choice. "Suit yourself."

"I won't sleep with you."

He quirks an eyebrow. "I am and have always been a man who gets what he wants, Corinna." He presses closer, his chest against my breasts. "One way or another."

"My name is Rin," I whisper, backing away from him. "And you may hold my body captive, but my spirit and my mind are my own."

He's either in motion, or perfectly still—it's eerie, honestly. He regards me in silence for a long moment. Then he turns on a heel and strides for the door.

"The remainder of the day is yours. Read, sleep,

bathe, as you wish. I will return for you when it's time for our evening meal."

"What's your plan, here?"

He doesn't reply, only closes the door behind him, locks it, and then I hear his steps receding.

Alone, I examine the room in more detail. I can see for miles in every direction: the vineyards extend almost out of sight, giving way in the far distance to orchards. A driveway winds through the vineyards and disappears over the hills, miles and miles long. At another window, I can see the castle—it's something of a cross between a lord's manor estate and a castle, there are no defensive walls or crenellations, but it's certainly well more than a mere home. It's absolutely massive, sprawling, with smaller towers here and there, gables and buttresses and secret balconies and hidden alcoves. It's old, well-kept and obviously restored and modernized.

On the other side of the free-standing wooden wall is, as suspected, a bathroom, complete with a hammered-copper soaking tub, glassed-in shower, a porcelain pedestal sink framed by ladder shelves laden with male hygiene products. A toilet. A huge mirror in a gilded frame with a gothic pointed arch above the sink.

The exterior wall is all window, here as well, bathing the bathroom area in natural light. There being no other structure in view for miles, privacy is clearly not a concern.

Also hidden behind the free-standing wall is a surprisingly small closet containing rows of chinos and dress slacks on hangars, button-downs and polos all in solid colors, no patterns or prints; there are cubbies containing dress shoes and boots, hiking boots, riding boots, and sneakers. Another few cubbies containing jeans, another of gym shorts, and several cubbies containing neatly folded plain black and white T-shirts. Simple and organized.

I have no clean clothes, so I'm not sure I want to get clean if I just have to put on this same smelly outfit—the shower looks divine, however, with multiple nozzles spraying horizontally and a huge rainfall head in the ceiling.

I opt to peruse the books. There's a history of the Visigothic occupation of Spain, a coffee table-sized book of photographs of Spanish Vineyards. A book of castle and cathedral architecture in Spain, Portugal, and France. A history of Moorish Spain.

Clearly, I'm in Spain, somewhere.

There are also paperback novels in English, Spanish, and Greek, ranging from Clive Cussler, Louis L'Amour, and Robert Ludlum to Lee Child, Dan Brown, and Brandon Sanderson. The assortment of languages is random, and these novels are dog-eared and well-read. Old favorites. Making the display of rarities and collector's editions in the library either a collection by a bibliophile, or just for show.

There are also books on leadership, an English copy of *The Art of War*, an Italian copy of Machiavelli, and dictionaries in all three languages as well as English-Greek, English-Spanish, and Greek-Spanish dictionaries.

I flip through the histories, browse through the books of photographs, and eventually end up reading one of the Ludlum novels.

Kidnapped in the middle of the night, transported in a tiny dark cell in a boat across the ocean, brought by helicopter and limousine to an actual castle, locked in an actual tower like an actual damsel in literal distress…

And I'm reading a novel.

The sun is setting, lowering itself into the hills behind the vines, bathing the landscape in a gradient of red to pink, with hints of orange and dashes of purple.

I'm hungry, I smell, I'm bored, and there's behind it all a constant simmering fear. It's impossible to forget that I'm a prisoner. That I don't know who my captor is, why he's taken me, or what he wants.

Judging by the wealth on display here, I feel it safe to assume he's not after money.

Darkness has fallen, and I'm still alone.

Then, I hear footsteps on the stair, the key in the lock, and the door opens.

He closes it behind himself. He has a wicker basket in one hand, piled high with packaged balls of fancy soap, bottles of shampoo and conditioner, bath oils, lotions, salt scrubs, candles.

He has a garment bag draped over his other arm, the key still clutched in his fist.

He moves past me without a word into the bathroom, depositing the basket of bath goods on the floor near the tub, and then hanging the garment bag from a hook on the wall near the entrance to the bathroom.

I lean in the opening, watching him.

He crosses to me, stops once again within my personal space, standing too close. "The journey here has not done your hygiene any favors, Corinna. You will be joining me for dinner within the hour, so please…prepare yourself."

I hesitate, refusing to back away from him, to give him the sense that I'm afraid of him or intimidated by him—that I'm affected by him at all.

"And if I don't?"

He regards me steadily, his body utterly still, only his eyes moving. "A hunger strike does you no good. If you wish to starve yourself, by all means, be my guest. You are a prisoner, yes, but you will be a prisoner in a gilded cage. If you choose to deprive yourself of the basic necessities which I am freely providing, such as the luxury of bathing, good meals, and a book to read? Well, by all means, suit yourself." He smiles at me. "You are a practical, sensible girl, Corinna. Let's not be petulant. It proves nothing to me, and only harms you."

I huff. "I don't understand the point of behaving as if this is some social thing between us. I'm your prisoner. I don't even know your name."

"The point is, I'm no barbarian. There is a purpose to this, which you need not concern yourself with at this time."

"My fate is not my concern," I say, my voice dry and sarcastic. "I see."

He does the eyebrow quirk, a quick arch of one eyebrow which I think indicates amusement. "If you wish to go unbathed and stinking, you will do so in the dungeon. If you wish to remain in my quarters like a civilized human being, you will, at minimum, smell like one."

"Fine." I lift my hands. "I'll take a shower."

A standoff, then. He waits expectantly.

I cross my arms over my chest. "You think I'm just going to strip down and take a shower in front of you? You don't get a free show."

"Your clothing is filthy. I'm going to have it incinerated."

"Fine. I'll toss it out there. I'm not undressing in front of you."

His eyes harden. "You are still a captive, Miss Roth. If I wish to view the property which I have acquired, I will do so at my leisure." His English is so formal, almost archaic at times, his accent lending it a very old-world aristocratic tone.

I almost miss it when it happens: his hands move in a blur, one bunching in the front of my tank top, the other lancing out and slicing down.

The whole thing occurs in an eye blink.

My tank top is sliced open from top to bottom, baring my belly and the insides of my breasts. I gasp, jaw hanging open. I'm too stunned to move, to react.

He reaches out with the knife, and I freeze stone still—he uses the tip of the knife to brush the strap of the now-ruined shirt over my shoulders on one side and then the other...the garment slips backward and tumbles to the floor.

I'm naked from the waist up. My nipples pucker as his eyes rake over me, lingering blatantly.

I'm trembling now, fear leaving me breathless and paralyzed.

He's not done.

His fingers hook into the waistband of my tennis skirt and his knife slashes downward—it's faster than a snake bite. At no time does the knife even so much as whisper against my skin.

Sliced open but for an inch or two near the very hem, the skirt slips past my hips to the floor.

Now I'm clad in nothing but a yellow thong, and I cannot even force my hands to move to cover myself.

That knife is too quick, and I've felt its razor-sharp edge.

I shake, and stare at him in fear.

His finger, the index, curls against my belly, slowly, as it hooks into the elastic of my thong, the tip of the knife a hair's breadth from my navel. "How intimately acquainted do you wish to become with this little knife of mine, Corinna?" he asks, his voice a low, caressing murmur.

Hands shaking, knees threatening to give out, I take the hint for the command it contains; renewed fear now breaks my paralysis, and I wrench my limbs into obedience. Tug the thong down past my hips, fear heightening every sensation, every sense. I feel the straps slipping over my hips, the string sliding down between my buttocks. I smell him, the soap and cologne and maleness spicy and heady in my nostrils.

I wiggle my hips to remove the undergarment the rest of the way, let it fall to the floor and step out of it.

I want to cover.

Huddle.

Cower.

I refuse to be cowed, however, even if fear creates prudent obedience in me.

I stand tall, hands at my sides, and meet his eyes.

His nostrils flare, and he breathes in sharply. Holds it. His eyes scour my curves, lingering, almost caressing. His expression gives nothing away, however.

Abruptly, he pivots on a heel and strides away. "Shower. Be dressed and waiting at the door in thirty minutes."

My clothing is still in a pile on the floor. "I thought you were burning my offensive clothing."

He halts. Turns back. Regards me steadily, his eyes now on mine rather than my naked body. He scoops up the shirt and skirt, and then the thong; without another word, he stalks away and I hear the door close and lock.

Despite the scalding heat of the shower, despite scrubbing until my skin is pink and raw with the salt scrubs, despite a thick lather of soap rinsed away and re-lathered half a dozen times, I cannot rid my skin of the feel of his eyes.

There is fear, yes.

But what concerns me most of all is that the feeling of his eyes on my skin is not, in fact, accompanied by the expected sense of revulsion or disgust.

He cut my clothes off.

Stared at my nude body, openly, frankly, blatantly.

And, unless I miss my guess, the fact that he

forgot the clothing he made such a production of cutting away means he was affected.

He's got a hell of a poker face, though.

Clean, hair washed and conditioned, I step out of the shower, and use a towel from one of the ladder shelves to dry myself, and wrap it around my torso. There's a hairbrush and dryer on one of the shelves as well—I take the time to brush my hair out and fully dry it.

Finally, I examine the contents of the garment bag: a scarlet dress, and matching shoes—the shoes are Louboutin, and my size. I remove the dress from the bag.

It's…breathtaking.

I slip it on and look at myself in the full-length mirror in the closet.

Straps cross over my chest in a halter, the bust low cut…so low it barely covers my nipples. The dress hugs my waist and hips, leaves my back bare down to the very swell of my ass, clinging to my thighs and ending just above my knees.

It's the sexiest thing I've ever worn, and it fits like it was custom-made for me.

Once I slip the heels on, my legs and ass look tight and toned, and the cut of the top props my admittedly impressive boobs and puts them on display—covered, but just barely.

I look goddamned incredible.

The man's got taste.

I mean, it's a pretty slutty dress, but holy shit, does it flaunt what I've got.

I don't really dress like this. I wear shorts, skirts, tank tops, and T-shirts. I wear bikinis to the beach, but they're pretty conservative, as far as bikinis go.

I don't wear heels.

I don't wear slutty dresses.

But, I have to eat, and now that he's cut my clothing to pieces, this is all I've got.

I hear the door unlock and open. I fluff my hair, tug the top of the dress a little higher to snug the girls into it more firmly, and then exit the bathroom.

He's standing in the open doorway, one hand in his pocket, the other holding his phone, which he's staring at.

I wait.

I know he's heard my heels clicking on the wood floor.

He looks up as he slips his phone into his back pocket—when his eyes land on me, he freezes, and his breath sucks in between his teeth in a sharp hiss.

His gaze takes ownership of me, slides down my form, landing last of all on my eyes. "You are simply… magnificent." His eyes glitter black in the lights, which are cleverly hidden in the vaulted ceiling far above.

A moment, then, his eyes on mine, then taking me in yet again, and again.

Finally, he turns and gestures at the stairwell. “Come.”

The stairs are steep and treacherous, and there is no railing. The first time I slip, I catch myself.

The second time, his hand catches me, lifts me. He waits until I’m steady, and then offers me his hand.

Instead of taking it, I slip off the Louboutins and hold them in the fingers of one hand, trailing the other along the wall.

He drops his hand.

Down, down, down the circling stair, to the heavy door; at the base of the stairs, I step back into my heels. Back through the covered walkway, beyond which now are the purple shadows of the gloaming, hiding the vines and hills. Through the winding, branching maze of hallways. We come a set of huge glass doors, currently propped open. I smell night-blooming jasmine. There’s an ancient, gnarled tree in the small, intimate courtyard, leaning to one side, stretching arthritic fingers heavenward, leaves rustling against each other in the soft breeze. Fairy lights drape over the lower hanging branches, casting a fae amber glow. Flagstones surround the tree, and a ring of irises, crocuses, and lilies—now closed for the evening—surround the base of the trunk. There’s a small, wrought-iron table with a marble top in the far corner, with a pair of matching wrought-iron chairs. A single candle burns on the table, flickering and dancing.

The jasmine is planted along the walls in a narrow stripe of cedar, the scent redolent and heady.

This courtyard is our destination, it seems, and I'm awed at it, despite myself. It's beyond lovely—it's magical.

My captor leads us to the table, slides out the chair, and tucks it in under me as I sit. His manners are, honestly, genteel and exquisite.

He takes his seat after me. On one side of the table is a silver stand with a bottle of white wine on ice, two stemmed glasses accompanying it. The bottle has been opened already and recorked, so all he has to do is remove the cork and pour, which he does with deft grace.

He hands me a glass. For a moment, I think he's about to offer me a toast, which would have probably made me burst into laughter at the absurdity of it all.

Instead, he puts his nose in the glass and inhales, swirling. Eyes me over the rim. "I am Apollo." He sips, swirls, sniffs, sips. Shrugs.

I sip the wine—it has a lush, soft body, and it's not too sweet. "It's good," I say, if only to fill the silence.

He nods. Gestures with a hand. "Grown and bottled here." A look at me. "Your parents own vineyards." It's a leading statement, not a question.

I nod. "In France, California, and Italy. I've only been to the vineyard in Italy, though."

His eyes meet mine, holding that poker face he's so good at it. "A lovely vineyard, indeed. The wine grown there is some of the best. The pinot noir, especially, is divine. Notes of blackberry and leather, with a long, elegant finish."

I frown—I heard the vintner at the estate once describe their pinot noir in almost exactly those same terms. "You've been there?"

"Of course."

At that moment, a middle-aged woman with graying black hair arrives, bearing a tray laden with soup and salad. She's dressed in all black, wears a long black apron, and addresses Apollo in Spanish.

He listens, nods, responds, and then she sets a soup and a salad in front of each of us, and then places a spoon and fork in precise positions on either side of the arrangements, finishing by laying napkins on each of our laps.

Apollo merely nods, and she retreats.

There's no more attempt at small talk from him. He eats slowly, as if savoring each bite, his eyes now and again flicking to me before returning to his place. There's no more staring at me, either.

The food is, as I would expect, of a quality found in a Michelin-starred establishment. The soup is a lobster bisque, the salad field greens and spinach with walnuts, diced fresh cherries, and a light vinaigrette.

I go slowly with the wine, and I notice he does as well, only sipping now and again. We've both barely finished the first glass by the time the main course arrives—salmon served on a cedar plank, with whipped feta, garbanzo beans, and some sort of tart pickled root vegetable. The salmon is so fresh it must surely have been caught within twenty-four hours, meaning we must be near one of the coasts, either Atlantic or Mediterranean; taking into consideration the Greek-language novels and dictionaries, I would assume the Mediterranean.

We're nearly through the meal when a tall man in a gray suit with a blue tie enters the courtyard—he's older, perhaps fifty, with hair that was once black but is now more silver. As he leans to whisper in Apollo's ear, I see a pistol in a shoulder holster under his suit coat.

Apollo listens, nods, and dabs his lips with his napkin. "Will you excuse me a moment, Corinna?"

I put down my fork. "All right."

God, it's all so odd. The weirdest kidnapping there surely has ever been. The manners, the aristocratic bearing, the tower, the food, the wine…

And slicing my clothes off.

Locking me up in, as he put it, a gilded cage… but doing so *politely*.

I sit alone in the courtyard for five minutes, maybe closer to ten.

Apollo returns alone, takes his seat. "My apologies, Corinna." He notices I've merely waited for him. "You should have kept eating."

"That would have been rude."

His smirk is faint, amused. "How mannerly of you."

"Just following your lead. You're the politest kidnapper I've ever met."

He arches that eyebrow. "You have met many kidnappers, then?"

I laugh. "No, I suppose not."

He picks up his fork and resumes eating, pausing after the first bite, frowning. "It's gone cold. How unfortunate." He gestures at me with his fork. "Please, finish."

Even his frown of displeasure is entrancingly beautiful.

As I, rather helplessly, watch him eat, I notice something which disturbs me. "Apollo?"

He looks at me.

"You've got…um…blood on your neck." I touch the left side of my neck. "Here."

"Oh." He uses the front-facing camera of his phone as a mirror, wiping the offending droplets away with his napkin. "Hazards of the profession, I'm afraid."

"Which profession would that be?" I ask, figuring it can't hurt to fish a little.

He only smiles, a small cold thing. "Nothing you'd like to know about, I'm sure."

I push the last of my food onto my fork with the knife, considering my words. "Well, I can make some assumptions."

Finished himself, he leans back in his chair and sips wine. "Do tell." He extends his legs out past me and crosses his ankles, swirling his wine as an idle gesture.

"You kidnapped me, for one thing. Which means you're definitely not…well, not above illegal activity, if you operate within the law at all."

I continue to sit properly, legs tucked under the chair, one ankle over the other, spine straight, shoulders back; I find myself mimicking his idle habit of swirling the wine, just for something to do with my hands, with my nervous energy.

He shrugs, waves. "All right. And?"

Not a denial, but not a confirmation either.

"Furthermore, the way you had me taken was… professional. It was too smooth and too flawless. My… uncle, I guess, I call him Uncle Harry—"

"Nicholas Harris. Yes."

I pause at the revelation that he knows Uncle Harry's full name. "Um. Uncle Harry takes care of situations like this—" I point at him and then myself, "professionally. And as my father's primary assistant, I've watched several cases get resolved. So I can say with a certain caliber of certainty that this is not the first time you've done this. Snatch jobs like this are expensive. The kind of professional who could get onto our island, past our security, take me without a sound, and leave again without raising an alarm? That guy costs a fortune. Which means you're very wealthy." I gesture around us. "This place is evidence enough of that."

"And what do these assumptions tell you about me, Corinna?"

"My name is *Rin*," I say, with no little irritation. "And I'm not done. You didn't hesitate to cut me to prove a point, in the vestibule. You cut my clothes off without qualm. You showed me surveillance camera footage of a former employee caught stealing, and instead of turning him in to the authorities, or firing him and seeking damages, or anything like that, you locked him in a literal dungeon in the basement of your *castle*…after beating him to a pulp. Judging by what I saw, I doubt he'll survive the night." I take a drink, then continue. "During dinner, a man with a gun under his suit coat summoned you away with a whisper. And when you return, you have blood on you."

He arches the eyebrow. "Astute observations."

"You're a criminal, Apollo." I smile, fake sweetly.

"You kill people. Judging by the wealth on display, I would guess you deal in either drugs or arms. Possibly people as well, either sexual slavery or prostitution rings—which amount to the same thing."

He lets out a breath. "You have me all figured out, do you?"

I laugh. "God no, not at all. I can't make heads or tails of you. What you want. Why me." I shrug. "I mean, I know why me—my parents. You took *me,* knowing who my father is and who my uncle is—and if you know my uncle's name, you must know what kind of man he is, what he's capable of. Which means you're either very certain of yourself, or very stupid." I make a gesture with my glass. "Or a very unfortunate combination of both."

"Do *you* know what kind of man your uncle is, what kind of man your father is?"

I consider my answer very carefully. "Does any child truly know their parents?"

His expression hardens. "I wouldn't know, I grew up without mine."

"I'm sorry for that."

"You aren't. But those responsible will be."

A shiver runs down my spine. "Who *are* you, Apollo?"

He stands up. "Shall we walk?"

He's walking away, and I follow him. A direct path through the house and to a different exit, this one leading to a cobblestone path lined with rosebushes. The path meanders seemingly at random, passing an occasional spreading tree, or an alcove with concrete benches, or fountains. We walk in a strange, thick silence for many minutes.

He's silent. Brooding.

"I'm not ready for you to know who I am just yet," he says, suddenly.

We've circled the castle and have reached the tower, approaching it sidelong, the covered walkway in front of us.

He stops. Looks up; the sky is awash with stars, twinkling and scintillating in countless millions. It's cooled off, the air now pleasantly warm.

"So, I'm going to just…sit in your tower and read your Jason Bourne books?"

A corner of his mouth lifts in a smirk. "An indulgence. To let my mind rest from more pressing matters." A nod. "That is indeed what you shall do. And you should be grateful your imprisonment is as boring as it is. You wouldn't like the kind of excitement it would be, otherwise."

"I just don't understand the goal."

"And you need not." He turns and faces me. "But if you really wish to know…"

"I do."

"You are bait, Corinna."

6

MAMA BEAR

The limousine takes me to the Miami airport, to the private charter flight area. Waiting idling is a small private jet. Funny how small and cheap it seems to me, now that I'm used to the hyper-luxury transportation provided by RTI—it's a six-seat Gulfstream, and by no means a cheap aircraft to fly in, whether owned or chartered. The limo pulls to a stop with the rear door even with the staircase which unfolds from the side of the jet. A pair of Mercedes-Benz G-Wagen SUVs are parked near the rear of the jet, and as the limousine pulls to a stop, three men emerge from each vehicle. They're damn near clones of each other, all of them about six feet tall, olive-complected with dark hair, wearing black suits and mirrored sunglasses. Each one is armed with a compact submachine gun. They form a three-sided box around the limousine and the staircase. I wait as the limousine stops. The driver emerges from the front and comes around to the rear passenger door, opens it and steps to the side as I get out.

It feels for all the world like I'm some dignitary arriving for a political event—except I can feel the hard gazes of the six armed men reminding me what's truly at stake here. My heart is in my throat, pounding and hot.

I do my best to portray poise and fearless dignity as I ascend the stairs into the jet—as expected, it's empty, all six seats vacant. The door to the cockpit is closed and I assume locked. I take one of the two rear-most seats and fasten the lap belt, and focus on breathing slowly, deeply, evenly.

The staircase whines as it folds up and clunks into place; the cockpit door opens, and a short, slender man in a pilot's uniform emerges to fasten and lock the exit door. This pilot's uniform, however, includes a shoulder holster with a large silver handgun, and his eyes flit to me before he returns to the cockpit—reminding me that I'm still being watched, still guarded.

I can do this, I tell myself.

I've survived worse. I survived Gina. I can deal with this. Whatever it takes, I will survive—and not just that, I will find and rescue my daughter. A cold hardness settles in the pit of my belly. There's nothing I won't do—anyone caught between me and my daughter is fair game.

The mama-bear rage is a boiling inferno inside me, pent up and fueling a rattling need to *do* something.

In the years since the war against the Karahalios clan and then Cain and his many goons, Valentine has insisted—against my wishes and personal comfort—that I practice at the shooting range on our island a few times a month, as well as keeping up with self-defense lessons with Sasha, as have both Cal and Rin.

So, I know I can strip and reassemble a pistol with speed and confidence. I can load and fire an entire magazine at multiple targets and keep my groupings tight, and I can do so quickly and smoothly.

My shooting training and practice is not just your average firing range instruction, obviously—I've been taught basic close-quarters combat skills by some of the most elite Special Forces warriors on the planet, both with handguns and hand to hand—I keep my shooting skills sharp at the small, indoor, reinforced range on our private island, but once every fiscal quarter Layla and I spend a week at Duke's CQB training facility outside Denver, working with Duke directly on our skills.

I'm no fainting daisy suburban mommy, is the point. We never took for granted our own safety, and after everything that occurred all those years ago, we've stayed ready in case someone else comes knocking.

Twenty years ago, I was a sheltered, innocent, naive twenty-something girl, ignorant of the true violence there is in this world. I did what I had to do to stay alive, but I wasn't ready for it.

Now?

Motherfuckers, you better watch me real close, because you're complicit in the kidnapping of my daughter, and I'm not taking any prisoners until I have my daughter back.

And I've been taught by the best.

The takeoff is smooth, and the flight long and boring. There's nothing to do, no books, no inflight magazines or movies or refreshments—this isn't a vacation, I'm a prisoner. So, I rehearse in my head the movements I've learned for disarming a bigger, stronger male opponent—how to wrestle his gun away from him and kill him with it. I go over room-clearing techniques. Unarmed takedowns. How to get out of a chokehold. How to escape from zip-ties.

I go over the basic advice Duke drilled into our heads, at the last training session a few months ago: "Ladies, if you're in a position where you're captive, where you're outnumbered and the bad guys have guns and you don't, you have two options at your disposal. One, just do what you're told and hope for the best. Or, bide your time and cooperate as far as is necessary to survive, and wait for your moment. It will come. There'll be one guard, and he'll be distracted. They'll leave you unbound, assuming because you've cooperated thus far that you're not a threat. When you see your opportunity, you fucking take it. When the moment comes, you have to be ready, mentally, to do whatever the fuck it takes. It's you, or them. It's kill or be killed. That's it. You've got to harden your mind. You take the civilian in you, the wife, the mother, the soft kind tender lady, and you lock her up deep inside you, inside a box. She's still there, but she's out of the way, where she can't see or feel or hear what you're about to do in the name of survival.

"She doesn't come back out until it's all over. The part that's left, the part that's operating you, she's a badass. She's unstoppable. She's a killer. You have to accept that, if you find yourself in that position. I know you've both been there, and I sincerely hope you never have to do it again. But if you do, you have to prepare yourself mentally. You've kept up with your training, and trust me when I say that if you commit to taking the necessary actions, your training *will* take over. It's the mental game you have to focus on."

So, while the jet flies over the ocean—east, over the Atlantic—I prepare myself mentally for what's about to happen.

Hours of boredom finally end when the jet lands, not at a major airport this time, but a small private airfield. I didn't recognize anything we flew over, so I have no way of knowing where we are. I continue my act of cooperation, descending the stairs and sliding into the waiting car, a Mercedes, this one a new S-class. The driver is different, but essentially the same type of individual, a hard, capable man who's as much of a guard as a driver.

I ask no questions, merely sit in the back seat, buckled, silent, watching out the window for any landmarks or features to tell me where we are. The car winds through a forest of pine, emerging to turn onto a two-lane highway. Hours of featureless highway, the road winding and curving gently but rarely veering from a general southerly direction, judging by the position of the sun. Finally, I see a sign on the side of the highway—I can't read it, but I get enough of a look to see it's in German. So, we're in Germany. Logical enough, I suppose, since Germany is a convenient location, since you can get by car, train, or plane anywhere in Europe quickly and easily. Certainly this is not my final destination.

What I have to decide is whether taking an opportunity to escape will further endanger my daughter. I could go along and miss my opportunity, only to discover there was never any chance of me surviving this.

It's not about Rinna, I know that much. It's about Valentine and me.

I just have to figure out who, and why.

Hours more of highway, occasionally passing an exit or a small town. Then, gradually, forest gives way to farmland and then rural suburbia, and then there's a city rising up from the horizon. Berlin, maybe? I don't know, I've never been there and honestly couldn't identify it by any major landmarks. An embarrassingly American lack of world geographical knowledge, I suppose.

There are apartment blocks and tenements, shops and restaurants and parks. Signs in German. Then, high rises, skyscrapers, a bustling business center of the city. Buses, cabs, private cars, and a whole hell of a lot of pedestrians on foot or bicycle. I spot a few signs near stairways going underground, indicating a subway—the signs call it the U-Bahn. I feel confident I'm in Berlin. Useful knowledge, actually—I have a handful of phone numbers memorized: my husband's, Anselm's, and Harris's. Anselm and Selah are here in Europe somewhere, last I knew, and if I'm going to get any help from my friends in anything like a reasonable time frame, it'll be Anslem. So my first order of business is to obtain a means of contacting Anselm.

Which means escaping my captors and staying

free long enough to beg, borrow, or steal a phone long enough to call him.

I have a goal, then. Step one. That's always step one—what's the first thing I have to do to get to safety?

Call Anselm.

How do I get money, for a cab or the U-Bahn? I have access to international bank accounts, of course, but I don't have my purse or any of those cards. So I'd have to find a bank that would allow me to make a withdrawal without identification. Also of note, I'm here illegally. So I can't get detained by the authorities—I have to assume my enemy will have a way of getting to me if I'm detained.

The car wends its way into the city, and I don't bother trying to keep track of the turns. Finally, age thirty minutes of driving through the city, we approach an underground parking structure beneath a ten- or twelve-story office building on the outskirts of the city. Not quite in what I would call a bad area, judging by appearances, but certainly not downtown, either.

The underground garage is sparsely populated by parked cars, mostly middle-class sedans and compacts. The car pulls to a stop next to the elevator and stairs—two men emerge from the stairwell. Both wear the same black suits as the men at the airport, and these two are similarly armed as well. One of them opens the door, and I step out. The other has called the elevator, which opens and I'm ushered on, flanked by both men.

My heart hammers now, and my hands shake, palms sweating. I resist the urge to rub them on my jeans—I refuse to give away any impression of fear or nerves.

I'm Kyrie Roth. I'm in control.

Neither man so much as looks at me. I can smell marijuana on one or both of them, faintly. A good sign. Means a more lax approach to discipline. If they're high, they're probably bored. They've probably been waiting for me for hours, if not days.

Not two-on-one, in an elevator, though. I'm not Duke.

Keep waiting.

The elevator rides four floors up, stops, and opens onto a generic office hallway. Muted wallpaper, thin carpet. Fluorescent lights in a drop-tile ceiling. One of the men leads the way, the other following behind—this floor, at least, is empty, the maze of cubicles vacant and unlit. We walk along darkened hallways at the perimeter, passing closed and darkened offices, a break room, and a room full of printers and copiers before coming to the only lit room, a conference room.

A long rectangular table with mid-range black leather desk chairs. A conference line phone, a projector, a coffee station; I smell coffee, actually.

There's one man in the conference room, sitting at the head of the table, facing away from me, sipping from a small white Styrofoam cup. He's tall and well-muscled, which is evident even through the pale gray suit he's wearing. His hair is blond, thinning, and swept back. A handgun rests on the table near his left hand.

I'm ushered in, and then the two men retreat from the room and close the door—assuming positions just outside, I imagine. I wait with my back to the door.

The man swivels to face me, catching up his gun, still clutching the coffee. His eyes are blue and cold. He's not shaved in a few days, and he's tired, his eyes heavy-lidded with dark circles under them.

He stares at me in silence for a moment, then gestures at the coffee station. "Coffee?" He has a distinct German accent.

I shrug. "Sure, thank you."

He nods, unfolds from the chair slowly, heavily, as if it's nearly too much effort. He slides a cup from the upside-down stack still partially enclosed in the plastic sleeve, fills it with coffee. Glances at me. "*Milch oder Zucker?*"

"No, thank you. Black is fine."

He hands me the cup, and I sip; it's strong, and cheap, but it's hot and I'm going to be awake for a while, I assume. "*Setz dich, bitte*," he says, gesturing at a chair with his gun.

I sit. He resumes his seat, after refilling his cup.

He eyes me expectantly. "No questions?"

I keep my expression carefully neutral. "A million of them."

"But you do not ask."

"You're not in charge. You didn't bring me here." I shrug. "You're here to watch me until the next phase of whatever this is happens."

He smirks. "You are very calm."

"Are you going to kill me?"

He rolls a shoulder. "*Nein.* I mean, if I have to, I can and will. But you are correct in that I'm only to watch you, for now."

I blow across the top of the coffee. "Exactly."

I have a feeling my moment is near at hand. Not yet, though.

"You are hungry?" he asks.

I shake my head. "No, thank you."

He frowns. "I should say, this is most unexpected. I have assumed when you arrived to here, you would be so angry, *ja*? Kicking, swearing. Ready to tear my eyes out. We have your daughter, after all." *Kickink, sverrink...vee haff your daughter, effter all.*

"Is she here? In this building?" I ask.

He shrugs. "*Nein*."

I shrug back at him. "Well, then."

He sniffs a laugh.

A long period of boredom. He drinks cup after cup of coffee, mostly ignoring me. Occasionally types out a message on his phone, one-handed.

Finally, a call comes through. He answers it in German, listening more than speaking, and when he does, it's only a series of *ja, ja, ja*.

He then, unexpectedly, hands me the phone. "For you."

I take it. "Hello?"

"Mrs. Roth. How nice of you to join us." The voice is low, cultured, with a Greek accent.

The accent, and something in the voice sends shudders down my spine. Reminds me of being locked in a cell on a Greek island. Being beaten, having my head shaved with a dull knife.

It can't be. We ended the Karahalios clan.

"Who are you, and what do you want?" I ask, doing my best to keep my voice steady.

"Let's start with…" a pause. "Ten million dollars."

I suppress the urge to laugh. It's insulting. You kidnap the daughter of a billionaire, take his wife hostage, and then ask for ten million dollars?

It smells off, to me.

"You didn't need to bring me to Berlin for that."

"You will have it delivered to you, in cash."

"How?"

"Call your husband. Tell him it's…a down payment."

"On what?"

"The life you ruined."

"And ten million dollars will fix it, will it?"

"Not even close." A pause. "Have your friend Anselm deliver it."

"I don't know how to get ahold of him." I don't give away my shock that he knows who Anselm is.

"Lies will not aid your cause, Kyrie Abigail St. Claire Roth." A quick silence. "Say hello."

A soft breath. "Hello? Mom?" Rin's voice, shaky, but clear.

Before I can respond, tears springing in my eyes, it's the male again. "So you understand. She's alive and well, for now. Ten million dollars, delivered by Anselm and received by you, within twenty-four hours."

"Let me talk to her."

"I think not."

"How do I know she's unharmed?"

"You will have to take my word for it."

"I think not," I say, echoing his own words. "I need proof."

A sigh, as if I'm annoying him. "Very well. Smile for me, beautiful girl."

The phone in my hand chimes, and I pull it away from my ear. There's a photograph of Rin. She's dressed in a sultry, sexy red dress, revealing and not at all like anything she'd wear. Her hair is down and clean and glossy. Her eyes betray confusion and fear, but she appears unharmed. The background has been blurred out via a bokeh effect, so there's no hint of where she could be from the photo.

"Have you touched her?" I demand.

"Make the call, Mrs. Roth." *Click*—silence.

I toss the phone onto the table. I don't like this. At fucking all.

I sigh, pick up the phone again, and dial the number I need. It rings four times. "*Ja*."

"Anselm?"

"Ja." A short, soft breath. "Kyrie. I have heard—"

"I'm in Berlin," I cut in. "Not by choice. They want ten million dollars delivered by you, to me, here, within twenty-four hours."

A short pause from Anselm. "That's all?"

"So far."

"This is not your phone, and being monitored, I assume."

"Correct."

Another silence, this one longer. "Are you okay?"

"So far."

He clears his throat. "Location?"

I hand the phone to the man beside me. "He needs to know the drop-off location."

The man takes the phone and rattles off a set of

coordinates, rather than an address, then hands the phone back to me. "*Das Ende*. Nothing funny, *ja*?"

"Anselm?"

"*Ja*, Kyrie. I am here."

"I need you to be safe, you feel me?"

A pause; this is a prearranged verbal code. "Understood. See you soon."

The code means extreme danger. That it's a suspected trap, essentially.

I end the call and pass the phone back. "Now what?"

The man pockets the device, stands up. "Now we go."

"When do I get my daughter back?"

Back through the empty office building to the elevator, now accompanied by all three men. The Mercedes is still waiting; another long, circuitous drive across Berlin.

My heart hammers. I can't just sit here, can't just do nothing. Ten million dollars is nothing to Valentine and me, and surely this person knows that.

The life you ruined.

This is definitely personal.

It's difficult to maintain a state of readiness and heightened awareness indefinitely. It's exhausting.

But I can feel the moment approaching. I sense it in the air, feel it in my bones.

We end up in another part of Berlin, this one much seedier, far less savory. A service drive under a massive overpass exchange, parked, idling.

"Now we wait," the man says. He's in the car beside me. There's the driver, and another car with the other two guards or soldiers or whatever.

An hour passes. I have no idea how long it will take Anselm to get here, to acquire the money and figure out a plan. Tension leaves me nauseated.

"I have to pee," I say.

He huffs, gestures out the window. "As you see, there is no toilet here."

I press my thighs together; this isn't an act. But it is an opportunity. Maybe. I just know I can't keep sitting around and waiting. I just hope I'm doing the right thing.

"Do you have a napkin? I can just go behind one of the pillars over there." I shrug. "I've got to go. I thought I could wait, but I can't."

He's got the gun in his hand—he's never put it away. He groans in annoyance, says something in German which sounds like cursing. "*Ja, ja*. Fine."

He says something to the driver, who digs in the console under the armrest and comes up with a few brown paper napkins and hands them back to me, then unlocks the door.

The man beside me points the gun at me. "You wait."

He exits and rounds to my side, opens the door for me. Gestures. I exit and head for the nearest concrete pillar some twenty or thirty feet away, and he follows me.

I go around the far side, and glance at him. "You're gonna watch?"

He hesitates. "I will turn away, but no funny business, *ja*?"

"No funny business, just potty business."

"A jokester, I see." He turns around, pistol held at his thigh. "Be quick."

"Why, are we in a hurry? I have no idea where Anselm is or how long we'll be waiting."

I lower my jeans and underwear to my ankles, lean back against the pillar and shuffle my feet forward so I'm doing a deep wall-sit.

Cut loose. It's loud, a forceful stream splattering noisily. Some splatters back on my butt and thighs.

The man snickers. "You were telling a truth, I think."

I use the napkins to clean myself as well as I can. Put my clothing back to rights and clear my throat. "All right. I'm done."

He turns back around, gun still held down at his thigh. Eyes the puddle of urine. "A lot."

I shrug. "I really had to pee. It was a long flight, and coffee goes through me, you know?"

"*Ja,* I know this. But I was *polizei,* so I can drink coffee all day and never have to piss. My doctor says this is no good." He gestures with the gun. "*Kommst du*. Back the automobile."

He waits for me, expecting to follow me.

Now.

My blood sings, adrenaline racing through me. I move as if to breeze past him. Instead, I turn abruptly and hit him in the throat as hard as I can with the web between finger and thumb, striking at his Adam's apple. At the same time, my other hand seizes his gun hand and twists it the wrong way. Stunned and gasping for breath, there's a split second where his reflexes haven't kicked in yet. I drive my knee up into his groin, using all of my weight with an upward drive of my braced leg, leaping upward to lend additional momentum to the strike. He doubles over, knees buckling. I still have his gun hand in mine, twisting it away—I finish the twist, stripping the gun away from him and jamming it into the side of his head.

"On your knees."

He shakes his head, but sinks to his knees, gasping, choking. "M-mis…mistake," he gurgles.

"Possibly." I shove the gun harder against his skull when his hand begins drifting toward his body. "Don't think I won't shoot you."

He lifts his hands. "What do you plan? He will kill your daughter."

"Will he? It's me he's after."

"And your husband."

"I figured as much." I dig in his suit coat pockets—he has another pistol there, a compact one.

I take it, shove it in my waistband at my back. He has a folding knife in his hip pocket, a pair of extra magazines, one for each pistol. ID, cash, and cards bound in a rubber band. His phone. I take everything.

"Now what will you do?" he asks. "A moment more and *meine freunde* will come."

"If you and your boss thought we'd all just go along with this nice and easy, that was a very big mistake." I grab a handful of his hair and yank his head back, jam the barrel under his chin. "Who is he?"

"I don't know."

"Bullshit. Wrong answer. I was planning on using you as leverage, but I'm perfectly willing to blow your brains out."

He frowns, eyebrows wrinkling. "You will? Really?"

"Doesn't he have files on us?"

"He does not share with me, if he does have this information."

Car doors open and close. Feet *click-clock-scuff* on concrete. A voice calls out a question—*What's taking so long?* I don't speak German, but that feels logical based on context.

"Don't answer."

"They will shoot me to get to you."

I put my back to the pillar, dragging him backward by the hair. "Fine by me."

"I know things." He scrabbles backward toward me to keep the pressure off of his hair.

The footsteps are close, now. They're repeating their question. "*Kai? Was ist los?*"

My lungs seize, and my hands want to shake; I force my lungs to work, force my hands to be steady. Kyrie is locked in a box, deep inside. Do what has to be done.

I check the safety; off.

Keep it pressed to Kai's temple.

Two men round the corner, coming into view from the car. Submachine guns out, at the ready.

Shit.

I swallow—too late to go back now.

Hunkering behind Kai, keeping his body fully in front of mine, I wait until they're both a few steps closer.

I think they're expecting me to negotiate—their guns are at the ready, but not trained on me, pointing in my direction but at the ground.

There are no negotiations.

BLAMBLAM!

One-two, the men drop with holes in their foreheads. Nausea roils in my gut at the spew of mess, at the wet thunk of bodies hitting cement.

"Sheisse."

Clear enough.

"Not expecting that, were you?" I wait. The drivers are next—doors open and I hear footsteps running.

They're trying to flank me, now, one each way. I shove Kai face down to the ground, his cheek in the puddle of my urine, and I kneel on his back, gun in both hands now, the way Duke taught me. Elbows in, support hand cupping the butt. One driver, coming my way as I'm facing him. I don't wait for a full view—I send a round at him the moment his torso in view; it hits the right side of his chest and he drops. Spin in place, still kneeling on my prisoner; just in time, I see the other driver coming around. This one actually gets a shot off, but it's high and wide, and his only one. He drops, clutching his gut.

"Can they contact what's his name?" I ask.

"*Nein*. They report to me, and I report to him."

I haul him to his feet, keep the gun trained on him. "Now that we're alone, let's see if you'll answer my questions."

He's still in shock—all four of his friends or subordinates are dead, and it happened in less than a minute. "You—what did you *do*?"

I press the barrel into his cheek. "I handled the situation, Kai." I hold his eyes, now, and let him get a good look into me. "Do you want to become one of those situations?"

"*Nein.*"

"His name. Start there."

"Apollo."

"Not good enough to keep breathing, Kai." I feel like an alternative version of myself.

I neither recognize nor like this version of me. But this version of me is cold and hard and efficient, and I need her to get through this. To get my baby girl back.

"I don't know."

What would Anselm do, in this situation? How would he make him talk?

"I would like to keep you alive, Kai, so you'd better start being worth my while." I press the gun to his shoulder where it meets his chest. "What's his name?"

"He doesn't tell us his name! He is Apollo."

"You said you know things. So far, nothing of use."

He ducks his head. "I don't know for sure. It's rumors, *ja*?"

"Such as?"

"The son of someone who was once your enemy."

"Our enemies are *dead*," I snap. "Because they did what this asshole is doing."

"It's what they say. This is revenge."

"For a life ruined," I say, remembering his words. "That doesn't help me. Tell me something that will help me find my daughter. *Now.*"

"You can't kill me, now," he says. "I'm no threat to you." A pause. "I have children."

I hold his eyes. "If you think I'm going to let *anyone* stop me from getting my daughter back, you're gravely mistaken."

"You would kill me in cold blood?"

"This isn't cold blood, Kai. This is the fury of a mother." I nudge him with the gun. "I'm running out of time and patience. Last chance."

He hangs his head. "Apollo Karahalios."

7

A SHARK IN THE DEEP DARK SEA

APOLLO TOSSES THE PHONE ONTO THE NEARBY couch. We're in the tower. I'm still in the dress, minus the heels.

He stands there a moment, head bowed, shoulders hunched, simply breathing. Then, he turns to me. "Your mother is a surprising woman, Corinna."

"Why?" I ask.

"She killed four of my men. *Four*. Armed, trained, combat-hardened men." He eyes me. "Did you know this about your mother?"

I swallow. "Intellectually, yes. I've heard stories."

His eyes burn. "Stories, hmm?" He turns to face me, stalks closer. That heat and crushing weight of his presence, the scalpel-sharp intensity of his eyes bears down on me. "Do tell."

I sit on the couch, smooth my dress under my thighs and cross my ankles under me. "It was all before I was born. They had enemies—my father did. Something to do with his life before he met my mom. I don't know the whole story. What I know is only what I've heard in bits and pieces, but my mom was kidnapped by a woman named...Jenny? Gina? Gina, I think." I notice, here, that his eyes narrow, one of them twitching. "It was an attempt to get back at my dad, from what I heard. Get back at him for what, I don't know. And, um. My mom killed some people while escaping. I guess the Gina lady was batshit crazy."

He turns away from me, hands going in his pockets. "You only know this from hearsay."

I shrug. "I mean, the hearsay is having heard bits and pieces of the story from multiple people who were there. So, it's not hearsay, it's just that I don't have the complete story. It happened twenty years ago and they don't really like to talk about it."

He turns back to me, composed once more. "Your mother doesn't seem to think I'm willing to harm you."

I swallow. "Are you?"

"I was hoping merely having you in my possession would be enough. It seems I was incorrect." He paces back to me. Stares down at me. "What am I to do with you, Corinna Roth?"

"I don't know," I whisper. "I don't know who you are. I don't know what you want."

He's utterly still, only his eyes moving, searching me, as if I somehow have the answers he's looking for. "Your father, perhaps."

"What about him?"

He shakes his head slightly. "She wasn't crazy."

"Who?"

He doesn't seem to hear me, turning away. "They *murdered* her."

"Apollo, what are you talking about?"

His chest rises and falls heavily, swiftly. He's troubled. His temple pulses, his jaw flexes and tics.

Fear twists inside me. What is going to do?

"Apollo, what are you talking about?"

"My *mother*," he snaps, whirling on me, eyes burning, wild, angry. "Your mother *murdered* mine."

I suck in a breath. "Holy shit."

He steps closer to me. His eyes bore into mine. "They ruined my life."

"I don't think they know you existed," I argue.

"Immaterial." He grabs his phone off the couch, unlocks it, brings up the keypad to dial a number, and hands it to me. "Call your father."

I swallow hard. Hesitate.

My hesitation costs me—his hand flashes, and the knife touches the thin, delicate skin of my throat, where the strap of my dress wraps around my neck.

A featherlight touch of the blade, and I can feel blood trickling down and pooling in my clavicle.

My heart pounds in my ears.

"Call…him." He bares his teeth—it's not a smile, it's a threat. "Or you'll spend your stay with me naked." His eyes flick down over my cleavage. "I'll enjoy it. You won't."

I dial the number for Dad's phone—a child of my generation, I don't have many phone numbers memorized, but I do know Mom's and Dad's by heart. It rings twice.

"Hello, this Valentine Roth."

"Daddy?"

His breath catches. "Rinna." A breath, not quite a sob. "Are you okay? Where are you? Nobody can find anything—we're trying, baby girl."

I look at Apollo. "I'm all right, Dad. I'm not hurt."

He snatches the phone from me. "Yet." A pause as he listens—I can't hear the other side of the conversation. A laugh. "Threats, is it? Yes, I know where your wife is. I'm keeping tabs on her, not to worry. She's causing a bit of trouble, actually, but it's only made the game even more fun."

He stares at me as he speaks. "Your daughter is ravishingly beautiful, Mr. Roth. Truly. Now, I'm a man who appreciates and…collects…beautiful things. I'd really rather not damage any of this…" he steps closer to me, and trails a fingertip over my throat, wiping through the blood, down, and horizontally across the swells of my cleavage, "…beautiful golden skin." His finger leaves a reddish smear.

I can't breathe. I'm afraid. So afraid. He's an unknown—will he hurt me? I don't know. I sense he may not. Threaten to, and maybe small things as evidence of his willingness to do worse. But if Mom killed his men in defiance of whatever he wanted her to do, and he hasn't punished me to get at her…maybe he won't actually hurt me.

But yet…

Again, I find myself not revolted by him, but almost…fascinated.

What's driving him? Revenge?

It's a twisted plot he's cooked up, if so. Kidnap me, and then what? Get money from my parents? He doesn't need money. It could still be a factor, because you can never count out greed as a motive. But…it just doesn't seem to be about money.

If it was pure and simple revenge, he'd have just killed me to hurt them.

But he's said several times he doesn't want to hurt me.

If anything, he seems as intrigued by me as I am him.

Which is…fucked up.

I can't breathe, with his finger sliding across my

skin, across my breasts. When did he put away the knife?

"You want your daughter back intact, Mr. Roth?" He holds my gaze. "Sell RTI."

A pause, and a laugh. "I'm perfectly serious. The proceeds will—" he halts, as if Dad interrupted him. "Don't think you understand me or my motivations, Valentine Roth. You do not. You'll put the money into an account I will provide to you. And you know what will happen to it then? It will be disbursed a hundred million, billion ways. Scattered like ashes on the wind. I don't want your *money,* Mr. Roth. I cannot be bought."

Another pause, and I don't have to hear what Dad says to know what his next question is.

"What *do* I want? I want your ruin." He ends the call and tosses the phone aside onto the couch. His eyes go to mine. "Do not hesitate, next time I ask something of you."

I say nothing.

His fingers touch my shoulders. Trace the crimson strap around my neck. My skin prickles at his touch. Every part of me is attuned to his nearness, reacting to him. It's physiological, chemical, animal. I swallow hard. My heart pounds.

I have no time to react or even flinch when his hand moves, the knife appearing, the flat of it pressing against my chest, sliding up to my neck. I don't breathe, don't dare even blink, watching the cold black metal skating over my flesh, nearer and nearer to the strap.

Closer, closer.

The tip halts a hair's breadth from my throat, where it already pierced my skin.

"Don't, please," I whisper. "Don't. Don't hurt me."

"Hurt you?" His stillness is uncanny—no part of him moves, except his eyes as he watches me, stares into me, his emotions guarded, hidden. "I'd as soon splash paint across an original Van Gogh, or smash a Ming Dynasty vase with a hammer."

"Then what are you—"

My voice gives out when he flicks the knife through the strap.

The dress sags, the weight of my breasts pushing the bodice down. I spill out over the fabric, the heat of his presence and fear and embarrassment at my nudity and a thousand emotions all conspiring against me—my nipples harden under his gaze.

My body is betraying me.

His exquisite features are carved from stone, betraying no emotion. His eyes skate over my breasts. His chest expands as he breathes in deeply.

That's a reaction.

He only looks at me for a long moment. Then his voice rasps out of his throat. "Remove it."

I don't dare hesitate. I clutch the fabric where it clings to my hips, preventing the dress from falling off. Tug it down, wiggling my ass from side to side to slip out of the dress. He watches every movement, every jiggle and bounce of my breasts.

When the dress is a pool of red around my feet, I stand straight. Resist with great effort the urge to cover myself. "Now what? I'm naked. Is this what you want? To embarrass me? Humiliate me?"

He took all my clothes, and when he provided this dress, he didn't include underwear. So, without the dress, I'm totally naked.

"You should not be embarrassed or humiliated, Corinna," he says. "You are a work of art. And art is meant to be displayed. Appreciated."

"If I so choose—I didn't choose to strip for you."

"You aren't attempting to cover yourself."

I lift my chin. Endure his scrutiny—which feels less like scrutiny and more like…a tiger eying its next meal. "I refuse to be cowed or intimidated by you."

He doesn't move. Only continues to look at me, eyes raking up and down.

"Haven't you seen enough?" I ask. "May I have something to wear, please?"

He turns away from me, stalks away a few steps. His clenched fists shove into his pockets—a habit to cover a reaction, I think. "I could never see enough." I barely hear him.

He whirls back to face me, takes a long, almost

angry stride toward me, hand outstretched, reaching for my breast—

He stops short. I can see his hand shaking.

His eyes go to mine, and I put all the dignity and pride I have into my gaze: I'm not scared of him.

Which, of course, is bullshit. Of course I am.

The threat of his touch leaves my mouth dry and my lungs empty, my heart pounding, my nerves singing.

His hand drops to his side, balls into a fist. Minute, fine lines of tension etch across his forehead, at the corners of his eyes, in the set of his lips—only because I'm looking at him closely, watching him carefully am I able to see the subtle hints of his emotions.

Such a careful, interior man.

Which makes the outburst about his mother all the more explosive, in comparison.

He clutches the collar of his polo shirt and rips it up and off. My mouth drops open, and a small breath escapes me. Perfection continues under his shirt; the musculature promised at by the set of his shoulders and toned sculpture of his arms comes to breathtaking fruition in the carved-from-marble beauty of his torso. Michelangelo couldn't have chiseled a more perfect male figure.

Neither overly brawny nor grotesquely lean, each muscle is defined and toned. His slacks sit just at his hips, a line carved in sharp relief angling over each hipbone and beneath his waistband. Abs pop, eight of them, rock hard. With each breath, his torso flexes and releases, ripples.

How dare he look this way? It's not fair. I want to hate him. But how can you hate perfection? It's like my body has forgotten what he's done to me: snatched me from my home in the middle of the night, cut me—albeit I've cut myself worse shaving my legs, but still—stripped me naked and gawked at me. Threatened me. Threatened my parents. Forcing my father to sell off his most valuable corporate asset simply out of some bizarre sense of vengeance, the provenance of which none of us have any clue.

Yet, simply removing his shirt has short-circuited my brain.

Momentarily.

I snatch the proffered shirt and shrug into it; the garment barely covers my sex, but barely is good enough for now.

A tableau, then. Apollo staring at me, me at him. Neither of us speaking. Less than a foot between us. Ice and fire war in the space between our bodies.

Then, abruptly, he stalks past me, into his closet, emerging a moment later slipping on a slate-gray button-down over his shoulders. I'm damned and triple damned, but I can't help but admire the way his torso twists and flexes as he adjusts the shirt and deftly thumbs the buttons closed. His strides are fierce, almost angry. He doesn't look at me as he passes me.

He leaves the shirt untucked, rolls the sleeves up to his forearms.

Pauses in the doorway, finally turning to regard me silently for an intense moment. I can no more divine what he's thinking or feeling than I could control the weather or fly away from the roof of this tower on my own.

He is a dark god, all coiled fury and coalescing thunderheads, with lightning in his eyes and a capacity for destruction in his hands—like a thunderstorm, there is a certain beauty in the chaos and wildness.

"You are a problem for me, Corinna," he murmurs. "One I must solve, and soon."

And then he's gone, locking the door behind himself.

He takes with him the oxygen in the room, the energy in my body.

Suddenly, I'm aware that I've been awake for I don't even know how long. Those long hours in the hold of the ship, I don't think I ever truly slept. Has it really only been one day since I've arrived?

I'm exhausted. My eyes burn, and my legs threaten to give out.

I've had enough—I'm going to bed. I'll take his, risks be damned.

I pull aside the comforter and slide in on the right side of the mattress, on the very edge. The moment my head hits the pillow, I feel myself drifting, toppling into sleep.

8

THE GRANDSON; AN ESCAPE

My blood turns to ice at his statement. "Vitaly's son?"

"Grandson." Kai shrugs. "So I've heard."

"What else have you heard?"

"I know that he is wealthy. I know he was not raised by the family—your people killed them all. It is legend, in the right circles." A sigh. "He has been increasing his presence in the underworld. Arms, drugs, these things. No one can connect him to anything—it's all rumors and suspicion. I know—I was investigating him."

"And then he bought you."

"He gives me a choice—work for him and make ten times the money, or…" a lift of his hand, a long stare into nothing. "I have a family. All I needed was the pictures he had of my wife, my boys. The decision was easy."

"Effective."

"Very." He looks at me, then. "I don't kill people, or hurt them. I connect people. I know everyone in this city, good and bad. I wouldn't hurt you. Or your daughter."

"But you can facilitate her kidnapping."

"What am I to do? Tell on him? Say no, he shouldn't do this?" A raspberry. "I am dead, and my family with me."

I can't stay here much longer. "Where is he keeping her?"

"I really don't know that."

"Guess."

"I have heard he has a castle or something like this. Spain, Portugal, France? I don't know. I really don't."

"But *he* has her? Not held, like, off-site?"

"So much as I know, *ja*."

"What's his plan?"

A laugh. "He tells me this?"

"Guess."

"Bait you all in. You, your husband, your friends. This Anselm comes for you, he is taken. Then we have you both. The others come, we take them. Then?" A shrug, a shake of his head. "I don't know. He kills you all, maybe."

"He really thought he could take us?" I shake my head. "How many are out there?"

"Men?" He gestures at the bodies. "Like them?"

"Right."

A shrug, a thoughtful pause. "Ten, I think."

He's been dragging this out—they're coming.

Shit.

I have to move. "Go remove the neckties from the bodies. Touch the guns and I'll kill you."

He does as he's told, moving slowly, keeping his hands visible. Brings me the ties. I use one to tie his wrists together, and another between his molars as a gag, and then I knot the two together, pulled taut.

"To the car," I say. He heads to the nearest car. I find the release for the trunk and gesture at it. "Get in."

He hesitates, and then awkwardly, laboriously climbs into the trunk—seeing as I've bound him, I have to help him. Once he's folded into the trunk, I close it.

Now what?

Call Anselm. But I know he'd tell me to keep moving, to not stay in one place for long. So I start the car and drive away. I don't know where I'm going—shit, I don't even know the street signs or the rules of the road, here. But I have to get away. So I just drive. I find myself on a one-way, two-lane road. Fortunately, the speed limit is clearly marked, so I can at least go the speed limit. I just keep driving, taking turns at random. When I've put a few miles between me and the bodies, I find a parking spot on the side of the road. I have Kai's phone, and Anselm's number was the last one dialed.

It rings twice. "*Ja*. I am near the location."

"Anselm, it's me." I swallow hard. "I'm not sure if I've made things worse or not, but…I, umm, sort of killed…everyone. Except one guy, who's in the trunk."

A pause. "You…" a huff of laughter. "Oh, Kyrie. How many?"

"Four."

"Where are they?"

"Where we were supposed to meet you."

"And where are you now?"

I laugh. "Not a damn clue. I just drove around randomly."

"Can you tell me the crossroads?"

I squint, trying to read the signs—the names are both long, and complicated, but I read them to him as best as I can. "Steg-ehh-weg, and, um…Mark… Schneider…strasse? There's a Volvo dealership down the road, and train tracks across from me."

"I know where you are." A pause, and I hear an engine revving. "You are a wonder."

"I'm not sure I believe what I just did, honestly. But, I do have the one guy who seems to know anything in the trunk. Anselm, he says the person doing this is Vitaly's grandson."

"You are fucking joking."

"I wish. He claims to not know for sure, that he knows the person as Apollo. But…I spoke to him. This Apollo, or Apollo Karahalios. He has Rin. And I'm scared I did the wrong thing, that I just got her killed."

"I don't think Rin is important to him. She's bait."

"That's what Kai said. That she's bait. That I'm bait."

"Did he say anything else?"

"That there's ten more guys out there. Converging on the drop, I assume. But now that I've skunked things up, I have no idea what's going to happen." Fear is taking over. "Did I fuck up, Anselm? Oh god, what did I do?"

"No, Kyrie. *Nein*. Be calm. You went on the offensive. It will be all right. I'm going to go to the coordinates and see if I can hunt down the remaining men. Stay where you are. I will call this number shortly."

"What if…what if he calls?"

"Answer. Tell him if he wants you, he's going to have to deal with you directly. Try to get a location out of him. Set up a meeting. Tell him you'll turn yourself into him. Promise him anything."

"He could be monitoring this line, you know. I have no idea what he's capable of."

"It is not so simple." A pause. "But, if he is listening, it is the truth. You would trade yourself for your daughter, would you not?"

"In a fucking heartbeat."

"Well then. Keep a sharp lookout. I will be to you soon."

Waiting is impossibly difficult. Every pedestrian I see is a possible assassin. My heart is in my throat and my hands are shaking and I keep seeing the first two men die, the backs of their heads exploding in a pink mist. I keep hearing Rin's voice, asking for me.

She's twenty. Not a child. She's always been precocious, always fiercely independent, but the more responsibility Valentine gave her, the more of an adult it made her. She lives at home with us, still, but only out of convenience.

Yet, in that moment, she just wanted to hear her mom's voice.

It makes the fury inside me boil over again.

The phone, resting on my thigh, rings—the sudden, jarring trill of it shocks me so badly I jump and gasp. The number is not saved as a contact, but I know who it is.

Shaking like a leaf, I answer. "Hello, Apollo Karahalios."

Silence. "Where is Kai?"

"In the trunk."

"I see." He sounds disappointed more than anything. "And my men?"

"Dead."

"Anselm did not obey his orders, then."

I laugh. "Oh no, he did. He has the money and he's nearly to the drop coordinates you provided."

"I am afraid I do not follow, Mrs. Roth."

"You've stolen my daughter from me, Apollo. Did you think I was going to take that lying down?"

"What I thought was that you valued your daughter's life." He pauses. "So you're saying *you* killed them?"

"Yes." I measure my next words carefully. "It's me you want, Apollo. If you hurt my daughter, it's only going to be worse for you. And if you kill her, you'll have no leverage over me at all."

"And you think this gives you power over me?"

"What is it you want, Apollo?"

"You, alone, in Madrid, two days from now."

"And my daughter?"

"Madrid. Two days."

"Lay one finger on Rin, Apollo…and your life is forfeit. It already is. But if you hurt her, I'll make sure your death is slow and painful."

A laugh of surprise. "I believe I underestimated you, Mrs. Roth."

"Clearly."

A pause. No way am I hanging up first.

"And, Mrs. Roth?"

"Hmm?"

"If you've finished with Kai, you can leave his body somewhere there along Flottenstrasse. I'll have someone collect him and return him to his widow."

Click.

Shit.

He knows exactly where I am.

9

STOCKHOLM SYNDROME

APOLLO IS IN THE BED WITH ME. HE'S TURNED AWAY, broad shoulders a tall cliff of male muscle rising and falling with each breath, his spine rounding slightly as he breathes. He's shirtless. His skin is naturally a deep copper tone bronzed further by the sun. He has scars on his back, thin lines in a maze of crosshatching. Strange.

The comforter is low over his hips—is he… naked?

I'm tempted to lift the blanket and look. But I don't.

I can't go back to sleep, though. I'm consumed by confusion and conflict—why am I not cowering away from him? Why is my skin not crawling?

There must be something wrong with me.

Stockholm syndrome? Is that the one where a kidnap victim develops a bond with their captor?

I don't have a *bond* with him. I don't like him. I'm scared of him. He's just…freaking gorgeous. The most beautiful male I've ever seen in my life, anywhere, whether online or on TV or in person.

He's just perfect.

Which isn't fair, at all. He's violent, and unpredictable, and arrogant, and…a litany of things, none of them good.

My brain knows this.

My body doesn't care.

The problem, my body doesn't know shit.

I'm startled when he rolls over, eyes hooded with sleep, and looks at me. I've never been in a bed with a man. I've shared a bed with Bryn, of course, any number of times. But that's different. We're twenty-year-old girls raised as sisters and thus comfortable with each other.

As seems to be usual for him, he just looks at me for a moment or two before speaking. "You snore."

I can't help a shocked laugh. "I do not."

"You do." The slightest hint of a smirk touches one corner of his mouth. "Just a quiet little…" and he imitates the sound he claims I make, a soft *snurk… sigh*. "Like that."

"Well, you're the one who locked me in a tower with one bed. I didn't sleep on the way here, seeing as, oh, I don't know, I was *locked in a dark cell on a boat*. Weird, I know."

He arches his eyebrow, a facial version of a shrug. "It amused me." That ghost of a smirk again. "The snoring."

"This feels oddly domestic, Apollo, you and me sharing a bed."

"You were in my bed. I was ready to sleep." A quirk of his shoulders. "I did not bother you."

Q.E.D., his tone suggests.

I have no response for that. I pluck at the polo shirt of his which I'm still wearing. "Do I get real clothes, or are you going to just torture me with near-nudity?"

"Near-nudity tortures you?" he says. "You seem rather confident in yourself."

I hold his gaze. "What do you gain by keeping me from having real clothes?" I'm tempting the tiger to eat its meal with this question, perhaps. "You've gotten your look at me naked. But you don't seem inclined to…" I swallow hard, force it out. "Rape me. Or anything. So…what's your plan?"

"Rape you?" He frowns. "I think not. I am not a good man. At all. But I am not that kind of man, Corinna."

"Above rape, but not above kidnapping and murder."

"One must draw a line somewhere." He stares

into me, with that impossible to read gaze of his. "Unwilling presence here with me notwithstanding, have you been egregiously mistreated?"

"Aside from forcing me to strip naked in front of you, burning my clothes, and cutting a dress off me, you mean?" I arch my eyebrow back at him.

A snort. "Aside from that, yes."

I shake my head. "I do not understand you," I say. "Am I supposed to just be fine with that, simply because you haven't beaten, raped, or killed me?"

I don't wait for a reply, I leave the bed and use the bathroom. When I'm done washing my hands, I look up and find Apollo in the entrance to the bathroom.

He's naked.

My lungs seize. Jaw again drops open.

He's naked.

I can't look away, can't blink or move or process what I'm seeing.

It's pointing at me, angled straight away from his body. Straight as an arrow, as thick as my wrist, or nearly so. Pink, with veins rippling through the skin. Broad, plump, round head. Heavy sac beneath it, taut against his body. Not shaved—a light dusting of black hair around the base, narrowing to a thin trail leading up to his navel.

As I stare at it, his member rises, lifting upward slowly, almost imperceptibly, thickening and lengthening. After a moment, it ceases to expand, standing flat upright against his belly, the tip touching his navel.

Several inches of thick, erect male flesh.

I swallow hard, trying to talk myself into turning away. Closing my eyes. Something.

React, damn you, I snarl at myself.

I turn around. "I'm sorry." I don't know why I said that—he came in here of his own volition, naked, knowing I was in here.

"I am not ashamed of my nakedness," he says. "I work hard to look the way I do."

"So do I," I say, whispering. "That's not the point."

"Then what is the point, Corinna?"

I shake my head. "Choice. Being here at all is not my choice—for all that this room is beautiful, you still lock me in here. When you threaten me with a knife and tell me to take off my clothes, that's not me having a choice in being naked in front of you."

"I see. But if I gave you a choice, you would leave." He's closer, somehow. I don't dare turn around—if I do, I'll keep staring at the monster between his thighs. "And that does not yet suit my purposes."

"Why are you naked?"

A huff, a soft breath of laughter. "Because I sleep naked. I'm not going to alter my habit simply for your prudish American sensibilities. Also, I'm about to take a shower. Which requires being naked." He's so close. I can almost feel his body against mine. "Are you afraid of my naked body, Corinna?"

"I'm afraid of you."

"Probably prudent." I feel his breath on the back of my neck; I don't move a muscle—If I do, I'll feel the thing push against my butt. "But that's not what I asked. Are you afraid of my nakedness?"

I don't answer.

"Are you, Corinna? Can you not answer so simple a question?"

"Yes," I whisper.

"Why?" I feel something soft and warm brush against my left buttock. I flinch, gasp. "I am not restraining you, yet you do not flee. You could go into the other room. You complain of being nude, or nearly so, but yet you do not avail yourself of the closet full of clothes mere feet away. They are mine, yes, but they would cover you." He pauses. Breathes. Each breath is warm on the back of my neck, making my skin prickle and tingle. "I admit I regret cutting that dress off you."

"Why?"

"Because you looked ravishing in it, Corinna." That brush against my buttock again. I flinch away, but yet as he pointed out, I cannot seem to move, to flee. "Surely you must know how incredible you are."

"I don't feel incredible. I feel like a prisoner."

"The door is not locked." He whispers it. "You can walk out of this room any time you wish."

At this revelation, I spin in place, searching his face as if I have a hope of diving the truth from his ever-inscrutable face. It is a mistake—turning around, I mean, not looking at his face. Why a mistake, you ask? Because now the appendage which was brushing against my butt is now nudging my thigh. So close. Too close.

I gulp, look down.

Good god, it's so *big*.

It seems impossible. Also impossible is the totality of the man that is Apollo—the depth of his physical perfection. Even just awake, his hair is mesmerizing, tangled and messy, sticking to the stubble of his jaw and curling around his neck just above his shoulders, wild and untamed. His eyes are deep and dark and unknowable, neither cold nor distant just now, but curious and heated yet still and ever guarded. His body…there are no words.

What—the—fuck—is wrong—with me?

This man *kidnapped* me, and I'm ogling him as openly as he has me.

"I can leave?" I whisper, finally finding the fortitude to back away from him, out of range of physical contact.

He smiles, a wolfish grin of amusement. "Sure."

"Your grin tells me there's a catch."

“The catch is, I own the land for miles in every direction. And as I am, as you may have noticed, a very private man, you could walk for hours and never see another person. Vines and orchards, and that’s it. Maybe a few farmworkers, but they won’t assist you. I doubt they’d even look at you.”

I deflate.

“But if my naked body frightens you, you may find another place in my home to bide the time.”

I turn around and go into his closet, searching his closet for something to wear on my bottom half. I find a pair of gym shorts with a drawstring and step into them. They hang to my shins, but with the drawstring pulled tight, they stay on fine. Thus attired in Apollo’s shirt and shorts, feeling I’m doing the walk of shame, I leave the tower. For the first time since the night I was taken, I’m doing something on my own, of my own volition. It feels…I’m not sure how to put it, even in my own mind…it feels strangely strange. As if I’ve always been here, in this castle, with this supremely unusual man.

When, in fact, it’s only been a day. A day and a half? I’m not sure.

Not so strangely, I find myself in his library. Good golly Miss Molly, what library. I’m shook. Three full stories, and not just floor to ceiling in a big box, either. He has proper stacks, like an actual, literal library.

We’ve taken quite a few vacations as a family,

obviously; my father designs and builds hyper-luxury transportation, so of course we have the best of the best in private transport—we've taken jets and boats all over the world. Most memorably, we took one of the crown jewels of RTI's fleet, the submarine from our island in the Caribbean to Rio de Janeiro. Which has one of the most beautiful libraries in the world: the Royal Portuguese Reading Room. Words don't do it justice—you have to see it. In person, preferably, if not online.

This library of Apollo's? Damn close, and similar in style, actually. Ornate, hand-carved shelf-ends, graceful arches spanning the posts supporting the balconies above—gothic arches, here, but delicate and almost insubstantial. The room is not an exact shape, the walls turning this way and that to create corners and nooks, each one featuring a small chair and end table lit by a floor lamp.

I peruse the first level for a while, scanning titles, wandering at random. The stairs are hidden in corners, and I ascend to the second level for a while, selecting a book and reading a few pages, or even a few chapters. Time doesn't exist here; does time pass at all, in a good library? How long do I spend, there? Hours, certainly. Up to the third level, then, and now I find a corner where the books are dusty and smell old, with cracked leather covers. There's a lectern and a pair of white gloves. First, I scan these ancient tomes.

Descartes, Hume, Virgil, Homer; Greek tragedies, Roman myth, and Renaissance philosophy; a folio of Shakespeare, Donne, a handwritten translation of Dante's *Inferno*.

The chair here is a well-loved one, deep with a high back and armrests, the brass-riveted maroon leather worn and scuffed and aged, with a matching footstool. A cork coaster on the side table, on it, a forgotten tumbler with a dried scrim of old liquor staining the bottom.

I choose the collection of John Donne's love poems; the gloves are too big, but a volume this old requires protection from the oils on my fingers, so I wear them. I turn the pages with extreme care, taking my time reading each poem. Just a month ago, I completed a survey course of English Poetry from the early Middle Ages through World War Two, and as I read, I can't help falling into the ingrained habit of close reading, prying meaning from the dense language.

I'm so entranced, I don't hear him arrive; that, or he's simply very light of tread.

"Ah, John Donne," he says, making me jump. "An old friend."

I frown up at him. "Really?"

He eyes the tome, upside down to him, then fixes his gaze on me:

"'I wonder, by my troth, what thou and I

Did, till we loved? Were we not weaned till then?
But sucked on country pleasures, childishly?
Or snorted we in the Seven Sleepers' den?
'Twas so; but this, all pleasures fancies be.
If ever any beauty I did see,
Which I desired, and got, 'twas but a dream of thee.'"

It's the poem I was reading, quoted verbatim.

He smirks at me. "You've pigeonholed me as a criminal, I presume."

"Well, aren't you?" I lean on the lectern without touching the book itself.

He shrugs. "Perhaps. Some of the things I do are outside the law. But not all. And those things are not all I am." He eyes me thoughtfully. "In fact, I am only a recently entree into the world of organized crime." A pause. "Well, my involvement in it, at least. The majority of my fortune was, I discovered, gained through crime."

"What do you mean, you discovered?"

He leans against the railing, arms outstretched along the top. "It's a long story."

I gesture around us. "I have nothing but time, it seems."

A wry smile twists his lips, and he sighs. "Do you really wish to know? Truly?"

I find that I do. Why? I couldn't begin to fathom

the psychology that's going into my curiosity. "Yes," I say, choosing to omit any attempt at an explanation.

He doesn't ask for one. He spends a moment considering. "I grew up alone."

"An only child?"

That doesn't surprise me.

The curve of his lips is not a smile, or not one of amusement or joy. "Well, yes, but that isn't what I meant." Another pause. "I mean *alone*. My mother was frequently gone. As a child, all I knew was that Mother was working. That's what I was told. I lived at the top of a high-rise in Athens, cared for by an *au pair* named Gemma. She would prepare my meals and see that I ate them. There was a tutor, a dour old Russian named Koslov. I didn't know any other name for him, just Koslov. He was unkind, strict, and unpleasant. He smelled of cigarettes and vodka." He looks away, gazing into nothing. "Koslov would come at nine in the morning, and drill into me lessons of mathematics and science and literature. It was a very…medieval… way of learning. As if I was the heir to some throne, meant to have this old-world education in the classics. There was no sense of the fact that I was but a child. It wasn't merely reading and writing and adding, it was reading *Aeneid* from a seventeenth-century translation, and algebra, and geometry when most kids my age were at recess and studying basic world geography and reading age-leveled primers."

"That sounds...unpleasant."

"I was certain I'd done something to anger my mother. Even though I barely saw her. She would come some weekends. Usually, I would wake up Saturday morning and there she would be, dressed as if she'd just come from a nightclub, smelling of booze and men and blood and cordite. I only know the latter two smells now that I'm an adult myself. Then, it was just the smell of Mother. She would behave as if it was all perfectly normal. 'Why good morning, Polly,' she would say. Polly." A derisive snort. "I hated that name. It felt like she thought I was a parrot. Or a girl." He sighs. "She would always bring me presents. The latest toys, video game consoles, a larger TV, stacks of comic books." Another of those wry, unamused smirks. "When I neared adolescence, the stacks of comics was replaced by stacks of American pornography magazines. *Hustler, Playboy, Penthouse*."

I blink. "Really?"

A shrug. "It was her way. She had no conception of normality. She would give me some of her drink. Or more usually, pour me my own. As if I was an adult and we were having a meeting, even though I was ten or eleven. She would talk to me, talk *at* me. Just rambling. If she decided to shower, she would strip down in front of me." A pause. "But she was gone again as suddenly as she would appear. I would go to bed with her drinking in the living room, and when I woke up Sunday morning, she was gone."

"Your father?" I ask.

His eyes narrow. "I've never known a single thing about him. Nor shall I ever. He is a nonentity."

Case closed.

He continues, after a moment. "That's what I mean by alone, Corinna. Gemma would be there, but she was distant. She did not foster affection between us. She looked at her job as merely keeping me alive, seeing to my physical needs. Koslov saw that I was educated—looking back, frightfully well educated. He even taught me the rudiments of Greek and Latin. But I had no friends. No companions. I rarely left the home. Once a week, Koslov would walk with me, a few blocks this way and that, drilling me in Latin conjugations or verbally solving math problems, or quoting long sections of literature at me."

I shake my head, unable to comprehend such a life. "So, it was just you and two adults neither of which was your parent, in a condo, alone, all day every day?"

"Yes."

"Did you get to play or watch TV?"

He rolls a shoulder. "Koslov instructed me from nine to four. After four, I was on my own. Gemma often left for long periods of time, shopping I suppose, or visiting friends. I was alone much of my life. I played with my toys, watched TV, played video games, and read books."

I put together pieces of what he's told me. "And your mother was Gina Karahalios. The woman who kidnapped my mother, beat her senseless, forcibly and violently shaved her head with a knife, and would have had her minion rape her to death had my mother not liberated herself."

His eyes flare. "That is not true."

I stand up away from the lectern, keeping it between him and me. "It is, though. My mother, my aunt Layla, my father, my uncle Harris, Duke, Anselm, Lear, Puck, Thresh, and Sasha...they have all told the same story, or pieces of it, over the years." I hold his eyes, and the anger I see in them worries me, frightens me. "What do you actually *know* about your mother, Apollo? She was absent most of your life. You said yourself she brought strange men around, showed up and vanished randomly, gave you pornography as a young boy...these are not the actions of a responsible mother."

"She was the only mother I had, though." He's utterly still, even his eyes frozen on mine. Barely breathing, jaw clenched.

"I know. I get that. But what do you *know* about her? We always want to believe the best of our parents. But they aren't perfect."

"Easy for you to say," he murmurs. "You have both of yours."

I feel a tense thrill of sympathy push up through the thick layer of fear. "You're right. I'm just saying—I know you may not want to admit it, but maybe...it is true, what your mother did to mine." I step around the lectern, and now there's nothing between us but a few feet of space; I approach closer to him like I would a half-tamed dog, cautiously, slowly, with no sudden movements. "My mother killed yours, Apollo. There's no denying that. And I know I can't possibly understand the effect that had on you. But...just... maybe it was justified. That doesn't lessen its effect on you. But...maybe you could try to understand that?"

He stares at me, expressionless and statuesque. Abruptly, he pivots on a heel and walks away. "Enjoy the library. Please reshelve the books when you are finished with them. I have business to attend to and will be gone for a day or two."

I get the sense that the things he shared with me he rarely, if ever, shares with anyone. He strikes me as an intensely solitary person—the isolation and solitude he says he was raised in never changed.

Mentally, I've compared him to wolves and tigers...but now, one comparison rises above them all.

Apollo Karahalios is a shark swimming in a sea of silence and solitude. He's most comfortable in the dark cold depths, rarely surfacing, and when he does, all one sees of him is a fin, slicing through the water.

Beneath it all, though, I think there's a hurting child. A psyche that was never shown love or affection. A man who grew to adulthood in near-total isolation with no reference point of humanity or emotional expression.

All a shark knows is hunger—the hunt. It holds no animosity toward its prey.

All Apollo has ever known is the silence and the isolation and the loneliness—himself, alone in the world, with no one to hug him or care about his feelings.

What if there was someone to do that for him?

What if I did?

Stockholm Syndrome indeed.

Or maybe I'm simply seeing the man beneath the mask—the hurting heart behind the island fortress that is Apollo Karahalios.

10

BERLIN TO MADRID; THE MONSTER UNMASKED

NIGHT HAS FALLEN, LONG SINCE. NO ANSELM.

I don't dare leave this spot, nor do I dare call him. I don't dare call anyone—I can't be certain this phone isn't bugged or tapped. All I want is to hear my husband's voice, to feel the reassurance of his presence, even over the phone.

I almost feel bad for Kai, trussed up in the trunk. I can't just kill him; I'm not that person. I don't know that I need him anymore, but I don't know what to do with him. I also can't just leave him in there, though. At some point, it becomes torture, and I'm not okay with that either. I have some boundaries, after all.

With a sigh, I exit the car and go to the trunk.

Pop it open. Kai blinks, bleary and sleepy. "Come on," I say. "Out."

He wiggles and inchworms awkwardly to the edge of the trunk, flops his feet out. I'm sure he's stiff and sore, if his limbs haven't long since fallen asleep. It takes a moment, but he finds his feet and stands facing me. I have his pistol in my hand, held down at my side. Now I point it at him.

He lifts his chin, eyes hardening. "Do it," he says, through the gag of the necktie.

"What would you do if I let you go, Kai?" I ask. "Don't lie. I'm a mother—I can smell a lie from a mile away."

I pull the gag out of his mouth but leave his hands bound.

He shrugs, working his jaw. "I can't go home. Apollo will…deal with me for failing him. But I worry too that he will punish my family instead of me. I can't go to him." A sigh. "I am not sure what I would do. I never anticipated you would turn out to be…" he gestures at me with a lift of his chin. "Who you are."

I hesitate. Letting him go could be a very serious mistake. But I can't just kill him. I don't know what to do.

"Take your chances," I say. "Go to your family. Go somewhere with them."

"Apollo will find us."

"No, he won't." I feel a frisson of cold certainty

shiver down my spine. “He won’t be alive to do so. Not once we’re done with him.”

He searches me. “Somehow, I believe you.”

“You think he’s worse than either his mother or his grandfather?” I ask. “Because I don’t. And we ended them.”

“He is not the same as them. He is an unusual man, I think. I have spent my career investigating organized crime—I was Interpol, based here in Berlin. Apollo Karahalios is…strange.”

“How so?”

“He has blood on his hands. You do not gain this attention in the world of dealing arms and shipping large quantities of drugs as he has without shedding blood. But he does not do so needlessly.” A pause. “And, from what I have heard and what I know personally, he does not hire out his dirty work to underlings. He oversees shipments himself. Negotiates the deals himself. If someone betrays him, if someone requires punishment or there must be an example made, he does it himself, with his own hands.”

I frown. “Forgive me if I don’t applaud his leadership skills.”

“I do not say so. I just say that he is complicated.” A shrug. “Not simply ruthless and ambitious like his grandfather, nor unhinged and bloodthirsty like his mad bitch of a mother.”

"You know *nothing* about how bloodthirsty and crazy Gina was," I snap. "Not a *damn* thing."

"But I do." He eyes me with something like a sympathetic wince. "I was newly hired into the ranks of Interpol twenty years ago. My first assignment was to investigate a disastrous mess on a small island in Greece. What we determined was that the Karahalios clan had kidnapped the wrong person, and paid the price." He lets a significant pause linger. "We had evidence of some of the assailants—the names and faces of the kidnap victim and the men who assaulted the compound. But somehow, the investigation just never…went anywhere. It was very strange, you know? But Vitaly was a bad, bad man. Wanted in many countries, yet we could never pin enough evidence on him to bring him down. So when he turned up dead? I think those who perpetrated the assault were seen as having done the world a favor. And if it were our girlfriend or our wife who was in that basement?" A shrug. "I saw with my own eyes the remains of Gina and her pet monster."

His eyes fix on me, communicating a wealth of things his words don't. "I could read well enough what had happened. They got what they deserved."

I frown at him. "So, you knew it was me who killed Apollo's mother. You knew he had kidnapped my daughter—and me, for all intents and purposes, even though I was going along willingly. As in, not physically forced. You knew he has something awful planned—for me, for my husband, maybe my daughter." I shake my head. "You knew all this, and you still went along with his plan?"

He frowns. "To protect my wife and my sons? *Ja*. I do not know for certain that Apollo would murder children. So far, he has not, so much as I am aware, at least. But can I take that chance? Would you?"

I sigh. "A rock and a hard place."

"Just so." He rolls his shoulders. "Will you let me go?"

"Will you betray me back to Apollo?"

"*Nein*." He bobs his head to one side. "If it is my life or my family's, or yours? *Ja*. Otherwise, I would not."

"Fair enough." I gesture with the pistol. "Go on, then."

"You are not going to untie me?" He looks around. "I am many miles from my home."

I shake my head. "I may understand your position, but you still were part of a plot to kidnap me and my daughter. My understanding only goes so far, as does my trust."

I walk backward to the driver's side door, open it, and lean in without taking my eyes or gun off Kai; I grab his wallet—or the rubber band-bound collection that serves him as a wallet—and remove all of the cash but a €20 note; this leaves me with a little over two hundred euros, which is decent little sum. I tuck his wallet into his hip pocket.

"There," I say. "Now start walking. Hit the U-Bahn and hope someone takes pity on you. I don't know. I'm letting you live, Kai—I'd count your blessings."

He sighs, nods, and turns to walk away. He only makes it half a dozen steps before he stops and looks back at me. "Spain." He rolls a shoulder. "I believe he is based in Spain. In my investigations of him, his personal holdings are all in his real name. It should not be so hard to find him, now that you know who he is."

He fades into the darkness, then, and I watch him go.

"I hope I'm not making a mistake by letting him go," I say to the night.

"I think not," the night responds.

I jump half a foot in the air, squealing. "Anselm! You scared the hell out of me!"

He's standing behind me, just suddenly there. His hair, somewhere between blond and brown, is not shot through with strands of silver, but otherwise the years have not touched him. You wouldn't look at him twice in a crowd, but if you did, you'd see the hard muscle and the lithe movements of a born predator.

I leap at him and hug him, startling him into a backward step, his arms going around my shoulders. "God, Anselm, am I glad to see you."

He lets me go. "You as well, Kyrie. Are you all right?"

I bob my head side to side. "I mean, I'm not hurt."

A nod. "This, I understand." He looks in the direction Kai had gone. "You let him go. Why?"

"I can kill when I have to, I can shoot if I'm about to be shot. But I'd taken him hostage and he wasn't a threat to me any longer. I couldn't just shoot him. Maybe I should've but I couldn't. He has a wife and sons—Apollo used them as leverage to make Kai work for him. I don't know. Something just told me I had to let him go."

Anselm nods. "It is best, I think. You have done well."

I poke his arm. "But now you're here, so I can let you do the yucky stuff, right?"

He laughs. "Hopefully."

"Did you get the other guys? Kai said there were ten."

Anselm nods. "*Ja*. The Berlin authorities will find ten bodies to deal with. This is what took so long—they were not all together, and I had to be sure of my targets."

"Kai said Spain."

"For this Apollo?"

I nod. "That's what he said—that Apollo owns property in his own name in Spain."

"Well, then, let's go to Spain." He gestures at the

car. “Not in that, however. It is most certainly being tracked. The cell phone from this Kai fellow as well. Leave it all here.”

“Can we get ahold of the others?” I ask.

“When we are *en route*. We must put distance between us and this last known location.”

Getting out of Berlin the way Anselm does things is a slow process. First, we use my cash to buy a burner phone, assuming the device Anselm had been using was now compromised. Then, we buy a stash of non-perishable food and bottles of water. Then, leaving me at a bus stop with the bags of food, Anselm vanishes into the shadows, returning a few minutes later in a late model BMW.

It’s a nice car, clean and well-kept, a few years old and fast.

“You don’t steal cheap cars, do you?”

He chuckles. “Not if I can help it.” He drives away at a sedate pace, as if in no hurry. “It is partly an ethical thing, however. A cheap automobile, what you in America call a beater? The person who owns that does so because he or she cannot afford anything better. A vehicle of that sort is often that person’s only lifeline, their only way to work and thus to stave off poverty. I would not steal from such a person, except in a case of a life or death emergency. A newer auto like this, an expensive one, it is owned by someone who can afford its loss. They would be inconvenienced, but it does not have the same deleterious effect."

"Huh," I say. "I never thought of that." We're heading west out of Berlin, now. "I didn't think it was possible to steal a car like this."

He just grins. "You can steal anything. You must simply know the tricks."

"Secret spy tricks, huh?"

A shrug. "Not so much this, no. There are devices, technologies. If I am off-grid, operating in the dark, so to speak, I often must steal automobiles to get where I must go without being detected when public transit is most certainly being monitored. So, I keep such tricks up my sleeve. These tricks also disengage the tracking and anti-theft devices." He taps the infotainment screen. "It disables this, as well, but I do not need navi to get from here to Spain."

"So now we call in?"

He nods. Holds out his hand for the burner phone. "I will dial. There are procedures in place."

He dials a long series of digits, listens, dials again, listens again. "Alpha-Tango-one-four-six-Kilo-Romeo." Listening again, another series of numbers, and then he hands me the phone. "It's ringing for your husband."

I put the phone to my ear, hearing it burble—not

a typical ringing sound. The elaborate process Anselm went through was to patch into a secure, encrypted line that couldn't be tapped into from the outside.

"Hello?" His voice is the most familiar thing to me on the planet. "Kyrie?" He sounds choked up.

"Yeah, honey, it's me. I'm okay." I clear my throat. It's not time to let my emotions out of their box, yet. "I'm with Anselm, en route out of Berlin. I've got a lead on who has Rin."

"So do I," he says. "Lear worked his magic. He got satellite imagery from the night Rin was abducted, and managed to track the boat from our island all the way to Cádiz."

"Spain."

"Right."

"That tracks with what I've learned." I hesitate. "Did Lear find anything on who?"

"The boat was chartered by a company called A-K-T-I, but it's just a shell. Whoever owns it does so through a massively complicated series of interwoven subsidiaries." His turn to hesitate. "The evidence points to this being personal." He swallows. "I spoke to him."

"You...did?"

"Yeah. He didn't identify himself, but...to keep Rin safe and to get her back, he wants me to sell RTI, and put the profits into some escrow account or something. He says he wants my ruin. Whatever that means."

"Did you?"

"Sell off RTI?" he scoffs. "Yeah. Well, it's in process." To someone in the room with him. "Is this line secure? How much can I say?...okay, thanks. I'm selling it to someone who owes me a favor. I'm not going to say too much even on a secured line, but...the favor he's going to do me is that once this is all over, I'll get it back. The corporation, that is. The essential stuff, the designs, the patents, shares, all that. The money I couldn't give less of a shit about."

"I know who it is, Val," I whisper.

He's silent a moment. "This feels like Gina or Vitaly. But they're dead. I saw their bodies myself. I had personal, visual confirmation of death."

"His name is Apollo." I swallow hard. "Apollo Karahalios."

"Vitaly had another kid?"

"I was told it's Vitaly's *grand*son. As in, *Gina* had a son."

"How the *fuck*?" he hisses. "All the time we were together, she never took any precautions against pregnancy—she almost seemed to relish in it. She never told me as much, but I always assumed she was infertile, because she never got pregnant. I remember her saying she had some illness when she was a kid. I don't know." Another pause. "Gina had a son."

"And we killed her." I swallow again, hard. Put it all down in the box. Keep it bottled up till it's over. "*I* killed her."

"And now he wants revenge." He sounds shaken. "For a life ruined. That's what he said to me."

"Will he hurt her?" I ask. "To hurt us?"

"I mean, the grab was professional. There's barely any evidence it even happened. It could have been bloody, but they took great pains to pull it off without firing a shot. He hasn't hurt her so far. I mean, I don't think we can bank on him not hurting her…but. I don't know, babe. We just have to get to her first."

"Anselm and I are on the way."

"Kyrie, how did you get away?"

"Let's just say all those sessions with Duke in Colorado paid off."

"I was afraid of that." A low growl. "He's going to pay for this."

"I'm fine, babe. Really." A husky laugh. "I mean, I'll probably be less okay once this is over, but for now, I'm holding out."

"She's going to be okay, Kyrie," he says. "She's tough and she's smart."

A pause, muffled background conversation.

"I'll meet you in Spain. Me and everyone else."

"What about Cal?"

A harsh sigh. "I don't think I could keep him out of this. He's…angry. They've got his sister, and you, and he and I have been holed up and hiding as he puts it, like scared little kids. He'd never forgive me if I made him stay here alone with a babysitter."

"Valentine. He's fifteen."

"I'm not giving him a gun, honey, but I can't leave him here by himself. Plus, I'd just feel safer with him in my sight at all times."

"And you'll have the full crew with you?"

He chuckles. "Yes, Kyrie. He'll have an honor guard fit for a Roman emperor."

"Promise me nothing will happen to him."

"I swear, Kyrie. He'll be safe."

I swallow hard. "Okay. I have no choice but to trust you on this. I just don't want him in on any action. I know that's what he wants, but he's fifteen. We can't let that happen. We can't expose him to that."

"I know. Believe me, I know." A sigh. "We shouldn't stay on too much longer, even on an encrypted line."

"I'm going to get her back, Val."

"I know, honey. I know you will." A hesitation. "Just…be careful, okay? No stupid risks."

"I'm with Anselm. He doesn't do stupid risks."

"Indeed I do not." Anselm holds out his hand for the phone. "I need to talk to Harris."

"Anselm wants to talk to Harris," I tell Valentine. "I love you. See you soon."

"Not soon enough," he says. "Love you too."

Anselm and Harris speak briefly, mostly in some sort of Special Forces bro code about threat assessments and recon and intel, and then the call ends with an agreement to rendezvous by phone again in a few hours, once Lear has done some digging with the information—excuse me, *intel*—I provided.

We take turns driving. Despite the urgency, we dare not attract attention by driving recklessly, so we're forced to behave as if this is simply a road trip. It's a twenty-two-hour drive from Berlin to Madrid; it's a beautiful drive, but it's hard to appreciate it.

Anselm takes the first shift driving, a marathon twelve hours behind the wheel, stopping to refuel twice. I try to rest, knowing I'll need it, but I'm too amped up, too worried. So I merely sit and don't quite doze, staring out the window at the scenery.

Finally, somewhere in France, Anselm turns the driving over to me. It's mostly rural highway driving, he says, so as long as I watch my speed and stay awake, I'll be fine. The moment he finds a comfortable position in the passenger seat, jacket balled up against the window as a pillow, he's asleep.

I envy his ability to fall asleep so easily.

11

DAMNED IN THE ORANGERY

He's gone the whole next day, which I spend in the library. There's a couch there, and I sleep on that rather than returning to the tower. The same woman who brought our dinner the first evening somehow finds me and brings me meals—oatmeal with blueberries for breakfast; a charcuterie tray piled high with fresh deli meat, cheeses, honey, fruit, and peasant bread with a crunchy crust and delicate, fluffy interior; and fresh fish of a kind I don't recognize, baked with a veggie medley and small red roasted potatoes. There's a pitcher of mimosas with breakfast, a large bottle of dark, Belgian, small-batch beer with lunch, and a decanter of crisp, fruity white wine with dinner.

Other than the woman who brings the food—I

never get her name, and she never speaks to me—I see no one. My time in the library is, honestly, refreshing. I can almost feel like I'm here voluntarily. Just enjoying a nice peaceful, relaxing day alone in a beautiful library in the countryside.

Almost.

It's just past dawn on the second day of Apollo's absence; I'm slowly rousing from sleep, still on the couch on the third level of the library. The woman appears, bearing a tray laden with a silver carafe that has steam writhing from the spout, a single white porcelain mug, a small jar, and a spoon. She sets the tray on the small side table next to the couch, pours coffee into the mug, and then lifts the jar in question.

I shake my head. "No, black is fine. Thank you."

She nods.

"Do you speak English?" I ask.

A small shrug of one shoulder. "Little."

"What's your name?"

"Consuela."

"Are you under some kind of instructions to not speak to me?"

A shake of her head. "*Don* Apollo, no speak with him. He like only…" she touches her index finger to her lips. "*Siempre silencioso.*"

"Well, I am not *Don* Apollo. You can talk to me."

A shrug. "You want…*comer*?"

I shake my head. "No, thanks. Maybe later."

A nod, a bow. "*Bueno. Comerás más tarde.*"

"Consuela?"

She turns back, face posing the question her voice does not.

"Is there anyone else here besides you and me?"

Her hesitation is noticeable. "*Sí.* Many others. You stay...*biblioteca*."

And so, I stay in the library. All that day. Much of the next.

I've dozed off in the library, in a chair in a corner of the second level, reading a white-glove copy of Voltaire. I hear a scrape, a footstep.

He's there, a few feet away. Gray trousers, black loafers, a white button-down, open to his chest. Hair smoothed back, simple black Ray-Ban sunglasses pushed up on the top of his head. He has a large brown paper bag in one hand.

"I brought you some clothes."

I stand up—I'm still wearing the gym shorts and polo shirt of his. "You did, hmm? More slinky cocktail dresses that barely cover me?"

He paces closer to me and sets the bag down. "No." A wry smirk. "Although you did look ravishing in that dress."

"If by ravishing you mean slutty, then yes."

He frowns. "To accentuate your lovely body is

not slutty, Corinna. Such a strangely prudish manner of thinking."

"It's just not how I typically dress."

"You typically live in bathing suits."

I laugh. "I do live on a Caribbean Island. I'm supposed to wear a parka?"

A shrug. "Perhaps not." He gestures at the bag. "This is not what you are accustomed to, but it is not a cocktail dress."

"Why?"

"Why what?"

"Why bring me clothes?"

A shrug. "We are lunching in the orangery in a few minutes. I thought you might like to be more appropriately dressed."

"The orangery?"

"Change, and I'll show you."

I withdraw the parcels in the bag—packages wrapped in thin brown butcher's paper, tied with twine. In one package is a complete outfit: black leggings, a sapphire blue tunic, a black belt, and a matching set of undergarments—not quite lingerie nor exactly plain utilitarian. The other packages contain similar outfits—stylish, comfortable, and neither formal nor loungewear or casual. At the bottom of the bag, a selection of footwear: some black ballet flats, white wedge sandals, a pair of heather-gray sneakers of some light stretchy material.

He's merely watching me.

"Am I supposed to change here? Go back to the tower? Is there a restroom nearby?" I ask.

He shrugs. "The tower is on the opposite end of the property from the orangery. There is a toilet nearby, but it is for the use of the kitchen staff, and not a very private place."

I huff.

But then…what do I have to hide? He's already seen all of me there is to see.

I won't be cowed. I won't be embarrassed.

I lift my chin and hold his gaze. "Very well, then."

I peel the polo shirt off, taking the time to fold it and set it on the couch. The shorts, as well. His eyes do not turn away—he provides no pretense of not watching me. His eyes are greedy and hot.

I step into the underwear first, a pair of yellow boy shorts. The bra is of a matching color, a T-shirt Demi bra. Surprisingly comfortable, and well-fitting. How he knows my exact sizes, I don't care to guess.

The leggings and tunic fit just as well, and it's marvelous to be properly dressed again. I pair the outfit with the black ballet flats—all I need to feel fully presentable would be to have my hair out of my face.

I don't have a brush or hair ties or a mirror, however.

As if he understands my dilemma, he moves to stand behind me, and I feel his hands gathering my hair, finger-brushing it with deft, delicate movements; to my shock, he then begins braiding it, quickly and without hesitation or fumbling.

"Hand me a piece of that twine," he says.

When I do so, he manages to keep the braided end of my hair pinched, holds the length of twine in the same hand, and produces his knife from somewhere to slice a smaller piece free. He then ties my hair off and knots the twine around the end.

"You can braid hair." It comes out as a statement, but is meant as a question.

"Yes." No explanation. "Come. Lunch awaits."

He leads the way—out of the library and down the long hallway which seems to run the width of the building along the back, one entire wall of the hallway is glass, looking out onto the maze of hedges surrounded by an expansive, rolling lawn. A door occasionally breaks up the glass, opening out onto a small veranda. We come to an intersection where a hallway bisects the one we're in, leading to what I believe would be the front door if we went right, and to the kitchen if we went left. I hear sounds from the left—the first sign of life I've heard anywhere in his mausoleum of a castle: rattling of pans, voices chattering in a smattering overlap of languages, laughter.

"Can I see the kitchen?" I ask.

He stops, arches an eyebrow at me. "Why?"

I shrug. "Curious. You and Consuela are the only

people I've seen." I frown. "Well, other than that one guy when you left during dinner to kill someone."

He regards me. "That man is Tomás, my…assistant, I suppose." He blinks, chews on the inside of his cheek. "I did not kill anyone, that evening."

"You didn't?"

He shakes his head. "To kill is distasteful to me—it puts me off my appetite. I would not be able to return to a meal if I was forced to kill."

"You had blood on you. Not yours, either."

A long penetrating gaze. "It was from the man in the dungeon."

"Tell me."

He tilts his head, turns to face me. "You wish to know?"

"I do."

"Why?"

"To understand you."

A frown. "Understand me." He says this as if chewing on the concept, as if it were an alien notion. "His name is Bruno. He was a deputy in my operation based out of Albania. He came up through the ranks—he was a runner, an errand boy. He did well, and moved up to a position of some authority. He showed himself to be trustworthy."

"What kind of operation?"

A pause. "Opiates of various kinds. Moving it from production to distribution—he ran the warehouse where the product was sent out for distribution to the local kingpins in Asia, Russia, and a handful of African localities."

"Drugs."

"A cash cow for my more favored businesses."

I snort. "Right."

He narrows his eyes. "You judge."

"Drugs kill people. Kids, mothers, fathers. They destroy lives."

"They will not ever disappear from our world, Corinna. When I run the business, I do so with a minimum of violence, and we prevent sales to children. It does not make it better, but it is something."

"So why get into it at all?"

A shake of his head. "A conversation for another time." A wave of his hand. "You wished to know about Bruno."

"True."

"I placed him in charge of many others. He had authority. I paid him very well. He could not do better with a university degree and twenty years of experience in a legal sector." A sigh. "I discovered he was skimming."

"Stealing, you mean?"

A nod. "Complicatedly, but yes. Having his men charge more for the product than I have authorized and keeping the difference. As if I would not know." A long, low sound, almost like a growl. "This was bad enough. But this, I could forgive. Stop stealing, do a job without the authority. Earn my trust again. I would not have had to punish him. Not through the use of pain, at least."

I frown. "He was stealing. You wouldn't have had him locked up and beaten for that?"

"I am not a monster, Corinna. Such things are a last resort for the worst of offenses."

"So what was his offense that landed him in your dungeon, beaten half to death?"

"How he was using the money."

"Which was?"

He sighs. "Girls."

"Like, prostitutes?"

A bob of his head. "That would not be a problem for me—if he wishes to pay for his sex, it is not any business of mine, as long as it is consensual." Another pause. "No, he was *trafficking*...in *girls*. Not women, but girls. He was part of a ring of detestable degenerates with a taste for children. When I discovered what he was doing, I ran my own little sting. One by one, I...dealt with...his compatriots. In this, I was not so peaceable." His eyes met mine. "These men, I did kill."

"But not Bruno?"

A shake of his head. "I have evidence he is part of a larger operation. He has been reluctant to speak of it, and I have been...convincing him."

"Why not take it to the authorities?"

"Because they will be too slow, and too politic. Such evil does not deserve the justice of the legal system. They deserve slow, painful deaths, which I am all too pleased to provide. Bruno is a key to this. That day during dinner, he had finally decided he would cooperate. He coughed, and some of the blood on his lips splattered onto me. I never touched him."

"What are you doing with him now that he's cooperating?"

"Once I've gotten all of the use out of him, I will turn him in to the authorities with plenty of anonymously provided evidence of his many wrong-doings. Once he is imprisoned, his taste for children will see to his demise, and my hands will be clean of his death."

"I see."

He eyes me. "You do not approve?"

I shake my head. "I didn't say that. If he was kidnapping, selling, and doing disgusting things with children, then he deserves whatever happens to him." I sigh. "You surprise me."

"I am not my grandfather."

"Clearly."

He gestures at the hallway. "Shall we?"

I indicate the kitchen. "I would still like to see the kitchen."

A frown, but it shifts into something not entirely

unlike but nearly a smile. "The kitchen, then. I assure you, it is merely a kitchen."

It's a short hallway, the stone walls, beamed ceiling, and aged floor transitioning abruptly to an industrial kitchen—nonslip tile floors, a high ceiling with exposed wires and plumbing and sprinkler system, a row of burners, a row of deep fryers, a section for cutting and prep, an assembly and presentation section, storage, refrigeration, dishwashing. It's a massive space, rivaling the kitchen of a five-star hotel restaurant.

It's bustling with people, men and women of a variety of ethnicities all dressed in the black and white chef uniforms found in kitchens the world over.

"Quite an operation for a little lunch for two," I remark.

He snorts. "They are not cooking for us."

I glance at him. "They're not?"

"Consuela cooks for me—I have a much smaller, private kitchen near the tower." He gestures at the kitchen. "They're cooking for my staff."

"Your staff?"

"This castle is my headquarters. I have a staff of over a hundred who live and work here. Not in this castle, but on this property. There are other buildings. Landscaping, housekeeping, maintenance, a construction crew which is renovating an old hunting lodge, as well as the operational staff for my various business endeavors. They are all fed by this kitchen."

"You provide their meals? The entire staff? Even housekeeping?"

A shrug. "A tidy home is vital to one's wellbeing. My housekeeping staff is important to me—they provide and vital and much appreciated service to me. They are well compensated, work reasonable hours, and yes, meals are included, as is lodging, child care, and medical care."

I blink. This is...unexpected.

He accepts my stare of confusion, and simply turns to walk away without explaining further. I follow, because the smell of the cooking food reminds me that I told Consuela I'd eat later, but never did, and it's now past noon.

The long hallway continues, more glass looking out over the rear of the property, which is now a garden full of flowers and flowering trees and small bushes, an explosion of color and greenery, now framed on one side by the hulking presence of the castle. Here, the castle wall is a rising face of glass, like a greenhouse, with even the roof a steeply-angled bank of glass soaring upward easily a hundred feet.

We round a corner, and the hallway simply...falls away. We're in...well, he called it an orangery. And I see why: a small orchard of orchard trees, growing indoors, covered by the glass, and surrounded by a wild profusion of flora. Vines writhe along the walls and creep across the floor and reach for the ceiling, dotted with huge blossoms. Terra-cotta pots explode with flowers. Small flowering trees shelter smaller, more delicate blossoms.

It's a huge, echoing place, warm and wild and smelling verdant and alive. There's a small wrought iron table with a pair of chairs tucked into an open space between the bowers of the orange trees, the seats cushioned. There's a door in the huge glass wall, standing open and leading out into the garden, which I realize is a continuation of the garden in here. I hear a bird and look up: a large red macaw perches on a vine far overhead, a piece of fruit in one of its clawed feet.

Apollo follows my gaze. "Her name is Maia."

I gesture at the door. "Won't she fly away?"

He shrugs. "She could. She hasn't." He looks up, clicks his tongue. "Maia. Here."

Dozens of feet overhead, the huge red and gold bird looks down at Apollo. She drops her fruit, and it falls to the floor with a loud splat; there's a flutter of wings and Maia settles on his shoulder with a loud squawk and a series of clicks and whistles. He rubs the side of her head where her ear would be, and she nuzzles into his touch, but her eye is on me. She allows his scratching a moment, and then turns and nips at his earlobe.

"Hey, quit that." He taps her beak. "Not nice, Maia."

"You interrupted her lunch," I say.

He tucks the edge of his hand under her talons, and she steps onto his hand, side-stepping to his wrist. Glances at him, squawking and clicking.

He flicks his wrist upward. "Fine. Go eat your fruit, then."

She rustles her wings as he moves his wrist, more to simply hold her balance, gives him another derisive squawk and a whistle, and then drops off his arm and floats to where her fruit had fallen, landing to scoop it up and gnaw it.

"I've tried to teach her to talk, but I've been told scarlet macaws aren't the best for that. She was a gift from a client, and she gives this room a better purpose. I come in here sometimes, but not nearly enough to justify it."

"You didn't build it?"

He waves a hand. "It was here, as were the orange trees. It was overgrown, so dense a jungle you couldn't reach the door without a machete and a guide. I had it pruned back, cleared of the unwanted vegetation, and filled with the more pleasing varieties. The credit for this place goes to my head gardener, Micha." He says the name *Mee-chhha,* with the consonant sound a guttural rasp at the back of his throat. "She is a miracle worker. This whole place was a jungle. The grass was waist-high, the hedges gone wild, weeds everywhere. It's taken her years of labor, but she and her crew have worked wonders."

"It is beautiful."

"I enjoy beautiful things," he says, his eyes landing on me. "There is much ugliness in this world. To be surrounded by beauty…it renews my spirit."

"But you're alone here," I say.

"I am always alone."

"Don't you choose to be?"

He shrugs. "I know no other way."

"You have no girlfriend? You've never been married?"

He turns away. "I have had…companions. For a time. And…for a limited purpose."

"Purely for sex, you mean."

"Just so."

"That's not companionship."

"No," he agrees. "I do not know what a companion is." A few steps away from me, his low voice echoing off the glass. "They do not come here."

"Why?"

"This place is mine. Only for me."

"It's an awful big place for just one guy all alone."

"There are many others here."

"But they're not your friends. They're employees. And Consuela told me you prefer silence."

"That you got so many words from Consuela is

both amusing and impressive. I hired her as my personal attendant primarily due to her taciturn nature. She speaks what must be said out of necessity and no more. Which I appreciate."

"I asked her questions. It's a surprisingly effective way to get people into conversation."

He glances at me with a small grin. "You do ask very many questions."

"And get very few answers."

"More than anyone else might expect from me, however." He gestures at the table. "Let us sit. Consuela should be here with our food shortly."

His eyes flit over me as we sit, his gaze settling on my eyes with curiosity.

"What?" I ask. "If you have a question, ask it."

"You are far more composed than I would have expected."

"Hysterics would do no good. Did you want me to scream and cry and…I don't know, run away? Try to attack you?"

"Yes."

"If you had tried to harm me, I would have made you pay for whatever you did. Don't think I'm defenseless."

"If you are anything like your mother, I would expect not."

"I am like my mother. And my father. And I've

learned self-defense from some of the most dangerous people on the planet."

"So I should step carefully, is what you mean." A wry smirk.

"Yes."

"Yet, when I held a knife to you, you didn't react in self-defense."

I shrug. "Once you go on the defense against a knife, you're going to get cut. You threatened, but that's it. I took my chances that you weren't going to actually try to maim or kill me with it. Correctly, it would seem."

"So if I had done more than nick you, or cut your clothing away?"

"I'd have gotten cut, but so would you have."

"You also allowed me to force you into nudity without argument."

"Lesser of evils, I guess," I say. "It was embarrassing and humiliating. But it didn't hurt me. I'll get over it—I *am* over it. It's just nudity. Better to allow that than force a fight. Even if I won a physical fight against you, I'm not sure of my chances of getting away. I don't know where I am. I don't know how many goons you have hiding here, and what they'd do to me in the name of recapturing me. I don't know where I'd go or how I'd get there. What I *do* know is that you haven't harmed me so far, and that my family is coming for me. And no matter what or who you can bring to bear, you won't win. Not against the people you've pissed off by taking me, let alone my mother."

"Your mother found her way free. I've allowed her to go, for now."

I snort. "You've allowed nothing, Apollo. You really, really don't understand what you've done."

He stands up, takes a few steps away. His hands go in his pockets. "If they attempt a rescue of you here, it will not go well for them. This is not merely a large house, Corinna. It is a true castle, with a castle's defenses." A glance back at me. "I'd rather not have to resort to those methods."

"Then let me go."

"That would not do." He turns back to me. "You should not be embarrassed by your nakedness, Corinna."

"Why not? We've already talked about this. I didn't have a choice. I didn't *choose* to let you see me naked. You presented it as a choice between being hurt or stripping. And that's not a choice. We are not lovers. You are my captor, Apollo. However gilded the cage, it's still a cage. So yes, stripping for you was humiliating. Having you cut the dress off me was scary. Having to wear your clothing because I had none of my own was embarrassing." I step closer to him. "Just because you think I'm attractive, it doesn't mean I'm not going to be embarrassed when I'm forced to be naked in front of a stranger—and not just a stranger, but a man who has taken me hostage."

He doesn't respond for a long while.

Consuela comes, places plates, silverware, a large bottle of beer, and a pair of glasses on the table, and leaves without saying a word.

When she's gone again, he turns and strides over to me. He doesn't stop until he's an inch from me, staring down at me. His chest rises and falls heavily. His brow is furrowed. Jaw clenched.

"I do not find you attractive." His eyes are fixed on mine, blazing like black fire, fierce yet unknowable, only the intensity readable

"No?" I arch an eyebrow. "The way you look at me says otherwise."

He swallows hard. His jaw grinds audibly. "Attractive? No, Corrina." His fingertip traces my jawline from earlobe to chin. "I am *consumed* by you."

His touch is exquisitely gentle. Yet, it sends a line of fire trickling over my skin, makes me shiver down to my toes.

"Could have fooled me," I whisper.

"Am I fooling you, Corinna?" Instead of his finger on my jaw, he now touches the pad of his thumb to my lips. "Can you not read the obsession in my eyes?"

"I can't read a damn thing in your eyes." I have to pause, suck in a breath; his nearness, the intensity of his eyes and the wild ferocity of his presence, the molten heat of his touch on my lips—my breath is scorched away. It's terrifying. "Why would you be… consumed by me?"

"It was a miscalculation," he murmurs. "I thought I could use you. I thought I could hold you hostage and use you for leverage against your parents."

"What was the miscalculation?"

"You." He's too close. I can feel his breath on my cheek. "Everything that you are."

"I don't understand."

"I had photographs of you. In St. Croix and St. Thomas. On the beach with your friends, from a distance. I thought you were…just a girl."

"I am just a girl."

He circles behind me. His nose touches the side of my throat; I smell him, his cologne and his body. "You are more than just a girl."

"Then what am I?" I ask, my voice a faint whisper.

"A siren."

"What do you want with me, Apollo?"

His hands grasp my arms, gently. "Everything," he whispers.

12

BEGRUDGING ADMIRATION

I'M WOKEN BY THE BURBLING OF A CELL PHONE. I finally was able to fall asleep after driving for eight hours, my eyes burning, starting to see double. We don't talk much—Anselm is typically a man of few words, and I'm too upset and angry and scared for chitchat.

"*Ja*," I hear Anslem say, as I sit up and rub my eyes. "*Ja*, good, okay. We will wait in Madrid for you and the team, then."

"The hell we will," I snap. "If they have a location, we're going in."

Anselm hands the phone to me, and I hear Harris on the other end. "Kyrie, listen to me."

"No, Nick, I'm sorry. No. That's my fucking daughter. Would you wait for backup?"

"In this particular situation, Key, yes, I would. I would hate it and I'd be as pissed about as you are."

"You'd better make a damn good case, then."

"Apollo Karahalios is new to the game, and he comes at it with a fresh perspective. He does things differently. He doesn't waste people. He doesn't tolerate his people violating his ethical code—rape is not allowed, and anyone in his organization who's even accused of that kind of behavior is executed immediately, by Apollo himself."

"That tracks with what Kai told me."

"Right. And the point of this is that it inspires rabid loyalty in the ranks. And in the populace of those who live around the places he operates. He shares the profits, Key."

"What does that mean?" I ask.

"It means he was left a colossal amount of money—Vitaly's will stipulated that his fortune went to Gina. And Gina's will stipulated that her fortune went to Apollo. Which means that even though Gina died before Vitaly, that the entire Karahalios family fortune, something like a hundred billion, went to Apollo. All of it. Except, from what I can tell, he wasn't raised by Gina as a Karahalios. As in, he knew nothing of his family's operations until he was already an adult, and had taken the fortune he inherited and made his own on top of it."

"Holy shit. So this really isn't about money."

"Not even close." Harris sighs. "He was a teenager when his mother died. But he didn't find out about who she was or who his grandfather was until he was in his late twenties and had taken the fortune he inherited and multiplied it through a bunch of different totally legal avenues. Real estate, commercial agriculture, shipping, imports and exports, construction, automobile parts supply for the European market. He's…honestly, he's a business prodigy. But other than the profile of businesses and money, there's very, very little known about him as a person. He's even more reclusive and private than you and Roth. He does business remotely, via video conference, and the screen is blacked out. Some report even his voice is filtered. If you live or work in the areas where he operates, you don't see him. If you interact with his business interests, it's through proxies."

"So then how do you know any of this?" I ask.

"Interviews with people who know people who work for him."

"It's been a day since I told you who he was."

"Lear works fast. It helps that he has Cuddy who can use her contacts with RMI—Johnny Raze sent some people out to do some hard and fast in-person digging. They couldn't find any direct contacts, so it's all hearsay, but it all tracks."

"So he's a ghost."

"Basically. But he's a ghost who inspires loyalty.

Because like I said, he shares. His people make a fucking fortune. If he owns a business, it's never in a big city, always in a smaller area, and he invests in that town. This we do have first-hand confirmation of. He owns a quasi-commercial fishing operation in the Mediterranean which operates out of Marseilles and Barcelona—by which I mean he has offices that handle the technical business end of it, taxes and payroll and the like. But the real operations are out of little villages outside the city. And in those little villages, he has personally invested millions and millions of dollars to upgrade things. Infrastructure, fiber optic, underground electricity, new plumbing, new schools. And he protects them. His soldiers, for lack of a better term, act as de facto police. If the real police don't handle a crime properly, his people will. The villages love him. None of them have met him, but not one person Raze's guys talked to had a bad thing to say. Crime is down, income is up. Kids are getting educated in brand new buildings, and the school systems have been given huge grants so the teachers get paid way more than anywhere else."

"Fuck." I hiss, frustrated. "There's got to be a catch."

"Well, yeah. Word is, he discovered his family's previous business, arms and drug shipments—after Vitaly died that vacuum was never totally filled. Not by any one person, at least, and none of the people who come in trying to take the space left by Vitaly are able to operate at the capacity he could."

"But Apollo can. He's got the money."

"Right. And he's slowly taken over." A laugh. "But he did it like he would take over an already operational legitimate, legal business—he didn't kill off his competitors, he hired them. Let them keep their own structures and people in place, but they received assistance from Apollo in the form of money and organizational people and such. He's taken over at least ten different arms dealers and drug dealers and put them under his umbrella. I guess things have improved for everyone."

"Except the general populace. More drugs and more guns out in the world."

A sigh. "Well, actually..." he grunts. "I've got what you might call a begrudging admiration for the man. Part of his takeover was instituting his ethical code all the way down—no rape, no kids, no innocent civilians involved. And because his takeover was monetary rather than through the usual violent methods, there's no grudges, no hostilities. Crime that could be directly related to his business practices has actually gone *down*. Because he directly and personally enforces his ban on any behavior that would negatively impact what you might call innocent people. As in, no one connected to his organization is allowed to sell drugs or guns to kids. If you have beef with someone, you'd better make damn sure no innocents get hurt because Apollo *will* come for you."

"Goddammit," I sigh.

"Yeah, makes it tricky, doesn't it?"

I snarl. "No, it doesn't. He has my fucking *daughter*, Harris."

"So you're still going in hot?"

"To get Rin back safely? Yes."

"You have to wait, Key."

"I can't."

"He has tons of muscle, Kyrie. I mean *tons*. A real deal army. You think Vitaly had unlimited resources and personnel? Apollo has double. More money. More connections." A hard pause. "You and Anselm go in cowboy, you're *going* to fucking die and you will *not* get Rinna back. I promise you. We need a different approach."

"You're not just trying to keep from taking a risk because you think I can't handle it?"

"Key, the fact that you'd even suggest such thing pisses me off," he says, and I can hear the ire in his voice, the strain it takes to keep his voice steady and neutral. "I know what you're capable of. If it was my wife and daughter out there, I'd say the same thing, and you know the respect I have for my wife in hairy situations. I'm telling you, my professional assessment of this situation is that a direct assault is suicide."

"We're not negotiating. He doesn't want money anyway."

"I know. I don't know exactly what the approach is, but I know we'll find one. So please, you and Anselm find somewhere in Madrid to lay low until we get there. So far, Apollo seems reticent to hurt her, so our timeline isn't rushed. If he wanted to and was going to hurt or kill Rinna, he'd have done so already. When you went rogue and killed his guys, right?"

"But what if he changes his mind?"

There's a clicking and a muted shuffling—the phone changing hands. "Babe." This is Valentine, now. "There's no other choice. The worst possible option is to attack without proper intel. Okay? We don't know enough about his position, the exact number of people, their locations, their loadouts, where she's being kept, or what he even wants. There's so much we don't know. What we *do* know is that he hasn't killed her yet, or even hurt her. And we know he's more into manipulation and power plays than he is outright murder. He actually seems to be against unnecessary bloodshed and violence. That works in our favor. There may be a way out of this without any more people being killed. I hate waiting. I can't imagine what it must be like for you, being so close, having gone through what you've been through and having to wait. But you *have* to. We go in hot right now, it may get her hurt or killed when a different approach could solve this peaceably. If he wants my financial ruin, I'll do it without hesitation to keep my family safe. Okay, Key? I can start from scratch. I'm not worried. You and Rin being alive and safe is all that matters. So just...wait. *Please.*

I pinch the bridge of my nose. "Okay." I sigh a shaky sigh, suppressing with brutal effort the tears pooling behind my eyes. "Okay."

"It's going to be okay, Kyrie."

"You can't promise that."

"No. But it will be."

"She'd better." My voice shakes. "If she's not, and I could have stopped it..."

"You can't think like that."

"How am I supposed to fucking think, goddammit?"

"Key." It's a gentle scold. "It's me."

I sigh, close my eyes. "I'm sorry, Val. I'm sorry."

"We'll be there as fast as this jet can get us there. We're about to go wheels up so I have to let you go. We're going supersonic once we're clear, so we'll be there soon. I promise."

"You'd better," I whisper.

"Hold on, Key."

"Hold on Rinna, you mean."

13

INTO MADNESS

I'M NOT BREATHING. I'M DIZZY. WHY AM I responding this way? What does the pounding in my heart mean? Why do my thoughts twist and tumble like dandelion seeds in a storm's wind? I can't make sense of myself. I'm supposed to remember that he's bad. That I'm a prisoner. That he scares me. That he could still hurt me. Or Mom.

I can't.

Everything that roots me to reality is being ripped up and burned away by the heat and ferocity of him. This close, the intensity of his presence is like standing in front of an open oven door at full blast—perhaps more like standing too close to the sun.

I suck in a gasping breath, the first in a long moment, and my pulse sets to pounding frantically.

All he's doing is standing behind me, holding my arms, nose against my throat.

"You feel it," he murmurs. "I know you do."

"Feel what?"

"Something burns between us, Corinna."

I want to deny it.

He skates his hands up my arms, over my shoulders. The neckline of the tunic scoops low to leave a generous portion of my cleavage bare—his fingers trail over the expanse of naked flesh. "Your skin burns." His palm presses over my left breast. "Your heart pounds." He brushes a thumb over my lips. "You have to remind yourself to breathe."

He spins me, crushes me against his chest. Pinions my right hand in his left. Presses my palm to the center of his chest in the opening of his shirt—his skin is on fire. "Feel." He moves my hand over his heartbeat. "Feel it pounding, Corinna?" He leaves my hand there, and thoughtless wildling that I am, I don't move it. "Hear my breath? Feel me gasping for breath?"

"What does it mean, Apollo?" I ask, meaning to sound sarcastic and failing.

He ignores my question. His face is close. His lips part. Brush mine. "If I kissed you, Corinna, would you flee?"

I don't answer.

"You think me a monster, perhaps." Those lips

graze mine again. "A big, bad wolf. You are frightened of me, you say."

"Yes."

He reaches behind his back and produces the knife. Without letting go of me or looking away from my eyes, he flips the knife to hold it by the tip and whips it at a nearby orange tree, the entire thing done in a single smooth movement, draw—flip—throw. It thunks into the trunk and sticks, quivering.

"I have not so much as touched you, except with that. Until now." He pinches my chin in his finger and thumb, and then that thumb brushes over my lips. "Yet you do not flee."

I swallow and try to breathe. My heart is beating out of my chest.

"You are not afraid of me." He touches his lips to mine, and I gasp a quiet, shrill breath. "It is *this* you are afraid of." He kisses me, then, a slow, inexorable slide of his lips on mine. "You are *not* afraid of me, and *that* is what you fear." Another kiss. "You like this. You want it. And *that* is what you fear. Not me."

I'm shaken, shaking. I suck in a sharp breath, but it's redolent with his scent, his presence. His breath. I could break away. I could knee him. I know moves that could take him to the ground and break his arm in three places. I do none of it.

I just shake in his grip, gasping for breath because

his presence leaves me breathless and now his kiss leaves me battered senseless.

Because it wasn't revolting.

Because he isn't wrong.

"I wonder how far I could push you before you break?" he muses.

"Apollo…" I breathe, but it trails off into nothingness.

He kisses me again, more deeply, more slowly. A touch of his tongue to mine leaves me whimpering, knees jellied. How can he do such things to me? Take my breath away, make me gasp, make my knees give out? I don't understand my body's reaction to him.

"Such sounds you make, Corinna." Another kiss, then, and I whimper again at the touch of his tongue—the sound is involuntary, drawn from me. "From a mere kiss, at that."

What's happening to me?

I'm leaning against him, hands pinned between my body and his. My face is tilted up to his—our height difference is just enough that I have to look up ever so slightly at him. His hands touch my face. Gentle, fingertips grazing my cheeks, my jaw. Almost a tickling touch. Another kiss, this one lasting and deep and probing, his tongue slicking against mine. And at this kiss, his fingers trail over my neck and across my shoulders, down my arms. His palms brush against my sides, and then his hands come to rest on the swell of my hips. His touch makes me shake. I gasp into the kiss, and he breaks it.

"Here you remain, letting me kiss you." A light squeeze of his hands, fingers dimpling into the swell of my hips. "Letting me hold you, letting me touch you. You could run, Corinna. Tell me to stop. Tell me you don't still feel the sting of my lips on yours, as I still feel it."

My lips burn from the sting of his lips.

"Will you kiss me back?" He nudges my lips with his. "Try it, Corinna. You have already fallen this far into madness with me, why not a little further?"

What is he saying? Where does this sorcerous poetry of his words come from?

"Kiss me back, Corinna. See how I taste. See how it feels to kiss me back."

This far into madness, indeed.

It is madness.

But I have fallen into this with him. Allowed it, and now I can't deny it. Can't say I don't feel it. Can't say he's wrong, because he's not.

He teases his mouth on mine. His tongue flickers against my lips. "Kiss me, Corinna." It's a whisper—It's hypnosis, surely. "Kiss me."

I kiss him. Damn me, I do.

I gasp, and my fingers curl against his chest—against his skin, digging into the firm muscle of his bare torso. And I kiss him.

I push up, lift onto my toes and surge against him and taste his mouth, feel the heat of his breath and the strong press of his tongue as he meets my kiss.

Some wall is broken down when I kiss him. The thing which tells me how terrible an idea this is, how irresponsible and crazy and even sick it is—it's bowled over and blown away.

There's only the kiss, then.

His hunger is a tangible thing. I feel it. It's in the way his fingers grip me and pull me closer, hold me against him. It's in the way his lips guide the kiss, taking us deeper.

My palms flatten on his chest, and as the kiss goes on, hotter and deeper, with more tongue and no breaks for breath, my hands scrape up to his shoulders. Push at the shirt.

I feel it give. Something pops, and ticks against the floor. His shoulders are bare, suddenly, and I'm greedy for them. The hard round muscle fills my hands and makes my mouth wild for his, and I couldn't stop kissing him if I tried. It's his arms in my hands, then, biceps firm and thick. His chest. The shirt strains against my wandering hands, stopping their downward journey.

His hands jerk apart, and I hear a rain of clicking and ticking, and all I know is that I'm allowed to touch his chest and his stomach, that my hands have been granted an unobstructed path across the furrowed plain of his abs, and my fingers trace them, circling each hard block, following each deeply-etched groove.

More.

I gasp for breath, but then I'm right back into the kiss, tasting him and lost to the wild wonder of his mouth seeking mine, seeking more of my kiss as if he's never tasted anything like it before and must have all there is, right now, forever. His hands score up my back, clutch me closer to him. I mirror his touch, and there is no shirt in the way. It's gone, somewhere. There's only skin—his skin under my hands, his muscle under my touch.

I'm hot—overheated.

Something opens within me—a void. A need. A gaping chasm that needs filling. It frightens me, the intensity of my need, but it's too demanding to be denied.

My voice is gone. Stolen by the fire of this kiss. It's a firestorm and I'm helpless before it.

What's happening? Who am I? What is this?

I don't know. I can't deny it, however. Can't stop it. Can only acknowledge the madness of this moment and its power over me.

Abruptly, he breaks the kiss. He doesn't pull away, however. His eyes meet mine, holding them, daring me to look away, defying me to stop him. I can't. I won't. His eyes are the wild infinite black of outer space, fathomless depths pulling me in.

His hands move at my waist. Unbuckling the belt tightening my tunic around my waist. It jangles to the floor. Nose to nose, his eyes unwavering on mine, he gathers the hem of the thigh-length tunic in his hands.

Then, in one smooth swipe, it's over my head and billowing to the floor at our feet, and I'm in leggings and a bra, and my skin is prickling, pebbling. My breasts ache, feel heavy. My nipples harden against the inside of the bra as his hands breeze over my bare shoulders. It's a light touch, an introduction. Downward, slowly, over my spine, his hands big and warm and strong, skating downward. His hands grasp my waist, and then his palms graze over my ribs and stomach, pausing again at my waist, just above the swell of my hips.

"You spoke of choices," he murmurs. "This is a choice, is it not? What choice will you make next?" His hands go to mine, cradling now, holding rather than imprisoning, guiding. "Would you touch me? Would you strip me further? Would you bare yourself to me?"

God, what?

I close my eyes—but it's too late. I remember him nude. He was a god, bare and unapologetic, carved to please my eyes. Hewn from heaven itself to fit into my hands. I remember his manhood rising erect and proud.

I remember standing naked in front of him, naked with him. His touch halting just short of my breast.

What would that feel like? To have his hand on me, there? I've been touched by men before—I'm no virgin…but never anyone like him.

My breath catches—what would it feel like to touch *him*?

What choice will you make next?

Madness. It's all madness. Surely I've gone mad, that's the only explanation for this.

How else would you explain my decision, consciously made, to fall further into this fever dream?

It is a choice, this time, when I free the clasp at my back and let the bra fall to the floor at my feet. I'm possessed, surely—possessed by some wild, hormone-crazed creature. Not me. Not rational, responsible, mature Corinna Roth. I can't rationalize this away. It's me. Just…some other me that's just now seeing the light of day for the first time—a tiny, tender, fragile little flame suddenly exposed to pure oxygen.

Because the truth is, this madness is intoxicating. I've never intentionally done wrong. Never taken the forbidden thing, never stolen that which was off-limits, never snuck out for the party I wasn't allowed to attend.

This is…the opposite of everything I am. This is

pure and utter insanity. Wrong. Terrible. Irresponsible. Forbidden. Everything about it is just…*bad.*

And it's what I would imagine a pure hit of ecstasy to be, a rush of some grade-A narcotic coursing through my veins.

I shudder uncontrollably as he pulls away enough to look at me, bare from the waist up.

"So…" he swallows hard. Starts again with a lick of his lips. "So fucking perfect."

One big, hard, powerful hand presses against my belly, low on the right side, just above my hipbone. Pauses there. His hand is hot, and I burn where he touches me. Shudder again. Try to breathe and cannot. His eyes are wide and deep and black, pupils dilated. His jaw grinds. His breath rasps past his teeth. With a nearly inaudible groan, his palm scrapes upward, catching the weight of my breast in his hand and holding it. I gasp, my eyes shuttering closed as billowing heat smashes through me, pooling between my thighs, tugging on my breast from the inside.

His thumb flicks over my nipple, the soft little nub going hard and erect. He lifts my breast and lets it fall, swaying. And now both of his hands reach to cup my breasts, lifting them. He fondles them reverently, thumbs against my nipples, lifting and squeezing.

I groan at his touch—it sends a flurry of heat into the void aching inside me; the void is at once in my soul and in my body, centered low, behind my belly button. The more he fondles and caresses my breasts, the lower the void sinks, the harder it pulls at me. Demanding my response.

And the more he touches me, the more I somehow know only his touch can fill that void.

I shake all over.

I touch him. Grasp his shoulders, fill my hands with his chest and his shoulders and his back—this too helps douse the wildfire hunger of the yawning void. So I touch more. His back, lower. His belly.

God, the void.

It's like hunger, but hotter, deeper. A more echoing emptiness, a more demanding need.

I've felt pathetic approximations of it with previous…lovers, I suppose I could call them.

But never anything like this.

And for…*him*?

This man?

Then, he kisses me again, with his hands busily and hungrily caressing my breasts, and I whimper into the kiss and I kiss him back, because I have to—the need caused by the void in me is inexorable and unstoppable and it's telling me I must kiss him back.

When he kisses me, when I kiss him, the feel of his hands becomes nearly unbearable—and I need more. The firm muscle of his body under my hands, too, is not enough. I need more.

I grasp his waist, stutter my hands across his belly, and catch at the button of his trousers.

He breaks, then.

Pulls away, gasping. "You consume me," he murmurs.

I can only gasp for breath and stare into his eyes. He doesn't return his mouth to mine, however. His lips touch my skin, just above the valley of my breasts. I can't even gasp, then, when his lips touch between them—despite their size, my breasts stand out straight and lift up, tips reaching upward. Apollo buries his face between them, nuzzling the tender skin where they meet, and then his lips kiss the inner side of one, and then the upper slope—I gasp a sharp breath of erotic shock when he closes his mouth over my nipple. My eyes close, shut tight, and I dig my fingers into his waist, head tipping backward. His hands cup the thick, round weight of my breasts and lift them, raise them to his mouth. He nuzzles them, then kisses across them to lap at my other nipple, and then his tongue licks around the half-dollar circle of darker skin that is my areola, flicks at the nipple.

God, this sensation.

I want to laugh from the wildness of it, but all I can do is moan, gasp. Head tipped back, thrusting my chest at him.

"Oh, Corinna," he breathes. "Such a goddess, you are. The things I could show you."

"Like..." I swallow my choking gasp; I know what, I just want to hear him say it. "Like what?"

"I can make your body sing, Corinna," he whispers. "I could make you scream until you faint."

"How?"

He stands up straight, looking down at me; his index finger hooks in the front of my leggings. "Don't you know?"

"Show me."

His other hand wraps around my braid and palms the back of my head, tilts my face up to his. He's not quite kissing me, but nearly. I feel his lips move when he speaks, feel his words as breath on my mouth. I'm writhing with the shaking intensity boiling inside me, the need to keep taking hits of this drug, this forbidden high.

I'm aware in some distant part of myself that I'm not thinking clearly—that I'm utterly consumed by... lust? Desire? Hormones? I don't know.

"Are you afraid, Corinna?" His voice is low, rough, throbbing with power and with promise.

"Yes," I answer.

"Of what?"

"This. It's crazy. It's wrong. I don't know what I'm doing. I shouldn't want this."

"But you do know what you're doing, and you do want it."

"Yes," I gasp. "I do."

He places his palm over my heartbeat, mine over his. “You feel this, don’t you? Between you and me. Something is here, in me and in you. It connects us.” His lips touch mine and I respond instantly, searching for the kiss. “You feel it, Corinna. It’s energy. We share it.” He kisses me, quick and light. “Don’t you feel it?”

I’m shaking with it, on fire with it. “Yeah, I feel it.”

“You think I wanted this any more than you do?” He shakes his head roughly. “I didn’t. I don’t. This is madness, Corinna. I know it, and you know it. But you can’t resist it, can you?”

I reach up and dig my fingers into his hair. Shake my head and groan a negative sound. “No, I can’t. I fucking can’t.”

“Neither can I.”

“What is it, Apollo?”

His mouth seizes mine, and I pull him down to make the kiss hotter, wilder, deeper. “I do not fucking know, and I wish to god that I did.” His hands skate down my back and under the elastic of my leggings and under the stretch of my underwear to cup my bare ass. Squeezes. “But I can’t ignore it. Damned to hell for it I may be, but I can’t.”

I cup his jaw, the stubble rough and delicious under my palm. One hand still buried in his hair at the back of his head, the other caresses down from his jaw to his throat, and I feel his pulse hammering wildly there; from his throat to his chest, over his shoulder, down his ribs. We kiss and we kiss, and our tongues tangle and taste and drive and probe and tease, and the impetus drives from him to me and back, Apollo taking over and then ceding to me. His hands cup my ass, kneading and lifting with equal reverence as he'd shown my breasts.

And god, is that touch intoxicating. If his kiss is drugging, his touch is something else yet. I lean against him, breasts flattening against his chest, the smattering of dark hair across his chest rough and scratchy in a heady sort of way that has me shuddering.

I'm leaning fully against him, and I can feel his cock between us—it's thick and fully erect, straining against the zipper and button of his pants. I remember the way it looked, bare and bold—the way it felt, brushing against me. A few quick movements of my hands and it would be free, and I could discover how he feels in my hands.

What choice will you make next?

I'm choosing this. I'm throwing myself down this hole, into this inferno.

I know I'm going to get burned, but yet I choose to soar toward the sun.

What choice, next?

It's made for me.

He spins me, presses my back to his front, the thick ridge of his cock against my ass, his big hard hands softly and gently cupping my breasts—there is a small wicker-and-cushion couch tucked between the orange trees, near the table where our lunch lies forgotten, and he drops back into it, laying on it with me on top of him. He lounges partially upright, my legs supported on his, his hands caressing my breasts.

His lips are at my ear. "Have you ever had an orgasm, Corinna?"

Yes," I whisper.

The fingers of one hand traipse down my belly to my navel, pausing to circle there before walking down further to the waistband of my leggings.

"You think so?" His voice is amused and hot.

"I have."

Words flee my brain, then, as he walks his fingers across my sex, over the thin stretchy fabric of the leggings and the thin silk of the underwear. Too many layers between his touch and my flesh, and not enough. I gasp when he tucks his touch between my thighs and traces upward, following my seam. His other hand still cups and toys with and fondles my breasts, one and the other in turn, tweaking my nipple and caressing the weight of the breast and tweaking again before moving to the other side.

I close my eyes in anticipation as he lifts his fingers upward over my sex to where the fabric ends and my skin begins. Those fingers dig under elastic, and I suck my belly in, knowing I'm going to let him touch me—wanting him to touch me. I know I'm going to let him. And if he were to try to stop, I'd ask him to keep going.

Ask? Shit, I'd beg.

I'm sold out to this, consequences be damned.

He slides his fingertips down, his touch now between layers, sliding over the slick silk of my underwear. He traces downward, now, and his index finger finds the shallow channel of the seam between my nether lips. Down, and down, until my pressed-together thighs and the prison of my leggings prevent him from going any further, and then his touch glides back up, again following the seam of my sex…until he reaches the apex. He pauses there, pressing in.

A gasp flees me, and my thighs clench.

"You want it?"

I can only moan.

He presses his hand flat against my belly. "Do you, Corinna? Do you want me to touch you?" A brush of his fingers over me, above my clothes. "Do you want me to touch you here?"

He's invoking that sorcery again, the words like needles slicing into me, words which penetrate my defenses and puncture my misconceptions and deflate my excuses, words which strip me bare, poisoning my mind and my body with knowledge of my own irrevocable, insatiable need. His sorcerous words show me my own lecherous lust, my own pulsating desire.

"Tell me yes, Corinna, or tell me no. Tell me yes and I'll show you things you've never even dared fantasize about."

"And..." I swallow and gasp. "If I say no?"

"Try it," he dares me. "Tell me you don't want me to touch you." His fingers slide against my skin, teasing under both layers of material now.

I growl, because I know I won't. I know I can't tell him I don't want him to. I won't tell him no. Not now.

He nips the shell of my ear. His voice is barely a murmur, but it's loud in my ear, hot and breathy and rasping and soaking me with dark power. "What will it be, Corinna?"

I press my hand over top of his, push it downward. "Touch me," I whisper. "Show me."

I'm damned.

Hell will welcome me to its ranks, when all this is over, perhaps. But in this moment, my need, the furious inferno of my desire, is all there is.

Slowly, giving me every chance to change my mind, he slips his hand under my leggings and underwear. His touch glides over the trimmed V of my pubic hair, index finger pressing against the inside of my left thigh, ring finger against my right, and his long middle finger delving against the soft damp seam of my sex.

I groan, aching. I'm soaked, down there, shaking all over, pulse a wild hammering drum, every sense attuned to Apollo, to his touch, his breathing, his scent in my nostrils and the scent of my sex as well. He curls his fingers, and his middle finger slicks through me.

I gasp, pushing my head back against his shoulder, spine arching. His hand cradles my left breast, cups it, his other between my thighs and teasing me with a finger slicing through my folds again and again. I want him to show me. But he's teasing.

I growl, arch my back and flex my hips to push my sex against his hand. "Apollo…please, just touch me."

Am I this begging thing? But I need it, need it, and if it means I have to beg, then I'll beg.

His hand slides up my chest to cup my throat, tilting and twisting my head until he can kiss me, a sudden and searing assault of his mouth on mine, and when I groan at the kiss, he drives a finger into my soaked sex, penetrating me and curling in. Dragging out, his long middle finger smears against my aching, swollen clitoris—I jerk at the touch, a cry leaving me.

"Ahhh, so sensitive," he whispers. "You'll come quickly, won't you?"

I can only whimper. Fire blazes inside me, burning me alive from the inside out. Only his touch can quench it.

His finger slides in again, until his knuckles nudge against my lips. Withdrawing, he grazes my clit once more—this time, though, when he drives his touch into me, it's two fingers. Stretching me. The heat inside billows, expands. Becomes sharp. Those two fingers graze my clit, and I flex impulsively against the quick touch, which, despite being light and swift, sends a Coriolis wind of arousal howling through my entire being.

My hands go to his—I need more. I grip his wrist, guide his hand from my throat and jaw to my breast, begging silently for more of his touch there. My other hand on his at my thighs, pressing, pushing, pulling.

"More," I whisper. "Please."

"Don't worry, Corinna," he whispers. "I won't deny you. I could no more deny you this climax than I could choose to quit breathing." His lips move at my ear. "I want your moans, Corinna. I need to hear you come. I need to feel you come apart for me. I'm going to make you come, now. I want you ride my fingers. Take it all from me, and don't hold back. Scream as loud as you want, Corinna—no one can hear you here."

I'm writhing on top of him, desperate and wild. While he was speaking, his fingers were slicking in and out of my channel, and his words almost drown out the wet squelch of his touch moving inside me, curling and spearing. It feels good, but it's not what I need.

Then, without warning, he presses his fingertips

to my clit and flicks side to side, a light quick touch. I gasp, a shrill breath of shocked pleasure. And now, finally, he doesn't stop. The side-to-side flicking becomes a slow circling, and at each circle my hips lift and lower in time with the movement of his fingers, and pressure mounts within me, heat and desperation building and building.

If this is what it's supposed to feel like, then I've been doing it wrong all these years.

It's a mountain of arousal rising inside me, a hurricane of erotic bliss smashing through me. Each touch of his fingers to my clit makes me whimper, each circle of his touch makes me shake and shudder.

Clothing is still in the way. I need to be naked.

I push at the waistband of my leggings, wiggle and growl in annoyance when they refuse to cooperate.

"You want them off?" Apollo whispers.

"Yes," I hiss.

"Allow me to assist you, in that case." His fingers withdraw from my sex, and I whimper at the loss, but he drags my leggings and underwear down and pushes them past my buttocks, and then I'm kicking them off, clumsily and desperately using my toe to hook them over my ankles and feet and kicking them away, and then I'm naked on top of Apollo and I can open myself to his touch, and I know I'm crazed, so wild that I don't recognize myself. Out of control. Desperate.

His hands scour my naked body, scraping from breast to sex, clutching at my hips, sliding over my sex and caressing my breasts and pawing my belly and prying my thighs wider apart. Two fingers touch my clit, then, and two more delve inside me, and now I'm so overcome by sensations that I can barely breathe, because he's also demanding my kiss, his lips touching my ear and then my jaw and then my cheek and I turn my face to his and I try to kiss him, but his touch pushes a whimper out of me.

My hips writhe.

I surge against his fingers, his talented fingers. His tongue tangles with mine. As I writhe, I feel him moan, as if my pleasure is almost too much for him, as my ecstasy is his own. And I feel his erection beneath me, ignored and enormous.

God, the desires within me are so foreign, so alien—unfathomable in their unexpected intensity. It's like they've been building up inside me all my life, pent up and boiling over without no outlet, and now the touch and the heat and the dark intensity and the primal sexuality of Apollo have opened the vent and let the powers within me loose. But, because they've been so pent for so long, the release is explosive and uncontrollable.

I feel out of control.

I have no power over myself. I am utterly at the mercy of my body's needs—and my body needs what Apollo is giving it.

Touch.

The more he touches me, the more I need it. His touch speeds against my clit while his fingers drive in and out of me with slow, sedate, unhurried consistency, and the dichotomy of slow versus fast, gentle versus roughening is enough to splinter my mind and body and soul. I hear myself keening as his touch speeds, no longer so sweet, no longer so gentle against the throbbing, aching button of my sex—my hips move, flex, push, writhe.

Faster, and faster, his touch circles.

I feel something approaching, some massive peak, some echoing abyss. An edge, sharp and explosive. The mounting pressure and heat behind my navel have spread to my fingers and toes and scalp, every muscle now taut with it, every synapse singing with it, until all of my being is utterly and furiously focused on the rough swipe of Apollo's flying fingers.

His breathing, felt as a rising and falling of his hard chest behind my back, quickens with mine. His voice in my ears is rough and primal.

"You're there, aren't you, beautiful?" His voice is a sensation unto itself, an erotic snarl in my ears that caresses every erogenous zone throughout my whole body, my whole being. "You're going to come for me, Corinna."

It's not a question. It's a command.

I explode, right then.

It begins with a scream, as a white-hot knife slices through my core, the long-pent pressure snapping free like the cable of a suspension bridge. I writhe, spine bowing upward as my feet press against the arm of the couch. His touch is unrelenting, no longer circling now but swiping side to side as fast as his hand can move. My arching thrust means he lost the angle necessary to keep his fingers inside me, but I no longer need that—all I need is the clitoral stimulation.

Faster and faster, and I'm screaming through gritted teeth as the hurricane of overloaded sensory stimulation batters me, an ecstasy so acute it is nearly painful, an explosion so wrenching my scream of pleasure crumbles into a sob.

Without warning, I'm lifted into the air. My eyes are closed and I'm writhing and shaking, gripped in the feverish wrack of my orgasm, and all I know is that I'm airborne. Briefly. Set down again, and now I feel the cushion of the couch under my ass and the rough cool wicker against my back—I'm sitting up.

I force my eyes open, and I see Apollo descending on me like a dark, vengeful god, his eyes wide and black and fiery, his skin glistening, his mouth set in something between a snarl and a smirk, the grin of a hungry animal spying helpless prey. He drops to his knees in front of me, and I'm trembling still, shaken with aftershocks. I can't take my eyes off him. His hair is wild and loose, curling around his jaw and shoulders in tangles, begging to be knotted in my fingers. He cradles an ankle in his hands, kisses a delicate touch of his lips to the ankle bone. The side of my calf. I gulp, swallow a breath, and he kisses the inside of my thigh. Sets my knee over his shoulder, foot and calf draping down his back. Lifts my other leg and kisses a mirroring line from ankle to calf to knee to thigh, until this leg too he drapes over his shoulder.

I know what he's about to do, and I still can't quite believe it.

I can't breathe. Can't look away from his mouth as it kisses my skin, slow wet kisses dotting my flesh from thigh to navel to thigh, dip of my hip to the other. Then to the top of the inverted V of my pubic hair—and now my gasp is a shrill whimper, a breathy cry of shock. The kisses don't stop—they descend. His eyes remain on mine, daring me to look away. I don't. I watch in rapture as his lips graze over my sex, as his lips trail along my pussy and his tongue slide against the seam. My mouth falls open, but no words come out—*oh god, oh god, oh god*...it echoes in my skull but I can't form words.

I'm still shivering with the tremors of the last orgasm, and now his tongue slithers against my clit and

I'm instantly at the peak, tottering on the tip of the mountain. His hands rush up my body, cupping my tits with greedy hunger, fondling them eagerly, desperately, and his mouth kisses my sex, tongue delving into my wetness and my heat, licking at it, slathering nimbly through my clenching channel to twirl with teasing slowness around my aching clit.

"Oh...*fuck* ..." It's a breathed snarl, barely audible, dropping from my lips.

His thumbs pry open my nether lips and his tongue flattens against me and he shakes his head from side to side, and then his fingers are curling into me and dragging against the higher inner walls where there lurks, unbeknownst to me, a secret. He touches me there with scraping rhythm in a counterpoint to his whipping, hungry tongue.

I shatter.

I can't even scream.

I can only shake silently, mouth open, eyes wide, brows furrowed, watching his mouth devour me, watching his fingers plunder me, watching him play my body like a violin.

If the last orgasm was a pleasure-like pain...this one is razor-sharp and sun-hot. I must only *endure* it. Wracked and splintered by it into breathless abandon, I finally find oxygen to scream and now with the rush of air to the fire, it blows hotter and wilder, as if my scream was a backdraft. I'm writhing and thrusting against his mouth, my movements wanton and erotic, my breathless screams coming hard and fast and loud as I helplessly desperately grind myself against his lips and talented tongue.

I can't take anymore.

I shake my head, try to pull away, but he's not done with me. His mouth continues to push me through the shaking and the shivering until I'm gasping again, until I curl my body inward and plead with him to stop.

"No more," I gasp. "Stop, please stop."

He prowls up my body and I feel him hovering over me and his eyes burn into mine. His stubble is wet from my juices, like a wolf with its prey's blood dripping from snapping jaws. "That," he whispers, "is how I will make you come—again and again, until you beg me to stop."

One knee is pressed into the couch beside my hip, the other stretched out the floor. His eyes are wild with lust. My eyes flit to his zipper, still bulging with his own arousal.

My need is not satiated.

Not nearly.

I've come, and the pressure within has been vented. But the snarling need of my suddenly insatiable sexuality has just come alive.

Before he can stop me, if he even would, I twist free the button of his slacks and tug down the zipper.

Immediately, his erection springs upright, and a pink broad head pokes out of the top of his underwear. I shove his pants down, my movements rough and eager, and then, more gently, hook my fingers into the elastic of his black briefs, pausing for a moment to assess his reaction.

"You think I'm going to stop you?" he murmurs. "I've dreamt of your touch since the moment I saw you in my vestibule, bound and gagged and helpless, yet still so proud, so fierce." He's motionless, that preternatural stillness he has. "Touch me, Corinna. I beg of you."

His voice contains not a single false note, not a hint of sarcasm, or play. His eyes are wild, seeking mine. His chest expands and contracts rapidly, panting raggedly. His hands curl into fists on the top of the couch, and I hear the wicker creak under his grip.

"Please, Corinna," he breathes. "Have mercy on me. Touch me."

I push his underwear down until his cock bobs free, swaying with his breathing. His brow furrows, his eyes on my hands as I graze them up his thighs. I hear his jaw grinding. His breathing is ragged, rasping in his throat, nearly growling with every breath.

My hands shake with equal parts need and nerves as they carve up over his hips, to his belly.

"You tease me," he whispers.

"No," I whisper back. "I would never."

And I fill my hands with him, wrapping both greedy fists around his cock. He lets out a slow hissing sigh, and his abs brace, go taut. He's thick and rigid, hard as steel in my hands yet soft as silk and so warm, nearly hot to the touch. I bring my fists down, and veins stutter under my fingers.

He huffs at the movement of my hands on his flesh, and now our eyes lock. I reach up with one hand and knot my fingers in his hair and pull him down to me and demand his mouth for a searing kiss. He groans into the kiss, and his hips push forward, jutting his cock through my fist. I stroke my fist down his length, and a growl morphs into a moan.

His other knee now lifts to press against the couch so Apollo is kneeling astride me, towering over me, still gripping the back of the wicker couch and hunched over me. I sit upright beneath him, gaze up at him as I learn what pleases him through slow exploration. With one hand, I caress his length in unhurried gliding strokes, top to bottom, a light touch. With both hands, simply plunging up and down. Up to the top, and then down with a twist. He watches, brow furrowed, jaw clenched, his breathing slow but rough.

His hips begin to lift in time with my touch, and I recognize that desperate, helpless movement as the first tremors of a pending climax. I want to know what his release looks like. What his loss of control means. I want to know. I want to feel it. I want to know what it feels like to make this man detonate beyond all lucidity.

I find a rhythm, then, and one that seems to make him grow the wildest: I cup the heavy taut balls in one hand, cradling their soft weight in one hand, and with the other I caress his length. Slowly, twisting now and then, sometimes pausing to caress the top, other times plunging a few short strokes at the bottom. His breathing is a long, continuous growl, now, and his hips are moving on their own. Thrusting his cock into my touch.

He's close.

He jerks himself away from me, throwing himself to his feet with a stomping twist to keep his balance, facing away from me. His back is rigid, his buttocks taut. His shoulders are bowed, hunched as if to ward off a blow, hands clenched into fists at his sides.

I find my feet and pad up behind him. I don't dare touch him, now, for reasons I cannot fathom, only some instinct inside me warning me not to. "Apollo?"

He shakes his head. "Not here. Not like this."

"Why?"

All I get is another shake of his head.

"Apollo, I don't understand." I dare—I touch his shoulder. "I…I wanted to."

He growls, and I yank my hand away. "You shouldn't."

"I know." I laugh. "Fucking trust me, I know I shouldn't. But dammit, I do."

"Here, in the orangery, like…" a bitter laugh. "No, Corinna. Not here, not like this."

I stomp around him, irritated now. "Why not? How is it different?"

He holds my eyes, and I can see him trying to find that distant coldness—he's failing. "It just is."

"So once again, you can get me naked and do what you want with me. Touch me, make me crazy. Seduce me into insanity until I'm writhing on top of you in broad daylight. You can do all that to me, here, in the orangery. But the moment I want something for myself, the moment *I* want to touch *you*…oh no, not here. Not like this." At that last, my voice is a gruff imitation of his. "You don't play fair, Apollo."

"It's different," he murmurs. "I didn't stop because it's not good enough for *me*. I stopped because it's not good enough for *you*."

"I don't understand."

His eyes search me. "I know. Can't you just… believe me?"

"Believe you, like…trust you?" I cackle. "You *do* see the irony in that, right?" I push at his chest. "So no, Apollo. I won't just believe you. Explain it to me."

He seems to grow, his presence swelling,

darkening, his aura and energy growing dominant and predatory. "You want to know?" He steps closer to me, his hard cock jutting upright between us. "Fine, I'll tell you."

I refuse to shrink away from him. I stare up at him, daring him, my pride and my arousal holding me upright even though this wild primal ferocity in him scares the bejesus out of me. "Please do," I hiss.

"I will." He grips my wrist, pushes it to his cock—willingly, I clutch him again. "You touch me like this, and I…I lose myself, Corinna. You know nothing of what lies beyond this merely touching, for me. You think this stops at just…my mouth on your sweet, delicate, little pussy, making you come? You think you can toy with my cock and I'll just…*let* you? I'd like to let you, you know. But that's not who I am and that's not how this works."

"How does it work then, Apollo?"

"Sweet Corinna." He cups my face, tenderly, eyes on mine with ferocity and intensity blazing in them despite the exquisite gentility of his touch. "You know what I want to do to you?"

"No," I whisper.

"No," he agrees. His nose touches my cheek, his breath whispering against my ear. "You can't fathom what I want." A wet warm tickle of his tongue to the inner shell of my ear. "I want to *fuck* you until you can't see straight. Until you're limp and boneless and begging me to let you stop coming. I want to have you from behind so I can spank your lovely ass till it's pink. I want to put your legs over my shoulders and fuck you so hard your perfect tits bounce until they hurt."

His words shiver through me, shaking me to my core.

"Is that what you want?"

I squeak a breath. "I…I don't know."

Such a damned, dirty lie. I do want that. All of it.

"I stopped because if I didn't…? I would have fucked you like that, here, now." His hand curls around the back of my neck, holding me close, and his other hand steals between us. Touches me where I'm tender and ultra-sensitive. "And I don't think you want that."

"Maybe I do."

A laugh. "You don't, Corinna, and don't lie to me." A slow touch. "Have you thought about me? About what it would be like to fuck me?"

He says my name in a way no one ever has. My full name from anyone else sounds like a scold. From him, it feels like a caress.

"Yes," I admit.

"Of course you have." My knees soften as he touches me, his touch as slow and as gentle as his voice is low and rough. "Did you imagine it would be slow and sweet, Corinna? That there would be nice little kisses and I would be so concerned for *your* pleasure that I think of nothing of myself?"

I groan at his touch, and at his words. "I don't know."

"*That* is why I stopped, Corinna," he growls. "Because a moment more and I would have had you here on this shitty couch in this giant stupid glass room full of flowers." His voice is so rough. Nearly angry. "I would not have been gentle. I would not have been concerned for you. I would have taken my pleasure from you and it would have been for *me*, not for *you*."

My knees nearly give out, because his voice is that wicked caress, matching the slow delve of his fingers playing my pleasure like a master violinist plays his instrument. So close. But I have to hear him.

"Did you think you would touch my cock and I would just…what? Come on your belly? Is that what you want?" His tone is harsh, his words vulgar. "Did you want to make me come like that? Jerk me off until I came all over these amazing tits?" He plays with one, fondling it in gesture. "You want me to paint them with my cum, Corinna?"

"I…I don't know. I wasn't thinking about that." I press up against him, cling to his neck for support as he drives me closer and closer to climax. "I was just…I wanted to touch you. That's all. I wanted to see how it felt to…"

"To what?" he demands.

"To make you feel the way you made me feel." I whimper. Keep admitting the truth. "I wanted to make you as crazy and desperate as you made me." I clutch his shoulders hard as I near the edge. "So yeah, Apollo. I wanted to make you come. That's all I was thinking about."

He releases me and holds my wrists, leaving me knock-kneed and weak, shaking. "I know, Corinna. I know." He yanks me off balance, tugging me forward so I fall against him, and he kisses me. "Do you want more, Corinna?" I feel his cock pressing against my belly, and grinds it against me. "Do you?"

Lust makes me rash and irresponsible, it seems. Because I do want more.

"Yes," I whisper.

"Then get dressed and meet me in the tower." He releases me, steps backward away from me. "If by the time you reach my room you still want this, with me, then I will take you into my bed and I will show you *everything*."

14

MAMA'S COMING

"How long am I supposed to just sit here while my daughter endures who knows what kind of hell?" I snarl, pacing back and forth across the hotel room.

Anselm is stretched out on one of the twin beds, hands folded across his middle, eyes closed, a gargantuan military-grade sniper rifle beside him like a lover. Where he got a rifle like that in the middle of the night I don't know—but this is Anselm. He very well could be asleep, but I know he's not.

"They'll be here soon," Anselm says without opening his eyes. "You need to try to rest. I don't say sleep, I know you will not. But at least rest. You will need it in the hours to come."

"How can I rest when my daughter is in danger?"

"It is, perhaps, counter-indicative, but resting is

the best thing you can do for Rinna right now, Kyrie. When it is time to act, you must be at full operating capacity. If you are too exhausted to function because you haven't taken care of yourself, you will be no good to your daughter when the time comes."

"I *can't*," I sigh, perching on the edge of the bed. "I don't have your training."

"It is not easy for me, even now." He turns his head to look at me. "Lay down, like I am. On your back, hands folded on your belly. It is not a posture of sleep, but of mindful rest."

Moving slowly, begrudgingly, I do as he says. "I'll last about thirty seconds like this, Anselm."

"Now you must assume a mental posture to match your physical. Tell yourself you are not attempting to fall asleep. You are allowing your body to recharge, that is all. You cannot sustain high-alert status all the time. We who have served in combat or other such modalities are forced to learn this—combat is long, long stretches of boredom followed by a few brief moments of brutal intensity, and you simply cannot be at full alert all the time. When you can rest, you must. It is not sleep, but rest. An important mental distinction."

I try—slow my mind, tell myself that I am not sleeping. I'm not wasting time. Just rest. Not relaxing, not sleeping, just resting.

"Now, if you have ever attempted mindfulness

meditation, this will be similar. Do not attempt to fight the activity of your mind. It will wander back to the problem at hand, perhaps obsessively. Let it. But begin attempting to bring it back to rest. To quietude. Slow, steady heartbeats—count them. Or your breaths, if you prefer. Something rhythmic and consistent. Now, start at your toes. Let them relax. The arches of your feet, now." His voice is soothing, hypnotic. "Your calves, and then your whole leg. Allow your belly to soften. Allow your spine to soften—let it mold to the bed. Your shoulders, next—let them melt. Your neck. Let your eyes weigh down into your head. Let your mouth go slack."

As he speaks, I follow his instructions, and I do feel a slowness wash over me. I couldn't fall asleep short of chemical assistance, but I do feel a sense of rest steal through me.

"Now, consider the face of your daughter. Envision your reunion. See yourself hugging her, both of you well and safe. Put that picture into your mind, and down into your soul. It will be the truth."

Slowly, I find a space in the madness, a bubble of something like calm in the swirling vortex of anger and fear and worry. I huddle there, mentally, in the small still bubble of rest.

I see my Rinna rushing to hug me, and I see myself hugging her back and kissing her. I see us wrapped up in Valentine's arms, all of us together.

The sound of a keycard in the lock and the door handle moving rouses me—I'm up on my feet and fully alert in an eye blink, and yet I feel strangely refreshed.

The first body through the door is my husband, crossing the room in a few long strides. His hands pull me to him, lifting me as I leap into his arms, and he clutches me against himself and his nose goes into my hair.

Safe in my beloved's embrace, I allow myself a moment of weakness. I shake all over, and a sob bursts out of me.

"I've got you, my love," he whispers, and even after all these years, he still has a faint trace of a British accent, especially when emotions run high. "I've got you. I'm here."

I give in to it, just a for a moment. Let myself finally feel afraid and small and weak, let myself feel disgusted at what I did, angry that I was put in this position. I let myself cry, just for a moment.

"It's all right, love," he murmurs. "It's all right. You're all right. Rinna will be all right."

I let it all wash over me, let myself wallow in it—but it's not over yet. In a way, it's just beginning. I push the sobs back in, shove the fear and the smallness and the worry and the weakness back inside, back in the box. I wiggle out of his embrace and find my feet, wipe my eyes, catch my breath. Slow my breathing. I focus on the anger and the hardness of doing what must be done. I hold onto Valentine's huge strong familiar hands and I settle myself back into a place of strength and equilibrium.

"All right, now?" he says, his voice a tender caress.

I nod. Smile up at him. "I am now. Mostly. I won't be all right until we have our girl back, but now that you're here, I'm better."

The room is full, suddenly, crammed wall to wall with massive, angry, armed and armored male.

They're all here, the whole A1S core gang: Harris, Anselm, Duke, Puck, Thresh, and Lear.

Sasha is here as well, a man who has been as much a constant fixture in our lives as the others. His face is troubled as he crosses to me.

"Kyrie…Mrs. Roth…" he stands in front of me, eyes haunted, his Russian accent pronounced. "I failed to protect your family. I have no apology for this."

His hands are thick and scarred and gnarled as I squeeze them. "Sasha, it's not your fault. I don't blame you."

"I was on guard myself that night. He walked right past me with your daughter." Anger clouds his features. "I blame myself."

"Sasha, stop." I hold his gaze. "You've stood guard over our family for twenty years. What happened was done in such a way that no one could have seen it or stopped it." I squeeze his hands again. "Did your attention lapse? Did you go lax in your dedication to your job?"

He shakes his head. "*Nyet*. Never."

"Then you didn't fail."

He drops his head. "Thank you." He steps back. "If you and Mr. Roth did not have priority claim over me, I would demand the right to end this bastard myself."

"Get in line, comrade," Duke growls. "Walked past me too."

Harris lets out a piercing whistle. "Enough. Blame and self-recrimination and vows of vengeance have no place here, gentlemen. We are professionals. This may be personal, but we will approach it with the same objectivity and rationality as we would if this was a job we were hired for. Put your anger aside. It will not help us, here." His blue-green eyes go to mine—this is meant for me as much as them; and to judge by the intensity in his gaze, he means it for himself just as much.

There's a silence, and I can see each man going through a mental process, putting the personal aside and putting on the professional detachment like he would a piece of body armor.

"We have a location," Harris continues, after a moment, "and we have some intel." He glances at Lear, who has set up his laptop on one of the twin beds. "Lear?"

"Intel is a loose term," Lear says. "I'm sending to each of you a file. You should have it in your inboxes. It's the totality of what we know. Here's the briefing version: Apollo Karahalios, grandson of our old buddy Vitaly, son of the mad bitch herself, Gina. Apollo is a legitimate businessman first, by all accounts, and a crime lord second. He does things differently, and he's shaking up the scene over here. This is good and bad for us, because he doesn't like violence if he can't help it, but it also means he's unpredictable at best. Also working against us is the fact that he was heir to a massive fortune from his grandfather and mother which he only multiplied through his own efforts. He has contacts in the European underworld and enough money to damn near rival even the big boss, here, Valentine Roth."

My husband snorts. "Not quite, Lear." He assumes the mantle of authority merely by speaking. "He's worth an even billion, I'd say, which is not chump change by any stretch of the imagination. But that's no closer to my net worth than someone worth a million is close in value to someone worth a few hundred million. Let's not give this guy more credit than is due him—he's got money, he's got resources, but is he on par with me? No."

Lear chuckles. "Dick measuring aside…" he

glances at Valentine with a snicker; Valentine just glares. "Teasing, boss, just teasing. Trying to lighten things up in here. Not working, got it. Anyway." He sets the laptop aside. "He's got soldiers. A lot of them. Well-armed, well-trained, and well-paid. And the location? A legit, real-deal fucking castle. All approaches are open—surrounded by vines in every direction for miles. Middle of nowhere, too, fuckin' miles from anything. So, approach by helo is out, 'cause they'd hear us coming and it won't be anyone but us. One road in, and you can't bet your sweet bippy that road will be monitored, if not actively guarded at several locations. Satellite imagery shows the doors are for sure fortified. So, even the seven or eight of us, being elite professionals with decades of experience, this is damn near impossible to approach. A frontal assault is not an option. Stealth insertion isn't much better. You could drop in from HALO height, sure, but that's not going to get you inside, and it bears repeating, every door I could get imagery of looks fuckin' massive, and I mean not even Thresh his ownself is gonna be kicking that shit in. You'd need serious explosives, and once you do that, you're swarmed."

"So what you're saying," I cut in, "is that there are no good options."

A shrug from Lear. "Near to it, unfortunately."

"He doesn't seem interested in negotiating," I say. "We don't have much idea what he *does* want other than revenge on Valentine and me for his mother's death. And his grandfather's, I would assume."

Valentine holds up his hand, and both Lear and I fall silent. "I think there's only one real play."

I know what he's suggesting, and I nod before he even lays it out.

"Kyrie and I approach, alone, on foot, unarmed. We exchange ourselves for Rinna. You guys will be waiting as close as you can get. We do our best to talk this Apollo character out of doing anything too… rash." He shrugs, hands lifting palms up as far as his shoulders, then flopping back down to his thighs. "Maybe we could get him to come outside, and Anselm, you could be in a helo with your rifle at the farthest distance you feel confident in taking a shot, and…bam. Done."

Anselm nods. "It is possible."

Harris growls. "I don't like it. You got no guarantee he's not going to just kill you both."

"Better us than Rin," I say, my voice hoarse. "She's innocent in this. We're not. It was brought on us, but I get how he may not see that. We just have to hope he's something like reasonable."

"That, or hope we can get him within range of Anselm's rifle," Valentine says.

I look around, a thought occurring to me. "Wait, where are Layla and the kids?"

Valentine and Harris exchange looks.

"Took a hell of a lot of convincing all around, but we managed to get Layla to stay with them at a different location here in the city," Harris says.

"Cal in particular was pissed off at being excluded," Valentine says, wincing, "but when I made it clear to him how this was going to go down, he finally agreed to stay with Layla. And let me tell you, she's no happier at being what she sees as sidelined than Cal is."

I sigh. "I can only imagine. But there was never a chance of this being a guns blazing operation."

"And he was never going to be a part of that even if it was," Valentine adds. "So they're in a safe house, guarded by two dozen of A1S's best."

I nod. "Okay. So, we approach by car as close as we can. Then you and I go the rest of the way on foot, and just hope he doesn't take us both hostage along with Rinna?"

"We set it up ahead of time. Get close and then get in contact with him. Agree to an exchange." Valentine shrugs and sighs. "I can't see a better way."

"I still don't fuckin' like it," Duke says. "We went in guns blazing last time. Don't see how this is any different."

"Last time, Gina didn't have a goal or a desire except to cause pain." Valentine holds Duke's eyes. "Kyrie was never getting off that island alive. Neither was Gina, for that matter. She was batshit crazy and wanted one thing and one thing only: to hurt me, and to hurt Kyrie to get at me." He gestures at Lear's computer. "This is different. There's a chance to end this without bloodshed, and I'll take it."

"Even if it means you two being the blood that gets shed?" Duke says.

Valentine looks to me, and I stand beside him, hand in hand. "If that's what it takes," I say.

Valentine nods in agreement. "We've had a taste of peace since we finished off Cain. I don't know about you guys, but I like it. And if we can end this without anyone else dying, to me, that's the best possible outcome."

I drop my eyes. "Hear hear."

Valentine wraps an arm around me. "Don't go there, Key. You did what you had to do, what you felt was right in the moment."

I can only shake my head and sigh. Somehow, those four deaths haunt me in a way the other lives I've taken don't.

"Let's work this plan out and get moving," Harris says.

And so, we set to planning.

I'm coming, Rinna.

Mama's coming.

15

THE MAN BENEATH THE MONSTER

HE WATCHES ME DRESS, AND HIS GREEDY HUNGRY eyes do not miss a single movement of my body. He himself makes no move to touch his clothing, merely standing there with his hands at his sides, cock standing up flat against his belly, straining and massive.

I hold his gaze as I dress—a challenge, perhaps. Underwear first. Bra. Leggings. Tunic, belt. My hair is still in the braid he put it in, tied with twine.

Our food is untouched.

I hesitate, before leaving. "You know what?" I say, sitting at the table. "No. I'm hungry." His usual lunch preference is laid out on the table: peasant bread, wedges of cheese, folded slices of roast beef, turkey, and ham, fruit, honey, crackers, and nuts, washed down with his favorite beer, the small-batch Belgian. "I'm sure you have work to do. I'll see you in the tower later."

I dig in, doing my best to ignore him. It's not hard, once I'm eating—hunger takes over, eclipsing even my still-raging lust.

He snorts, shakes his head. "Incorrigibly proud, aren't you?"

"I'm no one's plaything, Apollo."

"I had no thought that you were."

"Bullshit."

He lets out a sigh which sounds suspiciously long-suffering, and dresses himself, unhurried, each movement elegant and languorous. "It's not bullshit, Corinna."

"It is." I crack open the bottle of beer and pour myself a glass.

Once again dressed and composed, Apollo sits opposite me and breaks a piece of bread off of the loaf, matches it with a chunk of hard white aged cheddar and a slice of meat. "How so is it bullshit, then?"

"I think this whole thing is a game." I gesture at him with a piece of melon. "You're lonely. You have no one in your life who gives a shit about you. No one. Everyone who knows you, who's close to you—as in, proximity, not emotionally—is paid to be there."

His face darkens, and his chewing slows; I'm in

very dangerous waters, now. "Measure your words carefully, Corinna Roth."

"Oh, I am." I meet his eyes. "I'm telling the truth, and you know it. You just don't like it."

"The truth as you see it."

"Wrong. The truth as it is. There's only one truth, Apollo. Your opinion, your inability to see or recognize the truth doesn't change the essential nature of that truth."

He drops his eyes from mine and tears at a chunk of bread, ripping it free with his teeth, with a shake of his head, looking more than ever like a wolf in a poor approximation of mere man.

"The truth, then," he murmurs, pouring himself beer and taking a long draught of it. "What is the truth, since you know so much about me?"

I laugh. "I know only what you've told me, Apollo. Don't confuse truth with information—with facts. But the truth is easy to see. It's plain as the nose on your face." I search him, but he's not looking at me. "I told you the truth. You're lonely, and this whole kidnapping plot is all a big game to you. Maybe you don't see it that way, because you don't see yourself. But it's just a game." I forestall his protest. "A very dangerous game, and one that's turned deadly. And if you're not careful in how the next phase of it goes, I guarantee you, the next death will be yours. I'm not threatening you. Honestly, I don't want to see you dead, Apollo."

I let out a long, tight sigh.

"Fucking awful truth of it is, I'm fascinated by you. Intrigued. I'm attracted to you." I point at the wicker couch, a few feet away. "I knew exactly what I was doing, there, Apollo. I went into it eyes open. Once the heat of the moment took over, I admit I couldn't have stopped it if I wanted to, but the point is, I *didn't* want to." I lean over the table. "I see you, Apollo. You're not good. But who is? You're also not bad. You're not evil. I don't think you wanted anyone to get killed. You just didn't factor in the kind of people my parents are. You've got a tiger by the tail, and you're finding out exactly how big, how angry, and how vicious the tiger on the other end of the tail is."

"The tiger I've got by the tail is you." He manages a wry, small smirk.

I sit back, smear honey on a cracker and add a chunk of cheese. "My original point is that you thought I was a plaything. You thought you could take me hostage and that I'd just…go along. You thought I was the rich, spoiled brat and that my parents are nothing but vapid, self-centered, easily manipulated billionaires with more money than sense. You thought what happened to your mother was their fault. That your mother was misunderstood, maybe. What about your grandfather? I've heard bits and pieces of the story about him, too. And the story I'm hearing isn't a good one." I've got his full attention now, no more pretense of eating for either of us. “You thought you could kidnap me. You thought you could turn me inside out with your fucking smoldering looks and your…your stupid fucking perfect body. You thought I’d be too scared of you to fight back. Or if I did fight back, it’d be with my fists. You thought if my parents fought back, it’d be with their money.”

He frowns at me. “I don’t smolder.”

I cackle. “Oh, but you do. You smolder.” I wave at him. “Not the point, right now. You thought it would be easy. Take their daughter, play a little game of damsel in distress. Threaten and posture. Like playing chess. Get them where you want them, and get your petty, childish revenge. Make my father sell off the companies he’s worked his whole life building. Make him donate all his money. Whatever. Make my mom think she has to sacrifice herself for me. Playing on their emotions. Playing on mine.”

“Petty, childish revenge?” He pushes his chair back and stands up. “That’s how you see it?”

“That’s how it *is*, Apollo. Your mother died before I was born. This has nothing to do with me.” I stand up and move to face him, but I keep a couple feet between us; the tinder is easily sparked, and I dare not light the match of touching him. “How closely have you looked at your past, Apollo? Your history, your family’s history?”

“Close enough.”

"Bullshit." I shake my head, turn away. "You are such a liar. You lie to yourself as smoothly and easily as you lie to everyone around you."

"I'm honest about who I am. I do not pretend to be anyone but who and what I am."

"I know that." I turn back. "The lie you tell is *why*. Why did you get involved in the drugs and the guns, Apollo? You find violence…distasteful. Right? Killing people puts you off your appetite." I soak the words in sarcasm. "But yet, you've embroiled yourself in an industry that is inherently violent. And you've tried to change it. Maybe you've succeeded, to some extent. And good, great. Admirable even, in a twisted, fucked up sort of way. But have you ever asked yourself why you're even running drugs and guns in the first place? Is it for the money? The thrill of doing something illegal when all your other enterprises are aboveboard?"

He doesn't answer.

"Why, Apollo? Are you self-aware enough to answer me that? Why did you get involved in the family business when you didn't have to?"

His eyes crackle, spit fire and lightning. "I don't answer to *you*."

I hold my ground. "No, you don't. You answer to no one." I dare closer, but the anger and danger he's exuding makes it feel like I'm edging too close to a blazing fire. "Do you answer to yourself, though? That's the question."

"What would be the purpose in this game, Corinna? Tell me that, since you have me all figured out."

"I think you hoped you'd get your revenge *and* the damsel in distress."

"Meaning?"

"Meaning, get your revenge on my parents and have me fall for you."

He stares me down. "I had you naked and begging for me, only moments ago, Corinna." His turn to dare closer. "So it seems I was not wrong."

"You seem to think I'm going to be ashamed of it." I shake my head. Put my hands on his chest. "I'm not. I saw what was happening. I saw how you make me feel, physically. I'm not ashamed of that."

"Such a bold young thing." He's unmoving—I can feel him trying frantically to rebuild the island fortress walls around himself that I've systematically dismantled. "You are such a responsive creature, Corinna. You are a glory of sinful, delicious sexuality. "

I pivot back to face him, still a few paces apart. "The moment you took that fucking hood off me and I saw you, something in my…in my gut, my soul maybe…something inside me resonated, and I knew it was because of you. I didn't want it to be you. God, *anyone* but you. Anyone but a man who would kidnap a girl out of her bed. I mean, shit, what does that say about me? Why the hell do you think I was able to stand there, naked, letting you stare at me like some *boy* let loose in a girls' locker room? Why do you think I've been so calm through all this? Because I fucking *see* you, Apollo. And it's fucked up, and I'm scared of it, and I don't know what happens next, but I fucking see you."

"And what is it you see, Corinna?" His voice is razor-thin, razor-sharp, diamond-hard.

"I see a lonely little boy who has never known affection." I take a step toward him. "I see that lonely, unloved little boy who grew into an angry, isolated man with all the money in the world, all the power, all the influence anyone could ever want. But it didn't mean shit to him. Because he's *alone*."

Another step—and I see him tensing tighter with each step closer I take, with each word I say.

"I see the rich, powerful, educated, sophisticated man you are, the shrewd, successful businessman, the man with a taste for the beautiful things of the world—and I see that in the end, he has fucking *nothing* worth having, and he knows it."

Another step, and now he's stopped breathing, nostrils flared, brows drawn, jaw clenched so hard he's about to crack a molar.

"You know what I see, Apollo? I see someone who just wants to be…seen. Someone who wants to be hugged. Held. You just don't know what that looks like, and you know even less how to ask for it."

One more step, and now I'm in his space, my breasts brushing his chest. I look up into his eyes.

"For all that you're educated and sophisticated and worldly, Apollo, this whole kidnapping ploy was no more than a caveman clubbing a woman over the head and dragging her back to his cave. It was a Mongolian warrior raiding a camp and taking the woman he claimed as his wife and riding off with her."

"You know nothing," he whispers.

"You want to be seen," I say, ignoring him, "but now that I see you, you don't like it." I shake my head. "Why me? I've asked myself a thousand times. Why me? Why go to the effort of kidnapping me so precisely, so carefully, so nonviolently? Why me?" I shrug. "I'm only guessing, now. But I think it's because I'm the only person on this planet to whom you have any kind of a connection—through our parents. They are the thread that binds us. My mother, your mother—the story of what happened. Neither of us knows the whole thing. I don't think I want to, honestly. And neither do you, if you're being honest with yourself."

He shakes his head and backs away from me. "You don't know what you're talking about."

"Don't I?"

"I know what happened."

"Fine. Tell me what happened, then. Convince me."

"She was busy. She was in charge of a lot of people." He closes his eyes and turns away, hands going into his pockets. "She didn't mean to have me. She never wanted or intended to be a mother." His voice goes so soft I can barely hear it. "She said that to me, once. She was drunk, it was late. I was six. She didn't think she could even have children. 'I never wanted you, Apollo. You aren't even supposed to exist. You are an accident.'"

"Jesus."

He ignores me. "I did a DNA test, paid an investigator to find my father. The investigator narrowed it down to one of three men. All from Athens. I pieced together what happened to result in me. She essentially kept a harem of men. Poor, attractive nobodies. Men with no family, no future. Deadbeats, you Americans would call them. Drug addicts, losers, alcoholics. Men forgotten by everyone, with nothing to lose. She would give them a little…stipend, I suppose. And when she came to town for business, she would dress them up in suits and play pretend with them. My father was one such man. And my mother, she was not supposed to be able to have children. I found a medical record from her youth. She had a disease, a cancer, I think, in her childhood. She recovered and it never came back, but it was assumed she was infertile. There was, however, an accident. A fluke of statistics, and here I am."

"Did you contact him?"

He strides to the open doorway of the orangery and stands in it. I follow him, stand behind him.

"No." His hands are balled into tight fists in his pockets. Every line of his body is taut and tense. "He's dead. Long dead. And I said it was narrowed down to one of three men, not that I knew which one it was. I could have done further research, found out. But of the three men who could be my father, one was a heroin addict and died of an overdose around the time I would have been conceived, making it unlikely to be him. The second was a killer and a rapist, and I refuse to believe I could be related to such filth. The third was merely a hopeless alcoholic who couldn't stop drinking long enough to hold a job, and so relied on prostituting himself to my mother for income. If I am honest, it was most likely him." A pause. "He drank himself to death before I was out of diapers."

A silence.

"They were the very literal dregs off the bottom of the barrel. Not one of them saw his thirty-fifth birthday. There weren't even funerals because not one person on this planet cared whether they lived or died." He withdraws his hands from his pockets and grips the frame of the door, bracing himself to lean forward, head hanging; his voice is the rasping hiss of a blade across a whetstone. "It is from this I am descended. And my mother?" A harsh laugh. "She punished herself with those men, I believe. That, or she had such depraved sexual predilections that men such as they were the only ones she could find upon whom to entertain herself. I haven't been able to bring myself to find out that particular truth."

He turns, leans a shoulder against the door frame. Looks at me.

"My grandfather was a fucking monster." His expression is opaque. Hard as stone. "The stories of him are legendary, and the multiplicity of the stories detailing the monstrosity of his nature is too convincing to be anything but the truth. He relished in the vilest of things—allowed his men to rape the women he trafficked in, allowed them to murder at a whim, so long as it could not be traced back to him. His guns were put into the hands of child soldiers, and his drugs in the veins of the same. His empire was built on blood. The money I was raised on? It's blood money of the worst kind. It's fairly soaked in the blood of innocents. But it spends all the same as clean money, no? So I spend it."

Another long pause.

"And yes, my mother was just as bad, if not worse." A venomous laugh. "When I began digging into who I was, I would come across people who put it together before I did." His eyes go to mine. "There's a phrase I heard, in regards to my mother. Some have nicknames, you know? Like, The Ghost, or The Jackal, or Ripper, or shit like that, yes? My mother had her version of it. I would ask after Gina Karahalios and they would all say the same thing. 'Ah, that one. The mad bitch herself.' The mad bitch. One man called her the mad bitch from hell. Another said she was the evilest creature he'd ever met, and this was a man serving multiple life sentences for some truly brutal murders—or rather, executions would be the more accurate term."

"Yet when I told you what I'd been told about the situation which led to her death, you acted as if you didn't know who she really was."

He looks away. "She was my mother." A shrug.

"We are more than our DNA, Apollo."

His smirk is ugly—or as ugly as his perfect face can get. "You think so? And yet, here you are."

"Yet here I am." I pause. "Tell me about her."

"I just did."

"No, not Gina Karahalios. Your mother."

He frowns at me. "You *are* a glutton for punishment, aren't you?"

"I guess." I meet his eyes. "Because, here I am."

He closes his eyes with a sarcastic sniff and a slight shake of his head at the way I've twisted his own words. "She was a terrible mother," he says, looking away, out at the garden. "She was…arrogant. Vain. Shallow and materialistic. Selfish. She never once told me she loved me. She didn't hug me. I'm not even certain why I am here at all. Meaning, why she didn't abort me. Why did she carry me to term? She seemed to loathe the responsibility I represented. Perhaps even the fact of my existence, that I represent the continuation of her family line, the evil that is the Karahalios name."

"Do you have *no* good memories of her?"

A shrug. Staring into the vacant space of memory, an unfocused gaze. "Good memories? Mmm... not really. She was all sharp edges and hard words, when she was sober. But when she was drunk? I'd see the softer side of her, the dark, soft underbelly of the mad bitch from hell—and it was...far worse. The things she'd say to me...I brought her breakfast, once. She'd accidentally stayed through to Sunday morning, and I got up before Gemma, and I brought her yogurt and made her tea. And she asked if I was trying to be a good boy. Like that, hmm? 'Are you trying to be a good boy, my little Polly?' And then she laughed, as if she'd told the funniest joke. 'You *can't* be good, Apollo. So don't bother trying. It simply isn't in you. You are my son, and I am truly sorry for that. It's a horrible thing to be.'"

I choke. "She said that to you?"

He nods slowly. "It was a few weeks before her death. I was...ten? Almost eleven, maybe?" A frown. "No, younger. I don't know—I don't remember exactly."

A silence.

"It was better when she was gone. It was lonely and boring, but easier. Yet, I would always work myself into a mad state, wishing she was there, because I would always talk myself into believing she would be different. Like the children of addicts, you know? Maybe this time, they'll really get clean. And like the child whose addict parent always lets them down by relapsing, my mother always turned out to be the same awful creature she'd been the last time she turned up."

"Apollo…" I breathe.

He looks at me then, and for a brief moment, I see the unending wealth of pain his walls hide. "You still think there's a good man inside me?" He smirks, and it isn't pretty. "Like in the movies, yes? The crusader who sees good in the villain. The *Star Wars* movie. Luke…Sky…something. Skywalker? 'There's still good in you, I know it.' He says this to his father, the robot man with the red laser sword. Darth… something."

I laugh. "Darth Vader."

"Ah yes. But was there? How did that turn out for the orphan boy from the desert planet? Not well. There may have been something good in the remains of the thing that had once been his father. But if there was, it was too late, and buried too deeply under all the hate." He taps his chest. "*You* are going to redeem *me*? A few hard truths and I'm going to suddenly be something other than what I am? Which is a Karahalios. That's why I took on the family business. Because that's what I am."

He strides away from me into the garden, and now we're surrounded by fruit trees and an explosion of flowers of every color and variety. I follow him.

"You don't fool me, Apollo."

He barks a laugh. "Don't I? Do tell."

"You're deflecting. Pushing me off, because you think I'm going to be like everyone else—forced to be here. Your men, Consuela, your assistant or whatever…they have a choice in that you pay them. But without that money, how loyal are they to *you*? To the *man*, not the title, not the power, not the position or the influence."

He snorts. "Funny, I wonder that myself. And the answer is, not at all. That's why I pay them so well no one could ever outbid me. Their loyalty is assured, because I am their fortune's future."

"Right. Exactly."

A laugh, a wry arch of his eyebrow. "You are not making the case you think you are, Corinna."

"I'm still here, Apollo."

"Because I won't let you leave. You are a prisoner. Or have you forgotten?"

I stop short, stunned. He senses that I've stopped, and halts as well. A hibiscus blooms huge and wild behind him. Roses surround us, fragrant and violently crimson. "You know, I think I have, actually."

He laughs. "And I'm the crazy one."

"No, you're not crazy. I never thought you were."

"I'm really not following you, Corinna. Please at least *try* to make sense."

"What if there could be someone who was loyal to you? To *you*, I mean. To Apollo. The man. The man behind the castle and the soldiers and the money." I pause, and I wait until he turns to look at me. "What if, Apollo? What if someone could see beyond the name? What if someone could help *you* see beyond... beyond everything you've just told me?"

He swallows hard. "Sounds lovely." A slow blink, a deep breath, and then I see the emergency blast doors slam down behind his eyes. "And as fictional as *Star Wars*."

He turns then, and walks away. "I have business to attend to."

I see what he's doing—delaying, avoiding.

And I see past it.

He's gone, then, and I'm left alone in the garden, mind whirling.

If there's anything I know for certain, it's that if I don't change the course of this thing, Apollo won't walk away from this alive.

What frightens me is I know I'm not about to let that happen.

I can't.

I won't.

Because I *see*.

I see him.

I'm the crazy one, in all this.

Because where do I go?

Back to the tower…

To wait for the man beneath the monster.

16

WAITING

We have a plan. A shitty one, a desperate one, but a plan.

Sasha drives one SUV with Valentine and me in the back. No one speaks. Duke and Thresh are in another, following behind us, and Puck and Lear are in a third, preceding us. Harris is at the controls of a helicopter, along with Anselm and his rifle; there was no time to procure something from RTI's fleet, so it's a thirty-year-old Sukhoi bought with cash, but it will serve the purpose.

It's a long drive from Madrid to Apollo's castle, and I don't know Spanish geography at all, so I have no clue where we're going. I'm too wound up to care, and it's a relief to just let the men handle those details.

I use the technique Anselm taught me to tune out of the drive.

What feels like an eternity later, I feel the SUV begin to slow, and then we turn off of the paved highway and I hear gravel under our tires. I rouse myself from my not-quite-sleep and look around—it's night.

"We're here?" I ask.

"Yes," Sasha answers. "Dawn is a few hours away. I think the plan is wait till first light."

I can't see much beyond the windows, the headlights illuminating wine grapevines in endless rows. Stars scintillate in their trillions.

Sasha touches his ear, listening. "*Da*, I agree." He slows the vehicle to a stop. Turns to look at us. "We can go closer this night. Harris and Anselm are at an airfield some ten minutes' flight from here. We will wait till dawn."

I look at Valentine, and he's as on edge and pissed as I am.

"No," I snap. "I'm not waiting for dawn." I shove open the door and start walking. "Let's go, Val."

He's beside me in a heartbeat, but then his hands grab my arms and he's stopping me. His eyes are tortured. "I'm not losing you now," he murmurs. "Nor her. Just wait, darling."

I push at him, but he won't let go. "Wait, wait! All you assholes want to do is wait! How can I wait? My daughter is *out there!* She's close, Val. Can't you feel her?"

His eyes water. "*Yes*, Kyrie, I feel her. You think this is easy for me? I want to blow his doors off and take his head for a trophy." He pulls me into his arms. "We have to trust Harris. This is what he does, honey."

"I know," I whisper, miserably. "But this is *Rin.*"

"We'll get her back, darling. We will. Just a few more hours. Just till first light."

I crumple, sagging in his hold. "I can't, Val. What if he hurts her?"

"He hasn't. He won't."

"What is he doing? He hasn't asked you for anything else, has he?"

A shake of his head. "I don't know what he's doing, but no. No word. I think he's waiting for us to make our move."

Sasha exits the vehicle, goes around to the back and opens the hatch. A few moments later, he's dressed in layers of black and gray, carrying a suppressed assault rifle, wearing night-vision headgear.

"Recon," he explains. "I make no contact, only look and see what I can see." He flips the headgear down as he enters the shadows behind the pool of light from the vehicle's headlights. "Remain here until further word."

He's gone then, melting into the shadows.

Valentine turns off the SUV, and when the lights go out, we're bathed in the near-total darkness of a rural night. The only light is from the countless stars overhead. He leans against the hood and pulls me back against him, his arms around my chest, and we settle in to wait.

A couple hours later, a patch of shadows detaches from the darkness and resolves into Sasha's form, flipping the night vision gear up.

"To wait was the correct decision," he says, leaning his rifle against the hood and wiping sweat from his forehead. "This property is crawling with men. There is a guard hut a half mile down the road, three men in it. They patrol the rows along the road in pairs. There's another guard hut every half mile, each more heavily fortified and manned than the last. The castle itself is what Lear says to us it is—impregnable. The island Gina held you on?" He waves a hand. "*Pssssh*. Its defenses were porous. Like a sponge, *da*? We had many options. Easy in, easy out—only had to kill a lot of guys. Simple." He gestures down the road. "This? *Nyet*. He is smart, this one. Very careful. I am nearly caught several times. I would not assault this position without…oh, maybe thirty like us, but I would like fifty. And proper explosives. It would be a war, not only a shooting of bad guys. Many would die. Innocents would die."

"Shit," I hiss.

"This is why we're waiting," Valentine says. "This is why we're doing what we're doing. I'm not going to war—not that I'm not willing to, if that's what it took to get my daughter back. But it would only end up in Rinna getting hurt. And Harris, Duke, and the guys? They'd die for us, for Rin. But they don't need to. Baby, *every* instinct I have says to just wait. To go in at first light, just you and me. Like we said."

I swallow hard, nod. "Okay." I sniffle, let out a sigh. "I agree. I get it."

Sasha puts a hand to my shoulder. "It is best, Mrs. Roth." A rough exhale. "If I thought we had half chance of pulling off this thing, I would be first in line to take all the bullets to get Rin back. I would die to get her back. But…this plan is best."

"I get it," I say, suppressing the urge to snap at him. "I just don't like it."

"No one does," Sasha says. "It is all of our natures to go in and shoot the bad guys. But sometimes, discretion is very truly the better part of valor, Mrs. Roth. And this is such a time."

I turn and lean against my husband, face in his broad hard chest. "And so…we wait."

"And so we wait," Valentine echoes.

17

A GAME NO LONGER

Reading is just a pretense for impatiently waiting, and a poor one at that. I read the same page a dozen times without comprehending a single word. Stubbornly, I keep at it. Force myself to read the page, slowly. And the next one.

After an hour or two of this, I give up. Pace the room, from one section of window to another, watching the sun play across the vines. A cloud occasionally floats over the sun, sending shadows dancing and twisting and skirling across the hills.

He has no movie theater, no television. I've never seen a single piece of electronics other than his phone.

Bored to death in a gilded cage.

I can't help but think of him. What else is there

to think about? His touch and his words, working magic on my skin, soaking my sex with heated need.

And god, his cock throbbing in my hands. The way he groaned, moved. I had him close, I know. Yet he pulled himself back from the edge. He disguised it with his domineering attitude, but at the heart of the matter, he stopped out of…concern. For me. For how I would feel. For what I want. Or rather, what he assumed I would want.

Sweet and gentle.

He doesn't recognize the ravenous beast inside me, clearly, if he thinks that's what I want.

I've had that. My previous sexual partners have been that—sweet, gentle, considerate. Nice.

Apollo isn't any of those things. Or, well, he *is* considerate, in a weird, twisted way, and he does his damnedest to disguise it.

I don't want sweet and gentle and considerate and nice.

What I want is Apollo.

I know, I know—it's foolish, it's almost incomprehensibly irrational. But it's true and I'm prone to deluding myself. I don't lie to myself. I want him, and I'm going to follow this insane desire of mine all the way down the rabbit hole.

Every effort I make to distract myself fails.

All I can think about is Apollo. Finishing what I started.

I'm crazed with it.

Somehow, hours pass. Afternoon yellow-gold sunlight sifts through the endless rows of vines, morphs subtly into red-gold.

I'm left pacing, almost frantically. Waiting for the sound of his boots on the stair, the creak of the hinges.

Finally, I hear it.

The muted thump of his lithe tread up the stairs. The latch opens. The hinges creak.

He stands in the open door and stares at me. "Still here?"

"Where would I go?"

He steps inside the room, closes the door, puts his back to it. Arms cross his chest. "Is that why you're still here? Still in this room, I mean?"

I feel a tremor of nerves jangling in my veins. I feel desire pooling behind my navel and spreading through me at the very sight of him—his arms stretching the sleeves of his shirt, the breadth of shoulder and chest. But I don't see the clothes—I see the body beneath them. The body I had naked. The flesh I had in my hands.

"No," I whisper. "That's not why."

His eyes flick over me. "Then why?"

I'm breathing rapidly, shallowly. I know he must see the lust crackling and sparkling in my eyes. The way I'm looking at him. The way I prowl across the room to him. It must be in the sway of my hips. The way I accentuate my step so my breasts bounce for him.

I don't answer—not in words.

I halt when the tips of my breasts touch his chest, mere inches between us. So close I can see streaks of lighter brown in his black eyes. So close I can see his pulse pounding in his throat. His casual, insouciant posture hides his own ravaging desire.

He changed his shirt—we ruined his last one. This is another white button-down, crisp, clean, and pressed. Tucked just so into his dress slacks. I trace a finger down the line of buttons. I flick open the top button. He doesn't react. One by one, all the way down, I undo the buttons of his shirt until it hangs open, baring the magnificent sculpture of his torso. I push it off, but instead of letting it fall to the floor, I take my time folding it. Set it on the coffee table. Cross back to him. Shirtless now in just his slacks, shoes, and a Patek Phillipe watch, he's still motionless and expressionless.

So it's that game, is it? Get a reaction from the statue?

I smile at him. Run my palms over his chest, over his abs. He tenses them, but otherwise is immobile. He won't stop me, but he won't help me, either. As if he could delay or deny or avoid this connection he himself first pointed out exists between us.

What I want most is to free his beautiful cock

from the prison of his pants, but the game's afoot. So, instead, I tease us both by dropping to my knees. His nostrils flare and his eyes narrow. I run my hands over his hips, down the front of his slacks. Over his calves. He frowns, not comprehending. His shoes are loafers, easily slipped off. Then his socks.

This gets a small sniff of amusement from him, that I remove his socks for him.

Still on my knees, I look at him, hands resting on my thighs. He just gazes down at me, expressionless and motionless once more. So, I remain on my knees. Working slowly, I slip the end of the belt free of the loop, tug it aside to release the pressure on the tongue, and slide the end out of the buckle. Let the belt drape open, pausing, as if deciding what's next.

Trace his zipper, and I feel him respond. Feel him stir behind the metal teeth.

Not yet.

I pull the belt out of the loops, slowly, one loop at a time. Roll it into a neat coil and set it aside. Open the button of his trousers, blatantly teasing him now, once again tracing my fingertip over the zipper. This gets me an audible swallow of his Adam's apple, his tongue sliding over his lips. A reaction, at last.

Small victories.

My movements as I lower his zipper are exaggeratedly slow. One tooth of the zipper at a time, my eyes on his. I allow a small smile on my lips. He does not reciprocate, but I didn't expect him to. In fact, I appreciate his commitment to our little game—he's got his poker face on, not a single flicker of emotion showing. His breathing is measured, however. Careful.

Zipper open, black cotton bulges in the opening, stretched by the bent curl of his imprisoned cock. I tug the trousers down, and they pool at his ankles. I free them one foot, the other, fold them, and put them with the shirt. Now, he's clad in nothing but a pair of tiny black briefs. His thighs are thick and powerful and smattered with a dusting of curly black hair. It's masculine and manly, and I like it. I touch his thighs, caressing them from hip to knee and up his hamstrings. Cup his buttocks. Dig my fingers into the firm muscle. This surprises him, a little—his eyes widen, just a touch.

The front of his briefs is tented, bulging. His cock is bent sideways, caught at the elastic and trapped, prevented from straightening. Eyes on his, I trace the length of it, visibly imprinted against the cotton. His thighs bunch, and he shifts his weight as I continue to tease him, tracing the outline, the head, the length of it. It thickens, engorges further.

He sucks in his belly, and I feel his cock pulse as he flexes it. Trying to free it without touching himself.

I run my fingers around the waistband, then, slowly working my fingers under the elastic until I've got it hooked, my hands at his sides. Tug down, but so only the back of the underwear pull down, over his buttocks, continuing to imprison his erection. When his butt is free of the underwear, I caress it. Cup it, play with it. Then bring my hands to his thighs, run them upward and hook them into the elastic on either side of his straining arousal.

Pull the elastic away from his body, bringing the head of his cock with it, stretching and stretching… until the member pulls free, slapping loudly against his belly.

And now, finally, I remove his underwear. These too, I fold and place with the rest of his clothing.

He's naked for me, now, still leaning against the door. His pose is casual, weight on one foot, arms crossed over his chest. As if he was fully dressed. As if he didn't have a raging hard-on.

I stand in front of him. Just look at him. There's nothing to say.

Instead of touching him, I draw the game out further yet.

Undo my belt, fold it. Set it with his stack of clothing. Peel off my tunic, and that too joins the pile of folded garments. Leggings. I pause a moment and let him look at me in my bra and underwear—his eyes rake over me, and his cock twitches.

Rewarding.

I revel in the hint of eager desire hiding in the narrowing of his eyes as he watches me reach behind my back and unclasp my bra. His chest expands and holds, brow furrowing as I let the bra fall forward off my shoulders, caught in my hands and placed with the rest of the clothing. Another pause, in just my underwear, now. For his benefit. Let him look. Watch his jaw clench. His eyes narrow further yet to mere slits.

I can't resist the urge to taunt him. Tease him. I play with my tits for him, lifting them up and flattening them high against my chest, covering them with my palms and holding them there, then finally letting them drop with a heavy bounce. Squeeze them, squish and release, lift and drop again. Tweak and twiddle my nipples until I'm driven to near gasping from the stimulation.

He lets out his held breath with a sound that's suspiciously like a growl.

Underwear last of all, stepping out of them and now just tossing them onto the pile, because who folds panties? Not me. Now we're both naked. He's erect and hard as a rock and flat against his belly, and my nipples are standing on end, aching, sensitive, and my pussy is soaked, drenched with desire. I'm surprised I'm not literally dripping with it.

I step closer to him, hold his gaze and swipe a finger through my seam, gathering my juices. Remembering how hungrily he devoured me, I slide my essence-slick finger into his mouth. His tongue laps at it, and he suckles the juices away.

God, so fucking erotic.

I want him.

I want to shove him to the hard floor and ride him until we're both screaming. God, I can see it. His hands on my hips, jerking me down onto him, my tits flying and bouncing, his cock driving into me. He'd fill me to aching, stretching fullness. And then some, I bet.

I've literally never in my life wanted to be fucked so badly.

I'm shaking with it.

Neither of us has said a word in many minutes. I'm not about to break that spell. He'll break first—I'll make sure of it.

I rest a hand on his chest, just touching him. The first contact. I meet his eyes, make sure he knows to follow my gaze—which trips and slides downward to his erection. I caress his chest. His neck. His ear. Brush my thumb across his lips, ignoring the way his mouth parts as if begging to let him even suck on my thumb, to taste any part of my body. Slide my touch over his shoulders, feeling the hard cords of muscle. Down his chest again, to his belly, to the thick blocks of his abdomen. His belly goes concave again, anticipating my touch.

Instead, I touch myself.

I can't help a hissed inhale as I slide my finger into my channel and drag my essence over my clit.

A gasp as I flick the nub to send a searing flood of aroused pleasure through my body. I press my lips to his throat, leaning against him so my tits smash against his chest, and I kiss him—throat, slowly, cheek, corner of his mouth, chin, shoulder. Anywhere but his mouth. And I circle my clit.

Teasing him.

Teasing myself.

I'm hyperaware of his cock, bobbing between us, begging for my hand.

Dammit, I can't ignore the siren song of his cock. Can't. Not any longer.

I close my hand around him, and he sucks in a breath between his teeth, blows it out shakily between pursed lips. I stroke his length. As slowly as I can, I caress him from tip to root, and all the while the fingers of my other hand work soft, slow, fluttering circles over my clit.

Damn the man, he doesn't move.

I twist my fist on the way down, pause to cradle his balls in my palm and massage them before gliding my touch back up. My fingers press harder against my clit, their speed quickening. I gasp as lightning builds in flashing, searing bolts through my limbs and into my toes and behind my eyes, scouring my pussy with blasting bolts of white-hot arousal. I lean against him more fully, burying my nose in his neck, writhing against him as I dip helplessly at the knees.

Pump his cock, trying to keep it slow, to keep my grip loose and soft, and failing. His breathing is rough and ragged, but his body is otherwise stone-still.

My hips flex, now, pushing forward against my flying fingers. My fist clutches at his cock as I start the ascent to climax, squeezing until he grunts in protest, and I release him, forcing my touch to lighten. I'm gasping against the side of his throat, all my weight leaning against his body, tits flattened, knees threatening to give out as I gasp and whimper into orgasm. I can't help the whip-quick stroke of my hand on his cock as I come. He pants, and his abs tighten. A growl escapes him.

I mewl like a day-old kitten when my orgasm strikes me, hitting like a freight train. Not as good as the one he gave me, albeit. But it still has me shrieking through gritted teeth with the shocking intensity of it.

I force my caressing of his pulsing cock to slow, even as I come and come. It's a contradiction in needs—my orgasm wracking me into helpless twitching and thrashing and writhing against him, but I'm not ready for him come and I refuse to let go of his cock but yet also want to drag it out. Force a reaction from him.

The climax reaches a crescendo as my fingers fly side-to-side, and I feel everything inside me clench, crush with the furious intensity of it. My knees finally give out, and I drop to my knees in front of him.

Lean my cheek against his belly, gasping, and turn to look up at him. Palm his hips, and push away to kneel upright rather than resting on him. His eyes are heavy-lidded, hooded, sparking with arousal.

Precum leaks from the tip of his cock. I clasp his erection in both hands and keep my eyes on his…lick the clear fluid from the weeping hole at the tip. This finally results in a growl, a flex of his hips.

"Corinna…" he whispers, as I part my lips, telegraphing my intentions clearly.

My lips wrap around his cock, and I taste the salt of his flesh and the musk of his precum. Tongue him. Take him as far as I feel comfortable, and back away.

"Corinna," he murmurs again.

I caress him with both hands and meet his eyes. "Did you think you could get away that easily?" I ask. "That you could growl at me and be all gruff and terse, and that I'd just…let it go?"

He rests his hands on my shoulders, acquiescing to the need to touch me, finally. "Yes, I did, actually."

"You were sadly mistaken, in that case."

"So it seems."

I cup his balls in one hand, cradle and caress them. With the other, I stroke his length with slow twisting touches, bringing him away from his body and taking him into my mouth. Lower my mouth around him, lift away. Stroke the root, caress the heavy sac. All three at once, then, sliding his thick length through my lips in a slow rhythm and twisting short strokes around the thick base of him and massaging his taut balls in my cradling palm.

"Fuck," he whispers. "Corinna, I warned you what I would do, did I not?"

I don't let him free of my mouth when I answer, hum an affirmative around him as I gaze up at him. "Mmm-hmmm?"

"Is that what you want?" he growls, hips pushing as I feel the climax rising in him. "Are you *trying* to push me to the breaking point?"

I don't slow in my ministrations. I take him from my mouth and plunge both fists around his throbbing length, and hold his eyes. "Yes," I whisper. "I am."

He watches me caress his cock for a few moments before answering. "When I break, I won't be sweet for you, Corinna. I cannot be gentle. My need to be inside you is too great. Don't tempt me into something you're not ready for."

I look up at him with a frowning smirk, a wry twist of my lips and a puzzled frown of my brow. "What about me makes you think I want you to be anything but what you are? At what point have you shown me a sweet side, Apollo?"

"Right now," he says. "This is me being sweet. Letting you toy with me."

I take him into my mouth, take him deep, caressing and squeezing and stroking with my hands where

I cannot reach with my mouth, suckling and swallowing around him. Back away when he begins to grunt.

"I am toying with you," I whisper, licking the tip of him. Up the sides, as if he were a lollipop. "But this isn't you being sweet. This is you clinging to the notion that you're in control."

"You think I can't and won't stop you the moment I'm ready?"

I just smile at him. Lick upward along a winding blue-purple vein from root to tip, rolling my mouth over the broad plump head, wrapping my lips around the rim. Suckle, tonguing the tip. His groan is long and low. I find a slow rhythm, then, using the trio of touches he seems to respond to best, mouthing around his cock, stroking his length, cupping his balls. That last one seems to really get him—the more I cradle them, the more I massage and play with them, the heavier his breathing gets. Lord knows I'm not using my mouth any faster, nor my hands. But yet he's exhibiting all the signs of nearing climax: his hips flex and push, his thighs are tensed and bunched, his abs braced and tight, his breathing is rough and shallow.

It's tempting to think I've got him where I want him—about to come. But I don't take anything for granted where he's concerned. I took him to the edge with just my hands last time, and he pulled away at the last second, bearing down with remarkable control to stop himself.

I won't let him pull away, this time.

Now that I've found the combination that makes him respond, I keep at it. Swirl my tongue around the head on the upstroke, swallow around him when I take him deep. Stroke him faster with my hand, plunging my touch faster and faster.

He starts to growl, and I feel his hips pushing.

Yes, fuck my mouth.

I don't say it. I'm too busy to talk.

He finally breaks a little—his hands crown my head, as if he wants to bury them into my hair, but it's braided. He grunts as I work him faster, and roughly unties the twine binding the braid. Digs his fingers through the mass of blond, shaking the braid loose, and then he wraps the length of my hair around his fists and clutches at my head.

He doesn't guide my movements, nor does he try to force me deeper. He just holds and follows, and his hips flex harder now. I spit him out and back away, gaze up at him and use just my hands for a moment or two, fast and hard, until his brow furrows and his jaw tenses.

His hips are flexing nonstop now.

Abruptly, I let go of him. Nothing, no touch, no mouth. His groan is exasperated, desperate. His head tilts back but his eyes stay on mine.

"Goddammit, Corinna," his whisper is ragged.

I palm my breasts and gaze back. "You think I'd tease you like this and not follow through?"

I open my mouth, and lean toward him—his jaw drops open as if encouraging me to follow suit. I hold his eyes as I lean over him, until the last second, when I take him into my mouth. I slide my hands over his ass and hold him, pull at him. He thrusts, once, lightly, and I groan. It's fake, of course, meant for him. And it works. He thrusts again, and again, and I encourage this with my hands, pulling at the hard bubble of his ass with each thrust. My lips slide along his flesh and his ass tenses under my hands, and he grunts, groans with each thrust.

"Fuck," he whispers, his voice breaking.

He pulls away, as I'd expected him to, dancing out of my reach and pacing away a few angry, stiff steps. I just remain where I am, on my numb knees.

He stands facing away from me, shoulders hunched, heaving ragged breaths. "Sultry little siren, you are, Corinna," he murmurs, fists clenched. "You make me crazy."

I stand up, flex my legs to loosen my knees. Walk over to him. Embrace him from behind, pressing my breasts against his back, lips touching the base of his neck with kisses. I reach around him and find his waiting erection. "Who are you trying to convince with this, Apollo? And what is it you're trying to say?"

He doesn't answer. I lift on my toes to watch my hands caress him. He's panting hard.

"You think by refusing to let me make you come you're proving something to me? To yourself?" I bite his earlobe. Not exactly gently, either. "Or do you *really* think I'm afraid of what you'll do when you stop trying to hold yourself back?"

He can't help himself—he's close; he thrusts into my hands as I work his cock with two greedy, stroking hands.

"You don't know me," he murmurs.

"Not a bit." I don't slow. I kiss his neck. "I'm a complete and total fool. I am absolutely being ruled by lust. I know it. I know I'll likely regret this, at some point."

"You're a fool, Corinna. I'm giving you every chance to bail out of this inadvisable course of action."

"Why?" I let go of him and find his hands. Guide them to my ass. "Don't you want me?"

"More than is logical."

"And I'm telling you I want this."

"I just don't understand why you would."

"Me either, and I'd really like to. Maybe I'm just horny." I writhe against him as I resume caressing his length. "Or maybe I'm horny and attracted to you and I haven't been with anyone in a quite a while, and maybe something about all this is just turning me on like fucking crazy. Maybe I'm turned by the fact that this whole game between us is so fucked up and wrong and…forbidden."

"This isn't what I intended when I bought you here."

"Oh no?" I feel his hands grip, tighten. "You were hoping, though."

"In my wildest fantasies, I did not see this happening."

"Yet still you resist."

He's pumping into my hand. Grinding. Panting.

"Fuck!" he snarls, and twists away.

But instead of walking away from me, he lunges at me. His hands seize my face and his lips crush against mine, and I feel his hard, hot, throbbing cock dig into my belly. He pinions my wrists to prevent me from touching him, and then he's walking me backward across the room, his kiss hot and furious, tongue slashing against mine. It's rough, wild. Savage, even. I'm quick-marched backward, and I can barely keep up with the sudden onslaught of his mouth, the march backward, the assault of his tongue and the grip on my wrists. I want to touch him, to claw at him, to make him come. I fight him, fight to free my wrists, and this only makes his kiss all the rougher.

The seaman's chest hits the back of my knees and I sit abruptly onto it. He takes no mercy on me for the hard-edged discomfort of the position, leaning me backward onto it and pinning my hands over my head. One hand pinning mine, with the other he hooks two fingers against my opening and spears them inside me, curling them in a thrust deep inside, withdrawing to tap my clit. I cry out, writhing against his hand. Alternating between thrusting his fingers inside me to mimic fucking and circling my clit, he brings me to orgasm in record time.

By the time I'm able to draw a breath after the intensity of the abrupt orgasm, he has me in his arms and he's carrying me around to the bed. He tosses me, and I'm airborne for a moment, and then as I hit the mattress, he's on top of me. Kissing me. Touching me. One-handed, all the while, because he still has my hands pinned over my head.

He slowly pulls away from the kiss, and I'm gasping, hips thrusting with need—he's left me moments from another climax. He hovers over me, and then he reaches out and snags one of the lengths of gauzy white curtain at the headboard corner of the bed. In a lightning-fast movement, he wraps it around my wrist and ties it off. Before I realize what's happened, my other hand is bound.

Kneeling over me, a predatory smile steals across his lips. "Now, Corinna—*now* you are mine."

"Wh—what are you going to do?" There is, I have to admit, a slight glimmer of real fear that I've misjudged him, that I've just done the most foolhardy thing I could possibly do, in allowing him to bind me like this.

Yet, I'm still soaked with desire and shaking with the tremors of post-orgasmic rapture even as I clench inside with the unfinished heat of another impending climax.

The fear has me wild.

I must be really fucked up to be getting off on this.

He just smirks. "Anything I want."

No reassurance.

He kisses my throat, and I tilt my head back to accept it—his lips descend slowly, kissing here and there in random dotting touches until he reaches my breasts. And these, he plies with a thousand hot kisses, licking and suckling, fondling and caressing, flicking my nipples and twisting them until I'm aching, gasping. And then, when I can't stand it anymore, he kisses down my belly and over my hips. I fling my legs apart, and he delves down between them, and he licks me with a fat swipe of his tongue.

"You taste like honey," he murmurs. "Have you ever tasted yourself?"

I shake my head, but he's not waiting for an answer. He dips a finger inside me and puts it to my lips—I taste myself, musky and indeed almost sweet. His tongue slithers into me, slides up my seam. A finger enters me, his tongue circles me.

I writhe, pull at the bonds on my wrists, arch off the bed as he laps at me and fingers me to the peak of climax and pushes me over. He's not content with that, though. He pushes me to another climax, and another. Uses his fingers to give his mouth a break, and then when I'm close yet again, writhing and whimpering, thrashing and thrusting, he assaults me with his tongue all over again and licks away my climax.

I come so hard, so many times it hurts.

"Stop," I whimper. "I can't take anymore."

He doesn't.

This time, instead of a rise to orgasm and a quick topple over, it's different. It's a slow, difficult rise to the edge and he keeps me there for a long time, reading my desperation in the way I whimper and thrash, and pulling me back from the edge again and again, until it's akin to torture, until I'm openly weeping with the desperate need to come, to find release any way I can get it.

"Apollo, god, please…" I whimper.

He rises up from between my legs, his stubble wet and glistening black with my juices. "No, Corinna. Not yet."

"God, you bastard!" I snap. "Stop teasing me."

"You teased me."

"I did not. I would have made you come. I wanted to, tried to, and you stopped me."

"Not on my terms."

"And everything…" I break off and whimper as he teases me toward the edge I so desperately need. "Everything has to be on your terms?"

"Yes." He flicks me with his tongue, teasing, teasing—*flick, flick, flick*, then smears his tongue against my clit until I'm writhing and wailing.

Slowly, so slowly, he tongues me right to the very edge of climax, teetering, mad with it, screaming for it.

Instead of giving it to me, he crawls up my body, kissing his unhurried way up to my mouth—and all the while I'm losing the edge, and it feels like I might die if I don't get there, if I don't finally find the fucking orgasm he's been denying me for I don't even know how long, now.

His mouth touches mine, and I kiss him eagerly. His fingers slide into me, curling, gathering the seeping essence inside me. Kneels over me, licks at his fingers. "You taste so good."

I pull at the gauze around my wrists, straining to get to him, growling, and he just laughs. Touches his fingers to my lips.

"Taste."

I lick his fingers, tasting my own honey. "More," I whisper.

His eyes widen. "Dirty girl. You want more?"

I nod.

He puts his lips to my ear, whispers. "I've got you

tied up and helpless. I could do anything I wanted to you." He licks the shell of my ear, and I hiss, writhe. "You said I'd never shown you a sweet side. Well, here it is." He shelters me with his body, pressing himself to me, skin to skin, and I feel him nudging at my entrance, nuzzling, preparing to enter me. "I'll promise you something, to set your mind at ease."

I yank at the bonds in response.

"I'm clean, I promise you."

And then, I feel him enter me, a slow stretching slide of his massive cock into me, splitting me open and filling me and filling me until I'm crying out with the wild pressure of it, the burning ache of taking him, inch by thick, throbbing inch. When he's buried in me to the hilt, my legs move of their own accord and wrap around him, and he whispers to me again.

"Another promise I'll make you, Corinna." A kiss to my cheek, my jaw. "I won't come inside you without protection."

A thrust, then. Slowly withdrawing, pulling out until I'm trembling with the aching emptiness and already crazed to have him back inside me.

"I just had to feel you, Corinna." He arches his back, groans low in his chest as he thrusts back into me. "I had to feel your sweet pussy." Another thrust. "I couldn't wait."

"Oh fuck, Apollo."

He thrusts again. And again. And with each

thrust, I feel that edge I'd lost rise up at the base of my spine, and now it's hotter and deeper and wilder than before.

"Tell me something, Corinna," he murmurs, leaning upright, tucking my feet into his armpits. "Do you still want to taste yourself? You seem to like the way your own pussy tastes, don't you, dirty girl?"

A thrust, slow, angled downward, striking deep inside so I feel torn apart, split into pieces by him, made mad by the magic of this beautiful cock of his.

"Do you, Corinna?"

"Yes," I whisper. I'll say anything as long as he doesn't stop fucking me.

So what does he do? He stops fucking me.

He pulls out and kneels astride me. Shifts closer, bracing a hand on the wall. "Taste yourself now, Corinna."

His cock is at my mouth, glistening wet. My essence drips down his length in trickling rivulets. I have no shame, no decorum, no inhibitions. Anything, anything to taste him, to feel him, to please him—anything, so long as I never have to stop feeling the things he makes me feel.

I crane my neck and open my mouth, and he thrusts in. Now I taste him—I taste *us*, my honey and his musk mingling, a nectar I could only find sweet in a moment of madness such as this.

But sweet indeed it is to me, now, and I lap it all

away, suck it off of him, let him out of my mouth and lick at the sides of him and suck him down into my throat again until the only wetness coating his cock is my own saliva.

By the time I'm done, he's growling, chest heaving. "Fucking hell, Corinna. The things you do to me."

"Untie me," I snap, snarling at him like a rabid dog, "and I'll show you what I'll do to you."

"I don't know. I rather like this."

He settles between my wide-spread thighs again and delves into me once more, his bare cock throbbing between the tight-stretched lips of my pussy, sliding deep into me. Slow thrusts, each one an eternity, a thrust from tip to root, nearly falling out of me and then driving in until his hips meet mine.

He doesn't stop. I cry out with each one, cling to his waist with my legs, locking them around him so he won't ever stop. I don't care about anything—the kidnapping, that I'm not on birth control, nothing. Only the merging of our bodies, his perfect beautiful body on mine, big and hard and warm and so strong, his cock sliding inside me and filling me until I can barely stand it, his breath on my cheek, his hands on me, one bracing his weight and the other cupping my face and caressing my breasts.

"Corinna," he whispers, moving harder now, faster. "God…*fuck*, Corinna."

"Apollo," I whimper, legs crushing around him

to keep him close, my hips now slamming up against his. "Don't stop, Apollo, please, fuck, don't you dare fucking stop."

He's groaning and growling now, and I *know* he's close. Finally, I'll feel him wild and uncontrolled, feel him come with me, for me. It'll be so beautiful.

"Fuck…oh god, *Corinna…*" He's slamming into me, now, both hands braced. Fucking me with abandon, driving into me with power and wild release.

He roars, but instead of feeling him come, feeling the rush of his release inside me, he rolls backward. "FUCK!" he snarls.

"Apollo…what? Why?" I yank and tear at the bonds until it hurts my wrists. "Untie me, goddamn you! Why'd you stop?"

He's on all fours, arched, heaving. "Bare. No protection."

"I don't care!"

"You would, later."

"Come here," I whisper. "Please."

He looks at me, eyes tortured. "I have an unopened box of condoms in the bathroom. I don't keep them in here." A shake of his head. "I've never brought a woman here."

"Later." I writhe at the bonds. "Condom later. Just…come here. Untie me, *please*."

He frees one wrist, then the other, and the moment I'm free I tackle him, using a wrestling move

Duke taught me to flip him to his back. He's stunned at the speed of it, and I take advantage. Sink onto him in one move, crying out as he penetrates me. I sink down so my ass slaps onto his chest.

"Corinna, wait..." he growls, but he's helpless, his own need now taking over. His hands grip my hips and he thrusts.

"Trust me."

He shakes his head. "I trust no one."

I brace my palms on his chest and ride him, softly and slowly. "Trust me, Apollo." I drape my breasts against his chest, kiss him. "Just try. Trust me."

He's tense all over, warring with himself, seconds from throwing me off of him—he will, I know it. He has a line, and he will not allow himself to cross it.

I've no intention of making him cross that line. Because he's absolutely right. I can trust him that he's clean, but pregnancy is another matter.

Now, I have one focus: his release.

I ride him. He's wracked, taut, helpless to not move with me, but fighting the edge, pulling himself back again and again from it.

Finally, he grabs me by the ass and pulls at me. "I can't...Corinna. I can't stop myself."

I slide off of him and crawl down his body, tits dragging at his skin, until I reach his cock. He arches up, watching me. I cradle his cock in my hands and pull it to my mouth.

He groans, a ragged, broken sound, as I take him into my mouth. He flexes upward, and his hands bury into my hair and tighten, gripping hard. “Oh fuck, Corinna…god.”

It’s a plea.

I pump his base and massage his balls and suck him until he starts thrusting, helpless not to, and I let him thrust into my mouth. He cries out, a breathless snarl, and his hips flex, lock upward, and I wrap my lips around the head and stroke him—not hard, not fast, but slow. *Slow*. Twisting downward strokes while I tongue the head of him and suckle.

“Oh *fuck*, Corinna…Corinna.” I taste it moments before he warns me. “Oh fuck, I’m coming.”

He floods my mouth, and I can’t possibly begin to swallow it all, don’t try. It spills out of my mouth and trickles down my chin, and I keep the slow pace of my stroking fists around his thick root. He comes more, and more, and I stop trying to swallow it, let it spill out of my mouth and back onto him, until he’s coated and dripping with his own cum.

I give him the same treatment he gave me: I don’t let him stop, I keep plunging my fists around him and suckling the trickling, leaking head of his cock until he’s going soft and jerks away from me, twitching and gasping.

I collapse to my back next to him.

"Shit," he breathes. His head turns, and he looks at me. "You surprise me."

I wipe at my mouth, my chin. "I know."

He laughs. It's a beautiful sound, a burst of true amusement. "You know."

"You made assumptions about me, Apollo."

"I did. I assumed you were…a good girl." Another laugh. "It seems I was incorrect."

"Seems so." I roll toward him, and to my shock, he extends his arm around me and pulls me against him. "Thing is, Apollo—I *am* a good girl. Or, I was." I drag a finger through the sticky mess on his belly. "Then I met you. And I'm suddenly…not so good after all."

"I should go clean up." He doesn't move, however.

I laugh. "Legs not working?"

He huffs a laugh and shakes his head. "No."

I pat his chest and roll out of bed. "I've got it."

"Corinna…"

"It's fine, Apollo." I smile, pause, and then crawl back onto the bed to kiss him. "One, I need to brush my teeth and wash my face. Two, you need to rest." I flip his soft cock to one side. "I've got plans for you."

He watches me crawl off the bed and I feel his eyes on me as I walk away. I clean his cum off of my face and use his mouthwash to clean my mouth out. Not that he tasted bad—far from it. But I don't think anyone wants that after taste in their mouth for long.

I soak a washcloth in warm water and return to him, use it to clean him thoroughly—the mess on his belly, the stickiness from his cock.

Both of us something like clean, I get back in bed. He's on his side, just looking at me, head pillowed on his arms.

"What?" I ask.

He shrugs. "Nothing."

"Don't nothing me, Apollo. There's something."

"I already said—you surprise me."

"Why?"

"It's not that I thought you were good. I did, and you are." He gestures at the bed, at me. "This? It doesn't make you bad. Or dirty. It's just sex—liking it makes you human." He's quiet a moment. "What surprises me is that you..." a shrug, a shake of his head. "I'm not sure how to put it."

"Try."

"I suppose...it seems like perhaps you...care." It's said quietly. "You aren't just giving in to lust."

"I don't know what it is, Apollo. It's lust. I haven't had sex in months. And...I do like sex. A lot."

"I can tell." A smirk.

I slap his arm. "Don't be mean."

"I'm not. I appreciate it about you—I recognize that I am very much the beneficiary of the fact that you like to have a lot of sex."

"I didn't say I have sex a lot," I laugh, "I said I *like*

sex a lot. It's different." I shrug, sighing. "But I guess maybe it is a lot. Bryn and I go out with our friends fairly frequently, down in the islands. I hook up."

He shakes his head. "It's more than merely lust." He stares into me. "I should know. I've indulged in pure lust. It's all I've ever known. The meeting of needs, yes?"

I nod. "Yeah, I know what you mean. That's what it is, mostly."

"Not always?"

I shake my head. "There've been a few boys who captured my heart." I flip a hand. "For a while, at least. But they can't hold my interest, much less my heart. So it always ends up in an amicable enough break up, and there's someone new the next time I go out with Bryn and the others."

"How do they capture your heart?"

I roll to my back and look up at the ceiling. "They have a cute smile. It makes my heart go pitter-patter, you know?"

He shakes his head. "No, I do not know. My heart has never..." he flaps a hand. "Gone pitter-patter."

I snicker. "No, I suppose not."

He gives me a look. "And that's all it takes? A cute smile?"

"No. They're funny. They have good manners." I pause, think. "Inevitably, they find out who my dad is, and how they react decides a lot. If he's all awed and gooey about it, see ya. If he tries to get stuff out of me, see ya. But if he's cool about it? Sure, we can play."

"So you like nice, cute, good boys."

I snort. "Yes. Island boys with good hair and sexy skin and a killer grin and tight little bodies. Or tourist boys with expensive smiles and expensive haircuts who are only in the islands for a few days."

"Boys." He says this derisively. "Island boys. Tourist boys. All boys."

I nod. "Yeah. And maybe that's why they can't hold my interest."

"You said they can't hold your heart."

"Right. They can't."

"What does it take to hold your heart?"

I laugh. "Dunno. No one's ever done it."

"I am not nice."

"I've noticed."

"But I like to think I have good hair."

"And a killer grin, and a tight body, and a sexy skin," I say, smirking at him.

"If you insist."

"I do."

"What I am not, is a boy."

"I've noticed this as well."

"So, then…I don't seem to be your type."

I shrug. "I've already said I can't explain it," I say, gesturing between us. "I just know that at some point, I lost my damn mind. I can't seem to stop wanting you. Something about you makes me crazy. I know it's crazy. I know that this is…it won't end well. It can't. But I also can't seem to bring myself to care."

He sighs. "I've never known anyone like you," he says. "I don't know what I was expecting, but not you. Not the person you are. Your beauty. Your courage."

"It's not courage, Apollo," I say with a wry laugh. "It's insanity."

"What I was expecting least of all was this." He traces a fingertip over my breast.

I frown, giggling. "What, boobs? You didn't expect boobs when you kidnapped a girl?" I laugh. "Didn't you have photos of me or something creepy?"

A sigh. "That isn't what I meant, Corinna."

"I know that," I say, snorting. "You have no sense of humor."

"No, not really." A glance at me. "The photos I have of you are not creepy. Except in that you didn't know they were being taken. Standard surveillance photos, nothing more."

"Which is creepy."

A shrug, dismissing the topic. "What I meant was…" a puzzled frown, as he trails off and tries again. "Not sex, exactly, though I wasn't expecting that." Another silence. "I wasn't expecting the…quality of it. The intensity of it."

"The first time you touched me, I knew it would be intense, so I can't say I wasn't expecting it. But exactly *how* good and *how* intense? No, I wasn't expecting that."

He rolls out of bed. "I'll be right back."

He vanishes into the bathroom, and I hear him take a very long pee, wash his hands. He comes back with a box of condoms. Sets it on the bedside table.

Crawls onto the bed and prowls toward me. "Now. Enough talk. I've not had my fill of you, yet."

My heart hammers, and my body responds instantly, arousal kicking on and firing on cylinders. "Yet?"

"Yet," he confirms.

"So you may at some point get enough of me."

He laughs, an amused growl. "Remains to be seen. Thus far, that seems rather unlikely." He teases his tongue over my belly. "Now. Will you be good for me, or do I have to tie you up again?"

"I'll be good."

"In that case…" he puts his mouth over me. "Let me hear you scream."

18

THE SEEDS OF LOVE'S POTENTIAL...MAYBE

It's different, this time.

There's no power play, no tug of war for control.

He brings me to orgasm slowly, without hurry. His tongue moves in lavish, slippery circles, and he obeys my every subtle cue, speeding when I start to moan, backing away at just the right moment so I don't come too soon. No fingers, this time—all tongue. I clutch his hair and I ride his face and writhe against him and beg him to never stop. I feel no embarrassment as I plead with him to make me come.

And when he does, after a measureless time of edging me to it, it's with his name on my lips. My plea is his name, crying it out loud.

He doesn't let me down from the dizzy peak of

climax for a long time, until I have to push him away beg him to stop.

He does, this time.

He kneels beside me and reaches for the box of condoms. I take the string from him and rip one free, tear it open with my teeth. Roll the latex onto him with slow strokes of my hands. Instead of reaching to guide himself into me, he brings my mouth to his. Pulls me to him, and we lie down together, him beneath me. And for a long moment, we just kiss. Delicate and fraught at first, and then with increasing heat and building fervor. His tongue finds mine and I cup his jaw; he cradles my ass in his hand, pets it and caresses. I reach between us and clutch at his cock, stroke the latex-covered length, and he grips me by the hips and lifts me onto him. I straddle him and sit upright.

He stares up at me, and his hands cup my breasts. “So fucking perfect,” he breathes.

I gasp as he fondles them, thumbs my nipples to aching erection. Lift onto my knees and guide him to me, nestle the tip of him inside my lips. Lower myself onto him, just an inch or two. Roll my hips in wide circles, hands on his chest. He groans, caresses my ass with both hands, pulls at me.

“Need it,” he growls. “Need you, Corinna.”

I grin, and cup my breasts and play with them—and then sink down to take him all the way. “This?” I ask, breathless. "This is what you need?" I lift up, and slam back down.

"Fuck—*yes*, that." He holds my hips and helps me fall down onto him, harder. "That—I need that. Need *you*."

I give it to him, without reservation. I rise and I fall, slowly, and he greedily watches every jounce and bounce, every move of every curve of my body as I ride him. When I ache and can't find the edge, I lean over him and brace my hand on him and I touch myself, find the light quick circling touch that brings me where I need to be. He thrusts into me in a slow, steady rhythm, providing a lush counterpoint to the quick, desperate flying circles of my fingers.

Climax smashes through me with abrupt power, hitting me like a wrecking ball, crashing through me and tearing a scream from my lips. I can't move, paralyzed by it—he does it for me, for us, continuing to slam into me, and his fingers take over as mine clutch at his chest with clawed strength, and he keeps me coming until I break with a gasp.

I still on him, his cock sunk deep.

He just gazes at me, fierce and wild. "My turn."

And he throws me off him, toppling me to the bed. I land on my side, and he pounces, rolling me to my back and grabbing my jaw to seize a searing kiss. "Remember what I promised you? In the orangery?"

I can't think straight. "No?"

"About how I would fuck you, given the chance?"

"Ohhh," I breathe. "You told me…you told me you would take me from behind and spank me. And…something else. I don't remember." I reach for him, cup his balls and massage them. "I can't remember the other because the first thing you said sounded so good."

He kisses me again, and then pulls away. "Show me how you want it, Corinna."

I just stare up at him, defiant. "Make me."

He laughs, a dark growl. "I was hoping you'd say that."

He grabs me by the hips and flips me to my belly. His hands carve down my back from shoulders to waist, soft and smooth and gentle, and then he frames my ass in both hands. Caresses it.

Smack!

I cry out at the unexpected slap that leaves my ass cheek stinging. Before I can catch my breath—*smack!* He's spanked the other side.

"That hurt!" I whimper.

"Want me to stop?" His tone makes it a challenge.

I pause, think. Shake my head. "No."

Smack! The first side again. The stinging burn soaks through me—soaks my pussy with desire. Dear lord. The next spank I'm ready for, and it still shocks me. He's not being gentle—this is real, loud, resounding spanking—*hard*.

I fucking love it.

Especially when he grabs my hips and jerks them up and back, yanks me backward so my ass is in the air and my top half is pressed to the mattress. Kneels behind me, grips himself and nuzzles my opening with his cock, teasing it against my lips, feathering it in light circles until I moan and move my hips, seeking it.

"Please, Apollo," I beg. "Please. Let me have it."

He groans at my words, and sinks into me as if he can't resist my plea. As he drives in, he spanks me again—*smack-smack!* One side and the other in immediate turn. He pulls back, palms soothing where he's smacked my ass cheeks. Then he thrusts in hard and spanks me again. Just one side, this time. And the next thrust, the other side.

I touch myself. I can't help it—it's so hot, so erotic, so wild and dirty that I just *need* to. It only heightens the pleasure I get each time he fucks into me with a hard slap to my ass.

Faster, now.

Each thrust a spank, and with each spank I circle my clit with my finger and I cry out, scream, wail, whimper.

I explode again—harder than I've ever come, the wracking intensity of it wrenching sobs out of me, tears of overwhelmed ecstasy trailing down my cheeks as I thrust back against him, wild and crazed.

"Apollo!"

He growls. "Corinna, my god, Corinna."

"Come with me, Apollo," I cry. "Right now, come *with* me."

His hands cradle my ass, now, and hold me, pull me backward, and his thrusts seem to…stagger. As if he can't control them anymore. A thrust deep, and a groan…and then he's lost and out of control, slamming into me hard and fast, hips slapping against my tender ass as he drives himself to his climax.

I'm still coming.

When he joins me, I feel it. I feel him release, feel him unleash inside me. He cries out, roaring wordlessly, our movements in unison. Again and again. Until I'm weak and panting and he's pushed in as deep as he can go, as if he never wants to pull out of me.

We collapse to the bed as one, but instead of holding me and catching our breath together, he does something utterly shocking.

He rolls me to my back with a rough shove and covers me with his body, and he braces himself with one hand beside my ear, the other snarling in my tangled hair and jerking my face up to his. His mouth is hot and his tongue demands entrance. My hands seek him on their own, one tangling in his hair as fiercely as his is in my mine, pulling him down to me as roughly as he pulls me up. My other hand smooths down the muscled valley of his back, scratches and claws as he kisses me, smoothing over the claw marks and then clawing again. The harder I dig my fingers into him, the more he groans into the kiss and the harder he kisses me. I pull at his buttocks and he gives me his weight, his arm cradling under my neck and the other cupping my jaw.

It's an endless kiss—searing and soaring, a crashing and a coalescing of skin and soul.

Finally, we part, each of us gasping and breathless.

He rolls off me, pulls me into his arms. We breathe together, neither speaking.

I'm shaken to the core by what just happened.

He is too, I can tell.

I don't know how long we lie there entwined in silence, breathing. My thoughts are a chaotic whirlwind of confused emotion and frenetic arousal. You'd think after having had him twice in less than an hour I'd be sated, but I'm not. Not even close.

The opposite, if anything.

I want him. I need him.

I'm scared of him—of his life. Of the monster mask he wears—and it is a mask, I believe. I don't think it's truly him. A monster wouldn't hold me like this. Wouldn't have kissed me so ravenously—not *after* fucking me into oblivion. A monster wouldn't care about my pleasure before his own, and he clearly does.

But despite being merely a mask and not the true

man, he still chooses to wear it, to do dark and violent things. To those who deserve it, perhaps. But still.

Yet here in this tower, in this bed, I see beneath the mask, to the man he could be.

I want to see more of that man.

Layered over these thoughts is a thick, scorching blanket of erotic need. How can I want him, so? It's fierce and furious and untenable. It can't last. But it's insatiable and undeniable.

Merely lying here in his arms, I'm trembling with arousal. Soaked with it.

"Why are you shaking, Corinna?" His voice is a husky murmur.

My lips curl into a smile against his chest. "You've got a tiger by the tail." I reach down and tenderly scratch at his balls, tickling them. "And she's *very* hungry."

He groans, a low growl. "Permit me a moment to clean up, in that case."

"A moment is too long," I whisper. "Need you *now*."

He rolls out from under me and out of bed—he's beginning to unfurl while still wearing the condom from last time. "Very hungry tiger indeed."

I watch his tight ass move as he walks into the bathroom—I hear the sink running. My soaked core demands attention. He's taking too long.

God, who am I?

I've always revved high, sexually. I discovered masturbation rather young, coinciding with the advent of my period—and also my tendency to steal my mom's steamy novels. I started messing around with boys during trips to the nearby USVI and British islands not much after that, and I've taken every opportunity I can get to satiate my constant need for sexual attention. Or, rather, stimulation.

But this? Apollo does something else to me. Takes my already high-octane sex drive and puts it into overdrive—lights the afterburners and sends my arousal into the stratosphere.

I'm nearly writhing in the bed with the need to feel his mouth between my thighs, to taste his cock, to ride him—anything. Everything.

I slip out of bed and into the bathroom, find him cleaning himself with a washcloth. I move behind him, take it from him. "Allow me."

He chuckles as he surrenders the washcloth and stands facing the mirror watching me take over. "I've been gone all of thirty seconds."

"Thirty seconds too long."

I wash him gently, a little too thoroughly. Once he's more than clean, I toss the washcloth into the sink and quit the pretense—simply fondle his cock with one hand and his balls with the other. Gradually, taking perhaps a bit longer than last time, he rouses to life in my hands.

He stands with that stillness of his, watching my hands move on him. His brow is furrowed, his jaw clenched. I stroke him slowly, cupping his balls with the other hand, gradually sliding my middle finger along his perineum and pressing until he hisses, hips beginning their helpless thrust into my touch.

"Are you trying to make me paint the mirror with my cum?" he grumbles through clenched teeth.

I giggle—a sound very much unlike me. "That would be fun to see."

He presses backward and twists out of my touch. "Waste of a perfectly good erection," he mutters. "I have something better in mind."

He lifts me onto the counter and his hands skate from my thighs to my hips, up my belly to my breasts, and his mouth fuses with mine. His fingers find my sex and touch my clit while simultaneously pinching my nipple. He plays me to writhing arousal like this, until I'm shaking at the edge of climax.

He moves to sink to his knees, but I stop him. "I don't need that," I whisper, scooting my ass to the edge of the counter and pulling him to me. "I just need this."

He sinks into me, and I groan at the bursting fullness of his cock inside me. I clutch his face in my hands and demand his kiss—his hands bury in my hair and he meets my kiss with the crushing intensity I've come to expect from him. We move together slowly, unhurried—well, he does the moving, bending at the knees and lifting and the hips to drive up into me.

He pulls me closer, and my legs coil around his waist, and he stands up with me, and now I take over our movement, arms wrapped around his neck and bracing on his shoulders to lift my weight and let me sink down on him. And like this, I take all of him there can possibly be and then some, sinking so far down that I cry out with the ache of him so deep, so perfect. He walks with me, striding effortlessly as if I weigh nothing at all, but at each lowering thrust he staggers with a grunt.

We're in the closet, and he finds a section of blank wall near the doorway and presses my back to it, and now we move in concert, him driving upward as I sink down. He grunts and growls and I whimper and I wail.

He's bare, and so thick inside me, and his sliding thrusts are slick and powerful, driving into me and hitting me just right, making me quake from head to toe, from fingertip to toenail, making my pussy clench around him.

I've never felt this way before, never. The physical connection between us is unreal, as if our bodies were created for the specific intention of union, of completing each other. Each movement of his body is perfectly attuned to mine, each thrust of his cock designed to make me wild, each touch of his lips to mine crafted to send me soaring to ever more frenetic heights of desire.

It terrifies me.

Deep in my soul, I know this mastery of his body over mine is unnatural, too good, too perfect, too right. He knows my reactions. He knows my whimpers. When I begin to ache and cannot find the edge, he knows how to change his strokes to hit me in a new place, knows how to angle just so and I find a renewed shivering push toward the peaking wilds of climax.

Deep in my soul, I know this is so much more than merely fucking.

Does he know it?

Can he feel it?

Can he feel the frenzied force of our fucking in the dark, unknowable depths of his soul like I can?

I cling to him and bury my face in space between his jaw and his ear, his hair tickling my nose, and I whimper.

He holds me by the ass and pulls me apart to thrust deeper yet, and I feel him sagging, feel his knees giving out.

"Corinna," he gasps, voice ragged. "You feel too fucking perfect."

His legs collapse beneath us, and he sinks to his knees with me sitting on his thighs, and now I snake my arms around his neck and sit on my shins and kiss down on him with all the fury of my shuddering need, and he fingers my clit as I ride him. His groans are shaky, and I feel him throbbing inside me.

"Apollo," I sob, exploding around him, "my god, my Apollo, fuck, fuck, *fuck*—fuck me, Apollo, fuck me as hard as you can don't stop…"

I slam down on him, my ass cracking against his thighs, and he drives up to meet me, and I come around him, his fingers flying against me to push me to the mad, screaming, shaking, thrashing, sobbing clash of my climax.

"Fuck, Corinna, fuck, oh *fuck*—" His voice is breathless, and I feel him pulsating inside me, preparing to come.

He topples us to the side and we roll into the interior of the closet, and he ends up above me, pumping into me as hard as he can, spearing deep and groaning with each thrust.

"Fuck!" he shouts, head dropping to my breasts as he fights the edge, wanting as I do to drag this out, to make this last forever. "I have to…" he pants, "I have to come, Corinna. I can't stop. I can't…fuck, I can't hold it back any longer."

"Give it to me, Apollo," I whisper into his ear, the words as much a kiss as speech. "Come for me. Come for me, come right now."

He doesn't.

He pulls out.

Dammit—even now, he has more presence of mind than I do. His fist crushes on his length, and I know he's a couple quick movements from releasing. I knock his hands away and clutch his cock, lying beneath him. He's on all fours, head bowed, shoulders tensed, and now I pump his hard, thick length with everything I've got, scooting lower and clenching my tits together in one arm.

He thrusts into my hand, and then he can't thrust anymore, can only push forward harder as I stroke him faster and faster. "Oh *fuck*, Corinna," he grates through gritted teeth.

"Paint my tits with your cum, Apollo," I whisper. "I want it. I want it."

His eyes flick open and he growls. "You beautiful, incredible, dirty, perfect fucking girl," he hisses. "So goddamned perfect…"

I want him to come so hard he sees stars. I let go of my tits and cup his balls, press my finger along the underside and against the hard little knot of muscle—he gasps a broken moan, and I press harder, and stroke faster. I feel his arms shaking, feel his cock throbbing. I massage him with my middle finger, slow firm back-and-forth movements, and I feel him writhing, hunching and bowing spasmodically, trying to fuck my fist but too overcome to have any vestige of control over his movements.

He's growling, now—no longer a moan but a long unbroken growl.

"Oh f-f-f-f-*ffffuuuuuck*," he snarls, molars grinding audibly, "Corinna, fuck, Corinna, I'm coming. Oh fuck I'm coming so hard..."

He releases, then, a gush of hot cum splashing against my tits. Another, and another, and I slow my stroking so my fist crushes down to his root hard, and then I twist at the top, and he jets again, another lesser spurt of cum. I am indeed painted with his cum. It's dotted and pooling all over my breasts, splashed on each tit and between them and all over me.

He's still coming.

I keep caressing his length and massaging his prostate until he literally collapses to his back beside me.

He takes my hand, the one smeared with his cum, and holds it, heedless of the sticky mess on his hand.

"Ω Θεέ μου. Νομιζω σε αγαπω." His voice is a whisper, so low I'm not sure he spoke at all, and I can't tell if he spoke English or not.

"What?" I ask with a breathy laugh. "What did you say?"

"Nothing." His voice is suddenly hard, closed down.

I lift up, his cum dripping down to my belly in slow, sticky rivulets. "Apollo, what did you say?"

He shakes his head, forcing himself to his feet. He

stands, but on legs as shaky and unsteady as a newborn fawn. He staggers to the sink and grabs onto it. "Holy fuck, Corinna." This, with a gasping, breathy laugh.

He snatches the washcloth out of the sink, runs the water till it's steaming, soaks the washcloth and wrings it out. I lie propped on my elbows, watching him. He comes back to me and kneels beside me. Touches my shoulder to indicate that I should lie down, and I do. He gently wipes me clean, almost gingerly. Worshipfully. Discards the soiled washcloth in the hamper.

Then, he just kneels beside me, staring down at me. His gaze is guarded.

I touch his hand. "Apollo. Please. What did you say? Why won't you tell me what it means?"

He just stares at me, and sighs. Moves to his feet and walks away without an explanation, leaving me puzzled and not a little hurt. But he returns a moment later with his phone, opens it, brings up an app. Stands beside me, looking down at me with that opaque, unknowable expression back in place—the mask is back. For a moment, I'd been allowed behind it. Beneath it. Whatever he said, it freaked him out and he put the mask back on.

He repeats his statement—in Greek, I assume, since I know a smattering of Spanish and this isn't that—clearly, into the phone. Taps a button on the screen. He hands the device to me and turns away, twists the shower on.

Not looking at me.

Oh my god. I think I love you.

My hand goes to my mouth, a gasp escaping.

No wonder he's freaked out.

I mean, it was…a heat of the moment thing. Nothing more.

I stand up—my legs are as shaky as his—and stand behind him. He's at the shower, frozen in place, hand on the temperature knob, staring into nothing.

I touch his shoulder, and he flinches.

"I didn't mean it, Corinna," he murmurs. "I don't even know…why I said it. Shit, I don't know what that even…is. What it means."

"It was…" I think of a cute way of saying it. "Apollo, it was just a verbal ejaculation after a physical one." I lean against his back. "It's okay."

He snorts. "You're funny."

I wrap my arm around his chest. "It would be okay if you did mean it." I can't believe what I'm saying. "And it's okay if you didn't."

He just shakes his head. "I cannot…*mean it*, Corinna. I'm not capable of that." A harsh pause. "Of love. Don't think I am, because I simply will not ever have that within me. If you think you can heal me…fix me? That us fucking a few times—no matter that it was…" he trails off, as if he can't find the words.

I feel the sting of his words, but I don't let it seep into my heart. I feel his fear, and I know his reaction to fear is to lash out. To harden. To tighten the mask around his true self, to heighten the walls around the island fortress of his emotions.

"Apollo." I press myself up against him, breasts flattening against his back, arms underneath his to clutch at his chest, my lips whispering against his neck. "It was more than fucking. I know it, and I know you know it. You can deny it. You can pretend otherwise. That's okay. I get it. But it was still way, *way* more than just fucking. I mean, granted, it was the best sex of my life. I'll have dreams about the way you fucked me. It was…it was goddamned magical, Apollo. But it wasn't *just* fucking."

He inhales deeply. Holds it. Lets it out with tight control through pursed lips. Steps out of my hold and into the shower, adjusting the temperature.

I wait, and watch him wash, condition, and rinse his hair, water sluicing over his beautiful body, running in rivulets over his muscles.

Long minutes of silence in which he completely ignores me.

"So that's it?" I say, eventually.

He won't look at me. "That's it." A pause. "They're out there, you know. Your parents. In Spain and coming here. I had word earlier. That's what I came to tell you, when you…attacked me." Is there a hint of a smirk in the tone of his voice? Maybe. Not on his face, certainly.

I just stared at him, absorbing this information. "So…what's…what's happening?"

"That's up to them." He scrubs his skin with a bar of soap, not answering. Rinses. Steps out, leaving the water on. "Your turn."

He nabs a towel from the heated rack and dries himself with it. I'm frozen, unable to process this abrupt shift in him.

With a sigh, dabbing his face with the towel and then wrapping it around his waist, he turns to me. "Take a shower. Or don't. I have preparations to see to, and work to attend to."

"Apollo." I reach for him, but stop short of touching him. "You don't have to turn back into the asshole to prove a point to me."

He tosses the towel into the nearby hamper and stands naked in front of me; for all of his nudity, however, there is no vulnerability in him, no softness. He's as armored and guarded as if he were in a suit rather than as naked as God made him.

"That, dearest Corinna, is where you seem to have erred." He gives off no expression, neither cruel nor kind. Simply blank. "I am not turning *back* into anything, because I never stopped being anything but who and what I am. If you think you saw something… *else*…in the things we did, well…what you believe you saw in me is not anything to do with me." He breezes past me to the closet. "Now, if you'll excuse me."

I step into the shower, mind whirling, emotions boiling. I use his shampoo and conditioner, his bar of soap. Rinse off, and then simply stand in the hot spray, trying to get a grip on things.

I know what I saw.

What I felt.

I know I saw beneath the hard mask to the man he could be.

I am absolutely certain that for a moment or two, Apollo tasted what could be between us, and found himself desperately wanting it. But then…

He panicked.

The why of his retreat back behind the mask is complicated psychology I'm not qualified for, but if I had to guess? He's scared. He wants something he's never had, never known: love and acceptance.

He wants to be able to be that man, the one who gives and receives rather than simply takes and demands. The man with soft eyes and a tender touch.

But he doesn't believe he can have that, be that.

He doesn't believe I could possibly be truly and openly offering that to him.

He doesn't believe it.

He wants it—oh yes, I could see that plain as day.

So the question is…what do I do?

How do I convince him of what could be? That I'm for real, that I see him, that I'm not afraid.

I mean, I am afraid. Of being hurt, of being rejected—more, I'm afraid that I've misjudged him, that he was just playing a game, a part, getting what he wanted from me and now intends to do horrible things to me, to my parents.

No, I don't believe that—I'm afraid of it, but I don't believe it.

His fear is absolutely understandable, even if only a quarter of what he told me about his past is true. He has nothing upon which to base trust, or belief in love. Whereas I, on the other hand, have grown up surrounded by love. Being loved by Mom and Dad, by Cal despite our sibling squabbles, and by what you might call my extended family, the A1S crew. I also saw love acted out every, in the way Mom and Dad love each other. I've grown up seeing them take care of each other, put each other first. I've seen them get in fights and say stupid shit they don't mean, and I've seen them apologize and make up; well, I've heard them *verbally* make up and assume—icky—that they make up in ways I don't want to see or think about.

I've seen love, known love. Apollo hasn't.

Which one of us, therefore, bears the burden of courage?

I do.

It's not logical of me to assume he would

choose or risk for something he's never seen, felt, or experienced.

What we shared today was not love.

It was…the seeds of love's potential…maybe.

So, then. Am I going to let his surly, closed-off, man in the iron mask reaction to feeling something so unexpected and so intense scare me off?

You know what? No. I don't believe I will.

Nice try, Asshole.

I still choose the other guy. I just have to lure him back out from beneath the mask.

19

THE TRADE

First light. There's no sleep. No coffee. No breakfast. Just a too-fast-yet-too-slow wait for the darkness to bleed into dawn's gray. When the first sliver of sun shows on the horizon, we all stir as one.

Sasha stretches.

Valentine cracks his knuckles.

I look at my husband. "Call him."

A nod. He touches a previous call, sets the device on speaker. It rings a few times.

"Valentine Roth." The voice is cultured, with a distinct but elegant Greek accent. "And Mrs. Roth, I presume."

"We want our daughter back, Apollo." Valentine's voice is carefully modulated.

"I'll bet you do." A pause. "Say hello, darling."

"Daddy?" A slight crack, but her voice remains strong. "Mama?"

"We're here, honey," I whisper, my voice ragged and shaking. "We're here."

"What do you *want*, Apollo?" Valentine says.

"Well, I was rather hoping you'd be foolish enough to try and take her by force. Would've been quite the fireworks show, yes? And my men would have taken care of you for me."

"Quit *posing*, Apollo," I hear Rin snap, in the background.

Odd, it doesn't sound like the way a prisoner would speak to her captor.

I take the phone from Valentine. "Us for Rin." I swallow hard. "Better yet—*me* for Rin. I'm the one who killed Gina, anyway. Take me. You can do what you want with me. Just let my daughter go. She's got nothing to do with this."

"Mama, no!" Rin's voice, distant, as if he'd walked away from her. "You don't understand!"

"I think not, Kyrie Roth. Both of you. Walk down the road you're on. My men will not disturb you as long as your hands remain visible at all times. When you come to the castle, you will be approached by my second, Tomás. He will bring you in, at which time I will see that Corinna is delivered to your men."

"Do you think we're that stupid, Apollo?" Valentine snarls. "Try again, and do better, or I'll rethink my attempt to solve this without killing anyone."

"Oh, please do." He sighs. "Very well. I will meet you with her out front."

Sasha's eyes widen at this—he's playing directly into our plan.

"Apollo, don't." This is Rin, again distant, but pleading. "Just end it. There's nothing to be accomplished. Not anymore."

The way she says his name. My spine crawls.

"Can I talk to my daughter, please?" I ask.

"It's Mommy Dearest," I hear him say as he hands the phone off.

"Mom?" Rin's voice, surprisingly firm. "I'm okay. I promise."

"What's going on, Rin?" I swallow hard. "Something is going on. I know it."

"It's not what you think," she whispers.

"What isn't?"

"Any of this! It's not what you think."

"Enough." Apollo's voice abruptly cuts through. "The trade—we are agreed?"

Valentine and I exchange looks. I nod.

Valentine takes the phone back. "We are."

"Very good. We'll all meet soon, then, won't we?"

Click.

Valentine looks to Sasha. "Give Harris the signal."

Sasha speaks into a two-way radio set to a private channel. "Alpha Kilo, execute."

"Alpha Kilo execute, confirm." Harris's voice.

Sasha's jaw is grinding as he hooks the radio back on his vest. "The others will be moving in now that we've given the signal. The moment he's down, we'll get Rin to safety."

"No matter what happens to us," I tell him. "You get her to safety." I stare hard at him. "No matter what. Promise me."

"I swear it on my life."

Valentine nods, then takes my hand. "Ready?"

I let out a breath, squeeze his hand. "Let's go get our daughter back."

20

IT'S ALL ABOUT CHOICES

It was a long, sleepless night. Apollo didn't come back until just before dawn. He's in the same clothes as yesterday. He's tired-looking, as if he hasn't slept any more than I did. His jaw is heavily stubbled, and his eyes reflect turmoil. Now that I've seen the man behind the iron mask he wears, I see the pain in his eyes, the turmoil. The doubt.

He leans against a window, staring out at the approach to the castle, as if he can see something out there I can't—or *someone.*

His phone rings, and he pulls it from his back pocket, glances at the screen, then at me. "Valentine Roth. And Mrs. Roth I presume." His voice is something I barely recognize—not just icy, but zero-Kelvin cold, and hard and sharp as obsidian's edge.

A pause, to listen.

A glance at me again. "I'll bet you do." He gestures at me with the phone. "Say hello, darling."

There's no discernible verbal emphasis on the "darling" but there need not be. The word's existence on his lips at all says everything there is to say. Teases, taunts, tortures my parents. I can hear it, feel it.

He's on a path, and he doesn't know how to get off.

Maybe he knows this can only end in his death—and he's welcoming it.

He's never been hugged.

Never known love.

Yet…there are glimmers of someone else inside him. Hints of something more.

And something inside me calls to him.

It's crazy. I don't know what it is. I don't know anything except I can't let him die, and I can't let him do anything to Mom and Dad. I mean, obviously. But for him, too. There has to be another way out of this.

"Quit *posing*, Apollo," I snap, my voice betraying the host of emotions inside me.

He frowns at me, but then someone on the other end is speaking to him—I can tell by the way his gaze goes unfocused to listen, darting away from me to the road out the window, as if he could see them from here. He shifts the phone to speaker.

"…*me* for Rin. I'm the one who killed Gina,

anyway. Take me. You can do what you want with me. Just let my daughter go. She's got nothing to do with this."

"Mama, no!" I cry.

"I think not, Kyrie Roth," Apollo says in that quiet, cold voice. "Both of you. Walk down the road you're on. My men will not disturb you as long as your hands remain visible at all times. When you come to the castle, you will be approached by my second, Tomás. He will bring you in, at which time I will see that Corinna is delivered to your men."

"Do you think we're that stupid, Apollo?" Daddy snarls. "Try again, and do better, or I'll rethink my attempt to solve this without killing anyone."

"Oh, please do." Apollo sighs as if he's giving up something huge, out of the kindness of his heart. "Very well. I will meet you with her out front."

"Apollo, don't," I say, daring a few steps closer to him. "Just end it. There's nothing to be accomplished. Not anymore." I allow softness in my voice. Let him hear the real me, the me he saw in that bed, hours ago.

"Can I talk to my daughter, please?" Mama says, from the phone's speaker.

"It's Mommy Dearest," Apollo says, handing the phone to me and putting space between us.

"Mom?" I put strength into my voice. She can't worry, or she'll do something rash. "I'm okay. I promise."

"What's going on, Rin?" Mom's voice is shaky. "Something is going on. I know it."

"It's not what you think," I whisper. I don't want him to hear. I don't know why.

"What isn't?" Mama asks.

"Any of this! It's not what you think."

"Enough." Apollo's voice snaps over me, and he snatches the phone away. "The trade—we are agreed?"

Daddy's voice. "We are."

"Very good. We'll all meet soon, then, won't we?" Apollo ends the call and pockets the phone.

I go to the window which overlooks the vineyard, the spot he so recently vacated—I can see the road from here, the approach which one might term a driveway.

Far in the distance, I now see two small figures. Mom and Dad.

"Our little…game, as you called it…is almost over."

"And then what?" I take a step toward him. "You'll have my parents. Then what, Apollo? Torture them? Put them in the dungeon and go down there occasionally and beat my father? Rape my mother?"

He stands up. "I thought you understood me, Corinna. All that talk…I thought you'd come to know me better than that."

"And yet you continue on with this idiotic

scheme!" Another step. He tenses—because he feels my proximity every bit as much as I feel his.

"What is it you *want* from me, Corinna?"

"The real you." I take another step, and he takes another back—a dance.

He glowers at me. "The real me? You've seen the real me, Corinna. *This* is the real me."

I shake my head. "No, it's not."

He shakes his head. "Then...what is, according to you?"

I step closer again and he dances backward. "The Apollo who kissed me. The Apollo who held me in his arms."

He shakes his head. "*That* was the game, Corinna. Just a game."

"Bullshit."

He whirls away from me. "Say what you like. Believe what you like."

I tiptoe up behind him. I know he hears me, anyway. I see it in the tension in his body. "You're lying to yourself. But you can't lie to me."

"You know nothing, Corinna Roth."

I touch him, just my hands resting gently on his shoulders, but he flinches as if struck. "Try the truth, Apollo. Just once. Out loud, where both of us can hear it."

"What truth?"

"Any truth. Tell me one true thing, no matter how hard it is to say."

A long, long silence. "I saw you standing there at the window, and I know you were watching your parents approach." He lifts his chin, but his eyes darken, narrow. "I know it means you're considering your impending freedom from me. And I…" he swallows hard. "And I don't like it."

"You don't like what? My freedom from you?" I laugh and move closer to him yet again—he's got nowhere to go, now. His back is to the window. "Try again. I'll let you rephrase that, if you want."

"You'll let me."

"Yes, I'll let you." I close the distance again, so now there's no space between us. "It's not what you meant. Say it a better way."

"I didn't like…the thought of you…of you being gone." He swells, jaw hardening. The Alpha is back. But then, he's not really an alpha, is he? More of a sigma, I think. "I don't want to let you go."

"What if you—"

"Speak plainly goddammit," he snarls over me. "No more riddles. No more what if. Say what you fucking mean, Corinna Roth."

"You don't have to let me go." I whisper it.

"Just like that? You'd just…stay?"

I shake my head. "Is anything ever that simple,

Apollo? No, not just like that. You'd have to give some things up."

"Such as?"

"This silly, childish revenge plot of yours, obviously."

"And your parents just get away with it?"

"They already did, Apollo. It was twenty years ago, and it was self-defense. Your mother was a monster who planned evil things for mine and used my father to get to her. Yes, my mother killed yours, but only because she had to. You know this. You told me yourself you know what happened. So just accept it, Apollo."

"I can't."

"You have to." I look up at him. "Listen to me, Apollo. Listen to me, okay? You…are *not*…them."

"But I am."

"You've tried to be, and you've failed at it." I claw my fingernails into his chest. There's not much time left. "You took over your grandfather's empire of guns and drugs…and you made it *better*. You made it safer. You've attempted this whole kidnapping plot as an attempt to become your mother, but you can't even do *that* right." I touch his mouth with my fingertips to silence him. "Because *that's…not…you.*"

"You said…" he shakes his head like a punch-drunk boxer. Blinks hard. Looks away. "You said I didn't have to lose you."

"You don't."

"But you won't stay."

"Not here, not like this."

"I don't understand."

I gaze up at him. "Don't you?"

"Choice." His voice is a whisper; his eyes rake up to the ceiling—anywhere but mine.

The mask is wavering. There are gaps in the iron. Cracks in the façade.

"Exactly." I match his whisper.

"How?" He finally meets my eyes. "How, Corinna? I don't know how."

"Choose me." I take his hands. Hold them. "Let me walk away. Let my parents walk away."

"How does letting you go end in me *not* losing you?"

"You have to choose me by letting me go. And then, you have to prove to me that you can be the man I *know* is in here." I claw his chest so hard I'll probably leave marks. "Leave behind the Karahalios—all of it, the empire, the name itself even, if that's what it takes. The dark, twisted legacy of your family doesn't have to be who you are. You get to choose." My voice is as soft as the whisper of silk across skin. "It's all about choices, Apollo. Choose to be a man I could…" I blink, because these next words surprise even me. "A man I could fall in love with."

He sucks in a breath.

"And I will." I hold his eyes. "I *will* fall in love with that man. I *will* choose that man."

He shakes his head. His eyes are dark and dangerous. "Don't lie to me," he hisses.

I lift up on my toes, cup his face in my hands, and I kiss him. It is soft and slow and deep—and intimate. "Does that feel like I'm lying to you?"

"And all I have to do is change…everything?" His voice is drenched in sarcasm.

"You have to decide what you want, Apollo." I step away from him. "I can't make you do anything. And I wouldn't if I could." I look over his shoulder, and see that my parents are close, now. "Time to make your choice."

"And if I choose…the other direction?"

I walk toward the exit. "Then people will die." I stop at the door. Turn and look at him. "My parents. You. Me. Your men. The men who helped raise me, who are like uncles to me."

I walk down the stairs, and I hear him behind me. Feel him.

And I have no idea what he's going to choose.

21

THE TRADE, PART 2

THE WALK IS LONG, AND BY THE TIME WE'RE IN SIGHT of the castle, it's hot already and the road is dusty.

Fear hammers at my heart. My mother's intuition says there's something happening that we're not seeing.

It's not what you think.

"What if killing him is the wrong thing?" I whisper.

Valentine looks at me sharply. "What do you mean?"

"On the phone, Rin told me it's not what we think. 'It's not what you think.' That's what she said." I shake my head. "I don't know. I just have a feeling. What if killing Apollo is the wrong thing to do?"

"What else could it be?" He's angry. "He

kidnapped our fucking *daughter*. You killed four people to get away."

I shake my head again. "I don't *know*, Valentine. I don't know. I just…I'm…I don't know."

"The plan can't be stopped at this point. I have no radio, no phone, nothing."

The castle is huge. Not something out of a medieval fantasy, though, but an amalgam of a castle and a fortified country estate. It's still a castle, though, and no mistake about it. Towering, built of giant blocks of stone, hundreds of years old, with gothic arches at every window and door…and it's also clear Lear and Sasha were not exaggerating. It would require a veritable army to take this place.

There's a massive, circular tower at one end of the castle, with a pointed roof and windows running the rim beneath the roof. The driveway we're walking along arcs in front of the castle, past a fountain spewing water, and ends in a circular turn-around in front of the tower. Several big black SUVs line the drive, each with its doors open; armed guards stand in each door, wielding automatic rifles. At the end of the line of vehicles, in full view, is Apollo Karahalios. With him, our daughter.

She is not standing with the posture of a captive, of someone who's endured the terror of captivity in Karahalios's hands. She's calm, her back is straight, her head high. She's dressed in an emerald green tunic dress belted beneath her breasts, her legs bare, white wedge sandals on her feet. Her hair is clean and braided. She's unbruised, not so much as a scratch on her.

Apollo, meanwhile, looks…embattled. Not quite haggard, but it wouldn't be a stretch.

Even so, he's a shockingly handsome man. There are dark circles under his eyes, and his jaw is stubbled, his long black hair messy, as if he's run his hands through it. But yet for all that he looks the worse for wear, he's a simply stunning human being.

His eyes do not crackle with the evil I'd expected of him—of someone descended from Vitaly and Gina.

Beside him, Rin is calm and collected, hands folded in front of her.

In fact, she's standing a little too close to Apollo for my liking.

I look at my husband, and I see that he hasn't missed any of this.

"You have got to be fucking kidding me," he snarls under his breath.

I snicker. "You said it yourself—we'd be rescuing *him* from *her*."

He just growls. "That was a joke."

"Clearly not."

"He's a fucking *Karahalios*."

"Do you trust your daughter?"

He growls again. "It's a moot point. He's about to get a NATO round through his pretty fucking skull."

"Valentine."

"God*damm*it."

We're within earshot now, so we both fall silent. When we're ten or so feet away, Valentine and I both stop as one.

Rin is less composed than I'd thought, now that I can see her features more closely. She's got her fingers knotted up, which means she's trying to keep them from shaking. Her eyes are wide and she's only just barely hiding her nerves.

"Well." Valentine holds his hands palms up, drops them. "Here we are, Apollo."

"Here we are." He looks to his left, at Corinna. "A reunion, of sorts."

"Let her go now." Valentine's voice is harsh.

If you listen very carefully, you can almost hear the faint, distant thumping of a helicopter.

I touch Valentine's hand. "Trust me," I whisper.

He doesn't answer.

I take a step away from my husband. Hands out, in plain sight. "I'm sorry about your mother, Apollo. Really I am."

He just stares at me. "Choices," he mutters.

I'm not sure what that means, but I go with it. "Yes. I had a choice to make. It was life or death, and

I chose my life. I chose a life with the man I love. I just wish I hadn't had to take a life in the process."

"You've taken four."

"I have children now," I say. "I'm not about to go quietly. Surely you understand that."

The air fairly crackles with tension. I can almost feel Anselm preparing to take the shot.

Does he hear it? Does he know what it means?

"Choices," Apollo mutters again.

His eyes go to Rin's.

She looks up at him—and as a woman, I know the look she's giving him.

"Sir." One of the men is touching his ear. "Contact. Helo."

Apollo looks at me.

At Rin.

At Valentine.

My heart hammers. Rin's eyes widen as she comprehends what that means.

She moves…

In front of him.

22

MONTAGUES AND CAPULETS

In a horrid flash of icy comprehension, I understand my parents' plan. I know the contingencies they've worked out for many different scenarios. I've sat in on security briefings.

Lure Apollo out here.

Anselm, a mile away with a rifle, takes him out.

In the ensuing confusion, I'm whisked away.

Desperate, but better than doing nothing—in their eyes. And they don't know what I know. What being here has been for me. What I've found, here.

They've assumed the worst—justifiably.

There's no thought in the action, only instinct—I move to stand in front of Apollo, blocking him with my own body. I'm tall enough that there's no clear shot.

"*No*." I don't scream—can't. I'm barely breathing. "Not like this."

"Corinna?" Apollo's confusion is obvious in his voice. "What are you *doing*?"

"Strangely, I find myself agreeing with him," Daddy says. "What are you doing, Corinna?"

I hold my arms behind me, blocking him in. Stand tall. "Call him off."

"I can't." Daddy's voice is too calm—it's the *don't fuck with me* voice.

"I won't let you do this." I swallow hard.

Daddy looks at the men in the doors of the SUVs—the first visible sign I've seen of Apollo's supposedly overwhelming firepower. There's at least a dozen men, and it feels like the tip of the iceberg.

"Why?" He's pleading with me. "Move out of the way."

"Call your men off," I say, my voice low.

"I told you, I *can't*," Daddy answers. "I don't have a phone or a radio."

"Not you," I snap, turn my head slightly to glance at Apollo over my shoulder. "Apollo. Send your men away. The ones out there, all of them. Stand down."

"Malik is in position, sir," the nearest of the men says.

A surface-to-air rocket, I'm assuming.

"Apollo." I whisper it. "Make your choice. Do we

all die?" I turn in place, look up at him. "Or do you choose me?"

"Corinna," Daddy snaps. "MOVE."

I whirl back to my father. "*No.*"

"Don't you say it," he snarls.

I frown in confusion. "Say what?"

"'But Daddy, I *love* him.'"

I cackle, an unexpected outburst of laughter. "This isn't a Disney movie, Dad. I'm not Ariel—that's not what I was going to say."

I feel Apollo straighten behind me. I hear him take a deep breath, hold it, and let it out—the breath huffs on my hair.

His hands move to rest on my waist. "I choose you," he whispers. He steps out from behind me. "Stand down."

"Sir?" A gravelly male voice; a familiar voice—it niggles at my awareness. Like I've heard it before but can't place it.

"All of you, stand down. Get in and go away. Fingers off the triggers or I'll kill you myself." A pause. "Confirm that Malik has the command."

Silence.

"Confirmed, sir. Standing down." The same voice.

"Leave us."

"Sir."

A crunch of boots on gravel, doors slamming.

My eyes are closed—the moment he stepped

out from behind me, I'd been expecting the boom of Anselm's rifle. It never comes.

Engines roar, and tires crackle across gravel, and then we're alone, the four of us.

Apollo holds his hands out at his sides. "Corinna, get my phone from my back pocket, please." When I take it, he gestures to Daddy. "Give it to him."

Daddy takes the phone from me. "What's happening, Rin?"

Mom leans against him. "No one is getting killed, that's what."

"The code to open the phone is six-six-one-one-three-three. Call your man and ask him to not shoot me." A thick pause. "Please."

A beat, and then the digital beeping of a keypad. "Yeah, no, it's me." Daddy's voice is harsh, angry. "It's over. Your part at least. No—I know. It's…an evolving situation…yeah, we're good for now. I'll be in touch shortly."

Apollo speaks. "Tell them to come get you." Another short, heavy pause. "All three of you."

I move to face him. His expression is…tortured. "Thank you, Apollo."

He shakes his head. "You will go, now." His voice is heavy.

"Yes."

A nod. His eyes search mine. "You aren't coming back."

I hold his gaze. "You know where to find me."

"Corinna Abigail Roth," Daddy snarls. "*What* are you *doing*?"

"Hush, darling," I hear Mom say.

Apollo just stares down at me. "What if…what if I do the things you said…try to become…that man. But it's not enough?"

I've never heard him sound anything less than sure of himself. It nearly breaks my heart. "You quoted *Star Wars* at me earlier. Now it's my turn. 'Do, or do not. There is no try.'" I don't attempt to sound like Yoda, because this is a serious moment. I'm tempted to, though.

"I don't know *how*, Corinna."

"You just decide who you want to be, and you become him. Whatever is not that, you get rid of. Whatever is missing, you create it." I touch his face. "If you can wade into arms dealing and drug distribution with the most violent and brutal and ambitious men on the planet and come out on top, you can become a good man."

He smirks. "Those men do not frighten me." He looks past me, at my father, and the smirk fades. "He does." I don't think it's entirely a joke.

Daddy says nothing, to his credit. No posturing. No blustering.

I lift up and kiss him, once more. "Remember what I said, up there." I look up at the tower, behind us. "I *will*. Okay? If you can find the good man inside you, I *will* love him."

"Fuck me running," Daddy says. "I don't believe this."

"Hush, darling."

Apollo does that thing where he swells, filling the space, taking up all the oxygen. "Then, I will. You'll see."

"I believe you," I say, trailing my fingers down his jaw.

I have to back away, then. Out of his arms.

Tires on gravel. Doors opening.

Tension still writhes like serpents, flows like lava.

He stands and watches me; his hands go in his pockets.

I hear guns cocking, and turn, holding my hands up and stepping in front of him again. "Put them down. Please."

It's the whole crew: Duke, Thresh, Lear, Anselm, Harris, Puck, and Sasha rifles pointed Apollo.

I walk up to Duke, whose eyes blaze the brightest. "Duke, please. It's enough. You don't need it."

His blue eyes fix on mine, puzzled and angry. "He fuckin' *kidnapped* you, sweetheart. That ain't the action of Prince Charming."

I pull the muzzle of his rifle down, and he lets me. "Maybe not." I look around from face to face.

"But answer me this, any of you. Which one of you can say *you're* Prince Charming?"

There's a lot of shuffling, muzzles lowering.

"I say this with all the love in my heart for each and every one of you." I pause for effect. "You're all like bonus dads to me. I wouldn't change anything about any of you for the world. But…once upon a time, I don't think you would have …you wouldn't have classified yourself as *good*."

"Mebbe not," Puck growls around his cigar stump. "But we didn't kidnap any innocent girls. Shit, we kill the fuckers who do."

"His actions were wrong." I look at my father when I say this. "I'm not defending him on that score. But *I'm* the one who was kidnapped. And I'm saying while his actions were wrong, I understand why he did it. I don't expect you to, and I'm not asking you to. I'm not even going to try and explain it. But I don't want any of you trying to exact punishment on him."

Mom steps up to me. "What you're doing is… admirable, honey. But what he did wasn't just *wrong*. People are *dead*."

Apollo speaks up, then. "They were under strict instructions not to harm you. I don't tolerate the mistreatment of women."

"Yeah, well, I didn't fucking know that," Mom snaps. "All I knew was you had my daughter, and they had me, and they had guns."

"Got a funny definition of mistreat," Puck growls, "if snatching a girl out of bed and carting her across the world against her will isn't mistreatment."

Apollo shrugs. "I will not attempt to defend myself."

"Cause you fuckin' can't," Duke says.

"Perhaps not. Those men were hired guns. They were mercenaries, and not very good ones." He looks at Mom when he says this. "You did not kill good men."

"Doesn't make it any easier knowing I killed them," Mom says.

I hold up my hands. "No amount of talking is going to reconcile any of this."

"No Karahalios is ever—fucking *ever*—getting anywhere near my home or my family," Dad says, his voice low and acidic. "I hope you understand that."

I turn on him. "It's not up to you."

His eyes blaze. "Corinna."

I put my hands on his shoulders. "Daddy, please."

"You weren't there. You don't know what happened. What his grandfather did. What his mother did. What she was like. His mother was—"

"His mother is dead," I snap. "So is his grandfather. And he's *not* them."

He rocks back, throws his head back and sighs. "I just don't understand."

I pat his arm. "You don't have to."

I feel Apollo behind me, and I turn back to him, but I dare not touch him. Even now, the wildfire between us needs but a single spark to conflagrate.

He keeps his hands in his pockets, but his eyes caress me where his hands do not. "You had better go."

"Will you come?"

He nods. "I have a long way to go before I'm the man you seem to see in me." A soft smile, such as I've never seen from him. "But yes, I will. When I feel ready."

A harsh laugh from Puck. "Buddy, you ain't ever gonna be ready. You won't ever be what you think she sees in you. That there is some free advice from someone who ain't but a collection of rough edges and mistakes who somehow managed to get a damn fine woman to love him. You ain't ever fuckin' ready. So don't wait till you are."

Apollo's brow furrows in thought. "I see." He looks to Puck—short, broad, thick, scarred, bald with a long black beard going gray. "And how will I know, in that case?"

A laugh. "You don't. When you can't fuckin' stand it anymore, you just go and lay it all out there and hope for the fuckin' best."

"He's right," Duke chimes in. "You're never ready. You just go when you feel like you won't ever be any *more* ready than you are."

"You're giving this man *advice*?" Dad snaps. "What do I pay you for?"

"Hush, darling," Mom says.

He growls. "Stop telling me to hush, dammit. I'll hush you."

Mom snickers. "Ooh, threaten me with a good time, why don't you." She pats him on the chest. "He's not like them, Val. Can't you tell?"

Daddy's growl is still fierce, but I can tell a difference. "All I see is *her*." He gestures at Apollo. "Those damn eyes of his. Just like hers." A sigh. "But…you're right. He may be redeemable. She was not."

Apollo looks at the crowd of men, the guns—then Mom and Dad, Mom leaning up against Dad's side, his arm slung over her so his hand rested possessively on her hip. "You have quite a remarkable… family, Corinna."

"He always call you Corinna?" Thresh asks, the first words he's spoken thus far. "Last time I called you that, you bit my head off."

"It's different," I answer, not looking at him—only at Apollo. "You can't. He can."

Apollo's eyes heat. Fix on me. He steps into me, pulls me against him. A beat of hesitation, noses touching, and then he kisses me. It's a kiss meant to slay me, to lay me down and ravage me, to claim me. It's a kiss that takes no quarter. Demanding. Aggressive. Furious and full of fire.

When he finally relinquishes me, I'm breathless and sagging in his arms.

He waits until I've found my breath, and my feet, and then he steps away. "Until I see you again." His lips touch my forehead, slow, soft, and gentle—one last kiss.

He turns away and strides with that confident, arrogant swagger to his tower. Vanishes into it, and he's gone.

It feels like all the oxygen has been sucked out of the sky.

I feel eight pairs of eyes on me.

I stride to the rear passenger door of the nearest vehicle and get in without a word.

Within moments, we're rumbling away from Apollo's castle. I don't look back—I can't. I'll see him watching me go from the top of his tower.

"Of all people, *him*?" Daddy mutters, beside me. He points at Mom, on the other side of me. "Tell me to hush and I'll paddle you the moment we're alone."

Mom's laugh is dark and dirty and makes me extremely uncomfortable. "Not the way to win that argument, sweetheart."

I fake a gag. "God, you guys—gross."

"You just were just kissed by the son of my worst enemy." Dad's eyes are on me—I feel them. "Don't talk to me about gross."

"Your worst enemy is dead, Dad." I don't open

my eyes—I'm too tired, suddenly. "I don't want to talk about this right now, okay?"

Dad sighs, a long, deep release of tension. "Fine." He stretches his arm out and pulls me against him; Mom is, of course, already as close to him as you can get while clothed and in a car. "I'm just glad you're okay, and that we have you back."

"Can we take the fastest jet we have back home?" I murmur. "I want my own bed."

"Sure." Dad's quiet a moment. "Just tell me one thing, okay?"

I groan. "Okay?"

"Do you really trust him?"

I don't answer for a long time. "I'll know the answer to that the next time I see him. I don't have an answer for that right now."

"And when will you see him again?"

"I don't know, Dad."

Another sigh. "I don't like it. I'm not sure about him."

"Like I already said—you don't have to."

"You're my daughter."

"And I'm an adult." I finally open my eyes and look at him. It's not a sweet, daughterly gaze of adoration. "You aren't going to go all Montague and Capulet on me, are you? Because I will *not* be forced to choose."

Mom answers for him. "No, darling. That will not

be happening. If you decide he's changed and that you trust him, that will be good enough for us." A significant pause. "Right, darling?"

A begrudging grunt. "We'll see."

Mom sighs. "I think that's the best you're going to get right now, Rin."

I don't answer—I'm nearly asleep.

23

A FEW SHORT HOURS

2 years later

"Where are we with the launch prep?" Dad asks.

I shuffle a thick stack of papers, tap them on my desk to straighten the edges and hand them to him. "T-minus six days and counting. The payload has been calculated and recalculated down to the last gram, and the engineers are going over every bolt, circuit, and panel. So far, all systems are nominal."

"And the orbital substation?"

"It's reached geosynchronous orbit and is stabilized. The crew is quadruple checking their systems—I'm not directly monitoring that, though, but rather receiving reports from Michael."

"Very good." He sorts through the various reports. "The payload. You've said it's been calculated, but has the integrity of the payload itself been checked over?"

"A few dozen times," I say, sorting through a different stack of reports, find the one I need and hand it to him. "It all checks out. That's the meta report—I have the individual reports with data in a digital file. I can send it to you."

"No, that's all right. As long as you personally have verified it, I trust you."

"I have. Several times." I gesture out the window at the massive rocket visible in the distance. "It's going to go off without a hitch, Dad."

He perches on the edge of my desk. "It's hard to believe we're going to pull this off."

"Everyone said it was categorically impossible."

He laughed. "If we'd insisted on designing and building our own rocket, it would have been." His expression goes serious. "Someday soon, baby girl, you and I are going to be on one of those."

I cackle. "Okay, sure. You really think Mom is going to let you go to space, Dad?"

He growls. "We've discussed it. If every launch and every orbital docking goes off without a single hitch, she'll think about it." A huff. "Think about it. Valkyrie is my fucking company. I'm going."

I laugh and pat his arm. "I know you will, Dad."

He digs in the inside pocket of his suit coat—he had an investors' meeting just now. "This came for you."

It's an envelope. Plain, old school white envelope. My name is printed in neat block letters, in black ink.

My full name.

Not Rin. Not Rinna.

Corinna.

"It came for me…*here*? At work?" I take it from him, but just hold it. "In the mail?"

He shakes his head—his gaze is more serious than ever. Concerned. "Courier."

I stare at the envelope, heart palpitating. "It's from him."

"So I assumed."

"Has Uncle Harry…heard anything?"

I've intentionally stayed away from anything to do with A1S, with security, with that whole realm. And until this moment, I haven't heard a single word from or about him in two years.

I haven't been on a date. I haven't hooked up with anyone. I've helped myself through bouts of loneliness and long nights of restless arousal via vibrators and vivid memories.

Dad shrugs. "Rumblings. There's been…a reorganization, in the criminal underworld. It's hard to get much concrete intel, but it seems like he's done what you asked—divested himself of everything to do with the Karahalios criminal empire." A glance at me. "I've heard other stuff, too. Not related to the Karahalios side of things."

"Such as?" I trace the letters on the envelope.

"Well, I had a team of assistants do some digging into his legitimate business interests. Which are, to be honest, shockingly varied. Medical research, telecom, pharmaceuticals, VC investment, construction."

"And?"

"Well, it seems like he's streamlined things." A shrug. "Sold or merged a bunch of corporations and subsidiaries, acquired and merged and so on …the bigger deal is he's gone from a shadowy figure in the background, the kind of billionaire you would never know exists, to having a rather prominent public persona. He's appeared at several dozen charity events, always alone, where he's donated staggering amounts of money. He's allowed himself to be interviewed a few times…mostly in small-time industry journals, nothing in major media so far. But something. He has a presence in the world. And it's a good one."

"What kind of charities?"

"Mostly to do with kids. Troubled youth centers, orphanages, hunger programs, mentorship programs, things like that." He looks at me, making sure to catch my eye. "He does it quietly. There's no big fanfare, no giant checks or ribbon cutting. He just donates millions of dollars to these small-potatoes organizations and programs struggling to get by."

"So what you're saying is…" I prompt.

"What I'm saying is…" he sighs, rubs his face. "I admit I didn't think he was…capable of…of good. But it sure as hell seems like he's trying."

"Everyone is capable of good, Daddy. And you don't know him. I barely know him. But I saw enough to know he just needed a push in the right direction by someone willing to believe in him."

Daddy stares once more out the window at the jet. "God knows that was true of me, once upon a time."

"If and when he shows up, will you be nice?" I ask.

He sighs, and it's more of a growl than a sigh. "I'll try. But I'll have my hackles up. It's hard to forget whose son he is."

I hesitate. "The little he told me about his childhood is not my story to tell. But…I don't think it's fair to hold his last name against him. I feel like maybe he's just as much a victim as you and Mom were."

He turns to me leans in to kiss my cheek. "Do what you need to do, baby girl. I trust you." He grins as he turns away, re-buttoning the middle button of his suit coat. "And also, as you said, it's not up to me."

When he's gone, I slide my finger under the

flap of the envelope. Within, a single small square of paper, with more neat handwriting.

Corinna

Your friends Duke and Puck were right, it seems. I will never feel ready. I will never feel like I am…the man I saw in your eyes when you looked at me. But, if anyone could do more than I have over the past two years to grow into a man who could deserve you, I would like to meet him.

I miss you.

I have replayed the time we spent together in my mind a million times. Not just the moments in my bed (or closet). But the meals. The conversations. It seems impossible, but the time we shared was a matter of hours.

Those few hours with you altered the fabric of my very soul.

Hours, at most, and I am changed by you.

I have left behind all that is Karahalios. The businesses, the enterprises, the men, the money. Even the name, as you suggested. I did some further genealogical detective work and have determined the identity of my father. His name was Dimitri. Therefore, in accordance with Greek custom, I have changed my surname to Dimitriou.

So.

Did you mean it?

If you did, meet me at the address below, tonight, at 6pm.

Yours,

Apollo

A business card is paper clipped to the note—a restaurant here in Houston; since the majority of the work on Valkyrie as we near the first launch has been here, I keep a small condo here, near the offices, and a short flight to the South Texas launch site. Dad only flies in from the Caribbean when his presence is necessary, which means I live here alone, and do the bulk of my work as the CEO of Valkyrie Extraglobal Solutions without direct oversight from him. Not quite twenty-three, and I'm the CEO of a multi-billion-dollar spaceflight and construction start-up. It's the direct result of blatant nepotism, sure, but the board of directors of Valkyrie still unanimously voted for me, and yes, there was competition from more traditional sixty-year-old suit-and-tie business types, qualified men all. Yet, here I am.

I read the note again, and then check the time: 4:54. I don't have much time.

I collect my paperwork into folders and lock it all in my desk, collect my purse, stick my feet in my shoes—I always kick them off once I get to my office—and head out the door.

I pause at my secretary's desk. "James, would you clear the rest of my schedule for today, please?"

James glances at me. "Yes, Miss Roth." He looks at his screen. "You have a meeting with Michael at five thirty, should I reschedule?"

I consider. "Just tell Michael to put the important information in an email, and that I'll get back with him." I can't help feeling a little giddy. "Something's come up."

James frowns. Nothing ever comes up—I'm married to the work. "Yes, Miss Roth."

I drove here, but in the interest of time, I decide to indulge a little. "Can you call up and have Alexander get ready to fly me home? And then have someone shuttle my car home for me. Thank you."

He doesn't answer, he's already on the phone relaying my instructions.

I head up to the rooftop flight deck—RTI, reacquired shortly after we all returned from Spain two years ago, has developed a prototype personal aircraft using VTOL and sound dampening technology. The result is a four-to-six person aircraft that operates in four planes of movement as easily as a helicopter and flies as fast a jet—subsonic, although it's capable of supersonic flight—but without the destructive decibel levels of an average jet engine or helicopter. It gets me across town to my condo in a matter of minutes, a drive that normally takes me nearly half an hour.

Shower, hair and makeup.

I'm still in a bathrobe doing my hair and makeup when my door buzzes. I answer it in person, and find a young courier carrying a garment bag and a digital clipboard.

"Corinna Roth?" he asks.

"Yes."

"Sign here, please." I scrawl, and he hands me the bag. "A gift from…" he consults his clipboard. "Apollo Dim…Dimit…" a frown. "Dim-it-TRY-yoo?" He butchers the last name.

"Dim-EE-tree-yo," I correct. "Thank you."

"There's a note here I'm supposed to read." He clears his throat, peers at the clipboard. "'Corinna, I've had this made for you. See you soon.'"

"Got it, thanks." I pause, garment bag in hand. "Do I tip you?"

He shakes his head emphatically. "No, ma'am." And then he's gone without waiting for a response from me.

I bring the bag into my room and lay it across my bed. Open it.

It's a little red dress—no tag, no hint of the designer.

I put it on. It's elegant and sexy, showing a lot of skin without being too revealing, flaunting my curves, emphasizing my skin and hair tone. How did he get my measurements exactly right? Who made it? It fits like a glove, as if he'd had a dressmaker measure every inch of me first, when I know he hasn't.

Impossible.

Yet, here it is, a custom dress that fits better than anything I've ever worn.

Finished getting ready, I waffle on how to get to the restaurant—drive, or be driven? There's nowhere to land, so I can't fly.

My phone rings—Alexander, my personal pilot. "Hello, Alex."

"Ma'am. I've got instructions here from Mr. Roth himself. He says he's been asked, and I quote, by you know who, to fly you where you need to go."

"I know where I'm going and there's nowhere to land."

"That's been arranged, ma'am."

I sigh. Men. *That's been arranged.* "Very well."

I head up to the roof and find the jet waiting and warmed up. The flight is short, and I look through the footwell view-bubbles and see that the parking lot has been vacated entirely, leaving a space plenty large enough to land.

Which we do, smoothly.

Exit, fix my hair and the hem of my dress—there's literally a stripe of red velvet carpet leading from the exit of the jet to the front door, which is being held open by none other than Tomás, Apollo's assistant and second in command.

He nods to me, smiles. "Is my pleasure to see you again, Miss Roth." It was his voice I heard, outside the castle. The familiar one. I still can't place why his voice tickles at my memory.

I smile back. "Under these circumstances, I can say it's a pleasure to see you too." I gesture at the restaurant. "Wait, don't tell me—Apollo bought the whole restaurant for the sole purpose of this little display."

Tomás snorts a laugh. "He buys parent company which owns…" he trails off, hooking his index fingers around each other, hunting for the right word in English. "Chain? I think this is right word."

I nod. "If he wants to impress me with displays of wealth, I hope he understands he's going to have to do better than that."

Tomás gestures. "Say to him. He is there."

"Thank you, Tomás."

"But of course."

I head inside—the restaurant is a small chain-style Greek restaurant, mostly white interior with faux murals of Ægean life and cheap booths and Ionic columns seemingly at random.

The restaurant is empty, with the exception of three chefs on the other side of the kitchen window and a young woman wearing black slacks and top, a white apron, and a terrified expression. Granted, there are also two armed guards inside the door, and by armed I mean carrying fully automatic rifles, so I understand her terror.

"You could at least post the guards outside," I say, crossing the restaurant, gesturing at the young server, who can't be more than eighteen. "She's about to wet herself."

Apollo is lounging at a booth in the center of the restaurant, sipping coffee and scrolling on his phone. He snaps his fingers. "You heard her. Outside the door. No one in."

"Sir," the men say in unison.

I sit opposite him. "You didn't entirely eschew the trappings of the empire, it seems."

He smirks at me, and god that smirk gets me every time. "I'm worth several billion dollars and formerly dealt with, as you once said, the most violent, brutal, ruthless, and ambitious men on the planet. Security is a nonnegotiable."

I look around. "I must admit, Apollo, that I had envisioned somewhere slightly…more…than this for our first meeting in over two years."

He retains his casual, devil-may-care posture, slumped in the booth with a chipped porcelain mug clutched in his hand, but his eyes are sharp and heated and…emotional. "I heard you speaking to Tomás at the door."

I laugh, nod. "Well, I suppose I'm caught out by my own words. I'm the daughter of a billionaire. You'll find it rather difficult, I think, to impress me with displays of wealth."

"I know this," he says. "I did not choose this location in an effort to impress you." He waves at the window. "I could have bought any restaurant in the country and flown you to it. I chose this one for a different reason."

"And that reason is?"

"You are here, therefore you read my letter, yes?"

I nod. "Of course."

I'm holding back. I want to climb across the table and into his lap—he's more handsome than ever, and I've been oh, so lonely. He's let his hair grow, and now it's past his shoulders, bound back in a loose braid, a pair of sunglasses on his head. He's also grown a beard, short and neat. God, he's so fucking…*gorgeous*. His cheekbones are perfect. The beard emphasizes his incredible jawline. His eyes are deep and dark—and where they'd once been unknowable and impenetrable, they're now open and vulnerable and full of a thousand emotions, scanning me, searching me.

He gestures. "This chain is owned by a cousin."

"On your father's side," I surmise.

"Correct." He shrugs. "They were…struggling. As was the parent company. Poor management all the way around, many unsound investments, sloppy infrastructure. I bought the whole thing. I am reorganizing, streamlining, these things."

"Do your cousins know it's you?"

He looks away, shrugs again—this time it's uncomfortable. "No. I am not so sure how to...approach them. I am the bastard secret cousin no one knew existed. My father had a life before my mother. A wife, children. But he became so addicted to alcohol and gambling that he lost them. Or rather, they lost him, I think would be more accurate. He just...slipped away from them, drinking himself to death. My mother subsidized this, providing him money and a place to live so she could use him for her own purposes. For sex, if I am to be blunt." His accent is more pronounced, more thickly Greek than when I last was with him. "It prolonged his life by some years, I suppose. It did not do him any favors, and his family, my cousins and their mother, never saw him again, and never knew what became of him."

"So all they know is they've been bought by a mysterious benefactor."

He nods. "Quite. Their mother will discover some time in the next few days that her bank has somehow made an internal error which resulted in her mortgage being discharged to her benefit. I own that bank, of course. Another cousin is a builder in Athens. He will bid for a contract he would normally never have a hope of getting, and he will get it."

"But they'll never know *you*."

"I think not. Why? It would only create pain for them. To know the circumstances of my birth? No favor to them."

"I think maybe you're only looking at that through the lens of your own fear, Apollo." I swallow hard, reach out to rest my hand on top of his. "And that's understandable. But I can't help wondering if they've spent the last thirty or however many years wondering what happened to their father, with no way of knowing or ever finding out. Never having closure. Never knowing they have a cousin—who they would otherwise maybe come to accept. If not love."

He shakes his head. "You are too optimistic."

"Realistic."

He sighs, smiles. "Five minutes you are here and already you push me beyond my boundaries."

I withdraw my hand. "Sorry."

He shakes his head and catches my hand, holds it curled into a ball inside his. "No, don't be." He sets his mug down and abandons the casual posture, leaning across the table toward me. "I was worried that I'd imagined the connection I felt with you. I thought maybe it was…that it would not live up to how I remembered it being."

I swallow hard again. "I had the same worry."

"And?"

"And, so far..." I open my hand in his, press my palm to his. "So far I don't think I was imagining it."

He stares at me in silence for a long time. "You were with me in my castle for a day. Two? It's hard to remember precisely how much time has passed. How can it be real, Corinna? How can your soul have imprinted upon mine so swiftly, yet so indelibly?"

I shake my head. "I've asked myself the same question a thousand times since Spain, Apollo. I've never come up with an answer."

"I did not—and except for you, I think—still do not believe in love. My mother did not love me. My father did not know me. Gemma did not love me—she was tasked with and paid for the responsibility of keeping me fed and clothed. Koslov the same for my education. My life after them was professors at university, advisors for management of my wealth, business partners, associates, subordinates, hirelings, clients. No one who knew me. No one who could care. So... how love? Where? What is this love? Only those who wanted something from me. That's all." A harsh snort, wave of his hand. "So even less do I believe in love at first sight. But yet, I met you, brought you to my home and suddenly, somehow, you were...*inside* me. Like a parasite, you burrowed into my fucking brain. Into my heart. Into the synapses and the arteries."

I cackle. "Ah yes, that age-old metaphor from love poetry—being compared to a parasite."

He sighs. "Not what you were hoping to hear, I suppose. It's maddening. Because I do not know what to do with how I feel. Never have I needed anyone. Wanted anyone. Wanted any*thing*. I want, I buy. Cars, houses, businesses. I've never wanted something I could not simply purchase. Even so with… companionship. This too was purchased. Not in the sense of hiring prostitutes, but in a thin guise of it, nonetheless. I know nothing about caring for people. I use them. Pay them, discard them when they have served a purpose." He glances at the door, where Tomás stands discreetly just inside. "He is a sole exception. I pay him well, but he declines any offer of raises or bonuses or gifts—especially since…you. Since I have left the world of drugs and guns. This he approves of. He never liked that line of things or the tasks I occasionally assigned to him."

I know he's working toward a point, and I remain silent, let him make his own way there.

"You are the one thing I could not have." He swallows hard, looks at me. "When I told Tomás to bring you to me, and to not hurt anyone in the process, I could not have known this. That I would find in you a world of emotions I never knew existed. I thought you were a means to an end. Get to your parents and punish them, and I would somehow feel better about the past." A derisive snort. "I was a fool. I was not ruthless enough for this. I am too soft. My grandfather would be ashamed of me. My mother, too."

"A good thing, I think."

He nods. "I agree, now. Then, I was fooling myself into thinking otherwise. Thinking I could perhaps win the approval of their ghosts." A snort. "You saw through me as if I was made of glass."

My mind seizes on something he said. "Wait. It was *him*?" I glance at Tomás. "*He's* the one who actually physically took me?"

He has the good sense to blanch. "Yes."

I let out a breath, the tickle of memory now satisfied. "Bring him over here, please."

Apollo sighs. "Do not hold it against him. He was merely following orders."

"Apollo."

He gestures for Tomás, who comes over in a few quick strides.

"Sir?"

Apollo winces. "I'm afraid I have told her our little secret, Tomás."

Tomás sighs, drops to one knee beside me. "Miss Roth, I—"

I don't even know how to react. "The man in the boat."

He nods. "It was not part of my orders that you are not touched. He only says to me, bring her, but kill no one." His eyes are haunted. "Before him, I do many bad things. Then I am hired by him, and the bad things I do are to bad people, who do worse. Still not good, hmm? But better. To take you? I did not like it. Not to kill? Better. Harder, but better. Your island, the men, it was most difficult. I wanted to say to him that I am failing at this, it was to kill or to get away without you." A shrug. "I am fearing his response. In my life, always, to fail is no good. So…I bring. But the men who try to touch she who is not for them? I kill them. Is easy. The man on this little boat, the man when we reach Cádiz. On the journey over the ocean, others who think to go to your little room, that no one will know." He taps his chest. "*I* know. I stop." His eyes go to his boss. "Then he knows you, and he is changing. The drugs shipments, no more. The guns, no more. I am not killing anyone, since you. Since I am fourteen, I kill. Then you? No more killing. Maybe I am soft, but…in here?" He taps his chest again. "Is better."

Apollo frowns. "You've worked for me for fifteen years, and you've never said that many words to me all at once."

Tomás just snickers. "Neither you to me, sir."

"Ah, this is fair."

I let out another breath. "I forgive you, Tomás."

He closes his eyes, and deflates, sagging. "Thank you." He firms, straightens, stands, returns to his post.

"And you, too," I say, to Apollo. "I forgive you too."

"I have never apologized to anyone in my life, Corinna."

"This is not lost on me."

He closes his eyes. Breathes deeply. Opens his eyes and meets mine. "I am sorry, Corinna. My actions in kidnapping you were foolish, selfish, and stupid. I am sorry to your mother. Your father. It was all so…stupid. And I am sorry." He takes my hands. "Forgive me, please."

"I already did." I squeeze his hands. "The harder apology will be to my parents."

He holds my gaze. "This conversation is not going how I thought it would."

I smirk. "What did you envision? That I would just…fall onto your dick?"

He snorts. "Something like that, I suppose." A pause. "More…happy to see me, I guess."

I lace my fingers with his. "Apollo, I am happy to see you. I *did* miss you. But…two years have gone by. Sometimes it feels like…like it was all a dream. We cannot simply pick up where we left off—where we left off was a disaster. You've changed. I've changed."

"How have you changed?"

"I'm CEO of Valkyrie. I moved out of my parents' home and I'm living here in Houston on my own. I have a condo. A car. Responsibilities. I'm an adult. I mean, I was before, but…less of one. I worked for Dad but I lived at home and everything I did was run through him. Now, I'm fully and independently in charge of a company that's sending billions of dollars in parts into space, not to mention the people." I sigh, frown. "I can't just disappear. I can't just…run off with you."

He nods, and I hate the way his expression shutters a little. "I was not expecting you to."

I gesture at him, at me. "Where do we go from here, Apollo? What does the future look like for us?"

He doesn't answer for a moment or two. "I don't know, Corinna. I've considered this at length. Obsessively, even, one might say. And I've never come up with an answer. I've followed your career, of course. You have a launch coming up in a few days—exciting indeed." He pulls away, rubs his jaw. "I began this journey of mine for you. I started out divesting myself of any involvement with illegal activities. That was a lengthier process than I'd imagined, as it's not something you simply…sell off and walk away from. Then, I began examining my various business holdings, and my imprint on the world. I asked myself along the way, 'what would I imagine a *good* person doing?' I have no frame of reference for goodness, so I made it up. And to be honest, I often looked at what your father has done in his life, and attempted to find my own version of his decisions. I found that he does not always follow the money. He follows his interests and his instincts, and he makes that payout for him. But he always gives back. And not just in charitable donations for headlines, so he can point to them and say, 'look, I'm not just a rich selfish bastard.' He donates to make a difference. He knows where his money goes and how it's used."

"You *have* done some research, I see."

He nods. "I have. As I said, I began by doing this for you. So I could say 'look, look what I've done.' But after a time, it became its own goal. Being better, making decisions which leave a positive effect on the world…it doesn't and cannot erase the blood in my past or the wrongs done by my family, but perhaps I can offset their dark legacy, to some degree. I began making decisions for myself. To become someone I could be proud of."

"And are you?" I ask.

He nods, but also shrugs. "I think so. I decided it was time to contact you when I could look at myself in the mirror and not flinch. Not only think about who my grandfather was and what he did, who mother was and what *she* did. I could look at myself in the mirror and feel pride in what *I've* done."

"And what have you done, Apollo?" I ask, my voice softening.

"I no longer did things so I could tell you about them."

"I know. But I want to know."

"Many things." A thoughtful pause. "I purchased

several pharmaceutical corporations in a complicated series of acquisitions, mergers, and dissolutions. I did this so that I could control a dominant share of the market—and I have subsequently forced drug prices down." A wry smirk. "I left the field of illegal drugs and entered the even more sordid world of legal drugs. The more I forced prices down, the more my competition had to drop theirs to compete. Several smaller corporations went under, and I bought them, only to sell them to my competitors. It's always been a vicious industry, but now the competition is in the favor of the consumer. My focus has been largely on diabetes medication—one of my cousins who lives here in the States is diabetic. In a brief perusal of her finances, I discovered the amount she pays for diabetes medication, for insulin and the like, and I found it distasteful at best."

"And so you set out to do something about it."

"Exactly. And I have."

"What else?"

A sigh. "I have a corporation dedicated entirely to building low-income housing in poverty-stricken areas—improving ghettos. Where you have people who live in what cannot even be properly termed *houses*, just ramshackle assortments of materials to keep the rain off. I fund it through donations and run fundraisers. It's a model which loses money, and a lot of it, but it provides decent homes for people who otherwise would have none." A pause, another shrug. "I bought a telecom corporation and lobbied to have the government here finally invest in nationwide broadband access—of course, I saw that my company received the best bid, but I have plans. For every linear foot of cable we lie here, domestically, we will match it overseas, in areas which often have no internet access at all, let alone high speed."

"Remarkable."

"When you stop caring about only the bottom line, you can do remarkable things. As I sold off various interests, I set aside enough cash in easily-liquidated investments and shares that I will one day be able to retire in absurd luxury. I take a salary, of course, but it's nominal—enough to continue funding my retirement. The rest of what I would otherwise earn—the rest of my so-called net worth, is poured back into my various projects. My total net worth may never increase, but I consider it a net gain if I can continue to be a man who…" he swallows, looks at me. "Who you can be proud of—who you could, as you said, fall in love with, someday." A soft sigh. "But if you cannot, I am still proud of myself, of the things I have done. I have you to thank for sending me on this journey."

"What are you most proud of?"

He takes time to consider. "Something I think very few will ever hear of." He eyes me. "It is risky to even speak of it." A pause. "One of my competitors in the arms business...our competition was friendly, you could say. Business, rather than personal competition. He and I met for drinks a few times, and liked each other. He was into the bigger stuff, whereas I tended to deal mostly in crates of rifles and such. Well, one of the things we shared was an intense distaste for human trafficking."

"Distaste, huh?"

He snorts. "To put it mildly. Well, when I decided to get out of the business, I knew it was to him I would sell my stock. And I did, for pennies on the dollar, as they say. A steal for him, inventory he would be able to move at a profit and swiftly. My only caveat was that we take down a ring which with we were both familiar. When you move in that world, you come to know many unsavory figures. This man whom we both knew was one such. Mikhail and I joined forces and eradicated his whole ring, from top to bottom. It was, I admit, a bloodbath. I'm certain your contacts in the security business could tell you about it."

"I've stayed away from that end of things," I say.

A nod. "Understandable." A wave. "His men and his clients and anyone involved with human trafficking was eliminated. All of his erstwhile...*product*, meaning the human beings he was shipping in containers like so much heroin, we liberated, housed, and employed. Perhaps not always in legal employment, but we gave them choices, and a chance in this world where they had none." He nods. "I am proud of this. It was done in the shadows, made to look like an internal conflict among traffickers instead of the calculated raid which it truly was."

I consider. Pull out my phone, dial a number. It rings three times.

"Rinny, my dear. How are you, honey?" Auntie Layla asks. "Haven't heard from you in a while. When are you coming down to the Keys?"

"Soon. After the launch." I hesitate, eye Apollo. "I have a question for you."

She huffs. "Something sensitive, I think."

"Have you heard about something that went down with some human traffickers, recently?"

She's quiet a tense moment. "I think Uncle Harry should answer this. Here, honey."

I hear Uncle Harry's voice. "We heard about it. INTERPOL official ruling was internal conflict. Rivals going at each other."

"But?"

"But insiders, meaning my contacts in the less savory realm, say it was something else. No one who knows anything solid will talk, but the rumors we're hearing is that it was...an assassination, of sorts. Not of one person, though, but of an entire swath of the industry. Clients, foot soldiers, pimps, everyone connected to this ring died within a matter of days of each other. It was a hit, and no mistake. But no one's made any claims."

I glance at Apollo, who frowns, sighs, and nods. "It can't go any farther," Apollo murmurs.

"It was Apollo." I say this quietly. "This can't go beyond you. But it was him."

A silence. "You're certain of this?"

"I'm with him right now."

A low whistle. "That was a risky play he made, in that case. That's how you get enemies that'll make his grandfather look like Cinderella." A sigh. "But he's got my respect, that's for sure. He did a damn good thing and he did it quietly."

"Thank you, Uncle Harry."

"Sure thing, sweet pea. Come see us."

"After the launch." I pause. "I might not come alone."

"As long as he doesn't bring trouble with him, he's welcome."

"I think he's left that kind of thing well in the past."

"Our guest villa is always ready, honey," he says.

I end the call and put my phone back in my purse. I spend a long, long time thinking, and Apollo simply waits, watching me, heart in his eyes.

"What does our future together look like, Apollo? How do we do this?"

He shrugs. "I don't know. I travel a lot for the

things I do. But honestly, I currently have no real home. I still own the castle, but it's a boutique hotel, now." His voice is low, quiet. "I couldn't stand to be there without you. I will be wherever you are. I just…I've lived without you these two years. I haven't touched another woman. And I just…I thought maybe needing you would dissipate with time. But it hasn't. It has only increased. I can no more live without than I can choose to quit breathing."

He leaves his side of the booth and comes to mine, sits beside me. Faces me. Takes my cheeks in his hands. His nose slants across mine.

"Tell me you've changed your mind and I will go." He whispers this, and I see what it costs him to say it. "I will go and I will vanish from your life. I won't like it. I will never…I could never be the same, no matter what. But if you don't tell me no, right now, I am going to kiss you. You are mine, and I am yours, Corinna. We knew each other only a short time, but our souls became inextricably intertwined in those few short hours. We belong together." His lips touch mine. "Tell me you agree, Corinna. Please. Say something."

"Shut up and kiss me," I whisper.

I tangle my fingers in his hair, and I pull his mouth to mine.

He tastes like the future.

I pull away from the kiss an inch or two. "Take me home."

"Where is home?" he asks.

I laugh. "My home." Another delicate exploration of his lips with mine. "Ours, now. We can find another, if you like. Once we launch, I can take some time off. But for now, just…come home with me."

"Home." He whispers the word as if it's a foreign concept. "Wherever you are is home, Corinna."

"In that case, my home is wherever we can be alone, so we can take these damn clothes off." I touch his beard with my fingertips, his lips with my thumb. "I've spent the last two years alone and horny. And now I have you back."

He laughs and we stand up. "Will we make it all the way to your home?"

I shake my head. "Not likely. But we can try."

I haul him by the hand out of the restaurant, to the waiting jet.

He pulls back, turns to address Tomás. "See that the young woman and the cooks are all exorbitantly compensated. And then have business return to normal, if possible. Or just give them the day off. I don't know. Handle it."

Tomás nods. "Sir."

We board the jet, and I address Alexander. "Home, please. As quickly as possible."

Alexander nods. "Of course, ma'am." A hesitation. "When you say as quickly as possible…"

"Don't break the sound barrier. That would be impolite."

"Impolite, she says." A snort from Alexander. "Understood, ma'am." A grin. "I'd buckle the fuck up, in that case."

I tighten my buckle as we lift off the ground, rotating horizontally as we reach the flight height, and then we're pressed back in our seats as Alexander nails the throttle. Alexander displays his skill as a pilot, twisting and turning through the canyons of the city with consummate skill, ignoring the warnings from air traffic controllers. Feels like an eye blink, and then we're touching down, and Alex is cracking his knuckles.

"How's that, ma'am?"

I laugh. "Exciting. Hopefully we don't get in trouble."

"Nah. They know who owns this jet, and between you and your father, you employ half the city. It's all good. I wouldn't have done anything too risky."

"Thank you, Alex." I'm already pulling Apollo to the elevator which opens into my private foyer. "Take the rest of the day."

"Ma'am."

I hold his hand tightly on the ride down.

Apollo is smirking.

"What?" I ask.

He shakes his head. "Nothing."

"Don't you nothing me, Apollo Dimitriou."

"Can I get one of those?" he asks, jerking his head at the ceiling. "I'll pay any price."

I grin. "That's a one-of-one prototype," I say. "But version two, which fixes some of the technical flaws Alexander has pointed out, is nearing completion, and will need a test client to work out the bugs."

"I volunteer."

"I'll talk to Daddy. That's still his pet company. He loves playing with the designs." I squeeze his hand. "That's not what you were laughing at, though."

The elevator opens onto my foyer, a small space of marble and pale wood, with aged beams overhead, double doors standing open into my living room and kitchen.

I pull him into the kitchen. "Kitchen and living room." I point at the hallway. "Bedroom, workout room, and office." I lift my hands in a ta-da gesture. "You've gotten the tour. Now. What were you laughing about?"

He leans against the island and pulls me to him. "I was laughing at you."

I bristle. "You were laughing at me?"

"I was." He gazes at me with his face kissing distance from mine, and his fingers go to my hair, held up in a neat, smooth updo, and works it loose. "You had your pilot nearly break the sound barrier getting us here. You were playing it cool, back at the restaurant, I think."

I can't keep it in, anymore. I lift up and kiss him, the raging inferno of desire that's been pent up within me for the past two years now boiling over like a steam engine without a release valve. I rip at his shirt, a pale blue button-down, and send buttons pinging off the counter and floor. Shove the ruined garment off his shoulders. Yank at his belt, tearing it open and whipping it free. His slacks are next, impatiently torn open, underwear shoved down with them. He toes off socks and shoes and then he's naked, and I'm touching him.

"Does this answer your question?" I ask, kissing his neck, his jaw, his shoulder.

I kiss him everywhere as I make my way to the part of him I've dreamed about every night for years. I palm his ass and kiss his belly, rub his hips and clutch his cock—it's hard for me, thick and throbbing. Pulsing.

Already leaking precum.

"Corinna," he gasps, as I taste him, finally. "God, Corinna."

"Dreamed of this," I murmur, kissing the tip. "Every night, every day. I dreamed of this. Bringing you home and getting you naked and doing this. Putting my mouth on you."

He groans as I twirl my tongue around him. "I admit I've dreamed of this as well," he growls.

"Then shut up and let me do it," I mutter.

He growls again, and pulls me to my feet. "I don't think so."

He pulls the dress from my shoulders, kissing skin where he bares it. The garment pools around my feet, and he sucks in a sharp breath. "Not a stitch on underneath."

"The only way to wear a dress like this," I murmur, baring my throat for his eager kisses. "And a surprise for you."

He cups my breasts in gentle hands, and he groans a sound of utter relief as he does so, pressing kisses to my breasts, lovingly licking and kissing every inch of both of them.

He drops to his knees. "I would do anything for you, Corinna. Tell me to sell it all, and I will. Tell me to change my name to anything, and will. I will be Apollo Roth for you. I will work as a menial secretary in any building owned by St. Claire Industries, if that is your wish. Anything, Corinna. I dreamed of you for two long years. Needed you. Wanted you. I held my phone in my hand dozens of times, about to call you, and I never did, because I wasn't sure I was ready. And as your Duke and your Puck said back in Spain, I will never be ready. But I couldn't wait anymore. I couldn't not be with you. I dream of simply holding you in my arms again, Corinna."

I whimper as his mouth fuses to my sex. "Apollo..."

"I dream of waking up with you. I dream of... simply breakfasting together."

I gasp, snarling my fingers in his hair. "Apollo..."

He gazes up at me. "I can't sleep at night for needing to simply see you. To simply hear your voice. Say my name, Corinna, whisper my name the way you do, the way only you ever have, and I will be happy."

"Apollo."

He sighs, a broken, ragged sound. "Two years without you. It was the worst kind of fucking torture. Each day without you was hell, and worse than the last." He stands up, holds my face.

"I'm here with you now, Apollo, and I'm not going anywhere." I push him down. "Now get back down there and make me come so I can get my mouth back on this beautiful cock of yours."

He laughs and his tongue obeys my command.

I'm there, instantly. A touch of his tongue, a slip of a finger inside me, and I'm shaking, sobbing. It's been so long without him, and my own fingers, my vibrators...it's not the same.

He pries my pussy open with his thumbs and he devours my clit, and he makes me come so hard I see stars, so hard I collapse into his arms.

He carries me to my room.

Puts me on my bed.

And there, he makes me come again and again, with a tireless eager tongue and skillful, nimble, loving fingers.

When my need is more than I can bear, I pull him up my body. "Come here," I whisper.

He hovers over me. Kisses me.

I clutch his cock and I guide him to my opening. I hold his eyes and I hold my breath, and I take him into me. "Make love to me, Apollo. Make love to me and don't stop."

"We need—"

I shake my head, and I thrust my hips up against his. "No. Just you and me. I've dreamed about this for years."

He groans, and he buries his face in my throat, and he surges against me—sinks into me. "Corinna…"

"Oh *god*," I whimper, as he fills me. "Oh fuck. So perfect."

We move together, then, slowly. The desperation is in our voices as we cry out in tandem, as our bodies mesh into one. He fills me, completes me.

"Apollo, I whisper.

As if merely his name on my lips rips away the last of his control, he simply explodes inside me, fills me with heat, gasping helplessly and driving into me. I wrap my thighs around his waist and hook my feet around his ass and I pull him against me, refuse to let him go, to let him stop, and I come with him, weeping his name and meeting his wild thrusts with my own until we're complete and replete and we can't come any more.

It's an endless night.

We fuck till dawn, and we talk of everything in between.

He makes love to me, and he holds me.

We make plans for the future.

A home together, somewhere. A baby, someday.

First? We simply figure out how to navigate life as a couple. How to be together.

Epilogue

IT'S NOT THAT EASY

Six Months Later

I'M IN THE OFFICE, WRAPPING UP A FEW DETAILS FOR our next launch, which will see the last shipment of materials go up, at which point we will officially begin constructing the world's first orbital shipyard.

Life has been…amazing. Chaotic, fast-paced. Apollo and I bought a building in Houston and turned the top four floors into a combination of office space and home, with the rest of Valkyrie on the floors below.

There have been arguments over the usual things couples fight about, and make ups.

I've never been happier.

Apollo and my father are in business together

in half a dozen different ways, and Apollo and I have our own totally separate arm of businesses and charities and projects.

No baby, yet. Too busy.

I'm about to kick off for the day when my phone rings.

I answer without looking. "This is Rin."

"It's me, darling." His voice is…off. "You should screen your calls."

I snort. "You called my personal number. A dozen people total have this number."

"Come up to the house, please." Again, that odd, worrisome note.

I put the papers down and sit up straight. "Apollo? What's going on?"

"Best if you just come." A pause. "I've sent some men to escort you."

An escort? My stomach flips.

"I'll be right there."

I put on my shoes and snag my purse—four men are on the other side of my office door, each one in full body armor, and armed to the teeth. Four? In armor? Not good at all.

They box me in and escort me up to our personal quarters. Which is a madhouse of men with guns—all of them from A1S.

My stomach sinks further.

I find Apollo in the doorway to his personal,

private office in our home. I touch his waist. "What's going on? Why are they here?"

He's pale. Shaking. "I thought I could leave it behind. I thought I'd taken care of anyone who could have been my enemy."

"Apollo?"

He grabs my hand in a fierce, crushing grip. Looks at me with shaken, tortured eyes. "I don't want to show you."

"Show me what?"

He swallows. Shakes his head. "No. Don't look." He closes his eyes. "They got…Tomás."

"Who? Got him how? Killed him?"

I push him out of the way, and peer into his office.

It's painted red.

A severed head sits on the desk—Tomás.

One wall has a message written on it in blood:

It's not that easy, KARAHALIOS.

Apollo has something in his hand, I realize. I take it from him. It's a photograph of a little girl, no more than four or five. A sweet, cute little thing.

"Who is this?"

"My…my cousin's daughter." He's coming out of his shock, now. Anger is suffusing his features. "She doesn't even know I exist. None of them do."

This was a source of one of our arguments. I want him to contact them and he's not ready, still.

"They took her?"

"Flip it over."

There's a set of coordinates and a short note: *Be here in twenty-four hours, alone, or it's her head next.*

"What do we do?"

He looks over my shoulder. "We take care of it."

Behind me is the full weight of Alpha One Security's inner core.

"But I have to go," he says.

"Not without me." I shake my head.

He looks at me. "I can't ask you to—"

"You don't have to ask. She's family."

"Yelena," he says. "Her name is Yelena."

I turn and look at Uncle Harry. "How do we get Yelena back, Uncle Harry?"

His pale blue eyes are colder than ice. "We've got some ideas. We'll go over them in the air."

The End

Also by

JASINDA WILDER

Visit me at my website: **www.jasindawilder.com**
Email me: **jasindawilder@gmail.com**

If you enjoyed this book, you can help others enjoy it as well by recommending it to friends and family, or by mentioning it in reading and discussion groups and online forums. You can also review it on the site from which you purchased it. But, whether you recommend it to anyone else or not, thank you *so much* for taking the time to read my book! Your support means the world to me!

My other titles:

Preacher's Son:
Unbound
Unleashed
Unbroken

Delilah's Diary:
A Sexy Journey
La Vita Sexy
A Sexy Surrender

Big Girls Do It:
Boxed Set
Married
On Christmas
Pregnant

Rock Stars Do It:
Harder
Dirty
Forever

From the world of *Big Girls* and *Rock Stars*:
Big Love Abroad

Biker Billionaire:
Wild Ride

The Falling Series:
Falling Into You
Falling Into Us
Falling Under
Falling Away
Falling For Colton

The Ever Trilogy:
Forever & Always
After Forever
Saving Forever

The world of *Wounded:*
Wounded
Captured

The world of *Stripped:*
Stripped
Trashed

The world of *Alpha:*
Alpha
Beta
Omega
Harris: Alpha One Security Book 1
Thresh: Alpha One Security Book 2
Duke Alpha One Security Book 3
Puck: Alpha One Security Book 4
Lear: Alpha One Security Book 5
Anselm: Alpha One Security Book 6

The Houri Legends:
Jack and Djinn
Djinn and Tonic

The Madame X Series:
Madame X
Exposed
Exiled

The Black Room
(With Jade London):
Door One
Door Two
Door Three
Door Four
Door Five
Door Six
Door Seven
Door Eight

The One Series
The Long Way Home
Where the Heart Is
There's No Place Like Home

Badd Brothers:
*Badd Motherf*cker*
Badd Ass
Badd to the Bone
Good Girl Gone Badd
Badd Luck
Badd Mojo
Big Badd Wolf
Badd Boy
Badd Kitty
Badd Business
Badd Medicine
Badd Daddy

Dad Bod Contracting:
Hammered
Drilled
Nailed
Screwed

Fifty States of Love:
Pregnant in Pennsylvania
Cowboy in Colorado
Married in Michigan
Christmas in Connecticut

Goode Girls
For a Goode Time Call…
Not So Goode
Goode to Be Bad
A Real Good Time
Goode Vibrations

Billionaire Baby Club
Lizzie Goes Brains Over Braun
Autumn Rolls a Seven
Laurel's Bright Idea

Standalone titles:
Yours
The Cabin
The Parent Trap
Wish Upon a Star

Non-Fiction titles:
You Can Do It
You Can Do It: Strength
You Can Do It: Fasting

Jack Wilder Titles:
The Missionary

JJ Wilder Titles:
Ark

To be informed of new releases, special offers, and other Jasinda news, sign up for Jasinda's email newsletter.

Printed in Great Britain
by Amazon

75270070R00258